WICKED PLEASURES

Isabella's now restless fingers moved down across Damien's hard shoulders, feeling the sleek muscle and sinew. She tensed against him as the excitement within her grew to an almost unbearable level.

Damien pulled her completely down onto the carpet, then rolled her onto her back. He settled his body intimately atop hers, staring into her eyes with an intensity that made Isabella tremble. The air felt suddenly closed and heated.

"I'm going to remove the rest of your clothing, Isabella." The deep, sensual timber of his voice made her shiver.

"Wait!" Isabella insisted. "I want to remove some of your clothing first." When he offered no protest, Isabella reached for him. Curious and excited, she began to open the last few fastenings on his shirt. Damien shifted his weight and gave her an odd smile as she struggled with the buttons.

"Just rip it," he whispered in a deep voice, and he inhaled deeply as Isabella followed his commands. Buttons spewed about the room, and Damien laughed with delight.

Nervous but determined, Isabella continued her explorations. Deftly she reached inside the linen and spread her hands across Damien's naked chest. The springy dark hair tickled her palms. The flesh beneath felt smooth and very hard. Experimentally, she moved her hands lower, across the flat plane of his stomach to the top of his breeches.

A long shudder ran through Damien. "Enough," he whispered, yanking off the remains of his shirt and tossing it aside. He pulled Isabella closer and kissed her deeply, his passion becoming more urgent with each kiss, his need more overwhelming with each caress . . .

BOOK YOUR PLACE ON OUR WEBSITE AND MAKE THE READING CONNECTION!

We've created a customized website just for our very special readers, where you can get the inside scoop on everything that's going on with Zebra, Pinnacle and Kensington books.

When you come online, you'll have the exciting opportunity to:

- View covers of upcoming books
- Read sample chapters
- Learn about our future publishing schedule (listed by publication month *and author*)
- Find out when your favorite authors will be visiting a city near you
- Search for and order backlist books from our online catalog
- Check out author bios and background information
- Send e-mail to your favorite authors
- Meet the Kensington staff online
- Join us in weekly chats with authors, readers and other guests
- Get writing guidelines
- AND MUCH MORE!

**Visit our website at
http://www.zebrabooks.com**

HIS
WICKED
EMBRACE

Adrienne Basso

Zebra Books
Kensington Publishing Corp.

http://www.zebrabooks.com

For my grandmother, Angela DeStefanis Poni—
my biggest fan and best friend.
I love you, Nonna.

Prologue

Kent, England—1803

The stagnant air hung heavy with the smell of sickness and despair. Amid the tragic atmosphere of the small house, a young girl sat alone in the corner of the sitting room. Shifting her position, she sank lower into the faded chair, seeking to hide herself within the sagging stuffing and somehow escape from the constant pain and fear gripping her tender heart.

A boisterous shout from the front yard caught the girl's attention and she gazed listlessly out the half-opened window. Her three older stepbrothers were playing noisily in the front yard, yelling and screaming in excitement as they rolled a hoop on the overgrown grass, oblivious to the drama unfolding within the house.

"There is nothing more I can do, Mrs. Potts," a man's voice exclaimed in annoyance, as the man himself entered the room. " 'Tis in God's hands now."

The young girl lifted her violet eyes soulfully toward the man who had spoken such hopeless thoughts. "Surely there must be something you can do for Mama," she whispered softly, her voice laced with fear. "Please, Father."

The man's scowl deepened at the child's statement. "I am only a doctor, Isabella, not a miracle worker," he said harshly. "You know your mother is gravely ill."

The child turned her face away from the anger in her father's voice. Although she was used to the curt manner with which he treated her, for it had always been that way, she felt unable to cope with his coldness this day. This day her mother lay dying.

For a long, silent moment the man stared at the profile of the young girl. He could see the quivering of her bottom lip as she struggled to remain composed. The proud tilt of her chin reminded him so much of her mother. The resemblance caused him to pause a moment and relax his usual harshness.

"You may go and sit by your mother's bed, Isabella," her father said quickly, speaking before he had time to regret this rare instance of compassion.

Isabella instantly sprang up from her perch and crossed the room. She paused briefly next to her imposing father and, keeping her eyes downcast, whispered a dignified, "Thank you."

Charles Browning's shoulders sagged noticeably at her departure. He dragged himself across the room to sit in the chair Isabella had vacated, feeling every one of his fifty-two years. He looked down in despair at his hands. The hands of a physician, the hands of a healer. They shook slightly, and he deeply felt the need of a drink. Yet he mastered his craving. His beautiful wife, Marianne, lay on her deathbed upstairs. It would not do for Reverend Packard and the other members of this small community to find him drunk when they came to call later and offer condolences. Above all else, appearances must be kept.

He sighed deeply. Ah, Marianne. His frail, lovely wife. She had been only sixteen years old the first time he saw her. She was the youngest daughter of an earl and had been attending a house party given by one of the local squires. During an afternoon of riding, Marianne had taken a nasty spill from her horse and he, Charles Browning, the village's only physician, had been summoned to attend the young noblewoman.

Charles remembered clearly Marianne's startling blue eyes and the creamy alabaster glow of her complexion that blushed rosy when he asked to see her injuries. She had been so innocently sweet and demure, and extremely shy about showing him her ankle, which was sprained in the fall.

He had probably fallen in love with her that very instant, but he knew it was a hopeless situation. He was considerably older, socially and economically inferior, and above all, a married man, with three young sons. During the four weeks it took for Marianne's ankle to heal, however, Charles took advantage of every opportunity to visit his enchanting patient at the manor house. By the time Marianne and her family left, Charles had convinced himself that if the circumstances were different, the lovely Marianne would return his affections with equal ardor.

Charles never forgot Marianne. Neither, apparently, did Marianne's father, the Earl of Barton. Two years later, and now a widower, Charles was shocked to be awakened early one morning to discover the earl on his doorstep with a pale-faced and shaken Marianne by his side. The lovely, unmarried girl was pregnant, and her father was furious.

At first the earl tried to convince Charles to perform an abortion on his daughter, but the look of total horror on Marianne's face dissuaded Charles from attempting it. Instead, he offered to marry Marianne, and after a bit of persuading the earl agreed. The earl then emptied his pockets of all the coin he had on his person, placed the small amount of Marianne's luggage they had brought with them in the front hall, and left. Marianne never heard from her father or any member of her family again.

The wedded bliss and loving household Charles envisioned with his beautiful bride never materialized. Marianne was a nobleman's daughter and had been raised to live a far different life than the one a humble physician could provide. She tried very hard to fit into her new role but was never successful. She seldom complained about the lack of money or social standing, but it bitterly upset Charles that he could not provide his wife with what he believed she deserved. He blamed his wife's family for abandoning her to genteel poverty and social obscurity, and he blamed the child she bore for causing the chasm with her family.

The enchanting life Charles had fantasized about for years with Marianne proved to be nothing more than an empty dream. Over time, Charles convinced himself that Marianne honestly tried to return his affections, but it was obvious her heart had long ago been committed—first, to the child's unknown father, whose identity she would never reveal, and then to the child, Isabella. Charles deeply resented the unconditional love and attention his wife lavished on her child. As the years passed, his resentment toward Isabella steadily increased, until he could barely be civil to the child and did so only for the sake of keeping peace with Marianne.

"Oh, Father, she is gone!" Isabella's young voice quivered with pain as she stood in the doorway and made her pitiful announcement. "Mama is dead!"

Isabella ran across the room and threw herself into Charles's arms. His earlier compassion toward her, coupled with her overwhelming need for comfort, caused the young girl to seek relief from the man she called her father.

Momentarily startled, Charles allowed himself to embrace the child. He felt his emotions sliding beyond his control as sorrow, anger, resentment, and frustration rose to the surface. And settled on Isabella. Reaching his arms up, he disengaged Isabella's hands from around his neck and lowered them to her side. She shivered with her grief, and sniffled loudly.

"Get upstairs to your room, you little bastard," he growled at the child. "And do not show yourself again until it is time for your mother's funeral."

Not understanding his words, yet frightened beyond speech, Isabella raced from the room, her cries echoing throughout the room long after she had left. She reached the sanctuary of her small bedchamber and flung herself onto the bed, crying with great gulping sobs as if her heart would break. She had never felt so frightened and alone in all of her life.

Eventually she slept, and when she awoke, Isabella's head felt heavy with numbness. She forced herself to rise from the bed and straighten her rumpled appearance. It was time to go downstairs and face her father and brothers. Isabella was terrified, but she refused to allow herself to avoid the confrontation, instinctively knowing this was merely the beginning of her father's attempts to exclude her completely from the family. Isabella was determined to participate in all the necessary preparations for her mother's burial. It was her right. She would not be denied.

Isabella walked slowly but steadily down the staircase. She hesitated momentarily before entering the sitting room, her heart pounding with fear when she saw her father. But the Reverend Packard and his wife were in attendance, and Isabella knew her father would not create a scene in front of them. She entered the room and quietly sat down, forcing herself to look at her father with a direct, challenging stare. Charles gave her a dismissive glance but held his tongue, and Isabella allowed herself a tiny feeling of victory.

Isabella had never understood her father's brittle, often cruel attitude toward her, but she knew his reasons were no longer an issue. Life with him was going to be a constant battle and she was going to have to fight to survive. The safe, loving world her mother had created for her was now gone forever. It was time for her to grow up. She was eight years old.

Chapter One

London, England—1820

"You traitorous, lying, deceitful bitch!"

Damien St. Lawrence, eighth Earl of Saunders, shouted his frustration loudly before succumbing completely to his anger and hurling his nearly full goblet of brandy at the portrait hanging over the unlit fireplace. The flying glass hit the painting with remarkable accuracy, considering the lack of light in the room and the earl's inebriated condition, and he grunted in satisfaction.

Gleefully, Damien watched the shards of glass spray the portrait and several thin streams of brandy slither over the face and form of the stunning woman portrayed on the canvas. Only when the largest piece of broken goblet rolled to a stop on the floor, joining its seven predecessors, did the earl turn his back on the painting.

Damien took several unsteady steps toward the center of the room and literally threw himself into an overstuffed chair, the single piece of furniture in the dimly lit room. With a brooding expression on his darkly handsome face, the earl reached down for the brandy decanter he had left on the floor next to his chair. He lifted the decanter high in the air and eyed its contents, pleased to note it was still half full.

The earl reached down a second time, searching fruitlessly for his brandy goblet. He gave a loud snort when he realized that he had just flung the last remaining glass. Never even considering doing anything as uncivilized as drinking the brandy directly from the bottle, Damien instead bellowed for his servant.

"Jenkins! Jenkins! Get in here at once. And bring more glasses!"

Two young footmen, standing sentry outside the locked doors of the drawing room, exchanged nervous glances.

"I'll go get the glasses," the one called Manning volunteered. "You wait here for Jenkins." Before his companion had a chance to argue, Manning left his post, scrambling quickly toward the back of the house.

The other footman, Banks, even more nervous now that he was left alone, winced noticeably when the booming voice of the earl echoed through the house a second time.

"Is his lordship yelling for more brandy, Banks?" Jenkins inquired in a conversational tone, walking up to the drawing room doors.

"N-not yet, Mr. Jenkins," Banks stammered, his eyes lighting with obvious relief at the sudden appearance of the older man. "But he is calling for you, sir. And for more glasses."

Jenkins shook his gray head in understanding. "Been smashing them up pretty good, has he?"

Banks nodded eagerly. "Manning and I have been hearing the glass shattering for the past hour. I suppose it was the crystal," Banks responded slowly. "Of course, it might have been the windows breaking."

"Windows?" Jenkins stated with puzzlement. "I hardly think the earl—"

"I've brought the goblets, Mr. Jenkins," Manning interrupted, calling out to the two men as he rushed into the foyer. The young servant awkwardly juggled five mismatched crystal glasses in his arms while walking quickly across the large hallway. "Sorry I couldn't find a tray to put them on. Mrs.

Forbes has already packed all the plate and flatware. I found these glasses on top of an open crate.''

"Good job, Manning," Jenkins said with approval. He took the glasses from the lad and gingerly brushed off several pieces of straw. "Now go down to the wine cellar and bring up the rest of the brandy. There shouldn't be much left."

"More brandy?" Manning squeaked. "The earl's already had three bottles brought up since dinner."

"Aye," Jenkins agreed wryly. "Not to mention the two bottles of wine he drank *for* his dinner."

A telling look passed between the two young footmen. "I suppose his lordship will be f-falling asleep soon?" Banks finally ventured.

"You mean passing out, don't you, boy?" Jenkins replied with an easy grin. "Well, if he does, it will be the first time I've ever seen it happen. And I've been with the earl for almost twenty years."

With that said, Jenkins unlocked and entered the drawing room, leaving the two young footmen once again alone in the foyer, their mouths gaping.

"Where the bloody hell have you been?"

"And a pleasant good evening to you too, your lordship," Jenkins replied to the husky voice that spoke from the shadows.

The valet stumbled awkwardly into the room, blinking his eyes rapidly in the semidarkness. The only source of light, a single candle on the far side of the room, cast an orb of illumination throughout the vast, empty room. Jenkins suppressed a shiver. In addition to the gloomy darkness, the room was ice cold. "Good God, how can you see anything in here? It's like a bloody tomb."

"I prefer it this way," the earl retorted. Damien sighed and leaned his head back in his chair, restlessly stroking the neck of the brandy decanter he gripped tightly in his left hand. "And since when do you address me as 'your lordship'?"

"Since you stopped acting like one," Jenkins shot back. "I thought a subtle reminder that you are a peer of the realm might help you sober up."

The earl laughed loudly and lifted his head toward his servant.

"I swear, Jenkins, you have always held a romantic and unrealistic opinion concerning the conduct of the nobility. By drinking myself into a bloody stupor, I am acting precisely as a true earl would. Furthermore, you do not, as I recall, possess one subtle bone in your entire body." Damien reached out and took the glasses the valet was balancing in his arms. He carefully lined them up on the floor by his feet. "Besides, I believe I am still far too sober for my own good."

Jenkins made a face at that remark but did not comment. Instead he walked to the mantle and found a hand of candles with the majority of the tapers still a considerable length. The valet located a flint and lit the candles, then bent down over the cold hearth and started building a fire.

"Watch out for the broken glass," the earl warned, when he saw his servant kneeling in front of the marble fireplace.

"I would have to be a blind man to miss it all," Jenkins replied smoothly. " 'Tis everywhere."

"I think I actually hit her eyes with the last shot," the earl mused aloud, staring up at the portrait, now brilliantly illuminated. "I do believe, my friend, my aim has improved over the course of the evening."

"But not your temper," Jenkins insisted, kicking a jagged fragment of glass out of his way. "Young Banks thought you might be in here smashing the windows."

The earl paused, his fresh glass of brandy halting in midair. "Smashing windows? How positively barbaric." The earl shook his head, dismissing the servant's remark, and took a long swallow of his drink. Reaching down to the floor, he picked up a second goblet. After filling it, Damien silently held it out to his valet.

Jenkins stood up on his feet and accepted the glass with a rueful grin. He looked down at the earl, a man he had known and served for nearly all his adult life. A man whose sense of honor, intelligence, and strength of character were the finest Jenkins had ever encountered. "This behavior will accomplish nothing."

The earl nodded his head in agreement. "I know, Jenkins. It is a totally irresponsible, perhaps even idiotic way to spend an evening. Yet I am determined to drink every last drop of brandy on the premises. It is my way of bidding a proper farewell to this house."

"You didn't have sell the place," Jenkins insisted, still holding his untouched glass in his hand. "Lord Poole could have waited for his money."

"Ah, Lord Poole, my illustrious brother-in-law," the earl drawled, the name bringing a light of anger to Damien's steely gray eyes. "The only moment of satisfaction I have received from this entire fiasco was being able to throw that bank draft in Poole's face this afternoon. You have no idea what a relief it is to no longer be in debt to that swine. And his scheming bitch of a sister."

Jenkins's eyes traveled automatically toward the portrait of the stunning woman over the fireplace. "It is bad luck to speak ill of the dead," the valet suggested softly.

"Emmeline is not dead, Jenkins," the earl insisted vehemently. He tossed off the remainder of his brandy and refilled his glass. "I don't know what sort of scheme that bitch is playing at this time, but I firmly believe my traitorous little wife is still alive. Somewhere."

"Her death was an accident," Jenkins pressed on.

The corners of the earl's mouth curled up in a mocking grin. "Don't you mean suicide? Poole is still spewing that nonsense. He was exceedingly disappointed when his loathsome accusations didn't get a rise out of me this afternoon."

"It was an accident," Jenkins repeated firmly, but he could see his comments were being ignored.

Jenkins sighed audibly. He and the earl had already had this conversation more times than Jenkins could recall. Even after two years, Damien could not accept Emmeline's death. It had all happened so suddenly and unexpectedly. Two years ago, while making a rare appearance at Damien's country estate, Whatley Grange, Lady Emmeline had gone out riding. Alone. Several hours later, her horse had returned without her.

At first there seemed no great cause for panic. Damien himself led the initial search team. Although their marriage was not a particularly happy one, the earl took his responsibilities toward his wife, the mother of his two children, very seriously. By darkness that night, Emmeline had not yet been found and the atmosphere of The Grange changed to one of fear and trepidation.

Mid-morning of the following day, a gruesome discovery was made at the large lake bordering the edge of the property. Muddy horse prints and torn-up grass led to the possible explanation that Emmeline had been thrown from her horse and accidently landed in the lake. There was no sign she had emerged from the water.

For three weeks the reed-choked waters were dragged. Emmeline's riding hat, handkerchief, and left riding glove were recovered, giving further credence to the theory that she had somehow fallen into the lake and drowned. Because of the unusual depth of the water and the presence of thick, choking reeds, the local constable finally concluded the countess's body had been claimed by the depths of the lake and would forever remain on the bottom of its murky floor.

Damien adamantly refused to acknowledge Emmeline's death. After a few weeks, Emmeline's brother, Lord Poole, insisted on conducting a funeral service for his dead sister in the village church, but Damien would not attend, nor did he permit his two young children to be present. The earl's behavior infuriated Lord Poole, and he took it upon himself to spread all kinds of nasty rumors about the carl, hoping to discredit him in society's eye.

Damien considered Lord Poole's actions merely a nuisance, having little interest in the activities of the *ton*. He was more concerned over the fate of his missing wife. Over the next two years, Damien's search for Emmeline yielded nothing, and yet, although he had no evidence to substantiate his claim, the earl still clung stubbornly to the belief that his wife was alive.

"Almost from the first Emmeline was displeased with our marriage," Damien said reflectively, remembering with distaste his hasty courtship and wedding. "I know I am to blame for the coldness of our relationship. Emmeline told me often enough how unhappy I made her."

"As I recall, she did her fair share of spreading unhappiness," Jenkins insisted.

"Perhaps." The earl shifted in his chair, stretching out his long legs. "Emmeline craved excitement and romance. She longed for a grand passion. She told me once that she wanted an adoring husband, someone to spoil and cosset her. I am afraid I fell far short of the mark."

Jenkins heard the edge of self-loathing in the earl's voice and instantly responded. "You did not marry Emmeline because you loved her, Damien."

"No, Jenkins," the earl confessed softly. "I married Emmeline for her fortune. And she came to despise me because of it. Yet she knew of my motivation before we were wed. I never made a secret of my need for her money."

"You had to marry an heiress. It was the only choice left to save The Grange," Jenkins declared. "It certainly was a shock for both of us coming back from the war and finding your father had lost nearly everything."

Damien nodded in solemn reminder. "Poor Father. He had an endless streak of bad luck while we were fighting in the Peninsula. It was an almost unbelievable combination of several years of crop failure, falling agricultural prices, unwise investments, and lavish spending habits. At the time of his death, he was on the very brink of financial ruin. Emmeline's—or more specifically her brother's—money saved The Grange, Jenkins."

The valet took a long swallow of his drink. "Their money helped, Damien," Jenkins insisted. "But it's your hard work that has saved The Grange from complete ruin."

Damien modestly knew his servant spoke the truth. He had worked tirelessly to reduce the mortgages and repay the piles of debts his father had incurred before his death. Saving The Grange from the creditors had become an obsession for the earl. Still, Damien often wondered if the personal sacrifice he'd made had been too high a price.

"I've never been able to determine precisely why she married me, Jenkins," Damien continued. "With her looks and fortune, she could had her pick of young bucks of the *beau monde*. I have come to believe her brother forced Emmeline into accepting my suit, but I cannot think of one single reason Poole would do such a thing.''

''I always suspected Lord Poole had his eye on The Grange,'' Jenkins interjected, warming to the subject. He finished his glass and held it out for the earl to replenish.

''Naturally, I feel The Grange is an exceptional estate,'' Damien answered as he poured out the brandy. ''But there are many other choice pieces of real estate in Harrowgate. Poole is a rich man. He could have bought any number of estates that are far greater in value. There has to be another reason.''

''Perhaps,'' Jenkins ventured, ''but I doubt we will ever discover what it was.''

The room fell to silence as both men contemplated the idea. A soft knock on the door broke their concentration.

''I believe that will be young Manning with the rest of the brandy,'' Jenkins remarked to the earl. ''I told him to bring up the remaining stock from the wine cellar. I had a premonition you would attempt to consume it all tonight.''

''You know me too well, Jenkins.'' The earl flashed a genuine smile. ''When do we have to vacate the house?''

''I informed your solicitor that we would be gone by noon tomorrow.''

''Have you gotten all the staff settled?''

''Just as you requested,'' Jenkins responded. He opened the drawing room doors and accepted three bottles of brandy from the footman. Then he quietly shut the door. ''Those servants who were not offered positions with the new owners have all been offered jobs at The Grange.''

''Good.'' The earl rose from his chair and stretched. ''I don't suppose any of the housemaids will be accompanying us?''

Jenkins shook his head. ''Lord Poole's lies about your reputation are taken very seriously in London. The only reason we were able to keep any female staff at this house was because you came to town so rarely.''

''It doesn't matter,'' the earl insisted, hearing the trace of bitterness in Jenkins's voice. The valet's unwavering loyalty could still move the earl, even after all their years together.

"Since you have completed your duties so admirably, Jenkins, I was hoping you would keep me company for the remainder of the evening."

Jenkins smiled regretfully, knowing it would be useless trying to talk the earl out of his plans. Selling the London town house had been a very difficult decision for Damien. And if he was determined to spend the rest of the evening drinking himself into a stupor, no one was going to be able to dissuade him. Lord knew the man had been through enough in the past few days.

"I shall endeavor to keep pace with you, my lord," Jenkins responded soberly. "I cannot, however, guarantee how long I will remain on my feet."

Chapter Two

Miss Isabella Browning could not dispel the persistent feeling that she was being watched.

This unsettling feeling came upon Isabella soon after entering the small park with her three young charges in tow. She quickly made a sweeping glance of the immediate area, but did not spy anyone exhibiting the least bit of interest in her or the children. Yet the feeling persisted.

"We want to race our twigs in the water, Miss Browning," a young voice called out.

Isabella shifted her attention to the small boy addressing her. Master Robert Braun, age five, stood on the grassy slope near the shallow lake and fidgeted restlessly with the two sticks he held in his chubby hands. For once the child appeared to actually be waiting for Isabella to give her permission before he went blithely along his way.

Of course, Robert hadn't exactly *asked* if he and his two sisters could play in the water, but at least he had paused a moment to voice his intentions to his governess. Isabella sighed. Did she dare hope nine months of constant battling with Robert were finally starting to pay off?

"You and your sisters may race your sticks as long as you

promise to be very careful and not get too close to the water's edge,'' Isabella decided. ''If you become too excited and boisterous, however, you will not be allowed to continue. Is that understood?''

With a barely perceivable nod, Robert turned his back on his governess and ran toward the water. His two sisters, Guinevere and Caroline, trailed dutifully in his wake. Although both girls were older, seven and nine respectively, they blindly followed their parents' lead and deferred to Robert in all things. Consequently, the young boy was treated like a royal prince in the Braun household.

As the children's governess, Isabella strived constantly to temper Robert's spoiled and demanding attitude. It was a thankless and often frustrating task, but rare moments such as this morning provided Isabella with a glimmer of hope that she was finally achieving some measure of success with the headstrong boy.

Isabella followed behind the children slowly, climbing the sloping embankment where they were gathering. She kept a keen eye on their activities, but became distracted when she again felt prickles of awareness along her spine, and the uncomfortable sensation of being under the observation of a stranger's eye. She whirled around suddenly, half expecting to see someone standing behind her. There was no one, but the vague sense of uneasiness would not leave.

There was no obvious explanation for Isabella's unease since she was very familiar with this small park. She and the children came here at least three times a week, weather permitting. Still, Isabella would have felt calmer if the coachman, Hodgson, had been able to stay with them today as he usually did, instead of driving off to Bond Street on the orders of the mistress of the house. Hodgson would be returning to collect Isabella and the children after he finished his errands. She hoped the coachman would not be too long in arriving.

Isabella continued to experience an unfamiliar sense of foreboding, but she was determined to remain calm. The park was not very crowded at this hour of the morning, yet it was not deserted either. There were other nurses walking with their charges, as well as several gentlemen on horseback. Surely the gentlemen could be counted upon to lend assistance if the need arose.

Isabella shook her head and forced her mind to clear itself of these ridiculous notions. She was behaving skittishly and for no apparent logical reason. A sudden vivid recollection of a gruesome article she had read in the *Morning Gazette* about a young child being kidnapped off the streets of London caused a quickening of Isabella's heart rate. Perhaps she was not being foolish. Maybe she was being watched. Although not of the gentry, Mr. Braun was a very wealthy man, and devoted to his three children. He would, without question, pay any ransom necessary to gain their safe release.

Isabella spared an instant of pity for anyone foolish enough to target the boisterous Braun siblings for an abduction. After one hour of the girls' sniveling and Robert's belligerent shouting, any man, no matter how hardened a criminal, would be regretting his rash actions.

Isabella silently chastised herself for her unkind thoughts. The Braun children might not be the most likable individuals she had ever encountered, but she had a duty to care for them, and she would perform her duty to the very best of her abilities. Including keeping the children safe from kidnappers, real or imagined.

In all honesty, Isabella admitted to herself, she was very fortunate to have this particular position. At twenty-five, she had already been dismissed from three previous jobs, and she could ill afford to lose another post.

Isabella's eyes darted speculatively around the park, searching again for signs of danger. The Braun children were alone by the edge of the pond, engaged in a heated verbal battle Isabella feared would soon escalate into a physical one. She began walking toward them, deciding she had merely been allowing her active imagination to override her common sense, when a deep voice behind her nearly startled the wits out of her.

"My God, Emmeline, is it really you?"

Isabella stiffened in alarm. She jerked her head quickly

toward the voice, not certain what to expect. She held her breath in fear, but slowly let it out when she viewed the man who had spoken.

He was standing behind her, a fair distance away, but even at that range Isabella's experienced eye could see that his clothes were cut of the finest cloth, with a graceful, tailored fit that only Weston could achieve. A criminal would never be so well turned out. Besides, the stranger had called her Emmeline. He obviously had been observing her, not because he was waiting for an opportunity to snatch the Braun children away, but because he believed she was someone he knew.

"I am afraid you are mistaken, sir," Isabella stated in a prim voice that carried a trace of relief. "My name is not Emmeline. And I am quite certain we are not acquainted."

Isabella squared her shoulders and waited expectantly for the stranger to turn and walk away. As she waited, she studied him openly, from his muscular torso, with its forest-green, form-fitting jacket, to his skin-tight, fawn-colored leather breeches and high black Hessian riding boots. The cream-colored embroidered waistcoat called her attention to his flat abdomen, and his snowy white cravat emphasized his deeply tanned features. Although the fit and quality of his clothes proclaimed him a gentleman, he possessed an air of dishevelment that seemed oddly out of character.

The stranger was returning her direct stare with equal scrutiny. Isabella did not wither under his heated gaze, but when her eyes met his penetrating gaze, she felt a rush of uneasiness. She knew for a certainty she had never met this man before, and yet she felt he was clearly under the misconception that they knew each other.

"It *truly* is you, Emmeline."

The sound of the stranger's low, husky voice jolted Isabella out of her musing. His voice matched the rest of him—bold, strong and resonant. He advanced on her and she found herself looking directly up into his handsome face. Hard, steely gray eyes that held all the arrogance and confidence in the world focused intently on Isabella.

"I cannot believe I have finally found you, Emmeline. After all this time."

Up close, the stranger's features were uncommonly handsome—angular, chiseled, and decisively classic. He carried himself with a military bearing Isabella found both intriguing and intimidating. He did not openly threaten her, yet she had the distinct feeling he was holding himself in tight control.

As the stranger continued to regard her with a ruthless expression on his darkly handsome face, Isabella felt the hair on the nape of her neck raise. There was something dark and dangerous about this man. Everything about him seemed hard, unyielding and determined.

"I . . . I am sorry," Isabella stammered, annoyed at allowing a tremor to slip into her voice. "As I previously informed you, sir, you have me confused with someone else."

The stranger cocked his dark head slightly to one side. A stray lock of midnight-black curls fell onto his forehead. It made him look even more dangerous.

"Come now, Emmeline," he responded in his deep voice. "Is that is all you have to say to me after two long years?"

He took another step forward, and Isabella had the distinct impression he was having to restrain himself from taking hold of her. Instinctively she stepped backward. The stranger halted instantly when he saw her hasty withdrawal.

Damien St. Lawrence held his breath as he glared in mute astonishment at the women standing before him. It took every ounce of military training and discipline he possessed to control the desperate urge he felt to rush at Emmeline, grab her by the shoulders, and shake her until her teeth rattled. But the earl would not succumb to his baser desires. Silently, methodically, he cautioned himself to be very, very careful. He did not want to startle Emmeline. Now that he had finally cornered her, the last thing Damien wanted was for his victim to bolt.

The earl continued to observe her beneath hooded eyes, his face lined with hawkish determination. Damien could barely credit what his eyes told him. After all this time, here was Emmeline, standing calmly in front of him, denying she knew him. Hadn't he just been telling Jenkins he believed she was alive?

Damien had been drawn to her slender cloaked figure the moment he entered the small park. Drinking brandy with Jenkins into the wee hours of the morning had left Damien feeling numb and lightheaded, and he sought the fresh air to clear his head. After riding his favorite stallion through the streets of London, the earl stopped at the small park to rest his horse. And then he saw her.

At first the earl had been unsure it was Emmeline. Perhaps it was a trick of the morning sunlight or the effects of too much brandy. Damien continued observing the mysterious woman from a distance, with each passing minute becoming more and more convinced it was indeed his wife who stood a few hundred yards away. Finally he approached her, and when he stared fully into the woman's beautiful, deceitful face, the earl knew Emmeline was alive.

Of course, his wife had changed. The changes were subtle, yet noticeable. Her fair complexion was paler than he remembered and her nose looked smaller, her mouth fuller. She was dressed as Damien had never seen her before, demurely, almost somberly, in a long, loose-fitting navy blue coat and a matching bonnet that completely hid her glorious auburn curls.

Well, she could change her clothes and her hairstyle, but there was one thing Emmeline could not change about her appearance. Her extraordinary violet eyes. Damien had never seen their like before. And he stared ruthlessly into them now.

She returned his hard glare with a mixture of barely concealed confusion and fear, but Damien understood her reaction. After two years he hardly expected Emmeline to politely greet him. She was probably as shocked to see him as he was to see her. And she was determined to deny her true identity. But again, Damien was not surprised. Emmeline had gone to a tremendous amount of trouble to "die" two years ago. He hardly expected her to so easily give up her masquerade.

Before Damien could question her further, a young boy's cry shattered the turbulent atmosphere flaring between them.

"The children!" Isabella shouted in genuine alarm.

Dismissing the disturbing stranger, Isabella turned and raced down the embankment towards the pond.

She reached the edge of the water just in time to save Caroline from being pushed into the small lake by her brother.

"Caroline is cheating!" Robert shrieked in a high voice. "She said her stick won, but it was my stick that crossed the line first." He stamped his foot in anger and lunged for his sister.

Isabella thrust her hand out automatically to intercept the blows Robert aimed at Caroline. His young face was twisted in a mask of rage. "You will control yourself at once, Robert!" Isabella admonished in her sternest voice. "Your behavior is thoroughly disgraceful."

Caroline and Guinevere began sobbing loudly, frightened by Isabella's tone and the physical violence exhibited by their younger brother. Isabella managed to subdue the girls with a threat to cancel all outings to the park for the next two weeks. The girls sniveled noisily, but ceased their howling and Isabella focused her attention on young Robert.

She held the struggling child tightly by his collar, at arm's length, in an attempt to keep him from physically harming either her or himself. She shook him once, forcing his head back, and watched with relief as the blazing anger began to slowly recede from his blue eyes.

As the child once again regained control of his raging emotions, Isabella congratulated herself on adhering to her conviction not to use physical punishment to control intolerable conduct. Robert had tested her sorely on that point over the months, but so far she had not given in to the temptation to strike him. She was pleased to see him master his anger so quickly. Now if she could only prevent him from becoming so distraught in the first place, she would feel she had made real progress.

"Is everything all right, Miss Browning?"

Isabella raised her head tentatively, experiencing a vast sense of relief when she gazed into the familiar face of Hodgson, the coachman. His watery brown eyes were filled with concern.

"Is everything all right?" The older man repeated his question when Isabella did not readily answer.

"Everything is fine, Mr. Hodgson," Isabella assured the coachman. "The children have had a minor disagreement, but all is well."

Isabella relaxed her grip and relinquished her tight hold on Robert's shirt collar. She favored him with a stern, pointed stare. "Isn't there something you wish to say to Caroline?"

The boy's lower lip jutted out rebelliously, but after a few moments of tense silence, he muttered a somewhat ungracious apology to his sniveling sister.

It was not precisely the kind of apology Isabella felt was proper, but she was not about to press the point. She gathered the three children close to her and spoke to the coachman.

"I believe it is time for us to return home, Mr. Hodgson."

"Yes, Miss Browning." The coachman tipped his hat politely and began climbing the embankment toward the gravel path where the carriage awaited them. The children and Isabella followed close behind.

"And just where do you think you are going, Emmeline?"

Isabella groaned out loud at the sound of the now-familiar voice. Oh Lord, not him again, she thought with genuine dismay. The ruckus with Robert and the girls had momentarily distracted her from the stranger's disturbing presence. He had not, unfortunately, forgotten about her.

Isabella could feel him walking closely behind her, but she waited until they reached the carriage before addressing him.

"As I have explained to you before, sir, I am not Emmeline," she stated in a voice dripping with icy formality. Dismissing the stranger with a curt nod of her head, she deliberately turned her back on him and ushered the children into the carriage. Their young faces were shining brightly with curiosity, but they wisely did not question their governess.

Damien knew he had upset her. He did not miss the dark flush of anger on her cheeks, or the sparkle of annoyance in her beautiful eyes. Emmeline has learned to control her temper much better these past few years, he noted wryly to himself. But angry or not, he was hardly going to allow Emmeline to simply walk away from him. The earl sprang into action the moment he saw her raise her foot to climb into the carriage. Moving swiftly, he blocked her entrance.

"You cannot possible think I will let you go so easily," he said in a deliberately sarcastic tone.

He stood before her like a wall of granite. There was a challenging gleam in his steely gray eyes, a waiting look on the arrogant features of his handsome face. Isabella looked up at him and felt a cold fury sweep through her. She had been polite; she had been patient; she had been tolerant. Now she was furious.

"You have no choice but to let me go, sir," she spat at him in a scathing tone, "since I am not, nor have I ever been called Emmeline. And furthermore, I strongly suggest you refrain from accosting innocent young women in broad daylight or you might find yourself arrested and locked up in Bedlam, which in my opinion is precisely where you belong!"

Damien felt a flicker of uncertainty. Was it possible he had made a mistake? He attempted to look more closely into the woman's face, but she turned her head up to the driver. "Take us home at once, Hodgson," she commanded.

Isabella put a firm hand on Damien's sleeve and tried to push him out of her way. Her action startled the earl and in his confusion he unintentionally took a step back from the carriage. It was all the space Isabella needed. Seizing her opportunity, she jumped lithely into the carriage. Once inside she slammed the door loudly and determinedly pulled down the shade.

The earl turned a questioning eye to the older man who sat atop the box, holding the ribbons securely in his hand. "Are you in the lady's employ?"

"The lady you are referring to is Miss Isabella Browning, my lord," the servant answered readily. "Governess to the Braun family of Sparrow Court." After responding to the earl's question, Hodgson flicked the reins and the coach moved forward.

Isabella felt a vast sense of relief when the coach finally pulled away, but the astonished expression on the handsome stranger's face stayed with her on the short ride home. Try as she might, she could not shake the unsettling feeling this was not the last time she would see those steely gray eyes.

Chapter Three

The summons came before luncheon. Isabella glanced briefly at the potato soup, fenelle of fish, and fresh bread on her meal tray and sighed regretfully. Cook's culinary skills were somewhat limited, and Isabella had learned the food was infinitely more palatable if eaten hot. She was certain that by the time her meeting with her employers was concluded, her meal would be ice cold and unappetizing.

Before leaving the room, Isabella paused a moment to check her appearance in the tiny cracked mirror hanging on the wall. Several strands of her rich chestnut hair had come loose and were curled charmingly around her face. She immediately brushed them back and readjusted her severe hairstyle.

Isabella studied the rigid face of the prim, straightlaced woman reflected in the glass, hardly believing she was looking at herself. Her life had taken a far different turn than she had ever imagined it would. She thought wistfully of the plans and dreams she had as a young girl, dreams of a loving husband and children of her own. Only by escaping to her fantasies had Isabella been able to survive the bitterness and hate her father directed toward her after her mother's death.

Not her father, Isabella sharply reminded herself, her stepfather. Discovering eight years ago that Charles Browning was not her natural father had brought a ray of hope into her bleak world. On her seventeenth birthday, Charles Browning had told her the truth about her birth and then shipped her to her mother's family in York. "I've done more than my share," he said in a chilling voice. "Let your mother's snotty family care for their daughter's bastard."

Charles Browning was hoping to wound Isabella with his revelations, but she did not react as he planned. She was happy to go. She firmly believed escaping from him was going to be the beginning of a new and wonderful life. At long last she would have her chance to be among a family who would love and cherish her.

But it was not to be. Though bearing little physical resemblance to her mother, Isabella nevertheless was a reminder of her mother's disgrace, and her grandfather, the Earl of Barton, detested Isabella on sight. He chose to ignore her presence in his house and rarely spoke to her. Her two aunts, her mother's older sisters, were married and occupied with their own families and expressed little interest in Isabella. Her grandfather's sister, a formidable dowager who lived with the earl, was charged with supervising Isabella. The dowager, who was childless, resented Isabella and was not averse to showing her feelings.

Although the earl was a wealthy man, he was not generous with his granddaughter, and Isabella lived a miserly existence. In time she learned to swallow her disappointment and accepted the fact that she would never have a season in London. She hoped for an opportunity to be introduced into local society, but after accompanying the dowager to a few minor social functions, Isabella realized there was no place in this elite circle for a young woman who was such an obvious embarrassment to her family.

When she reached the age of twenty, Isabella realized her dismal situation was not going to change unless she took drastic action. In a rash act, Isabella made an impassioned speech to her grandfather and great-aunt about assuming responsibility for her own destiny and announced she was leaving to take a position as a governess.

Secretly, she had hoped her grand gesture would somehow jolt her family into taking an interest in her future, or at the very least shame her grandfather into providing her with a modest income and a small dowry, but he appeared vastly relieved to hear she was moving out of his house. Wounded, but not surprised, Isabella left, and her life as a governess began.

Isabella quickly discovered it was a tenuous existence. Technically she was an employee, but she was seldom treated as a servant. Yet she was not regarded as a member of the family either. As a governess it became necessary to learn to live somewhere between the two.

Her open nature and attractive person cost Isabella her first position. Lady Alcock did not approve of her, and when she realized that many of the young men calling at the house took more than a passing interest in the pretty young governess, she promptly dismissed Isabella.

Isabella learned from her mistakes. In her next post she took great pains to appear less attractive by wearing only modest gowns of dull colors. She also drew her hair back severely. This made her look older and more like hired help. Whenever she was called upon to supervise her charges in front of company, she always quietly removed herself to a corner of the room, taking precautions to avoid drawing any attention to herself.

The cool manner she adopted kept most of the young men at a distance. Yet the older males she chanced to encounter were more experienced, ignoring her when in the presence of others, but adept at catching her alone for a moment. Among gentlemen of society, governesses were considered fair game. It often amazed Isabella how normally civilized men could behave in such an uncivilized, boorish manner, especially when she told them in no uncertain terms that she was not interested in their scandalous propositions.

Isabella did not find all males repugnant, however. She was genuinely flattered by the subtle attention she began receiving from the eldest son of the house. He was a shy, earnest young man of twenty-two, and while she did not encourage him, she also did not discourage him. The climax of their mutual admiration was an innocent stolen kiss, unfortunately witnessed by her would-be lothario's overprotective mother. Isabella was immediately dismissed. Without a reference.

When searching for a third post, Isabella decided to try a different route, and she became a companion to the Dowager Duchess of Osbourn. That post had the distinction of being the shortest in duration. The dowager duchess was a cantankerous old lady who proved very difficult to work for and live with. By mutual consent, Isabella left as soon as she secured the position she now held with the Brauns.

Working for the Brauns was by far the most successful experience of her career, and Isabella finally felt a measure of security. The Brauns were of the merchant class, exceedingly wealthy but not socially elite, and that suited Isabella fine. There were no young bucks of the *ton* calling at the house to harass her, and the only male family member was the children's father. Mr. Braun always treated her with the utmost respect. Isabella long suspected he was enthralled with the notion of having the granddaughter of an earl caring for and teaching his three children.

The striking of the hall clock pulled Isabella's attention back to the matters at hand. Knowing she would be late for her meeting if she did not hurry, she quickly left her room. Summoning up her finely tuned inner discipline, Isabella succeeded in firmly pushing the emotional memories aside by the time she reached the large entrance foyer on the first floor.

She glanced briefly at the closed drawing room doors and wiped her damp palms on the skirts of her plain gray gown. Then she signaled the footman with a curt nod of her head and he opened the door.

"Miss Browning," he announced in a bored voice.

Mrs. Braun ceased speaking the minute Isabella entered the room. Wearing an over-bright smile, she greeted her children's governess breathlessly. Isabella could not help noticing how uncharacteristically nervous Mrs. Braun appeared.

Mrs. Braun was a middle-aged matron with an ample figure, yet she was attractive in a rather obvious way. This afternoon her black hair was dressed high up on her head, with several wispy ringlets artfully arranged around her ears. Her sea-green gown was cut low for a woman of her size and revealed more than a hint of swelling bosom. Even though it was early afternoon, Mrs. Braun wore an impressive array of expensive jewelry, attesting more to her husband's wealth than to her good taste.

Mr. Braun was the exact opposite of his wife. Tall, fair-haired, and almost painfully thin, he was hardly the image of a successful merchant. He was dressed in his customary somber black business suit, and Isabella belatedly realized that he normally was at his office down on Market Street at this hour of the day. He, too, seemed on edge.

"Thank you for coming so promptly, Miss Browning," Mr. Braun said. He cleared his throat loudly. "Please, do sit down."

With a questioning look, Isabella complied with his request, taking the seat directly across from Mrs. Braun. After Isabella was seated, Mr. Braun joined his wife on the settee. Isabella shifted her gaze back and forth between the two, from the grinning face of Mrs. Braun to the somber continence of Mr. Braun, trying to read from their very opposite expressions what was happening.

"Now then, Miss Browning, I would like to ask you—" Mr. Braun began, but he was cut off by a loud gasp of astonishment from Isabella.

Isabella could scarcely believe she had missed seeing the third occupant of the room until this very moment. He was leaning casually against the wall, a glass in his hand. When their eyes met, he flashed a slow and tantalizingly wicked grin. Everything else seemed to recede into the distance as Isabella stared in appalled silence at the rude man who had accosted her in the park.

She was conscious of a sudden feeling that the room had shrunk in size. There was something infinitely more unsettling about having to face this strange man in closed quarters. Instinctively she wanted to flee, but she had far too much common sense to allow herself to act in such an irrational manner in front of her employers.

The stranger's larger-than-life presence dominated the room. He was staring intently at Isabella, and when he caught her eye again, he gave her a mocking bow. Then he spoke.

"As you can clearly see, Mr. Braun, this woman knows me," he stated in an arrogant voice.

"Is this true?" Mrs. Braun asked. "Are you acquainted with the earl?"

"I have seen him before," Isabella admitted slowly, her mind whirling in confusion. An earl? This strange man who had spent the morning stalking her through the park was an earl. But what was he doing here? Was he a friend of the Brauns?

"Oh, dear," Mrs. Braun exclaimed breathlessly. "I am afraid we owe you an apology, my lord." She turned a jaundiced eye to Isabella. Mrs. Braun looked properly scandalized. "You must believe we had no idea who she really was when we hired her."

"Do not concern yourself, Mrs. Braun," the earl replied in an even tone. "I found it equally baffling to discover Emmeline was in your employ. And doing such a credible job." He shot Isabella a hard, challenging look.

Isabella gulped, trying to marshall her thoughts. It was obvious the earl had followed her to the Brauns' home to tell them his ridiculous story about her being some woman named Emmeline. Isabella took a steadying breath and attempted to assert a measure of control over the situation.

"Mrs. Braun, Mr. Braun, I can assure you this is all a bizarre misunderstanding," Isabella began imploringly. "When I said I had seen this gentleman before, that is precisely what I meant. Yes, I have *seen* him. I did not mean to imply that I know him. The one and only time I have ever laid eyes on him was this morning, during my outing with the children in the park. He stared at me for a considerable length of time before approaching me. He then addressed me as Emmeline and insisted he was acquainted with me. Naturally, I told him he was mistaken. As to why he has followed me here, I cannot even hazard a guess."

Isabella finished speaking and stared intently at her two

employers, trying to read their reactions to her explanation. Mrs. Braun's round face held a closed look, but her husband appeared to be wavering. Isabella addressed her next comments to him.

"I am not certain what the . . . umm, the earl has said about me—" Isabella began calmly.

"He told us you were his wife," Mrs. Braun bluntly interrupted.

"What!" Isabella's eyes flashed and she jerked her head up to look at the earl, who was still standing on the far side of the room. "My God, this man is obviously some sort of lunatic!"

"Really, Miss Browning," Mrs. Braun admonished. "It is hardly necessary for you to insult his lordship."

"Insult his lordship?" Isabella sputtered, unable to believe Mrs. Braun was defending the earl. "This . . . this man spent the better part of the morning stalking and harassing me, following me around a public park calling me Emmeline, which I might add, is not, nor has ever been my name. He now has somehow managed to track me to my residence and place of employment, and you have the audacity to imply I have insulted *him*. I strongly doubt he even possesses the wit necessary to be insulted!"

"That is quite enough," Mrs. Braun huffed. She turned to her husband in annoyance. "George."

Mr. Braun's expression revealed his shock at Isabella's angry response. In all the months she had worked for them, he had rarely seen her raise her voice to his children, let alone speak to anyone in such a passionate manner. The quiet, self-contained governess he knew appeared to be unraveling before his eyes.

"Did the earl hurt you this morning, Miss Browning?" Mr. Braun inquired. "Or threaten you in any way?"

"Not exactly," Isabella answered truthfully. "But he did try to prevent me from entering the carriage when we were leaving the park." She stared pointedly up at the earl.

He slanted a steely gray gaze in her direction and took a long swallow of his drink. His face gave no indication of his emotions other than the hint of amusement she saw in his eyes before a shuttered look took its place. It made Isabella furious.

"So the earl did not harm you," Mr. Braun stated reflectively. He was certainly in a very delicate position. Since she was his employee, Mr. Braun felt he owed a measure of loyalty to Isabella. After all, she was an unprotected female living in his household and clearly his responsibility. However, Mr. Braun was not unaware of either Damien's fierce reputation or his social stature. The man was an earl, and although he had a somewhat tarnished reputation, he was still a member of the English aristocracy.

True, Mr. Braun had heard about the mysterious death of the Countess of Saunders several years ago, but he also remembered hearing about Damien's obsessive insistence that his wife was not dead. Then there were all the wild rumors inferring that the countess had committed suicide, while some of the more sordid stories even hinted at murder, with the earl as the chief suspect.

Mr. Braun considered all that ancient history at the moment. Damien St. Lawrence had stated his case this afternoon, before Miss Browning had been summoned, in a very calm, very persuasive, and very civilized manner. It truly did not matter if Mr. Braun personally thought the idea that his children's governess was the missing wife of an earl was completely preposterous. He was certainly not about to disagree with a man who by every account was his superior. Mr. Braun had not earned his vast fortune by being a fool.

"As you can plainly see, Mr. Braun, my wife has reacted precisely as I predicted she would when I first explained this bizarre situation to you," Damien stated smoothly. "I ask only that you allow me to escort Emmeline to Lord Poole's house in Grovesnor Square. After she has seen and spoken to her brother, I believe she will be more reasonable."

The room remained silent as Damien pressed on. "Afterward, Emmeline will naturally be free to return here, if she wishes."

"That seems very fair, my lord," Mr. Braun replied slowly, pleased the earl had given him an easy choice. It was a reasonable request, asking Miss Browning to accompany him to Lord

Poole's. And it left room for the possibility, if the earl was somehow mistaken, then Miss Browning would be free to return, although nothing in Damien St. Lawrence's attitude or tone suggested there was even a remote possibility he was wrong.

"Fair?" Isabella repeated in a voice that sounded far too loud, even to her own ears. "You honestly think this man has devised a fair solution to this absurd situation?"

"The earl is only requesting your cooperation for a few hours," Mr. Braun insisted. "It can do no harm for you to visit Lord Poole this afternoon. He will be able to verify your identity."

"I don't need anyone to verify my identity," Isabella replied tensely, unable to believe what she was hearing. She sat very still while she considered the best course of action. Belatedly she realized her hands were trembling. She folded them in front of her. "I am sorry, Mr. Braun, but I must refuse to accompany *the earl* anywhere."

A charged, furious silence greeted Isabella's announcement. She could feel the resentment of both Mr. and Mrs. Braun, but it was the earl's fury that truly frightened her. His face was a taut mask of controlled anger. His steely gray eyes glittered with terrifying intensity and the whiteness around the edges of his mouth testified to his barely restrained emotion.

"You will accompany me, Emmeline."

Isabella flinched at the cold-blooded tone of the earl's deep voice. "I will not," she declared stoutly.

"I think it would be best for all concerned if you do as the earl requests, Miss Browning," Mr. Braun injected.

"I have already made my feelings quite clear about this," Isabella insisted softly. "And I must add that I would not feel comfortable working for someone who had so little regard for my personal feelings, Mr. Braun," Isabella added a trifle recklessly. She knew it was a gamble, but she also knew her only chance to avoid being hauled away by the earl was to convince Mr. Braun to support her.

Isabella waited tensely for Mr. Braun to make his decision,

beginning to experience a ray of hope when he did not immediately answer.

"If that is truly the way you feel, Miss Browning," Mr. Braun said with a regretful sigh, "perhaps it is best if you terminate your employment with us."

Isabella's heart sank at his announcement, but she listened to his answer with stoic acceptance. She was used to having her feelings and opinions disregarded; it had been that way for most of her life. But she had foolishly hoped it would be different this time.

Isabella sighed. For a brief moment, she thought she might have persuaded Mr. Braun to take her side. She rose regally to her feet and faced the Brauns. There was a hint of tension in the way she held her shoulders, and the hurt in her eyes was evident.

"Are you absolutely certain you wish to terminate my employment?"

Mr. Braun had the grace to look embarrassed. Before he could reply, his wife intervened. "We believe it is best for all concerned if you leave," she insisted.

"I'll go upstairs and pack my things immediately." Isabella turned and walked slowly toward the drawing room doors. It was over. She had just lost her fourth position. What would she do now? She felt dazed and a little sick to her stomach.

When her hand touched the door latch, the earl spoke. "I will await you in the front hall, Emmeline."

At the sound of his voice, Isabella's knuckles went white around the brass handle, but she forced herself to remain calm. She tried to reply, but her throat was too dry. She had to swallow a few times before answering.

"As you wish, my lord," Isabella replied in a wry tone. She shut the door quickly behind her and hurried up the stairs to her room, silently vowing she would beg on the streets before accompanying that dreadful man anywhere.

Chapter Four

Isabella wrenched a plain brown dress off its hook and flung it onto her bed. She swore vehemently and reached into the wardrobe for another gown. She yanked out the remaining three garments and cursed again. Then she pulled out her worn satchel from the bottom of the empty oak cabinet.

Growing up in an all-male household did have its advantages, Isabella decided, repeating a favorite curse of her eldest brother, the exact meaning of which she did not fully understand.

She kept her anger fueled by alternating her cursing and throwing, and within minutes all her clothing was scattered on the bed. After all her meager belongings were assembled, Isabella quickly gathered them up and stuffed them into the satchel.

Normally she would have carefully and methodically folded each and every garment before packing it, but Isabella was not about to take the time to pack neatly. It was imperative she vacate the house quickly, and neatness would be a deterrent to that goal.

Isabella embraced her anger, knowing it was buffering her from the true reality of her situation. If her anger left, it would be replaced by fear. Cold, unmitigated terror at the prospect of once again being without a job, without a home, without any security at all. And worst of all, the maniacal earl, the cause of all her recent distress, awaited her downstairs. Above all else he must be avoided.

Shuddering with emotion, Isabella jammed her straw bonnet on her head and hastily threw on her coat. She pulled too hard on a button and it went flying, but she did not take the time to search for it. Better to lose a button than lose a chance at escape.

You must hurry, you must hurry, Isabella repeated methodically to herself as she lifted her satchel. She paused briefly in the hallway outside her door, toying with the notion of saying good-bye to the children but rapidly discarded the notion. She could not afford to waste the time it would take to walk to the schoolroom at the opposite side of the house. Let the Brauns explain to their children why their governess had left so suddenly.

Quietly, efficiently, Isabella strode down the hallway to the servants' staircase. When she reached the first floor, she cautiously edged her way across the short hallway toward the kitchen at the back end of the house. She strongly suspected the earl had positioned himself at the bottom of the grand staircase in the front of the house, but if he moved to the side of the foyer, there was a slight chance he might see her at the back entrance.

Thankfully, Isabella reached the kitchen without incident. For once the busy room was deserted, except for the cook, who was sitting in a large rocking chair in front of the fireplace, snoring softly.

Isabella could scarcely believe her good fortune. She had neither the time nor the desire to exchange lengthy farewells with the household's servants and now it appeared she would escape the house without anyone seeing her at all. Silently she lifted the kitchen door handle and gingerly stepped outside into the small courtyard facing the rear of the house.

Isabella paused a moment, debating which direction to take. She would have preferred going straight ahead, walking through the Brauns' formal gardens, crossing the neighboring property, and emerging onto the street behind the Brauns' house. But a rather high fence divided the two properties and Isabella was uncertain she could scale it.

Instead, she turned to her right and rapidly walked along the shortest section of the house, crouching low to avoid being seen through any of the windows. Turning again, she followed the narrow brick footpath along the side of the mansion, heading toward the street front. She struggled for a moment with the iron latch on the gate guarding the entrance to the Brauns' yard but successfully swung it open on her third attempt.

"Going somewhere, Emmeline?"

Isabella was so startled by the earl's voice that she dropped her satchel. She jerked her head around and saw him standing in front of the house only a few feet away. He was leaning casually against the brick facade, his arms crossed over his broad chest. He looked very pleased with himself.

Drat the man, must he be everywhere? Isabella bent down to retrieve her satchel and slowly stood upright. She simply stared at the earl for a few minutes, feeling completely lost. His superior attitude grated on her nerves. She gritted her teeth and considered a variety of actions. Isabella glanced briefly down at the earl's strong, muscular legs and knew for certain she could never outrun him. Perhaps it was possible to outwit him.

"Ahh, I can almost see the wheels turning in that devious head of yours, Emmeline." The earl pushed himself off the wall and took a step toward her.

Isabella decided it was time to take a stand against him. She thrust her chin in the air.

"I give you fair warning, sir. If you do not allow me past you, I shall scream. Very loudly."

"You will?"

"Yes."

"I see." The earl stroked his chin thoughtfully. He appeared singularly unimpressed by Isabella's threats. Desperately, she tried again.

"I am not going with you, sir."

"You are going to do precisely what I tell you to do, Emmeline."

"For the last time, I am not Emmeline!"

Isabella shrieked loudly, but the fight soon left her. She brought her hand to her head and rubbed her temple vigorously. It was no use. No matter how many times she shouted the truth at this man, he would not relent. He would never relent. He would hound her until he got his way.

"What do you want from me?" she finally whispered.

Damien's eyes narrowed in suspicion as he observed her abrupt change of attitude. She had dropped her defiant stance and her eyes were lowered in classic feminine submission.

"Accompany me to your brother's house, Emmeline. I want to see his face when I confront him with you standing by my side."

"If I do as you ask, will you then leave me in peace?"

"Yes."

"Even if it does not turn out as you anticipate? Do you promise, do you swear to me on your word of honor, you will leave me alone?"

"I have already stated that I agree," Damien growled softly. "And I, unlike yourself, abide by my word."

"All right," Isabella sighed in defeat. "I will accompany you."

The earl gave a masculine grunt of satisfaction and moved forward to grab her arm. Isabella neatly sidestepped him and hurried toward the impressive carriage parked in front of the Brauns' house. She blinked resentfully at the coat of arms boldly emblazoned on the door of the shining black vehicle. It reminded her of the carriage her grandfather rode in.

A young servant dressed in elegant blue and silver livery eagerly jumped down from his position on the back of the coach when he saw them approaching. The servant respectfully opened the door, and against her better judgment, Isabella allowed him to assist her inside the coach.

She waited with a feeling of impending doom for the earl to join her. She could hear his deep voice outside the carriage as he gave his driver instructions, and she nervously adjusted the folds of her cloak on the cushions. Her heart began beating erratically at the thought of spending any length of time in such a close, confined space with the earl.

He entered the carriage all too soon, and to Isabella's dismay elected to sit by her side. The deeply padded cushions gave considerably beneath his weight, and Isabella found herself tilting precariously against the earl's leg. She let out a small yelp of surprise but managed to keep her balance with an effort and successfully avoided brushing against his strong, muscular thigh.

He glanced narrowly at her, and Isabella slid farther into her corner of the coach. Her body felt tense and awkward. She was aware of a growing sensation of lightheadedness, and her throat felt a little dry.

He is trying to intimidate me with his superior physical size, she decided suddenly. She slanted him an assessing glance, but he appeared oblivious to her stares. The carriage jolted forward unexpectedly, and Isabella instinctively thrust her arm out to prevent herself from being thrown to the floor. After regaining her seat, she turned her head away from the earl and fervently prayed their trip would be a short one.

After a mercifully quick and silent ride, the carriage drew into Grovesnor Square. Isabella viewed the impressive town house they pulled in front of from her window. It was a large building with six windows on either side of an ornate gray stone portico. A graveled courtyard set the house back from the street, and a charming fountain in its center merrily spouted clear streams of water. Due to the gloomy gray skies of the afternoon, glimmering lights could be seen in several of the downstairs windows, and the two flambeaux by the door were lit.

The earl swung the carriage door open impatiently before the vehicle came to a complete halt and lithely jumped out. He flashed Isabella a look of cold indifference as he reached in to haul her out of the carriage. Now that he had succeeded in bringing her here, his complete attention was no longer focused on her. Instead he seemed to relish the confrontation to come.

The earl pushed himself inside the house the moment his

persistent knock was answered, dragging a reluctant Isabella behind him. They were greeted by a startled footman.

"His lordship is not receiving callers this afternoon," the servant said in a formal tone.

"Oh, I do believe he will make an exception in my case," the earl stated in a defiant voice. "Inform Lord Poole the Earl of Saunders is here."

An elderly man who stood very erect and aloof entered the hallway. Isabella surmised he was the butler. "Is there a problem, Taylor?"

"No, there is not a problem," the earl replied in an authoritative voice. "Taylor was just going to inform Lord Poole the Earl of Saunders is here to see him. Isn't that correct, Taylor?"

"Was he really?" The elderly butler raised a questioning eyebrow. He glanced from the uncertain expression of the footman to the firm countenance of the earl and decided it was necessary to intervene. "Lord Poole is not at home, my lord."

The earl clenched his jaw at the news. "Then we shall wait for him to return. We will be in the red salon."

Ignoring the scandalous look of outrage on the butler's face, the earl grasped Isabella's elbow firmly and propelled her through the hallway to the second door on the left. Without waiting for assistance from any of the servants, he opened the door and pushed Isabella into the room, slamming the door shut behind them.

Isabella took only a passing notice of the opulent surroundings. Red and gold were predominant in the wall covering and heavy draperies. The thick, luxurious Oriental carpet echoed the same color scheme. The furniture was tasteful and elegant and very expensive. Apparently familiar with his surroundings, the earl headed directly for a Pembroke table and poured himself a hefty snifter of brandy.

Isabella scurried away from him to the opposite side of the room and positioned herself in front of a long French window. She had an excellent view of the meticulously groomed gardens, but she paid them no heed.

"Would you like me to ring for tea? Or would you prefer something stronger?"

"I don't care for any tea, thank you. And I seldom drink spirits," Isabella responded automatically.

"For God's sake, stop playacting, Emmeline."

"I am not playacting," Isabella insisted wearily. "And stop calling me Emmeline. It is a name I have come to heartily detest in the last few hours."

"As you wish, madam."

Damien made a mocking bow to her back and threw himself into a red brocade wing chair. He continued to drink methodically, his steely gray eyes never leaving the ramrod-straight back of the woman standing by the window.

Damien studied the enigma that was his wife through an alcoholic haze and wondered why he had no interest in plying her with questions. What had happened out at The Grange two years ago when she disappeared? Where had she been for the past few years, and how in the world did she end up as a governess to a merchant class family like the Brauns?

"How long will we have to wait here?" Isabella's gently asked question broke into the earl's thoughts.

"As long as necessary," he replied obscurely. "I have not come all this way to be denied." Damien set his empty glass down on the mahogany table next to his chair and propped up his chin with one hand. He suddenly felt a restless urgency to examine Emmeline more closely. "Turn around."

The earl spoke softly, but something in his voice set Isabella's teeth on edge. Yet, she obeyed him and gracefully pivoted on her heel.

No lamps or candles had been lit in the red salon, and the lack of afternoon sun produced a gray light in the room. During his previous encounters with Isabella, Damien had focused almost exclusively on her unique violet eyes. Yet in this fading light, he could not clearly see the shade of her eyes, and she looked different to him somehow. She did not look like the wife he remembered. It disturbed him.

"Remove your bonnet."

Isabella's dark brows drew together at the earl's strange command, but she lifted her arms and took off her hat.

"Now take down your hair."

"Really, sir!" Isabella sounded outraged.

"Just do it." The earl's voice was impatient.

A flicker of emotion passed over Isabella's lovely face, but she did not refuse his odd request. Slowly she removed the pins securing her rich chestnut hair. Once freed, it fell in long, thick waves down past her waist.

When the earl saw her unbound hair, he rose quickly from his chair, almost knocking it over. He looked very surprised. He was certain the deep chestnut color was different from what he remembered, as were the luscious length and curls. Color could be changed and curls added—Damien knew that much about a female's hair. But the length? In all the years of their marriage Damien had never seen Emmeline's hair reach any farther than the tops of her shoulders. Was it possible for a woman's hair to grow that long in two years?

"Your hair is different," Damien stated, his tone genuinely puzzled. "What have you done to it?"

"I have done nothing to my hair," Isabella replied steadily. "It is precisely as it has always been."

Damien took several steps toward the center of the room to gain a better view.

"You must have changed your hair," Damien protested. "I have never seen it as it is now."

The earl advanced a few steps farther until he stood only inches away. He reached out a long arm and grabbed a fistful of Isabella's hair. It felt like heavy silk. He brought the rich chestnut curls up close to his face to examine them, and he could see the threads of gold intertwined with the red and brown.

He tugged on the silken mass, using her hair to draw her closer to him. Positioned a scant few inches away, Isabella could not help but notice the almost terrifyingly powerful muscles of his chest and arms, the glint of determination darkening his gray eyes. He was a strong man, both physically and mentally. An immovable force.

Isabella felt the strange tension that seemed to emanate from the earl's solidly built body the minute she drew near him. She watched him closely with questioning eyes, unsure of what was going to happen next. Despite her inner qualms, she never moved, forcing herself to remain perfectly still.

Damien put his free arm around her waist and pulled her against his hard body, effectively making her his prisoner. Frightened and startled by the unexpected move, Isabella tried to twist away, but he held her hair tightly and her scalp tingled with pain.

"You are hurting me, my lord," she cried out softly. She stared up into his darkly handsome face, her eyes beseeching him to release her hair.

Damien saw the tears gathering in her eyes, and he let the shimmering mass escape his fingers. He moved his strong hand along her jawline and took her chin firmly in his fingers, tilting it upward. Then he increased the pressure of his other arm around her waist.

Isabella could feel the long, hard muscular length of him pressing closer against her body and it made her feel dizzy. Her breathing became unsteady as she stood transfixed, staring into his steely gray eyes for a timeless instant. And then, without warning, he bent his dark head and brought his mouth down on hers in a crushing kiss.

Isabella went rigid with shock. Yet the firm, insistent pressure of the earl's surprisingly soft lips against her own made her quickly forget every rule of female modesty she had ever been taught. Her shock gave way to fascination and she found herself relaxing against him, eager to experience the mysterious pleasure he so effortlessly brought forth.

His tongue moved delicately along the seam of her lips and Isabella heard herself whimper. Lost in her first real embrace, she felt the tide of passion sweep over her entire body as the earl's mouth moved more insistently, more demandingly on her own. Isabella was unaware that her hands moved upward to rest on his broad chest in a subtle sign of encouragement as the glittering excitement raced through her.

Never in her wildest dreams had she imagined a kiss could be so all encompassing. This heady mix of emotion and excitement nearly overwhelmed her.

With a low groan, Damien broke off the kiss. He raised his

head and looked down at the woman he held in his arms. Her eyes were closed and her whole body felt limp with sensation. He strongly suspected she would fall if he did not continue to hold her securely in his arms.

More than anything, Damien felt the need to kiss her again. And again. Kiss her more deeply, caress her more passionately with his mouth and his hands.

Her response had been genuine and passionate. She had returned his kisses with true ardor, but there had been a sweet innocence about her lips, a sort of wonder and awe in her response. She was obviously very inexperienced in making love. Her kisses had proven that.

They also proved beyond a doubt that she was not his wife. Carefully, Damien disengaged Isabella from his arms and gently pushed her away from his overheated body. She staggered a bit when deprived of his strong embrace but remained on her feet. Slowly, she opened her eyes. The sleepy, dreamlike quality in her lovely violet eyes disappeared the moment she saw the earl's rigidly controlled body and stern, unsmiling face. Her cheeks flamed with color and she hastily dropped her eyes to the carpet.

"You are not Emmeline," the earl stated unnecessarily.

"I am not Emmeline," Isabella repeated. Her breathing was still a trifle uneven, and she had not yet fully recovered from his devastating kisses.

Damien took a few steps away from her, needing to physically distance himself from her warm body.

"Bloody hell! What a damnable mess."

Damien ran his fingers through his dark hair and cursed again. How could he have been so wrong? Too little sleep and too much brandy, he admitted ruefully. "Naturally I shall accompany you back to the Brauns' house and somehow try to explain all of this."

"I am afraid it has gone too far for that, my lord."

Damien's apologetic expression altered slightly at Isabella's reply. "What exactly do you want me to do, Miss . . . Miss . . ?"

"Browning."

"Yes, Miss Browning."

Isabella shrugged her shoulders. "I don't really know."

Damien's face clouded and he felt his temper begin to rise. "It would be helpful if you could decide quickly, Miss Browning. Since my reason for confronting Lord Poole no longer exists, I prefer not to remain in his house."

"Need I remind you, my lord," Isabella answered in a cool tone, "this situation was not my doing. I told you repeatedly I was not your wife. Due to your obstinacy, I no longer have a position to return to!"

"I have already offered to make amends, Miss Browning, and you have refused my assistance. I fear you leave me no choice. My coach and driver are at your disposal. When you finally decide precisely where you wish to go, you may inform my servants." With hands clenched into tight fists by his sides, the earl made a curt, stiff bow. "Good afternoon, Miss Browning."

Isabella lifted her chin in response, then watched with wide-eyed dismay as the earl turned on his heel and marched purposefully from the room. It took a few moments for the events to register in her shocked mind. That arrogant, willful man had dragged her unwillingly to this strange house and had now abandoned her here.

Chapter Five

The elegant coach traversed the crowded London streets in a random manner. Isabella sat alone inside, barely noticing the milling crowds and variety of hackneys, carts, and carriages clogging the road.

The overcast skies of the early afternoon had fulfilled their promise of rain and a steady drizzle prevailed. The smell of wet pavement filled Isabella's nostrils and she sighed. The dull, gray weather matched her mood.

She had remained in Lord Poole's town house only long enough to rebind her hair and secure her bonnet on her head. Then she raced out of the house, offering no explanation to the astonished servants. She escaped to the safety of the earl's carriage, which was patiently awaiting her arrival, just as the earl had promised. As soon as she gained her seat inside the carriage, Isabella instructed the coachman to drive away. Since she gave no specific instructions as to her destination, the coach had been meandering about the city for the past hour.

"Should I drive down Bond Street, miss?" The coachman called down to her. "It's a bit crowded, but not impassable."

Isabella leaned near the half-opened window and yelled, "Bond Street would be fine."

She settled back against the comfortable squabs and forced herself to face reality. She could not very well continue driving around London in the earl's carriage for the rest of the day. She needed to make some important decisions about her future, and time was running short.

Isabella bit her lip nervously and admitted to herself that she was frightened. Her prospects for employment were dim, especially without proper references. It would most likely take her several weeks, perhaps even months, to find a suitable position. And London was an expensive city to live in given her meager savings.

Isabella knew she would have no choice but to return to her grandfather's estate in York while searching for a new post. Even though her mother's family had amply demonstrated their lack of regard for her, she knew they would not deny her temporary shelter. As much as it rankled her to ask for her family's help, Isabella knew she could ill afford to allow her pride to override her common sense in this instance.

Her decision reached, Isabella tapped on the roof of the carriage to attract the driver's attention.

"Take me to the nearest posting inn, please," she requested. "I need to catch the next available coach traveling north."

The coach made a sharp left turn and all too soon stopped. Isabella glanced speculatively out the window and was pleased to note that the establishment they had arrived at looked well-maintained. She sincerely hoped it would not be too long a wait for the mail coach to depart. No matter how respectable an establishment appeared, a woman traveling alone was often the target of unwanted attention.

"Thank you," she murmured softly to the young footman who assisted her out of the carriage. Turning around to pull out her satchel, she cast a final longing glance inside the luxurious coach. It would have been heavenly to ride to York inside this comfortable vehicle. Isabella spitefully wished it were possible, knowing it would infuriate the earl to have his carriage disappear for several days.

It seemed a fitting revenge to take the coach the earl so rudely placed at her disposal halfway across England, and Isabella was sorely tempted to commandeer the carriage, but her lack of funds prevented her from doing so. She did not have the necessary coin to provide food and lodging for herself, the servants, or even the horses on a journey as far as York.

As she took her final leave, Isabella gave the three male servants a curt nod of farewell and boldly began walking toward the entrance of the inn.

"Please wait, miss," an anxious voice called out.

Isabella turned around and curiously observed one of the earl's servants scramble down from the top of the carriage. "Are you certain this is where you want us to leave you? We would be happy to take you outside the city, or anywhere else you wish to go."

"That is most kind of you Mr. . . . ?"

"Jenkins," the man supplied.

"Mr. Jenkins." Isabella nodded politely at the introduction. "As tempting as your generous offer is, I must decline. I am traveling well beyond the city limits to York."

"I see," Jenkins replied slowly. "These inns can be rather rough for a genteel lady. I must insist you at least allow me to escort you inside."

Isabella paused a moment, observing the servant openly while she considered his offer. She judged him to be near fifty years of age, but he was a strong-looking man, obviously in good physical condition. She thought he was rather elegantly dressed for a coachman, but she decided to accept his offer of protection.

"Since I have no notion of how long I will be forced to wait, I would appreciate your company, Mr. Jenkins. Thank you."

Once they were inside the inn, Isabella was glad she had accepted the servant's assistance. The taproom was noisy and crowded, with an almost exclusively male clientele. A quick perusal of the area confirmed there were no unaccompanied women seated in the room.

Miraculously, Jenkins was able to secure a relatively private table in a corner of the crowded room. After a few moments, a harassed-looking barmaid came to their table.

"So what will you be having today?" she asked in a bored voice.

Isabella's stomach grumbled at the thought of food, and she realized she had not eaten since early morning. "I would like a pot of tea and something substantial to go with it."

"We don't have anything fancy, but the cook could fix you a cold plate, with whatever meat, cheese, and bread we have left."

"That would be fine." Turning to the man sitting next to her, Isabella inquired graciously, "Would you care for some tea also, Mr. Jenkins? Or perhaps a pint of ale?"

"I prefer ale."

After a considerable wait, the barmaid brought their refreshments. As Isabella lifted the heavy earthenware teapot and slowly poured herself a cup of tea, she became aware of the intense scrutiny of her companion.

"Do I look so very much like her, Mr. Jenkins?" Isabella inquired casually, while cutting a wedge of cheddar cheese. She delicately sank her strong white teeth into the tasty morsel and waited for a response.

Jenkins's face revealed his surprise at her direct question, but he did not pretend to misunderstand Isabella's remark.

"You do bear a distinct resemblance to the countess, miss," Jenkins replied, "especially the unusual color of your eyes. I can understand how the earl might have mistaken you for Emmeline. It was a credible mistake given the earl's condition."

"His condition?" Isabella remained silent for a few thoughtful moments and then nodded her head philosophically. "I strongly suspected there was something *different* about the earl. He was absolutely relentless in his insistence about my being Emmeline, and he acted in a most irrational manner. He was also excessively forceful and demanding toward me and my former employers." Isabella leaned in closer and whispered sympathetically, "The earl is unbalanced, isn't he, Mr. Jenkins?"

"Unbalanced?" Jenkins's face broke into a broad smile when he caught Isabella's meaning. "The earl is not addle-brained miss, if that is what you are implying. He was merely drunk."

"Drunk?" Isabella shook her head vigorously. "I am certain you are wrong. I can tell from experience when someone is inebriated. My stepfather had a great fondness for drink. I am quite sure I would have known if the earl was drunk."

"I am not very proud to confess I spent the better part of last night emptying three bottles of brandy with the earl. Believe me, he was under the hatches when he first spotted you in the park this morning."

Isabella raised a disbelieving eyebrow. "Does the earl often spend his evenings drinking with his servants?"

"I am his friend, miss, as well as his valet," Jenkins replied with obvious pride in his voice. "And no, the earl does not often spend his time drinking."

"What was so special about last night?"

Jenkins slowly set his half-empty tankard down on the table before answering. "We packed up the London town house yesterday. The earl was forced to sell it, and I think that bothered him a good deal more than he figured it would."

"He has pressing gambling debts?" Isabella could not keep the hint of scorn from her voice.

"These debts are not of his own doing," Jenkins responded defensively. "These obligations were incurred long before the earl assumed his title. Being an honorable man, he is determined to repay them."

"I beg your pardon," Isabella countered, hearing the note of indignation in the servant's voice. She could tell that her slur on the earl's character had insulted the valet. She was intrigued by the servant's unwavering loyalty. And by his admission that the earl was his friend. "It was not my intention to offend you, Mr. Jenkins. However, my ghastly experience with the earl today causes me to naturally assume the worst in his case."

"What happened?"

"The earl accosted me in the park this morning, insisting I was Emmeline, and when I informed him that he was wrong, he followed me to my place of employment. He shocked my employers with his outlandish accusations and then practically dragged me to Lord Poole's house where, thank goodness, the earl finally realized his mistake. Unfortunately for me, this realization came a bit too late. Thanks to the earl's overactive imagination and inebriated condition, I have been dismissed from my position as governess. Now I shall be forced to rely upon the begrudging charity of my family until I am able to secure another post.'' Isabella's troubled expression conveyed how distressed she truly was over the circumstances.

''You certainly don't look like any governess I've ever met,'' Jenkins blurted out. Up close, the fine porcelain skin and aristocratic features of Isabella's lovely face were striking.

''Unfortunately, you are not the only one who holds that opinion, Mr. Jenkins,'' Isabella admitted honestly. ''In addition, my references are almost nonexistent. I am afraid this time it will be a very long search for a new post.''

There was no trace of complaining in her voice, merely acceptance of the reality of the situation. As Jenkins watched Isabella chew relentlessly on a tough piece of meat, an idea began to form in his mind.

''Perhaps I might be able to assist you in finding a position, miss,'' Jenkins said in a tentative voice. ''I happen to be acquainted with a family that is sorely in need of a governess. And I don't believe they would be too concerned over your lack of references.''

Isabella's eyes lit with interest. ''Do you truly think I might be suitable for this post, Mr. Jenkins?''

''Yes, miss, I do.''

The way the valet scrupulously avoided Isabella's eyes caused her to become suspicious. ''This mysterious position wouldn't have anything to do with the earl by chance, would it, Mr. Jenkins?''

''Well, miss,'' the valet hedged, ''it could be an excellent solution. After all, you just told me the earl was responsible for your dismissal. The very least he owes you is another position. And he does have two young children who are badly in need of discipline and care.''

''I can imagine,'' Isabella whispered under her breath, wondering what kind of little monsters the earl's children were. ''I strongly doubt this would work, Mr. Jenkins. Besides, it is usually the lady of the house who engages the governess. I am sure that when the countess returns, she will not be interested in the bizarre justification for my employment in her household.''

Jenkins turned a puzzled grimace toward Isabella. ''I can assure you that will not be a problem,'' he stated with authority.

''Why not?''

''The countess is dead, miss.''

Isabella's fork clattered noisily to her plate. Her eyes never left Jenkins's earnest face as she swallowed hard, forcing the dry piece of meat she had been chewing on down her throat. ''I would like a full explanation, Mr. Jenkins. From the beginning, if you please.''

Two hours later, Isabella found herself once again comfortably ensconced in the earl's carriage, traveling at a brisk pace toward his estate in Warwickshire, not completely certain how she had allowed herself to be persuaded to make this journey. Jenkins's portrayal of the numerous tragedies and misfortunes the earl had endured touched Isabella's tender heart, and without taking the time to carefully consider her actions she had impulsively agreed to travel to Whatley Grange.

However, now that her common sense was reasserting itself, Isabella was having misgivings. Whatever had possessed her to agree to such an outlandish idea? Conjuring up the earl's steely gray eyes in her mind caused Isabella to shudder. As she remembered her initial impression of the earl's dangerous strength with utter clarity, Isabella's doubts increased.

And his kiss. The feel of the earl's lips and the force of his hard body had totally disarmed her. How could she possible consider placing herself in his household? Jenkins had already warned her there were not many female servants in the house, but she had been so caught up in the drama of coming to the earl's aid and helping him raise his motherless children, she did not question the valet too closely. Now she wished she had.

The carriage stopped at a comfortable inn just as darkness approached, but there was no further opportunity for Isabella to speak privately with Jenkins. She was given a small but clean room for the night and slept fitfully.

By the following morning Isabella was still having serious doubts about proceeding to the earl's home. While sharing a quiet breakfast with Jenkins, Isabella debated how best to voice her doubts. She opened her mouth to express her fears just as Jenkins noisily pushed back his chair.

"I'd best be seeing about the carriage, Miss Browning," Jenkins stated, rising to his feet. "If the roads aren't too muddy from all the rain, we should reach The Grange by midday."

Isabella quickly shut her mouth and her stomach jumped in nervous anticipation. Swallowing hard, she watched the servant leave without saying a word. Chiding herself for her cowardly behavior, she deliberately focused her thoughts away from her forthcoming confrontation with the earl. He probably wouldn't even offer her the position, she reasoned. And even if he did, she did not have to accept it. If she felt uncomfortable in his presence, she could merely proceed to her grandfather's estate in York and stay there until she found a suitable position. Feeling a bit less trapped, Isabella waited for Jenkins to return.

A shadow fell over the table, and Isabella glanced up quickly, expecting to see Jenkins. Instead, a tall, thin, fashionable dressed middle-aged matron was peering down at her with a quizzical expression on her pointed face.

"Pray, forgive my forwardness, but I saw you breakfasting with the earl's valet . . ." The woman's reedy voice trailed off, and she bent her lanky frame forward to obtain a closer look at Isabella's lovely face. She brought a gold-rimmed quizzing glass up to her eye and rudely scrutinized Isabella through the glass. "Extraordinary," the woman whispered in awe.

"Lady Edson." Jenkins's surprised cry suddenly filled the air. He approached the two women quickly, effectively interrupting before Lady Edson could say anything else to Isabella.

"Mr. Jenkins." Isabella gazed at the valet with undisguised relief. "Are we ready to leave?"

Lady Edson ignored Isabella's question completely and in a nasal voice commanded the valet, "Introduce us, Mr. Jenkins."

The matron listened with undisguised curiosity as the valet reluctantly complied.

"Lady Edson, may I present Miss Isabella Browning," Jenkins said in a formal voice. "Lord and Lady Edson are neighbors of the earl's in Warwickshire."

Isabella knew she should rise to her feet and make a proper curtsy to Lady Edson but the woman's pretentious behavior irked her. Isabella instead acknowledged the introduction with a slight nod of her head and fixed an unfriendly stare on Lady Edson, hoping the older woman would see her displeasure and take the not-so-subtle hint to leave.

"Are you related to the late Countess of Saunders?" Lady Edson questioned Isabella, seating herself in the only available chair at the table, without waiting to be invited. "Your resemblance to Emmeline is quite marked."

"No, Lady Edson, I am not a relative of the late countess," Isabella said tartly. The last thing she wanted was to encourage a conversation with the overly curious Lady Edson. And Isabella was becoming heartily sick of continually being informed of her resemblance to the earl's deceased wife.

"Miss Browning is the children's new governess," Jenkins supplied, obviously attempting to put an end to Lady Edson's growing interest in Isabella.

"A governess!" Lady Edson looked shocked. "You cannot mean to say you are actually going to live at The Grange, Miss Browning?"

"I believe it is customary for a governess to reside with her charges, Lady Edson," Isabella said, puzzled at the woman's odd reaction.

"Oh, my dear, I feel compelled to warn you that you are making a dreadful mistake," Lady Edson insisted dramatically. "No respectable woman would willingly become a member of the earl's household. Her reputation would be compromised beyond repair."

"Why is that, Lady Edson?" Isabella glanced over at Jenkins and saw the annoyed expression in the servant's eyes.

" 'Tis common knowledge that the earl cannot be trusted to

act with honor when it comes to his dealings with women,'' Lady Edson announced with pompous authority.

Isabella eyed Lady Edson thoughtfully, trying to determine if she was sincere. Jenkins had warned Isabella that the earl's self-imposed isolation had made him a target of wild rumors concerning his treatment of women, but Jenkins had not elaborated on any of the details.

"I assume you are speaking from personal experience, Lady Edson, when making such a serious charge?"

"Not precisely," Lady Edson admitted in a reluctant tone. "I have not actually spoken to the earl since his wife's accident. But I have heard, from a most reliable source, that the earl has seduced several innocent young maids in his household." Lady Edson leaned towards Isabella and whispered conspiratorially, " 'Tis said that three of these poor unfortunate girls are now carrying a child."

Isabella sputtered loudly, nearly choking on the lukewarm chocolate she was drinking. Her face flamed with embarrassment over the outrageous statements made by Lady Edson. Even given her own biased opinion of the earl, Isabella could not credit such a tale.

She glanced up at Jenkins. The gleam of fury in the valet's eyes confirmed that Lady Edson's accusations were as ridiculous as they sounded. Isabella furrowed her brow in annoyance. All her life she had encountered women like Lady Edson, who relished unsavory and damaging gossip about others and had no compunction in repeating those unverified barbs. Isabella felt ashamed to have listened to such drivel.

Pushing aside her own doubts about the earl's character, Isabella felt compelled to put Lady Edson in her place. She gritted her teeth and considered a variety of scathing retorts, the majority of which would have stunned and perhaps embarrassed Jenkins.

"I do thank you, Lady Edson, for warning me of the unfair, unfounded, and clearly untrue rumors circulating about the earl. Since I, like yourself, am a woman of good breeding and impeccable manners, I shall not demean myself by responding to such blatant falsehoods."

"I don't believe you understand, Miss Browning."

"Oh, but I do, Lady Edson," Isabella insisted, rising to her feet. She inclined her head regally, with mocking politeness. "I understand that rumors and innuendo of this nature can actually be believed by individuals who do not possess the brains the good Lord gave them to see these rumors for the vicious lies they are. Fortunately, I possess enough common sense not to believe such rubbish. I would like to assume you do as well."

Lady Edson bit her lip, clearly annoyed at being so neatly outmaneuvered. There was no way to respond without looking like a fool. She cast a chilling stare at Isabella and tilted her long nose skyward. Murmuring a hasty farewell, she rose quickly, turning her back on Isabella and Jenkins. Muttering under her breath, Lady Edson strode from the table.

Isabella seized the opportunity to make her own hasty departure.

"What a perfectly odious woman," Isabella muttered to Jenkins as she accepted his escort out of the inn. The valet cast a thoughtful eye at Isabella and grinned broadly.

The journey resumed. Isabella settled herself comfortably in the coach and watched the passing countryside with distracted interest. Every time she thought about her conversation with Lady Edson, she became incensed all over again, angry at the statements made against the earl. It seemed an ironic turn of fate that she would be his champion, considering all that had passed between them. But listening to Lady Edson malign the earl's character had caused something to snap in Isabella. She knew all too well the pain of being misunderstood and unfairly judged by others.

And yet, as the carriage carried her closer to the earl, a nagging voice inside Isabella insistently reminded her that most rumors, twisted and turned as they were, usually held a grain of truth.

Chapter Six

The warm sunshine improved the condition of the muddy roads, and the coach was able to travel through the western countryside at a clipping pace. To distract herself, Isabella concentrated on the scenic views outside her carriage window of rich pasturelands, grazing livestock, and lush green fields dotted by clumps of woodlands and divided by broad thorn hedges. Set back from the road on the hills, fine manor houses, in a vast array of architectural styles, peeped through the trees.

Before reaching the earl's estate, the carriage rode through the village of Halford. Cottages with dormer windows fronted by neatly tended walled gardens overlooked the narrow main street. Isabella was fascinated by the unusual village. It was a remote, windswept hilltop community, with red brick and gray stone houses that were clustered around a variety of spacious greens. As they rolled down the main street, Isabella's attention was snared by a simple Tudor cottage. It was a timber-framed building with leaded windows, a tiled roof, and walls that bowed visibly with age.

"We are approaching Whatley Grange, Miss Browning. We should arrive home within the hour."

Isabella's stomach clenched at Jenkins's innocent announcement. Now that the moment of encountering the earl was rapidly approaching, Isabella's doubts were returning. She imagined a variety of greetings from the earl, none of which were overly pleasant.

All too soon the carriage turned down the long gravel drive to the manor house. Even in her nervous state of anticipation, Isabella could appreciate the grandeur of Whatley Grange— an oddly modest name for such an impressive building. The vast mansion retained much of its Norman ancestry with its turrets and towers, but over the years symmetrical windows, decorative chimneys, and Renaissance ornamentation had been added to soften the fortresslike exterior. It seemed a fitting home for the earl—tall, proud, bold, and impressive. Even the gray stones of the exterior walls matched the earl's captivating eyes.

Beyond the lawns, Isabella could see the shimmering lake and extensive parklands, as well as the newly planted grain fields and numerous herds of grazing cattle and sheep. Clearly The Grange was as productive as it was magnificent.

When the coach finally came to a halt, Isabella was struggling to master her nerves. She chewed her lip in agitation, straightened her bonnet several times, and repeatedly smoothed the folds of her cloak. Suddenly, the carriage door opened. Isabella straightened her bonnet one last time, took a deep breath, and held out her hand.

Jenkins assisted Isabella out of the coach, and she was grateful for his support. Her legs felt stiff from the long hours of confinement in the carriage, and as she paused a moment to stretch her tired limbs, she heard a deep voice call out.

"So you have finally arrived, Jenkins. We were expecting you last night. I was wondering where you had gotten to."

Isabella did not have to turn around to identify the speaker. She recognized the earl's voice instantly. With her back still to him, she listened alertly to the steady crunch of his booted feet on the gravel as he approached, silently willing herself to remain calm. When she gauged that the earl stood no more than a few feet from her, Isabella whirled around, hoping to gain the advantage by shocking him with her sudden appearance.

''Good afternoon, my lord,'' Isabella exclaimed in a breathless voice.

''Miss Browning.'' The earl's voice was so calm and emotionless that for a moment she thought he must have been informed of her imminent arrival, but she did not think that was possible.

''Did you have a pleasant journey, Jenkins?'' the earl inquired conversationally.

Isabella kept a rein on her emotions with an effort. She was relieved the earl had addressed his question to Jenkins, instead of to her, since Isabella doubted she could have equaled the earl's casual tone. She was determined, however, to follow the earl's lead and tried to act as nonchalantly as he did at finding her, uninvited and unannounced, at his doorstep.

''The roads were quite passable, my lord,'' Jenkins responded to the earl's inquiry. ''Today's sunshine is succeeding in drying up some of the larger puddles.''

While the earl and his valet exchanged pleasantries, Isabella openly studied him. The earl's was a sizable, nearly overwhelming presence. Tall, broad of shoulder, and uncommonly handsome, he was a man who easily inflamed a woman's senses.

Isabella abstractly noted that the pale, tight breeches covering the earl's powerful thighs were stained with dirt and grass, and his well-worn riding boots were caked with mud. His dark blue jacket was open, and the white linen shirt he wore underneath was unbuttoned at the throat. She could see a sprinkling of dark, curly hair and a glimpse of tanned, muscular chest. It made her feel flushed. Damien St. Lawrence was a truly dashing figure, even in his soiled and half-buttoned clothes.

It would not have been possible to mistake him for a common laborer, even though he was sweating and filthy. The earl's bearing was commanding, almost regal, and even a bit threatening.

Isabella suddenly felt his gaze upon her, and she lifted her head. She met his frosty silver eyes calmly, with a facade of confidence gained through years of practice.

''Is there somewhere private we may speak, my lord?'' Isabella suggested, deciding to take the initiative, since the earl appeared to be content standing in the drive conversing with Jenkins until darkness fell.

"Of course, Miss Browning."

Mutely, Isabella followed the earl through the heavy oak doors of Whatley Grange. The foyer they entered was enormous in size, with massive pillars and round arches of dark carved oak soaring thirty feet into the air. Isabella's eyes were immediately drawn upward to the lavish mural that decorated the tops of the high walls and the ceiling. Mythical demons and animals, along with birds, lambs, and lions, were among the figures included in the elaborate design.

The enchanting paintings were unlike anything Isabella had ever seen, but the earl did not allow her time to admire her surroundings. Still wearing her traveling cloak and bonnet, she followed him across the massive hallway. He stopped at the end of a long corridor and opened the wooden door. Peering down expectantly at Isabella, he waited for her to proceed him into the room.

She scurried inside, deciding at once that this must be the earl's private study. The room had a masculine feel to it, from the sturdy, heavy wooden furniture to the plush, dark-hued carpets and mahogany-paneled walls. A richly carved desk stacked high with piles of papers, correspondence, and ledgers stood in front of a wide bay window. Isabella was relieved with the earl's choice of room. At least he understood that the reason for her unexpected appearance at his home was business and not social.

The earl politely indicated a seat, but Isabella shook her head. "I've been sitting in the carriage all day, my lord. If you have no objections, I prefer to stand."

"As you wish, Miss Browning," Damien responded, leaning against his desk and crossing his arms over his chest. He gave no outward sign of his emotions.

Instead, he looked carefully at Isabella. Her sculptured face showed signs of fatigue, but her brilliant violet eyes were sparkling. Damien's body tightened instinctively in masculine appreciation of her beauty. Surprised and annoyed at the sudden appearance of his baser inclinations, the earl resolutely pushed those feelings aside. "Now that we are alone, perhaps you will be kind enough to explain why you are here?"

Taking a deep breath, Isabella plunged in. "I have come to Whatley Grange in search of a position, my lord. It is my understanding that you have two young children. I would like to offer my services as governess."

The slight twitching in his jaw revealed his surprise.

"How do you know of my children?"

"Jenkins mentioned them to me," Isabella responded carefully. "You have two children, a girl and a boy. Six and three years old, I believe. Jenkins also said they did not have a governess. I was hoping you might consider me for the post."

"I am not looking for a governess, Miss Browning," the earl declared flatly.

His answer was precisely what she had anticipated, had even come to hope for, and yet for some perverse reason it rankled her. Isabella knew she should calmly accept the earl's rejection and be on her way, but she could not.

Apprehension flared momentarily in Isabella's violet eyes before she spoke, but she skillfully hid her feelings of self-doubt. Quietly she listed her qualifications. "I have received an excellent education, my lord. I am fluent in both French and Italian. I have studied Greek, Latin, history, and geography in addition to the more traditional female pursuits of piano, voice, painting, drawing, and several forms of needlework. I also have a sound knowledge of basic arithmetic, English, and French literature and poetry."

The earl scowled slightly, but Isabella valiantly continued. "Coupled with my extensive education is several years of practical experience. I have served as a governess in households with as few as three and as many as six children under my care."

"I am sure your qualifications are impeccable, Miss Browning," the earl replied, grudgingly impressed by Isabella's accomplishments. "Nevertheless, the fact remains, I am not searching for a governess."

"But you cannot deny that you need one. Surely you understand the importance of education. It is never to early for children to begin learning."

He knew she had a valid point. Most noble families engaged a governess to supervise the early education of their children, some when the child was just learning to talk. But the earl's was hardly a typical household. Damien tried a different approach.

"I strongly doubt you would be comfortable living here, Miss Browning. The Grange is an exceedingly unorthodox household."

"So I have been given to understand."

The earl straightened up from his causal pose. "By whom?"

Isabella felt a chill run up her spine, but she did not break their eye contact. "I met Lady Edson at the posting inn near Buckingham this morning. She was most anxious to relate some rather bizarre tales about you and your staff. Naturally, I do not believe such malicious gossip."

"Perhaps you should, Miss Browning." The earl spoke in an unemotional voice.

Isabella's color heightened as she remembered Lady Edson's preposterous accusations claiming that the earl impregnated three female members of his staff. Even though she felt certain these rumors were lies, she would have liked to hear the earl dony them, but Isabella knew she lacked the courage to directly confront him on such an indelicate personal subject.

"Idle gossip does not interest me, my lord," Isabella declared truthfully. "I am more concerned about securing a position."

"After what happened between us yesterday morning, I am very surprised you would wish to work for me," the earl said in a soft voice.

Isabella lowered her eyes, not wanting him to see how near the mark his words hit. "I bear you no ill feelings, my lord. Since our unfortunate incident, other individuals have commented on my resemblance to Emmeline. In retrospect, I have come to the conclusion that you made an honest mistake."

The earl's mouth formed a tight line. "If you worked for

me, Miss Browning, your reputation would in all likelihood be severely compromised, perhaps even ruined irreparably.''

Isabella shrugged philosophically. "A sterling reputation does not provide an adequate living, my lord. I need this job. Badly.''

Damien felt a twinge of guilt, knowing he was responsible for her current unemployed status, but he ignored it. ''Have you nowhere else to go, Miss Browning?''

''My stepbrothers are scattered throughout the country. It has been years since we've corresponded. I'm not precisely certain of their current direction." Isabella strove for lightness. ''I suppose my grandfather could be forced to tolerate my presence for a while. However, the earl's generosity is rather limited in my case. I prefer not to rely on it.''

''The earl? Your grandfather is an earl? Yet you insist you must earn your living as a governess.''

Isabella almost groaned out loud at her unintentional slip. She did not want him finding out about her parentage. It was too deep a wound, too personal a hurt.

''My maternal grandfather is the Earl of Barton. He and my mother were estranged before I was born. I did not even know of his existence until I was sent to live at his estate in York when I was seventeen. After staying there for three years, I took my first position as a governess. It was my only means of escape.''

Damien stroked his chin thoughtfully at her revelations. She was obviously alienated from her stepbrothers, and he heard the subtle contempt in Isabella's voice when she spoke of her grandfather. He got the distinct impression that if he asked her additional questions concerning her family and her past, she would truthfully answer him, but he did not press the point. It was none of his business, even if she did become governess to his children.

Damien stopped short when he realized where his thoughts were taking him. Could he actually be seriously considering offering her a job? The benefits to his children aside, did he really want this enchanting, disturbing creature living under his roof?

"I still find it difficult to believe you do not have grave misgivings about working for me, Miss Browning."

"I would not be here if I did, my lord," Isabella stated softly, surprising them both with her answer.

Damien considered her carefully as Isabella anxiously awaited his response. He supposed she could have tried to shame him into offering her a job, since he was ultimately responsible for her losing her position with her former employers. She might have pleaded with him or even wept over her predicament, although years of listening to Emmeline's crying on cue had hardened the earl against a woman's tears. But she had done none of these things. Instead she forgave him for his boorish actions. Damien made his decision.

"You are hired, Miss Browning."

The smile she gave him was dazzling. "Thank you, my lord. I promise you will not regret this decision."

"I sincerely hope you are right, Miss Browning," Damien replied with a frown, determined to repress the odd stirring he felt in his chest at her enchanting smile. The very last thing he needed was an attraction to his children's new governess. "I am sure you are tired from your long journey. I shall instruct our housekeeper, Mrs. Amberly, to show you to your room immediately." He reached out and pulled the bell cord to summon the housekeeper.

Isabella hesitated. "I would like to meet the children first, please."

Damien's frown deepened. This was an unexpected request. "I am certain tomorrow will be soon enough for introductions, Miss Browning. Besides, I wish to speak privately to my son and daughter before you meet." The earl reached over and pulled hard on the bell cord a second time, not about to reveal that he had no idea where his children were at the moment.

Isabella curtly nodded her head in acquiescence. Damien could tell she was displeased by his reply, but with an effort she held her tongue.

After an uncomfortably long, silent wait, the earl's summons was finally answered. A short, dour-faced elderly woman entered the study and was introduced to Isabella as the housekeeper, Mrs. Amberly. The women exited the study as Jenkins entered it, and Isabella gave the valet a warm smile when they passed in the doorway.

"Judging by the scowl on Mrs. Amberly's face and the sweetness of Miss Browning's smile, I assume you have engaged a governess," the valet remarked the moment the women were gone.

"Stop looking so smug, Jenkins," the earl warned. "I can clearly see your fine hand in all of this. And I intend to hold you personally responsible if this little arrangement blows up in my face."

Jenkins appeared unimpressed by the threat. "You worry too much. I predict the entire household will benefit from Miss Browning's presence, not just the children."

"Hmmmm." The earl was not convinced. "And speaking of my children, Jenkins, I require your assistance in tracking them down. It will be necessary for me to have a long talk with Ian and Catherine before they are introduced to Miss Browning tomorrow morning and I have no inkling as to their whereabouts."

"They are most likely down at the stables with Fred," Jenkins said. "I'll tell them you want to speak with them."

Giving the earl an exaggerated bow, Jenkins left the study with a smug grin of satisfaction on his face.

Isabella dutifully followed Mrs. Amberly up the long, winding staircase, attempting several times to engage the housekeeper in conversation. Her friendly overtures were met with unintelligible grunts and Isabella quickly abandoned her efforts. A less than warm welcome to a household was not an unfamiliar experience for her.

After taking numerous twists and turns down the long, narrow corridors, they finally reached their destination. Isabella glanced suspiciously at the housekeeper. The route they had taken seemed deliberately designed to disorient her, making it difficult, if not impossible, for Isabella to find the way back on her own.

The bedchamber was shrouded in darkness as they entered. Mrs. Amberly walked gingerly across the room, flinging back the heavy draperies and opening the leaded glass windows. Brilliant sunlight flooded the room, and the crisp, fresh air was a welcome relief from the musty odor. Isabella wondered if it would be necessary to sleep with her window wide open to dissipate the unpleasant smell.

Looking beyond the dust and grime, Isabella could clearly see that this had been an impressive room at one time. The heavy brocade draperies were a deep rose color and matched the delicate silk hangings around the canopied four-poster bed. The furnishings were of a style popular fifty years ago, but they were rich and elegant. The chairs and chaise were obviously designed for a woman; they were daintily proportioned and covered in silk patterned with blue, pink, and cream roses. The carpets echoed the same colors.

"There appears to have been a misunderstanding, Mrs. Amberly," Isabella said, waving her hand at the misty particles of dust floating in the late afternoon sunlight.

"I should be occupying a bedchamber next to the children's sleeping quarters. I am their new governess."

"There is no mistake, miss," Mrs. Amberly insisted briskly. Pointing diagonally across the hall, the housekeeper announced, "The children sleep in that bedchamber. The majority of the rooms on the upper floors are closed off. They haven't been used in years."

"If you're certain the earl has no objections," Isabella said slowly, "this room will do nicely once it has been properly cleaned."

Mrs. Amberly stiffened noticeably. "There is no time for cleaning today, miss," the housekeeper responded in a voice that brooked no argument. "I'll send one of the housemaids up with bed linens when I get a chance. That's the best I can do. If you have a complaint, I suggest you speak directly to Lord Saunders. His bedchamber is next to the children's." With a mocking smile on her thin lips, Mrs. Amberly left the room, leaving Isabella no opportunity to marshal a response.

The earl's bedchamber was across from her own! Isabella

felt a moment of unbridled panic, but soon convinced herself she was overreacting. Mrs. Amberly had already explained that most of the upper floors of the house were closed up. And it was important that she sleep near the children. It was merely a coincidence the children happened to sleep next to their attractive, imposing father.

Wasn't it?

By the time the maid arrived with her bed linens, Isabella had restored her sense equilibrium. She was annoyed with herself for allowing her strange feelings about the earl and the vicious gossiping of Lady Edson to influence her common sense.

"I've also brought some rags with me, miss," the pretty young maid said shyly. "After I've fixed the bed, I'll try to clean away some of the dirt and dust. As soon as I can spare the time, I'll come back with one of the other girls and give the room a thorough going over."

Isabella was relieved to hear the friendliness in the maid's voice. Thank goodness all of the household staff did not share Mrs. Amberly's surly attitude. "Thank you. I very much appreciate your help . . . ?"

"Maggie." The young maid made an awkward, off balance curtsy, her arms piled high with linens.

"Here, let me take those," Isabella volunteered, reaching out for the stack of linens. The large pile of bedding reached her chin, and Isabella gratefully breathed in the sweet fragrance of dried lavender that emanated from the sheets. At least she wouldn't have to worry about smelling mildew all night.

"I've never been in here before," Maggie remarked while pulling back the dusty bed coverlet. " 'Tis a pretty room."

Isabella nodded in agreement. She smiled shyly at the young maid, but her smile quickly faded when Maggie stepped out from behind the bed into the center of the room to tug on the edge of the coverlet. The pile of linens in Isabella's arms fell soundlessly to the dusty carpet. Isabella caught her breath in a stinging gasp and staggered slightly as she got her first unobstructed frontal view of Maggie.

The sweet-faced maid was tiny and very slender, except for her rounded and distended stomach. Though her experience in these matters was limited, Isabella estimated that it would probably be only a few short weeks before Maggie gave birth.

Chapter Seven

Isabella woke at sunrise the following morning. She dressed hurriedly, her ears tuned to the slightest sound outside her bedchamber door. Hoping for an opportunity to have a private conversation with the earl before being introduced to her new charges, Isabella listened eagerly for his footsteps. She was exceedingly curious about the earl's children and felt at a definite disadvantage since she knew almost nothing about them except for their sex and ages. She did not even know their names.

Isabella had first thought to question the servants about the children, but she had been so embarrassed and tongue-tied after seeing the maid in her very pregnant condition that all thoughts of the children had been promptly forgotten. The attractive young footman who brought her dinner tray last evening did not stay to chat, and Isabella had no contact with any other members of the household.

Although she had been expecting a summons, the knock at the door startled Isabella. She opened her bedchamber door expectantly, hoping to find the earl on the other side, but instead found the same footman from last evening waiting to escort her to the dining room for breakfast. Masking her disappointment admirably, she bade the man a pleasant good morning and followed him down the hall.

As Isabella and the young footman swiftly walked the complex route to the main dinning room, her apprehension mounted. Distractedly, she wondered how long it would take her to master the complicated maze of halls in the house, given her dismal sense of direction.

The dining room was already occupied when Isabella arrived, despite the unfashionable early hour. The earl was seated at the head of the table, his nose buried in a newspaper. Two young children were seated to his right; Jenkins was on his left. The sideboard was covered with a small array of tarnished silver platters that held the morning meal.

Isabella did not even question the homey arrangement of having the earl's valet sitting down to breakfast with the family. She had already learned that Jenkins occupied a unique position in the household that went well beyond that of a normal servant.

The room was silent as Isabella observed its occupants. Then the children suddenly noticed her presence. They immediately put down their spoons, ceased eating their breakfast, and openly stared at her. Isabella's spine tingled as mild tension began stirring in the room. Apparently the earl felt it also because he slowly lowered his paper and peered over the top. When he beheld the new governess hesitating in the doorway, he scowled slightly at her.

Isabella ignored the earl and turned toward the children. She pasted on a smile, hoping it conveyed the right amount of friendliness, and bravely stepped into the room. No one spoke a word. The floor boards creaked loudly with each step she took, but she boldly marched forward until she reached the unoccupied chair next to Jenkins.

"Good morning, Miss Browning," Jenkins called out cheerfully, as Isabella seated herself. "I trust you slept well last night."

"Very soundly, Mr. Jenkins," Isabella lied. She murmured appropriate greetings to the children and then focused her attention on the earl. He had already resumed his intent perusal of the morning paper, but Isabella was not about to allow him to hide behind his newspaper for the duration of the meal. She cleared her throat loudly and stared boldly at the top of the earl's head, the only visible part of his anatomy.

After a few awkward moments, he tentatively lowered his reading material.

"Was there something you wanted, Miss Browning?" the earl challenged, a touch of annoyance in his deep voice.

Isabella's violet eyes sparkled with fury, but she did not indulge it. The earl was being particularly difficult this morning, but he was not her first concern. Isabella inclined her head pointedly toward the children, waiting impatiently for the earl to grasp her meaning.

"Oh, yes, of course," he responded. "Miss Browning, these are my children, Catherine and Ian. Children, this is Miss Browning, your new governess."

The brief introductions completed, the earl snapped his paper loudly and once again buried himself behind it. The children shifted their attention from their father to their new governess and stared at Isabella as though she were some strange, exotic creature.

Eventually Catherine, the older of the two, mumbled an incomprehensible greeting while staring rudely at Isabella. Ian did not speak at all, but his small face gleamed with undisguised curiosity. Isabella flashed them a warm smile, which caused them both to quickly lower their heads and resume eating their breakfast.

Isabella was disappointed with their reaction but she took it in stride. Not an encouraging beginning, to be sure, but she had endured far worse. The first time she had met the Braun children, young Robert had thrown a screaming tantrum. At least the earl's children had remained calm, if somewhat unresponsive.

Damien observed the entire exchange from behind his raised newspaper. He was inwardly pleased that Isabella did not make an issue of Catherine and Ian's lackluster greeting. Damien's children were independent by nature, as well as circumstance, and would certainly rebel at being fussed over by a stranger.

Feeling for the first time that he had made the correct decision in hiring a governess, Damien threw down his newspaper and stood up.

"If you are going to work with me today, Jenkins," the earl said, "I suggest you change your clothes. I plan on completing the new section of stone fence on the eastern borders by darkness."

The Grange was a working, productive agricultural estate, and all the men who served within the house also worked out of doors when needed, including the earl.

"I thought I would stay in today and help Miss Browning get acquainted with Whatley Grange," Jenkins announced, ignoring the earl's frown.

"That is most kind of you, Mr. Jenkins," Isabella said diplomatically, "but I am sure one of the other servants can show me about the house. Besides, I shall be spending the majority of my day with Catherine and Ian."

Jenkins wiped his mouth with his cloth napkin and rose from the table. "If you are certain you do not need my help, Miss Browning, I suppose I must accompany the earl today," Jenkins replied in a disappointed tone.

"How kind of you, Jenkins," the earl muttered sarcastically under his breath, as Jenkins walked past him. The valet chuckled softly.

After Jenkins left, the earl turned a critical eye toward his children and their new governess. Catherine and Ian were still glued to their seats and Isabella was pushing her food absently around on her breakfast plate.

"I shall see you all later this afternoon." He strode to the door, but turned toward them before he left the room. Staring hard at Ian and Catherine, he admonished in a strong voice, "Children, behave." Then he closed the door with a resounding bang.

A great amount of the tension eased from the room with the earl's departure, and Isabella felt relaxed enough to finish her meal. The food was mediocre and not very hot, but she was hungry and within a few moments her eggs, kidneys, and toast were gone. Daintily brushing the remaining crumbs from her fingers, she looked across the table at the children, who had long since abandoned their meal in favor of watching her consume hers.

"After you have finished your breakfast, children," Isabella began in a soft voice, "you may show me around the manor. I don't think I have ever been in such a large house before."

Catherine and Ian exchanged quiet glances, then nodded in agreement. "I don't want any more porridge, do you?" Catherine questioned her younger brother. When the little boy agreed that he too was finished, they stood up and moved away from the table. Carefully picking up their plates, they began walking toward the door.

"What are you doing?" Isabella asked, curious at their odd behavior.

"We are carrying our dishes into the kitchen," Catherine answered.

"I see," Isabella replied, although in truth she had no idea what was going on. She had never seen any of her charges lift a dish from the table, dirty or otherwise. There were always a bevy of servants to attend to every domestic need. "I am sure the kitchen staff appreciates your assistance, children."

"What is a kitchen staff?" Ian whispered to his sister as he followed close behind her.

Catherine shrugged her shoulders and replied in a loud whisper, "I don't know. I guess she means Mrs. Amberly. Or maybe Maggie and Fran."

Deciding to follow the children's lead, Isabella picked up her cutlery and dirty dishes and trailed dutifully behind Catherine and Ian. The kitchen was empty. The children walked without hesitation to the large, scarred oak table in the center of the room and placed their dishes upon it. Isabella imitated their actions.

"What about the rest of the dirty dishes on the table? Do you usually clear all of them?"

"No," Catherine answered. "Just our own plates."

"All right. If you are finished in here, you may take me on a brief exploration of the house," Isabella requested in a cheerful voice.

Again Ian and Catherine exchanged meaningful glances, but they did not protest.

"What do you want to see?" Catherine asked.

"Perhaps we can start with the schoolroom," Isabella suggested.

"What is a schoolroom?" Ian whispered to his sister.

With an effort Isabella managed to refrain from answering Ian. Since the boy addressed his question to his older sister, Isabella did not feel it was prudent to offer an explanation. She knew that she needed to gain the children's trust and confidence before she could effectively establish a relationship with them, and Isabella instinctively sensed that they would not react well to her sudden interference. Catherine and Ian appeared to be extremely close and dependent upon each other, and any unrequested information thrust upon them by the new governess could be perceived as a threat to their sibling relationship.

"We don't have a schoolroom, Miss Browning," Catherine declared bluntly.

"Oh, I am fairly certain a house this size has a schoolroom, Catherine," Isabella countered gently. "I imagine your father used it when he was a young boy. I am sure if we search together, we shall find it."

Catherine seemed dubious, but willing to try. "I know where Father's study is," she volunteered. "It is across the great hall and three doors over."

"I too have been in your father's study," Isabella said, pleased that Catherine appeared to know a few of her numbers. "Although I am not certain I could find my way to it on my own." She smiled encouragingly. "Generally the schoolroom is located on the upper levels of the house. Shall we climb to the top and search there first?"

At Catherine's acquiescent nod, the trio set out on their quest. As they climbed the numerous steps, Isabella could not help but notice the dusty furniture, abundant cobwebs, tarnished brass wall sconces, worn and stained flooring, and areas of soot-blackened walls. It was obvious The Grange had been neglected through the years and had not had a thorough cleaning in a very long time.

The children paused when they reached the third floor landing. "Molly, Fran, Ned and Joe, Penny, Maggie, Fred and Norman all live up there," Catherine explained, pointing toward the fourth floor.

It took a few moments for Isabella to realize Catherine was showing her the servants' quarters. "In that case, I believe we should begin our hunt on this floor. All right?"

Catherine reached for her brother's hand and admonished in a mature voice, "Stay close to me Ian. You don't want to get lost up here."

The little boy nodded solemnly and tightly clutched his sister's hand. Isabella was touched by their need and trust in each other. She followed quietly behind them, assisting with a stubborn latch or stuck door as needed. At the fourth door they located the schoolroom.

"Here it is," Isabella declared brightly, as she crossed the sunny, dusty room. She struggled mightily with the window hinges, finally succeeded in opening several of the leaded glass windows. The warm, fresh air helped to displace the musty odor.

"I am sure that after a good scrubbing, the room will be quite adequate," Isabella said. She continued exploring the room while Ian and Catherine watched in silence. Reaching into a wall cupboard, Isabella found several slates and a few pieces of chalk.

Mentally, Isabella began compiling a list in her head of supplies that would be needed. Writing tablets, ink, watercolor paints, drawing paper, primers and other appropriate books. Isabella hoped the castle's library would hold many of the reading materials she needed. She always enjoyed reading aloud to her charges, especially at bedtime.

Ian and Catherine also began exploring the room, and Catherine gave a loud shout of enthusiasm when she discovered a large tin box filled with toy soldiers.

"Aren't these wonderful, Ian?" Catherine said excitedly. "They are ever so much nicer than the other soldiers we have. With all of these soldiers, we shall have much larger battles."

Ian nodded in agreement and eagerly helped his sister sort

through the box. In a short time, the children's hands were filthy, covered with the dust and dirt of the toy soldiers.

"I think we should get some soap and buckets of water so that we may begin cleaning up in here," Isabella announced when she saw the children's blackened hands. "You and Ian may give your soldiers a bath. I am sure Mrs. Amberly will be able to provide us with all the necessary cleaning supplies. Perhaps one of the maids can be spared to help us also."

The children seemed unimpressed with the notion of cleaning up. "We will wait here for you to return, Miss Browning," Catherine decided, lining up several infantrymen.

It was not an unreasonable request, and normally Isabella would have been inclined to agree. But she was reluctant to leave the children alone and besides, she could not find her way back to the kitchen without the children's guidance.

"I believe it would be best if we all go find Mrs. Amberly together," Isabella insisted. At first she thought Catherine would continue to protest, but with a last longing glance at the dirty soldiers strategically lined up on the floor, the little girl stood up. Ian instantly imitated his sister's actions.

They took a different, more direct route down to the kitchen. As they negotiated around numerous wooden crates cluttering one hallway, Catherine abruptly stopped. A large painting, carelessly placed among the crates, claimed the child's attention. Leaning over, she stared closely at the painting, a sober expression on her sweet, innocent face.

After a careful examination of the picture, Catherine announced importantly to her younger brother, "This is our mother, Ian. I remember Jenkins showing it to me when it used to hang in the long gallery."

The little boy moved toward the painting. His expression was unreadable as he stared at the beautiful woman on the canvas.

Unable to hide her curiosity, Isabella also stepped toward the portrait, exceedingly interested in viewing the likeness of the woman she was suppose to so closely resemble.

"It smells funny," Ian said, wrinkling his nose.

Isabella bent her head and caught a heady wiff of brandy.

How odd. Ignoring the strong scent of spirits, she squinted in the dim hallway and stared in amazement at the stunning, vibrant woman painted on the canvas. Isabella felt a strange twisting in her stomach.

Isabella acknowledged there was a faint, distant resemblance between herself and the woman in the portrait, especially the shape and color of the eyes, but in Isabella's opinion that was the extent of the similarity. How could the earl possibly have mistaken her for this exciting, beautiful creature? He must have been very drunk indeed to believe she was the enchanting Emmeline.

"Your mother was a very beautiful and elegant lady, children," Isabella remarked, still not believing the earl had mistaken her for this woman.

"Yes, she was pretty," Catherine agreed nonchalantly. Continuing in the same tone, she added, "but she was also a meddlesome, disloyal, spoiled little bitch."

"Catherine!" Isabella admonished in her sternnest voice. "What a positively horrible thing to say. And about your own mother. You must never, never again speak of your mother or anyone else in such a disgraceful, ill-bred manner."

The little girl raised confused eyes toward Isabella, obviously not understanding why her governess was so angry. "That is what father says about her, Miss Browning."

Isabella bit her lip hard to prevent herself from shouting at the child. "I am certain you have misunderstood your father's remarks, Catherine," Isabella insisted, yet she suspected the little girl had most likely repeated precisely what the earl had said. "In future, you will not repeat such malicious words."

"All right," Catherine agreed, with a shrug of her shoulders.

The incident momentarily forgotten, the trio proceeded to the kitchens. They managed to reach their destination without further incident. Mrs. Amberly was rocking comfortable in a wooden chair by the fire, while two young maids were washing and drying the breakfast pots and dishes.

"We found the schoolroom, Mrs. Amberly," Ian told the housekeeper in an excited voice. " 'Tis up on the top floor. Father used it when he was a little boy."

"We found a large box of soldiers, too," Catherine added importantly. "Miss Browning said we may give them all a proper bath."

"Sounds as though you children have had a busy morning," Mrs. Amberly remarked. "I've missed you. Come and sit by the fire and tell me all about it." She turned her attention away from the children and regarded Isabella with narrow eyes. "Was there something you wanted, Miss Browning?"

Isabella refused to be intimidated, deliberately ignoring the uncomfortable tension. For some reason the housekeeper had taken an instant and rather strong dislike to her. Isabella was determined to answer her hostility with a civil, polite voice, no matter how much she was provoked.

"The children and I will need rags, soap, and water to begin our cleanup of the schoolroom," Isabella instructed, knowing there would be no servants to do the work. "And any members of the household staff that can be spared to assist us would be appreciated."

Mrs. Amberly stood up, stiffening her spine. "Penny and Molly are cleaning the earl's bedchamber. And as you plainly can see, Maggie and Fran are still busy with the breakfast dishes."

"Fran and I are nearly done, Mrs. Amberly," Maggie volunteered. "We can come upstairs as soon as we put away the last of the china."

"I for one would certainly be grateful for your help, Maggie," Isabella answered the maid. She turned to the housekeeper and added, "I assume you will be joining us, Mrs. Amberly? I am sure the earl would prefer his children to have their lessons in a clean environment, rather than a dirty, dusty schoolroom."

Mrs. Amberly fairly bristled under Isabella's criticism. "If the schoolroom isn't a fit place for the children to be, then they should stay here in the kitchen with me, like they always do."

"Catherine and Ian are under my care now, Mrs. Amberly," Isabella replied firmly, realizing the housekeeper had just revealed the cause of her underlying hostility. Isabella felt a pang of sympathy for the housekeeper, but she had no intention of allowing her position to be undermined. The sooner Mrs.

Amberly accepted her presence and her authority over the children, the better for the entire household. "The children and I will be spending a great deal of time in the schoolroom."

Isabella's calm statement of authority increased Mrs. Amberly's anger, and she rose from the chair in mounting emotion. The inevitable clash of wills between the two women was momentarily diverted by Fran. The young maid stepped forward, carrying two large buckets, each brimming with sudsy water.

"I'd be glad to bring these up to the schoolroom if you'd like. May I go now, Mrs. Amberly?" Fran asked.

There were several tense minutes of silence while everyone awaited the housekeeper's reply. After casting Isabella another scalding look, Mrs. Amberly finally agreed with a curt nod of her head. Isabella tactfully decided not to pursue the matter further. She turned to Fran to express her gratitude, and her eyes widened in surprise.

Fran was a country lass, a tall girl with a large, sturdy frame. She was pretty, in a robust, fresh way and she held the heavy buckets of water easily, with no apparent discomfort. Yet even Fran's wide hips could not conceal the fact that she, like Maggie, was in an advanced stage of pregnancy.

Chapter Eight

With a conscious effort, Isabella retained her control. There was no cause to panic or overreact, she insisted to herself, just because Lady Edson's gossip about two of the maids at Whatley Grange being pregnant had proved true. It could be nothing more than a bizarre coincidence, couldn't it?

Firmly relegating the incident to the back of her mind, Isabella stepped forward and relieved Fran of one of the heavy buckets of water she carried.

"Would you be kind enough to lead the way to the schoolroom, children?" Isabella requested in a voice that sounded strained to her own ears.

The children eagerly complied, anxious to return to their new toy soldiers. Mrs. Amberly huffed in disapproval and rebelliously resumed her seat in the rocking chair by the fire. Isabella paid her no heed.

Once in the schoolroom, Isabella assigned everyone a task and the cleanup began. Isabella donned a borrowed apron and spent the remainder of the morning focusing her attention on cleaning the dusty room and avoided dwelling overlong on the pregnant condition of the two women working beside her.

Fran, like Maggie, was a friendly girl, and both woman were

obviously appreciative of the assistance Isabella provided. The maids and Isabella worked hard, and within a few hours, the room was sparkling clean and fresh smelling. When their task was nearly completed, the two other maids, Molly and Penny, joined them.

"Fine time for you both to get here," Maggie teased with a smile. "We're nearly done."

"Well, Molly and I have had our fill of cobwebs and dusty rooms today," Penny replied. "We spent all morning cleaning that new governess's room. Mrs. Amberly said she was a very fussy, demanding type and would be sure to speak harshly to us if the room was not found to her liking."

Maggie's eyes widened in distress at Penny's words. She glanced nervously over at Isabella, who had heard every word.

"Please, Penny, do go on," Isabella requested in a pleasant tone. She felt too overcome by a sense of giddy relief as she viewed the slim-waisted Penny to be offended by the housemaid's remarks. It was certainly a pleasant change to meet a housemaid at Whatley Grange who was not heavily burdened with child. The fourth maid, Molly, was equally slender. Isabella's smile broadened as she asked, "What else did Mrs. Amberly have to say about the new governess?"

"Not anything nice," Penny readily answered, but her voice trailed off when she realized it was not Maggie or Fran, but another woman, a stranger, who had spoken. Clearly embarrassed, Penny asked, "I don't suppose you are the new maid from the village Mrs. Amberly been trying to hire for the last few months?"

"No, I am not the new maid, Penny. I am Isabella Browning, the demanding, fussy new governess." Taking pity on the maid's discomfort, Isabella lightly added, "and I sincerely hope your opinion of me will not concur with Mrs. Amberly's."

Penny's face turned a deep shade of scarlet.

"She meant no offense, Miss Browning," Maggie interjected, walking up to Penny and placing a comforting arm around her shoulder.

"Then none was taken," Isabella replied. She turned to the

slight, pale-faced girl standing next to Penny. "You must be Molly."

Molly said nothing, but dipped a curtsy in Isabella's direction. Hastily Penny did the same.

Molly spoke up. "I hope you won't feel it necessary to tell Mrs. Amberly about Penny's impertinent remarks."

Isabella waved her hand in the air in a dismissive gesture. "The incident is already forgotten," she assured the maids, secretly believing Mrs. Amberly would probably be pleased to know the maids had spoken ill of the new governess.

"Penny hasn't been herself lately," Molly continued as if Isabella had not spoken. "She's been feeling poorly these last few days."

"I've just been a little tired and sick to my stomach at times," Penny said. "It will pass soon enough, though, won't it, Maggie?"

"As I've told you before, 'tis different for each woman," Maggie replied philosophically, rubbing the small of her back vigorously. "I had the morning sickness real bad the first four months, but Fran wasn't sick for a day, were you, Fran?"

"Not one day," Fran agreed with a wide grin. "I swear I have never felt better in my life." Fran patted her rounded stomach lovingly. "Of course I am getting fatter than a pig."

The maids all giggled. "How about you, Molly, are you still getting the morning sickness?" Maggie asked conversationally.

"Haven't thrown up in six days," Molly confessed shyly. "I sure hope it lasts."

Isabella turned a frantic eye from one maid to the next as she began to understand the nuances of their conversation. Molly, it would appear, was getting over her bouts with morning sickness, while Penny's morning sickness was just beginning. That meant, of course, that both girls were expecting children.

Isabella's own stomach felt decidedly queasy at the realization. Not two or three, but all four of the maids working at The Grange were pregnant. Her mind reeled with the implications. Was it in any way possible, as Lady Edson had so scandalously suggested, that the earl was responsible for the housemaids' conditions? Isabella shut her eyes in mortification, knowing that since she had now been confronted by the possibility, she was obligated to discover the truth.

The earl did not return home that day until sunset. He spared only a brief greeting to Isabella and his children before sequestering himself in his study. Marshaling her courage, Isabella breached the sanctuary of the earl's study a few minutes after his dinner tray had been delivered by Jenkins.

As she entered, the earl was sitting in a leather wing chair in front of a blazing fire, a book in one hand, a glass of claret in the other. His dinner lay untouched on a small table by his side. His thick black hair was disheveled and falling over his forehead. Both his boots and the knees of his breeches were muddy. He was coatless, and Isabella could not help but notice the muscular strength in his forearms as he turned the page in his book. He did not appear aware of her presence. She coughed loudly to gain his attention.

"Yes," the earl grumbled impatiently. He turned another page in his book and finally glanced up when he heard no response.

Isabella met his gaze without flinching, determined to show him she was not intimidated by his rude, unwelcome attitude. All her life she had dealt with men who were decidedly displeased to be in her presence, starting with the man she had called Father and her maternal grandfather. She was not about to let the earl's disdain upset her.

"I need to speak with you, my lord." Isabella's request was courteously and firmly spoken.

The earl did not reply, but gestured for Isabella to seat herself in the matching wing chair flanking the fireplace. He scrutinized her intently as she did so, his gray eyes narrowing in anticipation of their conversation.

Damien was physically and mentally exhausted and had no desire to listen to the new governess's complaints. And the earl felt certain Isabella was going to complain about something, most likely his children. Damien could only imagine the sort of day she had experienced trying to control the high-spirited

Catherine and Ian. Damien was sure he was about hear a long list of the children's transgressions, and quite possible a lecture about his unsuitability as a parent.

The taut lines of the earl's body conveyed to Isabella his mounting annoyance, and the icy look he flashed chilled her, yet she forced her features into a bland mask. She openly challenged him with her calm demeanor, deftly rebuffing his attempts at intimidation. She would show the earl she was no skittish miss.

"The children have already been bathed and put to bed, my lord," Isabella began, deciding to begin the conversation on a more neutral topic before mentioning the pregnant housemaids, which was the reason she had sought the earl out. "Catherine and Ian were tired, but I am certain that if you go up to their room within the next half hour you will be able to say good night to them."

"Fine," Damien replied, surprised at her words. Bedtimes were a haphazard event at The Grange. More often than not, Catherine and Ian were awake well into the night before their father thought to chase them off to bed. "I will visit the children shortly." Damien dropped his eyes to his book in a dismissing gesture, expecting Isabella to comply with his silent command.

"There are a few things I would like to discuss with you, my lord," Isabella continued, deliberately ignoring his wordless dismissal.

"I feel compelled to caution you, Miss Browning," the earl remarked in a neutral tone, not lifting his eyes from his book, "that I am tired and not in the most congenial mood. And I cannot abide chattering females."

"Neither can I, my lord."

Unwittingly, Damien's firm mouth curved into a small smile. Miss Browning was very persistent and not easily intimidated. He shut his book with a resounding thud and placed it carelessly in his lap. He settled back in his chair, steepled his fingers under his chiseled jaw, and focused his full attention on the lovely governess seated across from him. "What specifically do you wish to discuss, Miss Browning?"

Isabella's confidence wavered slightly under the earl's steely gaze. His was such a dominating, forceful presence. She licked her lips nervously while frantically searching her mind for a diplomatic way to broach the subject of the maids. One could not simply blurt out an accusation.

"I would like to discuss the housemaids, my lord," Isabella finally said quietly.

"Is there a problem?"

"Not exactly a problem, my lord," Isabella hedged. She felt her face growing warm, but she boldly plunged forward. "It is just that the housemaids are all . . . umm . . . that is to say, they are . . . um, well, all . . . expecting."

"Expecting? Expecting what, Miss Browning?"

"Babies, my lord. Babies. All four of the housemaids are with child!" Isabella was aghast at the earl's lighthearted tone. She felt this was a very serious matter indeed, yet she could almost swear she saw a smile cross his handsome face.

"I was under the impression that most governesses liked children. Are you an exception?"

She looked at him levelly. "I like children very much, my lord." Isabella stiffened her back and sat up straight in her chair. "Since I have been hired to care for your own children, I was wondering if I will also be responsible for these yet unborn babies."

Isabella had the satisfaction of seeing the earl shocked into stunned silence as it took several moments for him to realize what her question implied. She could clearly see the precise moment when the meaning of her question registered in his mind.

Sending Isabella a piercing stare, the earl said harshly, "Maggie, Fran, Molly, and Penny are all married women, Miss Browning. Their husbands are employed in various capacities at The Grange. Each couple occupies a small suite of rooms in the servants' quarters on the fourth floor."

Isabella made a slight sound to clear her throat and her violet eyes flickered uneasily. Her cheeks blushed an even brighter shade of pink as she lowered her gaze to the carpet.

"I was unaware that the maids were married, my lord," Isabella responded quietly. "However, that makes little difference.'' Recalling vividly that the man who had married Isabella's own mother was not in fact her natural father propelled her to ask a direct question. ''Are they your children, my lord?''

The earl appeared so taken aback by her directness that he had difficulty formulating an intelligent response. ''You actually believe I am the father of these children?''

''Someone informed me that you had fathered several children from your housemaids,'' Isabella answered with a slight quaver in her voice. She forced her eyes from the rug and cast a long, doubtful look at the earl. ''I do not know if you are responsible, my lord. That is why I have asked this question.''

The earl was instantly suspicious. ''Who told you I have fathered these children? Certainly not the maids?''

''I did not question the maids about the father of their children, my lord,'' Isabella said, bristling at the suggestion she would be so insensitive. ''Lady Edson informed me before I arrived at The Grange that three of the housemaids were carrying your babies. At the time I dismissed her gossip as pure slander, but after discovering all four of the maids were in truth with child, I did not know what to believe.''

''Lady Edson is a meddlesome, gossiping fool!'' the earl shouted, obviously struggling to master his temper. He shifted suddenly in his chair, and the book on his lap fell to the floor. He ignored it.

''I am not sure if I should be flattered or insulted, Miss Browning,'' the earl finally declared, his temper tightly leashed. He shook his head ruefully. ''Bedding four different women, all of them living under the same roof. Extraordinary.''

''It does seem rather incredible,'' Isabella mused, beginning to wonder if she had made a very serious mistake. ''Exhausting actually.''

The last she had whispered under her breath, but the earl heard her. And it struck him as absurdly funny. He should be angry with her, furious really, for first crediting and then repeating such an absurd tale. And then having the unmitigated gall to face him directly with her allegations. Yet he suddenly found the entire situation ironically humorous, though he had no clear idea why.

His shoulders shook a bit with amusement as he recalled the shock on her face at his reaction to her questions. Damien decided it was time to put things to right, but first he intended to put the fear of God into the very proper Miss Browning. A teasing glint of anticipation entered the earl's smoky gray eyes.

Stretching his back languidly, he threw Isabella an assessing glance. "What if these accusations are true, Miss Browning?" Damien inquired smoothly. He leaned seductively toward her, a calculated, lecherous grin on his handsome face. "Will you now flee from my house in abject terror, my dear, frightened beyond your wits at the thought of being seduced by such an unscrupulous rake as myself?"

Isabella hardly dared to breathe as the earl moved closer to her. He was so near, she could feel his warm breath on her cheek, could smell his distinctively masculine scent. She clearly felt the underlying tension emanating from the earl's solidly built body, and it made her decidedly uneasy.

"I feel certain I can protect myself from any of your attempts at seduction, my lord," Isabella finally choked out, "though in truth I see no reason why you would have the slightest interest in me."

Isabella was pleased that she had managed to formulate some sort of response, given the intense pounding of her heart. Yet she felt her statement certainly would have been more effective if she hadn't sounded so breathless and meek when she uttered it.

"Come now, Isabella, there is no need to be coy. You are an attractive woman. Surely you are aware of your feminine allure," the earl continued silkenly, clearly enjoying this intimate bantering with the lovely governess.

His eyes glistened with excitement, and he felt a strange exhilaration in his broad chest. Damien deliberately moved himself even closer to her, studying Isabella's wide-eyed expression with a certain satisfaction. By God, if the woman thought he was capable of bedding all four of his housemaids, he would not disappoint her expectations.

"You have not answered my question, my lord," Isabella whispered back, ignoring completely the earl's intimate remarks. She was aware of a growing sensation of light-headedness, caused, she was certain, by the deep timber of his voice and the sensual intoxication of his nearness. Her throat felt parched, her pulse was racing, her breathing was shallow. She had never before encountered a man who inspired such feelings within her.

"I have never bedded any of the women in my employ, Isabella," the earl continued in the same mesmerizing tone, enjoying himself too much to stop now. "But that is the past. Who knows what the future will hold?"

Isabella's violet eyes widened even further at his remark, and she was shocked to the core to hear herself whisper throatily back. "Who knows indeed?"

"Almighty God!"

The earl swore loudly at her completely unanticipated response, and his lips descended swiftly on her own. His assault caught her by surprise, but she did not protest. Her lips parted slightly, and he boldly slipped his tongue inside her sweet mouth. Isabella flinched at the invasion, but the earl wrapped one strong hand around the back of her neck to prevent her retreat.

Pleasure soon overcame any doubts as a shiver of pure passion seared through Isabella's taut body. She moaned softly in the back of her throat and willingly returned his kisses.

The hard, almost painful ache of his swollen manhood forced the reality of the moment into Damien's consciousness. When he realized precisely *who* was arousing him to such acute passion, he wrenched himself away and abruptly stood up.

The earl deliberately dragged himself away from her, knowing he was only seconds away from taking her into his arms and thoroughly seducing her. The little game he had instigated was fast progressing beyond his control.

He strode purposefully toward the fireplace, needing to place a physical distance between himself and Isabella. He rested his arm against the mantle, keeping his back to her.

Isabella was grateful to escape. The reckless excitement she derived from the earl's kisses was easing, although the indefinable sense of heated awareness flowing within her body lingered.

"I shall have my belongings packed and ready so I may leave at first light tomorrow morning, my lord." Isabella could not keep the trembling from her voice with her softly whispered declaration. She felt certain the earl was going to dismiss her, and she wanted to save herself from that final humiliation. Whatever had possesed her to first make such brazen accusations against him and then respond with such wanton abandonment to his thrilling kisses was beyond her comprehension.

The earl felt a sharp pang of guilt. He had goaded her too far, and now she thought it was necessary to flee from him.

Stoically, he turned and faced Isabella. "If I give you my solemn promise never to repeat such boorish behavior, Miss Browning," the earl inquired quietly, "will you reconsider your decision to leave Whatley Grange?"

"I was merely anticipating your actions, my lord," Isabella said, noting with a strange sense of loss that he had again adopted the formality of calling her Miss Browning instead of Isabella. "You are not going to dismiss me?"

"For an incident that was utterly my fault? That would be grossly unfair."

"The fault was on both sides, my lord," Isabella responded gently, knowing she could not allow him to take full responsibility.

Isabella rose to her feet and met him squarely, her beautiful eyes soft and apologetic. In her heart she knew the correct course of action would be to leave Whatley Grange as fast as possible. But she did not want to leave.

"If you would be kind enough to excuse *my* unpardonable behavior, my lord," Isabella said plainly, "I will gladly continue as Catherine and Ian's governess."

"I am pleased you want to stay with us." The husky masculine whisper sent a tingle through her. In some ways the apologies they exchanged were as intimate as the kisses they had shared. Isabella nervously dropped her eyes from the earl's and turned to leave the room.

She paused at the doorway. "I shall see you in the morning, my lord."

"Good night, Miss Browning."

Damien reached automatically for his glass of wine the moment the room was empty. His thoughts were filled with images of Isabella. He was genuinely appalled at his actions toward her. She was employed in his household, under his protection, and he had treated her with utter disrespect.

Isabella's response to his blatant sensual assault on her person had been the biggest shock of all. She had responded honestly, with passion and desire. A very dangerous reaction, indeed.

Damien drained his wine glass and instantly refilled it. He eyed the full decanter of claret and wondered if he would be able to restrain himself from consuming the entire bottle. The earl was glad Isabella had elected to remain at The Grange, but he questioned the wisdom of requesting her to stay. Was it really necessary to keep a woman in his household who simultaneously intrigued him and drove him to drink?

Chapter Nine

Isabella did not set eyes on the earl again for five days. He no longer joined his children and their new governess at the breakfast table, and he returned to The Grange long after Catherine and Ian had eaten their supper and been sent to bed.

At first Isabella wondered if the earl had journeyed from house, but discreet questioning of Jenkins revealed the earl remained at Whatley Grange.

"His lordship has been especially busy with estate matters these past few days, Miss Browning," Jenkins told her. "I could tell him you wish to speak with him," the valet added helpfully.

"Thank you Jenkins, but I don't believe that will be necessary," Isabella hastily replied, wanting very much to be the one to choose the time and place of her next meeting with the earl. "I am certain I will eventually encounter his lordship."

Isabella waited an additional two days before admitting to herself that the earl was either working excessively, as Jenkins had claimed, or doing a plausible job of avoiding her. For herself, Isabella soon discovered that not seeing the earl did not alter the fact that she found him impossible to forget. She remained in a conflicting state of emotions as she anticipated their next encounter, experiencing feelings of euphoria and dread almost simultaneously.

By day Isabella was far too busy to dwell overlong on what was, in her opinion, an irritating fascination with the earl. Yet, when she was alone at night, the earl's handsome image haunted her. Isabella's undeniable interest in him was something she neither welcomed nor understood; quite frankly, it amazed her.

Her cheeks flushed with color whenever she relived the scandalous excitement of the earl's kisses. She remembered with startling clarity the warm, sensual taste of him, the hard masculine strength of his muscular body, and above all the strange and wonderful feelings he evoked in her of being swept away by an exhilarating, mysterious passion.

Her puzzlement over her strange reactions to the earl did not overshadow her genuine desire to remain as governess to Catherine and Ian. She clearly saw how much the children needed her, and for the first time in her life she experienced a true sense of belonging that she was determined to preserve.

The major obstacle to overcome was learning to control the attraction she felt for the earl. To Isabella's way of thinking, it was imperative that she develop a relationship with her handsome employer that was totally respectable and morally correct. And did not include stolen, heart-melting kisses.

Isabella presumed the earl was thinking along similar lines and thus was avoiding contact with her. While she appreciated his efforts towards resolving the problem, she knew that avoidance was not a practical approach. As governess to his children, she would need to confer with the earl often and privately. Deciding that she had put off this important encounter for too long already, Isabella rose one morning before dawn, determined to waylay the earl before he left the house.

Isabella strode silently down the darkened corridors, following the one and only route to the main dining hall she had mastered in the week she had resided at The Grange. The dining room was empty when she entered, but the lamps had been lit and a tiered hand of candles illuminated the sideboard. A china place setting was haphazardly arranged at the head of the table, and next to it rested a Spode china coffeepot with a large chip in its spout.

Isabella assumed the seat next to the earl's and waited expectantly, determined not to dwell on the events that had occurred the last time she sought out the earl for a private conversation.

The servants' door swung open suddenly, and Mrs. Amberly entered the room, awkwardly balancing three large serving platters in her arms. Isabella rose automatically, intending to assist the housekeeper, but after a quelling look from Mrs. Amberly, she quietly resumed her seat.

The housekeeper cast her a final disapproving stare before leaving the room. Isabella in return favored her with a dazzling smile, causing the desired effect of completely mystifying the sullen housekeeper. Thwarting Mrs. Amberly gave Isabella a boost of confidence, and she felt a bit more relaxed as she waited for the earl to appear.

The earl entered the room quietly, as was his custom, and was halfway into the room before he noticed Isabella. His body tightened with awareness at her nearness, but he recovered quickly, barely breaking his stride. His handsome face was a polite mask of curiosity.

"Good morning, my lord." Isabella's voice was steady, but escalating nerves at seeing the earl made it low and husky. To his ears it sounded sensual and inviting.

"Miss Browning." The earl nodded curtly in her direction. If he was surprised to see her at the breakfast table at this exceedingly early hour, he gave no outward indication.

Stretching his long, muscular frame across the mahogany dinning table, the earl retrieved the china plate that had been placed in front of his chair. Straightening up, he peered down at Isabella and inquired politely, "May I fix you a breakfast plate, Miss Browning?"

"No, thank you, my lord. I shall eat my breakfast with the children." Isabella prudently decided her already fluttering stomach would not tolerate Mrs. Amberly's heavy cooking at this early hour of the morning.

She waited until the earl had filled his plate with a decidedly unappetizing array of food before speaking.

"My lord," Isabella started, but the earl held his hand up in silent command.

"Enough," he pronounced, as he took his seat. "Your formality of speech and constant 'my lording' of me every minute is beginning to grate on my nerves. I insist you call me by my Christian name." The earl plowed his fork into a pile of greasy potatoes and thrust them into his mouth. "It is Damien, by the way."

"I know what your name is, my lor—ah, sir." Isabella watched the earl struggle to swallow his potatoes. "However, I do not think it is proper for me to address you so informally."

"If you desire propriety, *Isabella,* you should not be working at The Grange." He cast her a challenging stare.

"I suppose you have a valid point . . . Damien." The name forced itself off her tongue slowly, but at least she succeeded in uttering it.

Damien, pleased that she had succumbed to his wishes, flashed her a slight grin and forcefully cut into an overdone, dry piece of steak. "Now, tell me why you felt it necessary to rise before the sun this morning."

"We need to discuss Catherine and Ian. Since you have been so preoccupied for the last few days, I decided to catch you before you left the house."

Ignoring the gentle rebuke in her tone, Damien asked with a slight smile, "Are my children proving too much for you to handle, Isabella?" He knew all too well how difficult his high-spirited children could be.

"Quite the contrary," Isabella insisted, experiencing a strange warmth in her chest on hearing him address by her given name. "The children have been quiet and polite, deferring to me in all things. In the week that they have been in my care there have been no arguments, no pranks, no disagreements, no signs of rebellion, no attempts at independence, no questioning of my authority in any matter."

Damien leaned back in his chair, a puzzled expression on his handsome face. "And you find this behavior cause for complaint?"

"I find this behavior most unusual," Isabella replied earnestly. "Especially after Maggie and Fran related a few of the children's previous scrapes. Given their history, I feel Catherine and Ian are now acting in a manner that can be classified as—well, abnormal."

The earl was instantly offended by her remark. "There is nothing wrong with my children," he declared forcefully.

"You misunderstand me," Isabella interjected. "I think Catherine and Ian are both normal, intelligent children. I am merely pointing out that they are not behaving naturally. They are suppressing their innate curiosity and enthusiasm because they are fearful of seeming disobedient." Isabella leaned forward in her chair. "And I believe that you are the cause."

"Me?"

Isabella unconsciously placed her hand on the earl's arm. "Catherine mentioned to me the other morning that you had instructed her and Ian to follow my orders without question and obey me in all things. If not, they would suffer the consequences."

Damien wrinkled his brow. "This was the wrong thing to say?"

Isabella let out a small sigh. "Of course not. But it seems obvious the children are so intent on pleasing you that they are suppressing their natural inclinations toward fun and adventure. I find that unacceptable."

Damien gave Isabella a searching look. "Are you saying you want me to instruct Catherine and Ian to misbehave? To ignore your authority and act however they wish?" Damien's deep voice was filled with genuine wonder.

"Naturally, I do not wish them to turn into undisciplined little monsters. Yet I want them to know that it is acceptable for them to indulge their natural curiosities at times. It is even acceptable for them to make mistakes. I want you to tell them they do not always have to be perfect." A fleeting glimpse of pain crossed Isabella's features as she remembered the pain of her own childhood. "It can be a rather exhausting task for a young child to constantly strive for perfection."

Damien looked at Isabella doubtfully, but she continued speaking.

"There is something else we need to address," Isabella said softly. "Concerning Catherine."

"Yes?"

"Are you aware of her exceptional memory? It is quite extraordinary. She can remember with the most astonishing detail nearly everything I teach her, especially when numbers are involved."

A slow grin crossed the earl's face. "My grandfather had such an ability. I did not know Catherine shared his gift."

"Well, she does. And while I certainly feel it is an amazing and potentially useful talent, Catherine applies it in the oddest way."

"How so?"

Isabella let out a long breath. "She is obsessed with battles. Warfare of any kind intrigues her, but the recent conflict with France seems to be a particular fascination. Catherine and Ian stage numerous mock battles with the large collection of toy soldiers they have, and her attention to detail is overwhelming. Catherine knows precisely how many troops are on each side, how the action of the battle takes place, which generals issued what specific commands. It is remarkable." Isabella looked down at her hands. "She is also intrigued about the number of causalities after the battle, wounded as well as dead. Her insistence on accuracy can be positively chilling at times."

"That seems very peculiar." Damien swallowed the last of his coffee. His brow wrinkling in confusion, he asked, "What do you think this means?"

"I am not certain." Isabella shrugged her shoulders helplessly. "Yet, I cannot help but feel this obsession with death and dying is not healthy."

The earl wiped his mouth with his cloth napkin and tossed it casually on the table.

"I agree that Catherine's behavior is unhealthy and should not be tolerated," Damien said. Pushing his chair away from the table, he rose to his feet. "I shall speak to Catherine this evening and instruct her to cease this odd behavior immediately."

"Oh, no!" Isabella jumped up in dismay. Her knee hit the

edge of the dining room table and the earl's breakfast dishes rattled noisily. "You cannot simply order Catherine to stop."

Damien raised a brow. "Why not? As her parent, I am responsible for her conduct. If she is acting in an unacceptable manner, then it must cease. At once."

Isabella flashed him a look of pure consternation. How typical of him to pursue the easiest course by demanding the strange behavior stop, instead of searching for the underlying cause.

"I do not think ordering Catherine to stop playing with her soldiers is the correct solution. While she and Ian are reenacting these rather bloody battles, she always mentions your role in the conflict."

"My role?"

Isabella nodded her head. "It is my understanding that you and Mr. Jenkins participated in the fighting in the Peninsula." At the earl's curt nod, Isabella continued. "Catherine's main focus of interest is the actual battles you participated in."

Damien looked totally bewildered. "Those conflicts took place years ago, long before she was born. How can Catherine possible be aware of my involvement?"

Isabella squirmed uncomfortably under the earl's intense gaze. Even though she felt no loyalty toward Mrs. Amberly, Isabella was reluctant to reveal the housekeeper's connection. Yet seeing no alternative, she disclosed the truth.

"Apparently Mrs. Amberly kept a scrapbook of newspaper clippings while you were away fighting. Over the past few years, she has read the printed accounts of these battles to the children and Catherine has committed the details to memory."

"How very extraordinary," Damien muttered to himself.

"Yes, it is amazing." Isabella bit her lip nervously before uttering her next remark. "However, I think this peculiar behavior only illustrates how deeply the children, especially Catherine, crave the attention and love of their father."

The expression on the earl's handsome face was guarded. "I may not be, in your opinion, the most attentive parent on earth, but I can assure you, Isabella, I cherish my son and daughter."

The remoteness in the earl's eyes betrayed his inner feelings, and Isabella realized suddenly that she had wounded him. It surprised and disturbed her, for it had not been her intention.

"I did not mean to offend you, Damien," she insisted contritely. "I have merely observed that Catherine and Ian miss their father. They have seen very little of you this past week."

"This is an exceedingly busy season at The Grange," Damien said abruptly, obviously still feeling the sting of her remarks. "I have numerous responsibilities on the estate that cannot be ignored."

"You also have a responsibility to your children, sir," Isabella replied quietly. "They have not spoken with you in days."

The earl turned his back on Isabella in annoyance. Her words rankled him, yet he knew in his heart that she spoke the truth. He had allowed his duties on the estate to monopolize his time, and apparently Catherine and Ian were suffering because of it. There was no excuse for neglecting his children, no matter how busy he was. And it was even more annoying to have a new governess point out his shortcomings to him.

Damien strode to the door and swung it open, but paused for a moment before leaving. "I shall return to the castle today for tea. I expect you and the children to join me in the drawing room at the appropriate time." The door closed quietly behind him.

Isabella collapsed in the chair after he left, a feeling of exhaustion overwhelming her. She could barely believe she had the nerve to call the earl to task on his parental obligations. And he had listened to her. But she had truly believed Catherine's odd behavior was caused by the absence of her father's love and attention, and she had no intention of letting that disgraceful condition continue as long as the children were under her care.

Thwack! Thwack! The sound rang rhythmically through the quiet woods as the earl raised his ax and swung hard at the thick tree stump.

"She wants me to spend more time with my children," Damien muttered as he brought the ax up for another swing.

"She thinks I neglect them, and because I have been such a poor parent, Catherine has developed this strange obsession with soldiers and battles and death."

"Miss Browning said you are neglecting the children?" Jenkins asked in amazement. The valet sat up, abandoning his relaxed pose against a giant elm, as the earl hacked away at the stump. "She actually called you a poor father?"

"In so many words," Damien replied, making contact again with the thick tree stump. Small chips of bark flew in all directions, but the earl did not seem to notice. "Then in the next breath she was berating me for being too strict with Catherine and Ian. She told me that by demanding perfect behavior from them, I was suppressing their natural curiosity and stunting their growth, or some such nonsense."

The valet winced at the earl's annoyed tone and shook his head regretfully. "So you have dismissed Miss Browning," Jenkins stated slowly, his voice tinged with disappointment. "I must confess Damien, I shall miss her. I have grown rather fond of her."

"In one short week?" the earl questioned sarcastically, not wanting to admit to himself that he was also developing a fondness for the pretty young governess. Taking one final swing at the now split tree stump, the earl grinned at his valet.

"There is no need to look so downhearted, Jenkins," Damien told his servant. "I did not fire Miss Browning. Although I certainly had grounds." Damien dropped the heavy ax and wiped the sweat off his brow with his shirt sleeve. His muscular body felt strained and tired from the intense physical exertion, but his mind was still tense. "I always thought governesses were timid creatures, Jenkins, the sort of employee one would barely notice. They have always struck me as gray, drab women who glide unobtrusively through the household, often disappearing into the background entirely."

"Miss Browning is not a typical governess," Jenkins replied, clearly pleased that his employer had not sent Isabella packing. "If she were, she would not have lasted more than one night at The Grange."

The earl chuckled at that remark. "No, I don't suppose an

ordinary governess would feel comfortable in our household.''
Over the years, the oddness of his staff had become an eccentric
point of amusement for the earl. ''Did you know she thought
I was responsible for the housemaids being pregnant?''

''All four of them?'' Jenkins uttered a short laugh and passed
a wooden bucket of water to the earl. Damien dipped a ladle
into the bucket and took a long swallow. Then he poured the
remainder over his head, enjoying the feel of the cool water
on his heated skin.

''Isabella might have misunderstood about the maids, but
she is right about my neglecting Catherine and Ian,'' the earl
admitted. Damien picked up his ax and started walking towards
the clearing where the rest of the work crew was eating their
lunch. Jenkins quickly fell in step with him. ''I suppose I should
be grateful that she cares enough about the children to call me
to task on it.''

''You spend more time with Catherine and Ian than most
parents of your class,'' Jenkins was quick to defend the earl.

''That is not a very good comparison, Jenkins,'' the earl
retorted. ''In my experience, most members of the *ton* are too
frivolous and preoccupied with social events to spare much
time or thought for their offspring.''

''Good Lord, Damien, you have been occupied with countless estate matters this past week, not a round of social obligations. The children understand your many responsibilities. And
so should Miss Browning.''

''I don't think it particularly matters to my children or Miss
Browning how I spend my time. The point is that I have not
been with Catherine and Ian.''

Jenkins eyed the earl curiously as they reached the clearing.
''How do you propose to remedy the situation?''

''I am going back to The Grange this afternoon to have
tea with my children and their governess,'' Damien replied
smoothly, his eyes twinkling with amusement at the stunned
expression on Jenkins's face. It gave the earl a certain sense
of satisfaction to know that after all their years together, he
still possessed the ability to surprise his valet.

Chapter Ten

Afternoon tea was a disaster. The quiet, demure children Isabella had previously voiced her concerns about were boisterous, loud, and rude from the moment their father entered the drawing room. Catherine and Ian bickered passionately with each other over who would sit next to the earl while tea was served, and both grumbled noisily over the compromise of allowing him to sit between the two. They continually interrupted each other's sentences and unabashedly tried to outmaneuver each other for their father's undivided attention.

Damien remained perfectly calm amidst the chaos of his undisciplined children, listening with avid curiosity to their stories and making appropriate comments when necessary. He made no move, however, to correct their appalling behavior, even as Catherine threatened to hurl her teacup at her younger brother when Ian attempted to eat the last remaining strawberry tart.

"You already ate two pastries, Catherine," Ian insisted, in a sharp tone Isabella never before heard the young boy use. "This one is mine."

"Oh, no, it is not," Catherine retorted, raising her empty china teacup. "I want the tart, Ian. And if you do not hand it

over to me this minute, I'm going to cosh you over the head."
Catherine swung her arm higher in the air to emphasize her
resolve.

"Catherine!" Isabella exclaimed in a voice filled with indignation. "Put that tea cup down this instant!"

Catherine opened her mouth as if to protest Isabella's command but remained silent when she caught a glimpse of the
earl's stern features. Reluctantly, Catherine lowered her arm,
although she continued to glare challengingly at her younger
brother.

Isabella let out the breath she had been holding as Catherine
resumed her seat. The momentary calm was shattered as Ian
and Catherine both made a sudden, simultaneous grab for the
pastry. Isabella saw their intent and somehow managed to be
quicker than either of them. Impulsively, she snatched the
offending pastry off the tray, and in a final desperate attempt
to prevent the children from coming to physical blows, stuffed
the strawberry tart into her mouth.

Her completely unexpected action stunned the children into
silence. Catherine, Ian, and the earl stared openly as Isabella
struggled to keep from choking while she chewed and then
tried to swallow the large, dry tart.

Isabella refused to allow the embarrassment she felt to show.
Boldly, she returned the shocking stares she received from the
earl and his children, her jaw moving ferociously as she chewed
the tart, her deep violet eyes sparkling with anger, daring any
one of them to make a comment. When at last her throat was
clear, Isabella announced in her sternest, most proper governess's voice, "Children, tea is over. However, before you take
your leave of this room, you will apologize to your father for
your rude behavior and unmannerly display this afternoon."

Isabella braced herself for a tirade of protest, intending to
stand firm, but one stern look from Damien and the children
begrudgingly complied with Isabella's request.

The welcoming silence that descended on the drawing room
after Catherine and Ian departed helped sooth Isabella's ragged
nerves. She had spent the past two hours correcting, admon-
ishing, and outright threatening her charges in an effort to make

them behave in a civilized manner. In the end her efforts met with very little success. She felt drained and agitated and was certain these emotions were plainly written on her face.

Isabella glanced speculatively at the bottle of brandy on the sideboard as she poured herself a cup of lukewarm tea. Even though she rarely consummed them, the idea of strong spirits to calm her ragged nerves held definite appeal. Yet she would never be so bold as to pour herself a glass, especially in front of the earl.

Isabella was, in fact, afraid to look at Damien, not wishing to see the disapproval and reproach he must certainly be feeling reflected in his eyes. What must he think of her! Was she so poor a governess that she could not keep two young children under control long enough to have a civil cup of tea with their father?

The earl rose from the brocade settee and stretched his long legs. He walked carefully toward the sideboard and poured two generous portions of brandy. Wordlessly, he crossed the room and held out a glass to Isabella. She looked up, startled, as he pressed the goblet into her hand, but offered no protest.

"You look as though you could use this, Isabella," Damien said with a distinct twinkle in his eye. "I know I certainly need it."

Isabella did not miss the amusement on his handsome face. "I can see you find this entire situation humorous, sir," she said dryly, "though for the life of me I cannot imagine why."

"Come now, Isabella, I thought you would be pleased," Damien replied with a teasing smile. "Catherine and Ian were acting like their mischievous little selves again. Wasn't it just this morning you were saying how concerned you were because the children were not exercising their . . . um . . . how exactly did you phrase it? Oh, I remember . . . their 'natural curiosity.' "

Isabella stifled a groan at the earl's remark. For a brief moment she wondered if Damien had put his children up to this afternoon's antics but she quickly ruled out the possibility. No father in his right mind would willingly encourage such appalling, obnoxious behavior.

"Encouraging a child's natural curiosity is one thing, sir,"

Isabella insisted, as she took a small sip of the brandy. "Tolerating their unruly and rude behavior is an entirely different matter."

"They weren't all that bad today," Damien said in a conversational tone. He drained his glass and refilled it before reclaiming his seat. "If I remember correctly, the last time my children fought over a pastry, Catherine lost a clump of her hair."

"Ian pulled out Catherine's hair?"

"Only a small amount," Damien clarified calmly. "Of course, he was provoked. Catherine bit him on the arm. Twice, I believe."

"Hair pulling and arm biting over Mrs. Amberly's dry strawberry tarts," Isabella said, shaking her head in amazement. "I shudder to think what would occur if Catherine and Ian sampled a competent pastry chef's wares."

"It could very well mean war."

Isabella could not prevent the small laugh that rose to her lips. She took another sip of her drink. "Yes, I can picture it clearly. Teacups being thrown, hair being lost, numerous body parts being bitten."

The earl indulged in a low chuckle and Isabella felt her heart lurch at the rich, intimate sound. Why did she find him so incredibly appealing? Deliberately focusing her attention away from the restless churning in her stomach, she cleared her throat loudly and said in a serious voice, "I don't intend to treat this lightly. It was amply demonstrated this afternoon that I need to exercise greater control over my charges. Yet, I feel strongly that the reason for the children's appalling behavior is their quest for your attention, sir."

"I believe you are making far too much of all this," Damien insisted, trying not to concentrate on her delicate face. Her cheeks were flushed from the brandy, and a wisp of chestnut hair grazed her temple. Damien thought she looked lovely, disturbingly so. "My children are merely high-spirited, Isabella."

"I prefer them disciplined. Are you going to support me in my efforts?"

"Yes," Damien whispered softly.

"Good," Isabella replied with a satisfied nod. She lifted her chin defiantly and gazed directly into Damien's bold gray eyes, determined to conquer the strange emotions he inspired.

It was a mistake. Damien met her direct stare with an intense, powerful look that sent chills up and down her spine. His eyes held a challenge she did not fully understand, yet she admitted honestly to herself that she was intrigued. Though they were separated by several feet, Isabella swore she could feel the heat of his powerful body.

They would have sat there indefinitely, if not suddenly interrupted by Jenkins's voice.

"Are you going to ride out and inspect the work on the south fence before darkness, my lord?"

"Certainly, Jenkins," Damien replied, tearing his eyes away from Isabella to answer his valet. "Miss Browning and I have a few matters to settle first. I will ride out shortly."

Freed from the hypnotic power of the earl's glance, Isabella rose from her chair and stepped to the far side of the drawing room. Fearing to look at the earl again, she deliberately turned her back to him, starring unseeingly out the window.

Damien remained quiet for a long time. Each time he was alone with Isabella, she had a decidedly unsettling effect on him. Somehow she managed to stir up smoldering emotions and passions that he had almost forgotten he possessed. With just a few innocent glances, Isabella had shown him just how close to the surface these feelings lay, and how quickly she could bring them to life.

Yet Damien was determined to resist her, no matter how appealing he found her. He would keep his feelings firmly in check and remain immune to her charms. He fought for and regained his self-control.

"How do you propose to reconcile this problem of my children's need for attention and my obligation to run this estate?"

Isabella shivered visibly at the sound of his voice. She swallowed several times before answering. "Is it possible for Catherine and Ian to accompany you when you attend to certain estate matters? Perhaps they can ride with you when you visit your tenants?''

Damien thought a few moments before answering. "Generally, I leave the house very early in the morning and am often miles away before Catherine and Ian even awaken. And I only visit my tenants if there is a problem."

"I don't suppose you could return for afternoon tea each day?"

"So I can referee the fights over strawberry tarts?"

Damien's lighthearted remark eased the tension within Isabella, and she summoned the courage to turn around and face him.

"Well, sir, if I promise to do my best to prevent the fights, will you promise to come to tea?"

"I will be here at least twice each week," the earl declared. "Perhaps Catherine and Ian can join me for dinner Saturday evening?"

Isabella rolled her eyes at the notion. Visions of mashed potatoes and peas being flung across the dining room table filled her head. "The children are a bit young to be eating dinner so late in the evening," Isabella hedged. "It might be better to wait until Sunday. I am sure you can find some free time after we return from Sunday services."

The earl stiffened at her remark. "I do not attend church services, Isabella," Damien said tersely. "And neither do my children." He held her gaze for a chilling instant, allowing no emotion to cross his face. "Is that clearly understood?"

Isabella blinked uncertainly. "You have made your point, sir." Isabella was astonished by his vehement declaration and very curious. Too curious to resist asking, "Is it merely church you object to, sir, or do you have something against God?"

"Not personally," Damien replied with a note of temper in his voice. "It is my opinion that the majority of individuals who attend services in this community act as though spending an hour in pious prayer absolves them of a week of sinning. I'd like to think I'm not quite so hypocritical."

Isabella raised her eyebrows questioningly. "Surely that cannot be the only reason you do not attend Sunday services?"

Damien gave a harsh laugh. "You are very aware of the ugly gossip that surrounds my name, Isabella. I refuse to bring my children into the village and expose them to all those malicious lies."

"I would think the people of this village could find a more worthy subject of conversation," Isabella said lightly. "And I highly doubt anyone would have the audacity, or the courage, to insult you or your children directly. If you faced the gossips head on, Damien, they might just move on to more juicier scandals."

The earl was not convinced. "I will not subject Catherine and Ian to any scrutiny," Damien declared in a firm voice.

"Do you object to my attending services?"

Damien frowned slightly. "Your presence will certainly cause comments." When Isabella did not respond, the earl concluded impatiently, "Ultimately, it is your decision to make, Isabella. As long as you do not involve my children, I have no right to object. In fact, I insist you take my carriage."

"Thank you," Isabella replied, inclining her head with icy politeness. "I should be honored."

"Fine," Damien replied, slightly annoyed because she appeared determined to follow a course he felt certain would cause her discomfort. "I wish to have supper with Catherine and Ian on Saturday evening. I shall instruct Mrs. Amberly to serve the meal promptly at seven o'clock." He cast her a sly look. "Naturally, I expect you to be in attendance."

"Naturally," Isabella repeated faintly, her heart fluttering anew at the thought of spending an evening in the earl's company.

Damien walked to the door. "If you will excuse me, I should like to see about those fences before darkness falls." The earl hesitated, but departed the room without another word.

With shadowed eyes, Isabella watched him leave.

"I have finished drawing my flowers, Miss Browning. Can I paint them?" Catherine looked with undisguised longing at the fresh box of water colors Isabella was using.

"Certainly." Isabella shifted the position of her easel, allowing Catherine easy access to the paints. "Light, even strokes," Isabella advised as the young girl jammed her paintbrush onto the canvas.

Isabella offered a few more tactful suggestions before shifting her attention to Ian. The young boy had elected to forgo the watercolor lesson and instead was practicing his writing. Isabella joined him on the stone bench as he leaned intently over his slate.

"That looks good, Ian," she praised the child, as he proudly displayed his writing. The letters were disproportionate in size, and two of them were written backwards, but they were legible. Certainly a fine effort for a three-year-old boy. "Now let's concentrate on our counting. One, two, three . . ."

Dutifully Ian chimed in, and Isabella's voice gradually faded away, allowing him to recite the numbers on his own.

Isabella returned to her canvas, pleased she had decided to conduct the afternoon's lessons outside. The weather was sunny and inviting, and Isabella was enjoying the fresh air as much as her young charges.

Catherine and Ian had suggested the rose garden on the north side of the castle for their lessons, and Isabella approved of their choice. It was the only garden on the estate that showed any attempt at maintenance. There were still many weeds in the flower beds and the unclipped hedges were unusually high, but the stone path was passable and the rose bushes healthy and blooming.

"Father!" Catherine's voice rang out with excitement. She dropped her paintbrush heedlessly and hastened toward the earl.

Damien appeared suddenly from behind a tall hedge. He sauntered casually into the rose garden, slapping his riding crop idly against the top of his muddy boots as he walked. He greeted his daughter warmly, then turned his attention to Isabella.

She hid her astonishment at his unexpected appearance and felt the now familiar pounding of her heart begin. "We are having our lessons outside this afternoon," Isabella explained.

"So I gathered," the earl replied with a slight smile. He

moved in front of Catherine's easel to gain a better view and commented on her watercolor.

"Seventeen, eighteen, nineteen, twenty." Ian, who had wandered behind a large, overgrown hedge, was not visible, but his singing numbers could be clearly heard.

"Ian is practicing his counting," Isabella remarked unnecessarily.

"Yes," the earl remarked. "I can hear him." Damien parroted his son's unusual numerical sequence with a smile. "Twenty-eight, twenty-nine, twenty-ten, twenty-eleven. A new system I am unaware of, Isabella?"

"He is making progress," Isabella proclaimed breathlessly, her color heightening. "Ian, come back here, please."

"I've come to take the children riding this afternoon," the earl said when Ian appeared. "If they have finished with their lessons for today."

"I'm done, Father," Catherine declared with a final swipe at her painting. "We'll change into our riding clothes and be right back. Hurry up, Ian." Catherine threw down her paintbrush with a flourish, grabbed her brother's hand, and the two rushed off.

Isabella correctly interpreted the earl's frown and intervened before he could reprimand the children for leaving without waiting to be dismissed. "We really are finished for the afternoon," she said softly.

"Will you join us, Isabella?" Damien stood by Isabella as she packed up the paints and paintbrushes.

"I don't ride."

"Taken one too many bad spills?" Damien inquired with sympathy.

She did not answer immediately, frowning intently at the materials in her hands. "Actually, I don't know how to ride," she finally admitted in a soft voice. She sat down on the stone bench and gracefully adjusted the skirts of her plain gown, hoping Damien would simply let the matter drop.

He lifted a dark eyebrow in surprise. "Didn't your grandfather, the earl, insist you learn?"

"No," Isabella replied curtly. Damien moved closer, and

Isabella slid along the stone bench away from him. Ignoring her movement, he braced his booted foot on the bench. Casually resting his elbow upon his upraised knee, he gazed down at her.

"And why is that?"

Isabella saw the open curiosity in his handsome face and contemplated her options. She was well within her rights to tell him to mind his own business, but she hesitated to do so. She was fast becoming attached to The Grange and prudently decided that if she wanted to make a home for herself here, it would be far better if the earl learned of her strange parentage sooner rather than later. If Whatley Grange was truly as unconventional as the earl claimed, it should not matter that the new governess was, for all intents and purposes, a bastard.

"My maternal grandfather, the Earl of Barton, took no interest in me," Isabella stated flatly. "If memory serves me correctly, he spoke directly to me fewer than a dozen times in the three years I lived on his estate."

Damien thought her statement rather odd and wondered at its accuracy. Emmeline always loved to be dramatic. Surely Isabella was overstating her case. "Did he take offense at your bold manner?" Damien asked, searching for a cause.

"No, my lord," Isabella replied slowly. "He took offense at my illegitimate birth."

The statement was calmly, almost casually given, but Damien was not fooled. Isabella's hands were white-knuckled with tension as she awaited his reaction.

"You were ill-treated?"

Isabella contemplated her reply. "On the first morning I was in residence at the earl's estate, my great-aunt Agnes summoned me to the morning room. She greeted me hurriedly and instructed me to stand by sunny windows on the east side of the room so she could view me clearly. I wanted very much to make a favorable impression, and though puzzled, I did as she bade me."

Isabella took a steadying breath before continuing her story.

"Great-aunt Agnes then paraded each and every male member of the household staff who was in service at the estate while my mother resided there through the room and told them to stand next to me.''

"Whatever for?"

Isabella squeezed her eyes shut. "Apparently, my aunt had formulated her own opinion concerning my mysterious parentage." Isabella lifted her head and forced herself to open her eyes and look directly at Damien. "Aunt Agnes was searching for the man who had fathered me. She hoped by viewing me next to these male servants, she might notice a resemblance."

"What did you do?"

Isabella gave a short, self-mocking laugh. "Nothing. Not at first. I didn't understand what was happening." Her lovely face sobered and she continued. "When I finally realized what Aunt Agnes was doing, I stormed out of the room. In a most undignified manner, I might add."

"You had every right."

"My aunt did not see it quite that way. Things deteriorated from that point on."

Isabella made her comments with forced lightness, but Damien could see that the scars ran deep. He was moved by the hollowness of her voice, and he felt an odd twist of pity for the cruelty and humiliation she had suffered.

"Jenkins told me your father was a physician."

"The man my mother married was a doctor," Isabella corrected. "I have no knowledge of my true father."

"That must be a difficult burden to bear," Damien replied, trying to keep the sympathy from his voice. He did not want to further injure her pride by letting her believe he pitied her.

"I spent many a long night lying awake, wondering about my real father. I confess I often fanatisized about his identity," Isabella responded in a faraway voice. Lost in her memories, she inadvertantly revealed secrets she had never dared to speak aloud.

"I remember at one point hitting upon the notion that my father was a royal duke. They were all known to have a great fondness for women and for siring numerous illegitimate children. I rather liked the idea of having royal connections. Of course later I overheard a gentleman repeating the Duke of

Wellington's remarks concerning the old king's sons. He called them 'the damndest millstones about the neck of any government that can be imagined.' After that, I quickly revised my theory.''

Damien was amazed that she could speak so calmly about an incident that was clearly a deep and scaring wound.

"Why have you shared this with me?"

"I'm becoming fond of my life here at The Grange." Isabella swallowed reflexively and forced her chin up. "I wanted you to know the truth about me, Damien. If you care to dismiss me, I'd like to leave before I become too attached to my charges."

"Is that what happened? In your previous positions?"

"Not exactly," Isabella hedged. She wiggled uncomfortably, not eager to recite her history of dismissals, but the earl obviously was waiting.

"My first employer thought I was attracting far too much attention from the men visiting the house, and my second employer falsely believed I had my sights set on capturing the affections of the eldest son of the household."

"Did you?"

"Certainly not," Isabella insisted emphatically. "There was only one small, stolen kiss, nothing nearly as passionate and exciting as those you have . . ." Her voice trailed off in horror as Isabella stopped herself.

"Do go on," Damien prompted, secretly thrilled that his kisses were far more stimulating than those of some nameless young dandy's.

Rattled, but forcing herself to ignore the earl's intense stare, Isabella continued. "My third post was as a companion, and my employer and I mutually agreed that I was not at all suited to the life. I am infinitely more successful coping with children than spoiled old dowagers. And I do believe you are aware, sir, of the circumstances surrounding my dismissal from the Brauns' household."

Isabella couldn't be sure, but she thought the earl blushed. "Their loss is our gain, Isabella," he responded gallantly.

Isabella acknowledged the compliment with a slight nod of

her head. "Now that I have shared a secret with you," she said, "I expect you to return the favor."

Damien's body stiffened instantly in suspicion, but he kept his voice neutral. "What precisely do you wish to know?"

"Why does Jenkins address you by your given name?"

The guarded, wary look slowly left the earl's silvery eyes. "Jenkins managed to pull my injured body from beneath my fallen horse after the battle of Vitoria. If not for his stubborn insistence and perseverance, I might have been left for dead, like so many of my comrades. During my long recuperation in Spain, he began calling me Damien. Once we returned to England, it seemed ludicrous to insist he again adopt the formality."

An ironic smile tugged at her mouth. "Impending death is a great equalizer," Isabella murmured softly.

During the ensuing silence, a comfortable warmth settled over Isabella. She felt a closeness with Damien, a sharing of memories with the absence of judgment.

"We're ready, Father." Catherine's voice rang out loud and clear.

Regretfully, Damien pulled himself away from the softness in Isabella's eyes. It had been oddly comforting to share this moment with her and unexpectedly establish a bond of understanding and respect between them. Damien couldn't remember if he had ever spoken of his wounding with so little pain at the memory.

"If you ever decide you are interested in learning to ride, I'd be pleased to instruct you, Isabella." With that said, the earl pushed himself off the bench and stood upright. Before Isabella could muster an appropriate response, he was gone.

Sunday morning dawned gray and overcast. Nevertheless, it was a large group that set out from The Grange bound for the village church. Isabella rode inside the earl's carriage with Jenkins by her side, while the maids Fran and Penny, accompanied by their husbands, rode on top. Penny's husband, Joe, handled the ribbons.

"Did you enjoy last evening's supper with the earl and his children, Miss Browning?" Jenkins inquired politely, as the carriage ambled down the dirt road.

"No food or drink was thrown, Mr. Jenkins," Isabella replied wryly. "I suppose that marks the occasion as a success."

Actually, Saturday night's supper was not quite the disaster afternoon tea had been, but it was not without its mishaps. Catherine upset the gravy boat, which in Isabella's opinion was no great tragedy, since the gravy was bland and far too thick. But Ian made such a fuss over his sister's accident that he truly embarrassed her, and Catherine in turn promised retribution.

This time Isabella managed to stop their fight with a quelling look of her own, but overall she was disappointed in the children's behavior. A stern lecture to them before the meal had not ensured a peaceful dinner. Isabella sighed softly.

"The children are perfectly well behaved when they are alone with me and during their lessons. Yet I'm afraid, Mr. Jenkins, I have yet to devise an effective way to control Catherine and Ian's unruly behavior when they are in their father's presence," Isabella admitted.

"I am certain you will find a solution, Miss Browning," Jenkins proclaimed kindly.

Isabella gazed with undisguised skepticism at the valet. Her confidence had been shaken during the last two encounters with the earl and his children. Compounding the problem was her own personal desire to succeed. It was fast becoming an obsession to prove her competence to the earl. Isabella did not want to explore her reasons for this need too closely, not ready to deal with the consequences of what she might discover.

Seeing Isabella's preoccupation, Jenkins sought to distract her by relating some of the history of the village.

"Much of the Norman influence remains in our local buildings," Jenkins began, as they passed several stone houses, some thatched with mullioned windows.

Isabella obligingly turned her head. Even from this considerable distance she could distinguish the soaring stone shafts of the church, with its massive pillars, round arches, and small windows in thick walls.

"The church was built by a Norman knight, one Ruark De Mohun. In the chapel, an alabaster effigy carved on the coffin lid of the last of the male line of this same family, who was killed at the Battle of Boroughbridge in 1322, is prominently displayed."

Isabella made an appropriate comment of interest, and Jenkins continued. "Of course, much of the history in the village has been overshadowed through the years by the fascination with Whatley Grange."

"Whatley Grange?" Isabella echoed, certain Jenkins was about to depart more gossip. "What else can possible be said about The Grange?"

"Have you not yet heard the tale of Lady Anne's treasure?"

Isabella drew her brows together. "I do seem to recall Maggie making a reference to Lady Anne, but I paid it no heed at the time."

"The legend of Lady Anne's treasure is a fascinating tale, Miss Browning."

Isabella was obviously intrigued, but they were fast approaching their destination and there was no time for an explanation. The carriage drove by a regimented line of clipped yew trees, and Isabella could see the lovely stone archway to the churchyard. They drove through it and as they entered the churchyard, Isabella's nervous excitement turned to pure shock.

Perched regally upon the church steps, looking every inch the lord of the manor, from his polished Hessian boots and form-hugging breeches to his expertly tailored coat of black superfine, stood the earl.

Chapter Eleven

Damien waited patiently for the carriage to come to a complete halt before swinging open the coach door and reaching inside for Isabella. He was smiling brilliantly.

"Do close your mouth, Miss Browning," Damien whispered softly, as he held out his arm. "Although everyone in the churchyard is making a valiant attempt to ignore my carriage, I feel certain all eyes are trained upon us."

The earl's words gave her pause and Isabella hesitated inside the coach, casting an assessing gaze about the busy churchyard. It was true that everyone stood in small groups, seemingly occupied with their own conversations, but when Isabella caught the eye of a well-dressed matron, the woman abruptly dropped her gaze to the hymnal in her hands.

Isabella felt a faint blush cross her cheeks. Determined to remain unaffected, she placed her gloved hand in Damien's and gracefully alighted from the carriage.

"Whatever are you doing here?" Isabella hissed at the earl, as she forced a tentative smile toward a portly man who was openly staring at her.

"You didn't think I'd leave you to face the gossips alone, did you?"

Isabella turned her face up sharply in surprise. Surely he was jesting with her. He had made his feelings about attending services more than plain the other day. Yet here he was.

"Catherine and Ian?"

"Are at home where they belong," Damien replied firmly.

Without further conversation, the earl took Isabella's gloved hand and placed it on his arm. As they stepped inside the church vestibule, Isabella grew aware of the sudden hushed silence of the congregation. Her knees felt weak, and she was very glad for the strong support of Damien's arm. She was overwhelmingly conscious of the entire crowd staring at her.

The earl's arm felt strong and solid beneath her fingers, but a slight trembling drew her attention. Although one would ever know by looking at him, the earl was nervous. Isabella could sense it, could feel it. To the world he might present a totally calm, totally in-command facade, but in truth he was hiding his fear. This newly revealed vulnerability hit her with a blinding force.

Damien was only here because of her, because he felt she needed his protection. He had put his own misgivings aside in order to lend her his support. She had rarely, if ever, experienced any sort of unselfish consideration. Isabella's tender heart soared.

Still reeling from her turbulent discovery, she did not at first realize that the earl was leading her toward his family pew at the front of the church.

"You know, of course, this is highly improper," Isabella said pointedly as they slowly began the long walk down the center aisle. Feeling the gawking eyes of the congregation on her back compelled her to add in a quiet whisper, "I should be seated in the same pew as the other household servants from The Grange."

"And deprive me of the pleasure of your company?" Damien declared with a wounded look. "Besides, we both know you are far more than a servant in my home."

Isabella was startled by the remark, yet, conscious of the many eyes upon her, she kept her expression plain.

"Some of these people will probably misinterpret your

actions and think I am your mistress," she hissed, wondering if somehow that obvious conclusion escaped the earl.

"I rather hope they do think that," Damien replied smoothly. "Although bringing one's mistress to church must surely be considered the height of bad taste. A crime I imagine all my pompous neighbors would think I am quite capable of committing. Still, if they believe I am keeping a mistress, it might be the single piece of gossip that finally squashes the nasty rumors about my impregnating all the housemaids."

Isabella made a squeaking noise, and Damien flashed her a wicked grin before continuing.

"Of course, there is also your striking physical resemblance to Emmeline." The earl reached over and squeezed the hand that tightly gripped his arm. "Please, Isabella, at least allow me the pleasure of startling some of these old gossips into speculation. I was hoping some of the more nearsighted members of this holy congregation might actually believe you *are* Emmeline. Ah, there is Lady Edson now. She has a decidedly pinched look about her aristocratic nostrils, does she not?"

Isabella could not prevent the gasp of astonishment that escaped her lips. She turned her head up sharply, intent on chastising Damien for his outrages words, when she saw the teasing glint in his smoky eyes.

"You are trying to distract me, my lord," Isabella accused him primly, trying to conceal a smile.

"And I have succeeded, Isabella," the earl countered triumphantly as he paused in front of the ornately carved wooden pew.

It was an interminably long service. Damien held his tongue and made no further comments about the assembled worshippers, and Isabella was grateful. Her stomach already felt knotted and she was having difficulty appearing so calmly unaffected sitting next to the earl without a proper chaperone.

Throughout the long service, she felt various eyes straying to the family box they occupied and the persistent edge of self-consciousness remained with her. She suspected Damien shared her feelings, although his steady, regal continence never once suggested any discomfort.

As the final hymn began, the earl leaned toward Isabella. Pitching his voice so low that only she could hear, he whispered, "The service will be ending shortly. I will have Jenkins ride my horse back to The Grange so I can accompany you in the carriage. Shall we bolt for the coach, or stay and make inane conversation with the locals?"

Isabella was pleased he asked her opinion. "While I certainly don't feel the need to linger, it would be bad form to rush away. A few moments exchanging social pleasantries with the congregation would not be amiss."

Damien nodded in agreement, his admiration for her courage growing. He had slept restlessly last night, worrying over her reception at the church this morning, yet she proved far more adept than he had imagined.

The earl and Isabella lingered in the churchyard for several minutes, but no one approached them. It was probably idiotic to care so much, but the longer they waited the more Isabella regretted suggesting they stay.

"There doesn't appear to be one lone brave soul amongst the entire village," Damien remarked softly, bending close to whisper in Isabella's ear. "Even the vicar has deserted us."

"Perhaps we should leave," Isabella replied with a taut smile.

She cast a bold eye toward a cluster of people and saw their closed, curious expressions. Her heart started hammering. They are all cowards, Isabella concluded angrily. And fools. Nothing more than a bunch of sheep, believing all those horrid, viscious lies, acting with unwarranted sanctimony. They were truly beneath his notice, absolutely unworthy of the earl's consideration.

"We should leave," Isabella repeated.

"We cannot leave now," Damien insisted. "I believe I know how I can change the tide of my social disregard, and I'm curious enough about the outcome to test my theory. As you may already know, I never like to leave my curiosity unsatisfied. Besides, I've decided I can no longer tolerate having my neighbors view me as something they must avoid at all costs. Like the plague." The earl casually adjusted the cuff of his jacket, then offered her his arm. "I've learned it is always best to confront unpleasantness directly. Come along, Isabella."

Arm in arm, they walked with great purpose through the milling throngs of people. The crowd easily parted before them. After several steps, Isabella realized the earl's destination. They continued walking at a leisurely pace until they were positioned directly in front of Lady Edson. The crowd noticeably hushed in order to overhear the exchange.

"Good morning, Lady Edson."

Damien's voice nearly startled Isabella with its loudness and firmness.

The earl's greeting drew a blank stare from the rigidly stiff Lady Edson. She refused to speak, yet refused to look away. So they stared each other down. Two strong-willed adversaries, each determined to best the other. Isabella felt a trickle of perspiration run down her back, but she cautioned herself to remain perfectly still.

Just when Isabella thought the standoff would never end, Lady Edson blinked. The older woman momentarily lost her iron composure and flushed visibly under the earl's stare. Isabella exhaled.

"It has been rather a long time since you've seen fit to attend services, my lord," Lady Edson commented tartly, struggling unsuccessfully to regain the upper hand.

"Indeed." Damien's stare remained rigid. "I have been remiss in my duties. But rest assured, I have every intention of making Sunday service part of my weekly routine."

That comment brought a loud murmur of comments from the interested crowd of bystanders. Lady Edson tried to regain control over the group, to no avail. Those who had previously been spectators of the little drama now promptly joined the conversation. The earl had successfully accomplished his mission.

Introductions were made, and they all managed a polite, meaningless discussion. Isabella noted, however, that Damien seized the first opportunity to make good their escape.

"It was not as bad as I anticipated, yet I must confess I am glad to be away," the earl confided to Isabella as his carriage

pulled out of the churchyard. They rode alone inside the coach
with the rest of the servants on top.

"I think you enjoyed yourself far more than you let on, sir,"
Isabella remarked, remembering the earl's boldness. "You took
great delight in confronting Lady Edson."

Damien's somber gray eyes lit up with amusement. "It was
rather delightful forcing the old witch to acknowledge me. I
doubt anyone will dare to snub me openly now. Perhaps the
gossip that surrounds my name will finally begin to fade."

Isabella smiled with relief, infinitely pleased the outing had
been so successful. She felt a sense of pure elation at the turn
of events. And a closeness to the earl that went beyond simple
friendship.

They rode for the next mile in silence. Searching her mind
for a neutral topic of conversation, Isabella blurted out the first
thought that popped into her head.

"Please, Damien, tell me the story of Lady Anne's treasure.
I've heard Maggie and Fran make passing remarks, and Jenkins
mentioned it again briefly this morning, but he did not have
time to relate the entire tale."

"Lady Anne's treasure?" Damien replied with a twisted
grin. "To my knowledge it has been several years since the
legend was openly discussed at The Grange. I suppose it is
time to resurrect the tale."

Isabella gave him an encouraging smile.

"Lady Anne is one of my more colorful female ancestors.
She was the great-granddaughter of Henry VIII, descended
through the illegitimate Seymour line, but inanely proud of her
Tudor blood nonetheless. She came to The Grange as a young
bride of fifteen, and it is said her husband was completely
besotted with her."

"A love match?"

"So the story goes." Damien's tone implied he did not agree.
"Yet, for all her supposed love for her husband, Lady Anne was
also greatly devoted to Prince Charles, possibly improperly."

"With the prince's reputation for womanizing, tis no wonder
there was speculation."

"Perhaps," Damien grudgingly conceded. "There was no

disputing Lady Anne's loyalty to the Stuarts. She was a fierce defender of the crown, a stanch royalist to the end, and while her husband was off fighting with Lord Fairfax—''

"Pardon me," Isabella interrupted. "Did you say the earl fought with Fairfax?''

Damien nodded.

"But Fairfax was Cromwell's man. They fought against the king!''

"There were numerous aristocratic families that sided against the Stuarts, Isabella, though not many will boast of it today. Yes, the earl took up arms against the king, but his wife vehemently opposed his views. Lady Anne was a unique woman for her time, an independent thinker who was not ruled by her husband. She aided the royalist cause by collecting, hiding, and routing monies for the crown.''

"Was she a spy?'' Isabella leaned forward eagerly.

"I don't think so," Damien replied thoughtfully. "But we really can't be certain. Undoubtedly her actual involvement in the war has been greatly exaggerated over the years.''

"What about the treasure?''

Damien grinned broadly, amused by Isabella's gathering excitement. "The largest and supposedly most valuable collection of coin, jewels, and gold plate was hidden somewhere at Whatley Grange for safekeeping until the king's man could collect it to pay for arms for the royalists. Apparently the contact died before the treasure could be retrieved—murdered, the story contends—so Lady Anne was forced to bury the entire treasure somewhere on the estate.''

"Then what happened?'' Isabella prompted.

"Lady Anne fell ill and took to her bed. There was no one she trusted to divulge the location of the treasure, and she greatly feared her husband would use the funds against the crown. According to the legend, she died before the treasure was passed on, telling no living soul of its whereabouts.''

"Are you saying the treasure has never been found? After all these years?'' Isabella squirmed with unconcealed excitement. "Did Lady Anne leave any clues as to where she buried the treasure?''

"She kept a journal. The final entry is reported to be a poem proclaiming the location of treasure. Solve the riddle of the poem, discover the hidden treasure."

"Oh." Isabella sank back in disappointment. "I imagine the journal has long since been lost."

"Quite the contrary," Damien replied in an offhand manner. "The last time I saw Lady Anne's journal, it was in The Grange library."

Isabella clasped her hands together in undisguised glee. "How wonderful! Can you just imagine how exciting it would be if we solved the riddle and discovered the treasure?" Suddenly she sobered, reality taking hold. "Of course, it must be a very long and complicated poem."

Calmly, Damien recited, "Oh, Gloriana of titian hair, thy savior I shall be; for through the rose of the noonday sun, thy enemies shall flee."

"You know it!"

"By heart." Damien's deep voice echoed with laughter. "I believe that at one time or another each child of every generation of our family attempts to make the monumental discovery of the treasure."

"Well, I am not a child." Isabella straightened up in her seat and eagerly repeated the verses. "Gloriana with titian hair—that must be a reference to Elizabeth the First. I suppose the rose might refer to the Tudor red rose."

Isabella continued muttering to herself for several minutes and then shot up like a spark. "Good Lord, the treasure is buried in the rose garden on the north side of the castle."

"Stop right there," Damien insisted, smothering a laugh. He was impressed by her quick mind. It had taken him hours to reach the same conclusion. Of course he had been ten years old at the time, but Isabella's rapid conclusions were still impressive.

"Rest assured, Isabella, during the past one hundred and fifty years this story has existed, each and every one of the rose bushes at Whatley Grange has been uprooted and the ground beneath thoroughly searched. I can say, with a fair amount of certainty, there is nothing beneath any of the roses on my estate other than dirt.''

''Every bush?'' Isabella's voice held a trace of skepticism.

''Every one,'' Damien insisted emphatically. She wilted visibly at his words, and Damien felt strangely bereaved as he watched the glow disappear from her sparkling violet eyes. ''I am sorry,'' he finally whispered in a soft voice.

''Pray, forgive my foolishness,'' Isabella replied with a nervous laugh. ''I'm afraid I tend to get a bit carried away at times.''

''I rather liked your enthusiasm, Isabella,'' Damien confessed quietly. He glanced down at her tightly clutched fingers. ''Please, feel free to avail yourself of Lady Anne's diary. Perhaps you will discover a clue that has eluded us all these years.''

Isabella studied his handsome face for a few moments, testing his sincerity. Convinced he was being honest, she favored him with a dazzling smile. ''Thank you, Damien. I do believe I shall take you up on your kind offer.''

''Come along children,'' Isabella prompted. ''Your father is expected for tea and we all must get cleaned up before we join him.''

Isabella looked with undisguised dismay at her two dirty charges. She imagined she looked just as unkempt. They had spent the better part of the morning and early afternoon out of doors collecting various flowers and fauna to identify and study in the schoolroom.

Ian, in his exuberance over discovering a water lily, had nearly toppled into the lake. Isabella managed to save him from falling, but his walking shoes, socks, and short pants were covered in mud. Catherine fared no better, tripping over an exposed tree root and ripping out a substantial length of the hem of her light blue gown. Her previously neatly braided blond hair was loose and straggly, and a drying streak of brown mud crossed her forehead. Isabella shuddered to think what horrors would be revealed about her own appearance when she viewed herself in the mirror.

"Let's cut through the garden, Miss Browning," Catherine suggested. "It will be faster."

At Isabella's affirmative nod, Catherine grabbed tight hold of her brother's hand and the two raced ahead. Isabella's heart lurched at their obvious excitement over the impending visit with their father. Despite the earl's promise, he had not been spending very much time with his children. To Isabella's knowledge, the children had spoken with their father only at bedtime in the past five days.

At least Catherine and Ian have each other, Isabella mused, watching Catherine deliberately slow her pace to match her younger brother's. It never ceased to amaze Isabella how devoted these siblings were. They fought often and occasionally violently, especially in the presence of their father, but Isabella knew how much they meant to each other. No one would ever be able to sever the special bond that existed between Catherine and Ian.

Isabella reached the outer edges of the rose garden just as Catherine swung open the heavy French doors on the upper terrace.

"I shall be in your room in five minutes to help you change," Isabella called out loudly. Catherine paused a moment, waving her free hand in understanding before she and Ian entered the house.

Isabella slowed her pace once the children disappeared. She wandered along the narrow gravel path through the rows of roses, her eyes alight with speculation as they darted from bush to bush.

"I will never to able to walk among these lovely blossoms without thinking of Lady Anne and her blasted treasure," Isabella muttered to herself. Her enthusiastic start to discovering the treasure had met with very little success. Curiously, the diary the earl had spoken of was not where he remembered it to be in library and thus far, Isabella had not had the time to search among the thousands leather-bound volumes for it.

Instead, Isabella concentrated her efforts on deciphering the simple poem, convinced that if she found the elusive rose in the clue, she would find the treasure. She quickly discovered, however, there were roses of all kinds, shapes and sizes among the furnishings of The Grange—wood furniture with roses carved in it, stone-and-wood moldings featuring a rose motif, stained glass windows with roses prominently and subtlely displayed, stone carvings of roses on the face of archways both inside and outside the castle walls.

She also learned in the course of her brief investigation that there existed a rose bedchamber, a rose sitting room, a rose drawing room, a Queen Elizabeth bedchamber, a Tudor bedchamber, and innumerable rooms supposedly named for Lady Anne.

Surprisingly, Jenkins was able to supply much of the information she required about the history of The Grange and its various rooms, but Isabella was no closer to arriving at any conclusions than when she had first begun her search several days before. She conceded honestly to herself that greatly hampering her efforts was her appalling sense of, or rather lack of, direction. Isabella knew she could not go mucking about the castle alone. She would surely get lost after a few turns.

Jenkins had gallantly volunteered his assistance, but he was preoccupied with estate matters, and as yet was unable to spend any time with Isabella.

"I could use some hot water if there is any to spare, Maggie," Isabella said to the maid when she entered the warm kitchen. Isabella had deliberately made this detour through the kitchen to acquire fresh water for washing herself and the children. She knew from experience there would be no male servants about the castle to perform this simple task at this hour of the day.

"I'll fill a bucket for you right away," Maggie replied. Placing the basket of beans she held in her lap on the floor, Maggie struggled awkwardly to rise from her low chair.

"No, no, I can get it myself," Isabella insisted, rushing forward before the maid could gain her feet. Lately, it pained Isabella greatly to watch Maggie. The young women's body was so large and distended from her pregnancy that she appeared to be in a continual state of discomfort. It should only be a matter of days before Maggie's baby was born, and Isabella prayed fervently every night that it would be a swift and uncomplicated birth.

"Don't know why you'd be needing hot water in the middle of the afternoon," Mrs. Amberly grumbled as she stirred a black pot simmering on the stove.

"Good afternoon, Mrs. Amberly," Isabella said sweetly. She pointedly ignored the housekeeper's comment, not wanting to ignite Mrs. Amberly's barely concealed hostility. The house-keeper's attitude towards the new governess had not changed. She greatly resented Isabella's influence over the children and was not averse to showing it.

"The earl will be home for tea this afternoon," Isabella announced. She gave Maggie a stern look. "You must promise me you will have Molly or Fran bring in the tea tray, Maggie. And if for some reason they are unavailable, don't hesitate to call me. I don't want you lugging a heavy tray up all those stairs."

"All right, Miss Browning," Maggie replied shyly, her cheeks blushing pink with pleasure at Isabella's concern.

Isabella could hear Mrs. Amberly's grumbling objections as she left the kitchen, but she paid them no heed. Arms straining with the heavy bucket of hot water she carried, Isabella carefully climbed the staircase, heading directly towards the children's room.

Isabella helped Catherine and Ian change out of their soiled garments and wash the dirt off their hands and faces. Freshly scrubbed and neatly dressed, the children were eager to race to the drawing room to await their father. Isabella restrained them.

"I expect both of you to behave in a suitable manner this afternoon. There will be no arguing, no shouting, no teasing, no physical roughness." Isabella paused dramatically for effect. "In short, there will be no unpleasantness of any kind. Is that clearly understood?"

A telling look passed between Catherine and Ian. They regarded their governess with somber, innocent eyes, but Isa-bella was not fooled. Catherine and Ian could behave with total restraint and decorum when the mood suited them, but a few minutes in the company of their imposing father could reduce them to unbridled hellions. Sternly, Isabella made her final proclamation.

"I give you fair warning, children. The moment you begin bickering, I shall make you stand in the corner of the drawing room, with your noses touching the wall, until the hall clock strikes the hour."

Isabella waited several moments for her dire threats of punishment to sink in before dismissing the children. Then she hurried across the hall to her bedchamber. She fretted for several moments over her appearance, sighing with regret as she looked into the wardrobe. No magical occurrence during the night had produced any fashionable and flattering gowns. Only the same dull, serviceable garments awaited her. Vainly she wished for something soft and gossamer to wear, something that would ignite the flame of passion she occasionally glimpsed in Damien's eyes.

Blushing at her wayward thoughts, Isabella concentrated on washing the dirt from her face. She brushed her long hair slowly, savoring the comforting feeling of the soothing strokes. Her thoughts, as always, drifted again to the earl. Damien. Always Damien.

Isabella had been obsessing over it for days, but now it no longer seemed important to determine when she realized the true extent of her feelings for the handsome, arrogant earl. Perhaps she had fallen in love with him as she observed his dark head bent solicitously toward his children as he patiently listened to them recount the events of their day. Or maybe it occurred when she saw him lift a heavy tray of soiled dishes for the very pregnant Maggie while the maid blushed with gratitude and shyness.

Actually, Isabella suspected that she opened her heart to Damien the morning he appeared on the church steps to accompany her to services. He was nervous that day, but he put aside his own misgivings for her.

In truth, it didn't matter when she began to love the earl, the fact was that she did. And it caused a combination of joy and pain within her heart the likes of which she had never known before. For Isabella knew she lacked the courage and self-confidence to ever reveal her feelings to Damien, and she never dared to hope he would somehow, miraculously, reciprocate her devotion.

Determinedly, she shook off her melancholy thoughts and deftly secured her hair in a tight coil. She knew she had no cause for complaint. All in all, she was living a satisfactory life. The earl and his unconventional household fully accepted her and she was allowed a freedom of expression she had always sought, but never attained.

Casting one last look at the mirror, Isabella turned and headed downstairs, her heart beating in familiar excitement at the thought of spending a pleasant afternoon in the earl's company.

Chapter Twelve

"What do you mean, you can't stay for tea?"

Isabella stood in the entrance hall, hands propped on her hips, and fairly shouted the words at Damien as he began the long climb up the staircase.

He paused suddenly in midstride and looked down on her, an expression of true exasperation marring his handsome features.

"I do believe my statement is very plain, Isabella." There was an audible note of anger in the tone of his voice, but Isabella unwisely decided to ignore it. Lifting her skirts in an undignified manner, she raced up the stairs after the earl, stopping one rung below him.

"Catherine and Ian are at this very moment waiting for you to join them in the drawing room," Isabella said in a brittle voice. "You cannot possible disappoint them."

"I have no choice," he said with a grim twist of his mouth. Taking full advantage of his superior height, Damien deliberately loomed over her. His steely gray eyes were glinting strangely. "Send my regrets to the children and inform them I shall attempt to speak with them before they go to bed this evening." Casting Isabella a final dismissive glare, the earl turned away.

She stared at the broad expanse of his retreating shoulders for several moments. Stamping her foot in frustration, Isabella cursed loudly. How dare he act this way? The children had been looking forward to this all week. Damien had already canceled an outing two days ago. Now he was intending to do so again. Isabella decided she could not simply let it pass.

Cloaked in righteous indignation, she chased after the earl, her temper rising with each step. She reached him just as he entered his bedchamber.

"You have made a promise to your children, sir," she said bluntly. "And I have every intention of making certain you keep your— Good lord, whatever are you doing?"

Amusement momentarily replaced the anger in the earl's eyes. "I am changing my shirt," Damien retorted, shrugging out of the unbuttoned garment and deliberately flinging it toward the corner of the room. "It is wet and ripped."

"Oh." Isabella sputtered with embarrassment, suddenly realizing she had unwittingly invaded the earl's private chamber. She deliberately averted her eyes, but the glorious sight of Damien's naked chest still burned in her memory. Her cheeks blushed pink and her breast rose and fell with her rapid breathing, yet Isabella stood her ground. She instinctively knew Damien expected her to turn and flee in maidenly horror, but she refused to cower.

"We were discussing Catherine and Ian, my lord," Isabella said irritably, trying to regain her equilibrium.

Damien made a small gesture of disgust. "No, I believe it is fair to say you were lecturing me about Ian and Catherine," Damien insisted, donning a clean shirt. Harried and distracted, the earl made a valiant attempt to marshal his emotions. He was cold, he was wet, he was tired. He was definitely not up to arguing with Isabella. Summoning up every ounce of self-control he possessed, Damien faced his adversary.

"There is a break in the north fence, and several hundred sheep have wandered on to Lord Gilmore's property. I am needed there."

"Can't it wait? Just for an hour? Catherine and Ian will be crushed if you break your promise. Again." A lock of chestnut hair escaped the confines of Isabella's neatly plaited hair, and she impatiently pushed it back. "Surely you can spare a scant hour for your son and daughter?"

Damien's jaw tightened. "I don't have an hour to spare. If you would care to look outside, you will see the storm clouds threatening even as we speak."

Isabella gave a cursory glance out the window. "If it is going to storm, then it makes no sense for you to leave in the first place." She took a small step toward him. "Please, Damien, don't dismiss your children so lightly."

"I have already explained why I must leave," Damien growled, his patience giving way. "In my opinion, you are making far too much over my missing one afternoon tea." He gave her a scathing look. "And I, for one, would greatly appreciate it if you would stop acting so damned melodramatically. It ill becomes you."

Isabella shot him a furious glance. "You made a promise to your children, sir. And I fully intend to see that you keep it," she reiterated fiercely.

"Is that so?" Damien rounded on her. "I have also made a promise to take care of them. Will you kindly explain to me how well off they shall be without a roof over their heads?"

"What utter nonsense," she returned nastily. "Now who is acting melodramatically." Isabella narrowed her violet eyes. "I hardly think the welfare of the entire estate rests on a few sheep. You are merely using that as a convenient excuse for neglecting your parental obligations."

The earl stilled instantly. The cords on his neck stood out, and a pulse was beating visibly at his temple. Isabella knew she had pushed him too far. With perceivable effort the earl maintained his control. Across the room, their eyes met.

"Well, you are correct about one thing, Isabella," the earl finally stated coldly. "You hardly think." He lurched past her and Isabella watched him in silence, lacking the courage to utter another syllable.

The palpable tension remained in the room after Damien's departure. Isabella regretted allowing her overset emotions to rule her tongue, but her first obligation must always be toward the children. Who else would look to their welfare, if not she?

A deep, familiar coldness came over Isabella as painful memories of rejection from her own unhappy childhood surfaced and mingled with her concern for Catherine and Ian. She knew they would be very hurt when they found out their father would not be joining them this afternoon. How could a child be expected to understand that other things came first, before them? Especially from a father they clearly worshiped and saw far too little of to begin with.

Smoothing back the imaginary wrinkles in her dove gray gown, Isabella turned to begin the long walk to the drawing room where Catherine and Ian were eagerly awaiting their father's arrival. She paused a moment outside the closed door, intertwining her fingers and twisting them until they ached. Summoning up her inner strength, she masked her face in an unreadable expression and opened the door.

Two little heads turned in eager expectation toward the door. Catherine and Ian were seated side by side on the brocade love seat, their hands folded neatly in their laps. The tarnished silver tea service sat on the high butler's table in front of them, along with four carefully placed china teacups. Isabella's heart constricted as she took in the scene, knowing her announcement of the earl's departure would soon extinguish the eager light in the children's eyes.

Reasoning that it was useless to postpone the inevitable, Isabella began quietly, "Children, I am afraid your father won't be able to join us this afternoon. Apparently, there is a problem with the fences in the north pasture . . ."

The first fat raindrops hit Damien long before he reached his destination. He cursed long and loud as the cold water sprayed his face. *Serves me right,* he thought glumly. *I should have stayed at home with my children and the wandering sheep be damned.*

He rode in restless, brooding silence for the next few minutes, his emotions in turmoil. He was a man who prided himself on accepting responsibility, and he had never before questioned his priorities. Estate matters came first; too many livelihoods depended on his ability to keep The Grange financially afloat. But lately Isabella was causing him to rethink the carefully constructed order of his life. That he loved his children was not the issue. He truly would have suffered any sort of pain if it meant sparing his children. Yet, as Isabella so doggedly pointed out, by willfully breaking a promise to them, he was hurting them, albeit unintentionally.

His role as father had always been clear-cut and well defined. He was their provider and protector. Yet Isabella insisted they required more from him, and Damien was unsure how he could give this to them. He could not neglect the affairs of his estate to mollycoddle his children at every turn. On the other hand, was it truly necessary for him to personally supervise the herding of the sheep? Had he made the right decision, placing the needs of the estate above Catherine's and Ian's? What bothered him most, Damien admitted honestly as the wind and rain engulfed him, was that he strongly suspected he had not.

Damien rapped his knuckles forcefully on the door, but the raging thunderstorm drowned out the knock. He waited a few moments before opening the door; then, univited, he slowly entered Isabella's bedchamber, hoping to find her awake. Once inside, the earl strode silently across the room to her bedside, holding his candle high in front of him to light the way. The heavy bed curtains were pulled back, and Isabella lay burrowed deeply into the soft mattress, snuggled contently beneath the warm coverlet.

Damien placed the lit candle on the bedside table, pausing a moment to look at the slumbering governess. The glimmering light from the candle illuminated her shimmering chestnut hair and highlighted her fair, porcelain complexion. He admired the charming curl of her long, dark eyelashes and the high set of her cheekbones. He studied her in quiet contemplation. She was truly breathtaking. Damien swallowed hard.

''Isabella. Isabella,'' he called softly, trying to awaken her without unduly starling her. ''Wake up, Isabella.''

Isabella murmured incoherently in her sleep and rolled languidly onto her back. The earl called to her again, and a delightful smile crossed her face. She stirred restlessly and sleepily blinked her eyes. ''Damien,'' she muttered groggily. ''My own sweet Damien.''

Isabella was having a simply wonderful dream. She was majestically seated upon a high-spirited horse, and Damien was praising her skill as a horsewoman. Catherine and Ian were also with them, behaving perfectly, and Isabella reveled in the wonderful sense of family and belonging they all shared.

She easily jumped a particularly difficult hedge, and the earl applauded her daring, then gently scolded her for taking such a risk with her person. Yet his tone was sweet and caring, and Isabella did not mind his censure, for she knew he spoke only because of his concern.

The children pleaded for permission to ride ahead, and with a quick smile the earl acquiesced. As soon as they were alone, Damien pulled his mount next to Isabella's splendid horse. With a strong, muscular arm, he reached out and plucked her off the animal's back. Isabella laughed at his stunt, willingly lifting her arms in gentle surrender and nuzzling close to his bare neck.

''Oh, Damien, my love,'' she sang out merrily.

The earl took a startled step back from the bed, his dark eyebrows shooting up in surprise at Isabella's words. He peered down at her, scrutinizing her lovely features, but her eyes remained closed and he realized she was still sleeping. Damien's mouth curled up in a devilish grin.

''Ahh, so I am part of your dreams, my prim little governess,'' he whispered in a deep voice.

The sound of her beloved's voice caused Isabella to stir again, and Damien could see the curves of her breasts outlined against the thin fabric of her nightgown. It was a tantalizing sight.

She looked so free and open and giving. Damien felt captivated by the sensual warmth radiating from Isabella's expressive face. Her invitation was simply impossible for him to resist.

Against his better judgment, the earl leaned down and drew her carefully into his arms. She moaned her approval and pressed herself closer to him. Damien felt himself starting to tremble with anticipation. His long suppressed passions momentarily overtook his common sense as his mind conjured up erotic sexual images of the two of them. Shaking his head violently, he threw those wicked thoughts aside. Yet he could not help himself from wondering. Could he steal a kiss before she awoke?

Encased in her delightful dream, Isabella sighed contently and snuggled closer to the earl. She could feel his warm breath in her hair as his lips pressed fervent kisses on her temple. Isabella shifted her body and tightened her grip around his neck. In a faraway voice, she whispered to him urgently, "Kiss me, Damien. Please, kiss me."

Isabella's sensual request ignited the banked fire within Damien. He grasped her chin firmly in his fingers, lifted her head, and brought his mouth swiftly down on hers. He kissed her hard, torn between his sense of honor, hoping she would awake, and his raging passions, praying she would not. Isabella automatically parted her lips for him, and his tongue eagerly penetrated her mouth. She responded immediately with her own tongue, and Damien softened the kiss, skillfully stroking the escalating tension between them.

Nearly overwhelmed by her response, Damien regrettably broke the kiss. "God only knows how much I want you," he muttered thickly.

He was breathing fast, and his body felt heavy and taut with arousal. Unable to resist, he nuzzled her delicate throat and flattened his large palm on her shoulder. Isabella again responded to his touch, lifting herself against his hand, moving her body under the warm strength of his fingers. Slowly, with a will of its own, Damien's hand inched toward Isabella's chest. When he softly touched her breast, she moaned and moved closer.

Sweat broke out on Damien's forehead. He should stop.

Now. This very instant. Yet he could not. Again he caressed her rounded breast, and her nipples tightened. Caught up completely in the moment, Damien's fingers deftly unfastened the tiny buttons down the front of her nightgown, exposing her glorious breasts.

His mouth went dry as he viewed the creamy white flesh. He tightened his hold across her back and lifted her eagerly to his mouth. Just one small taste, he fiercely promised himself. His tongue darted out, and then he took the entire nipple in his mouth and suckled her gently, his groin hardening painfully as he tasted the sweetness of her flesh.

Isabella suddenly felt a darting blaze of heat throbbing deeply within her body, centering on a growing dampness between her legs. She groaned loudly in restless excitement, thrashing her head from side to side. The sharp movement, coupled with the sound of her own voice, abruptly woke her. Isabella's eyes flew open in surprise. Confusion reined within her as the compelling fantasy of her dreams suddenly became a startling reality.

Nearly lost in his passion, Damien nonetheless felt the change in Isabella's body. She stiffened noticeably in his arms, and he knew she had awakened. He muffled a curse and lifted his head to look at her. Isabella stared back at Damien in total shock, an expression of horrified bewilderment etched on her beautiful face.

Isabella's unbound hair was tousled, her lips puffed and red from his kisses. Her nightgown was open to her waist, and Damien could see the creamy flesh of her breasts peeking out. His fully aroused manhood tightened painfully.

"Isabella."

The sound of his husky voice unfroze Isabella, and her violet eyes widened even more. She opened her mouth to scream. Correctly reading her intentions, Damien reacted instantly, covering her mouth with his large hand. Her eyes darted frantically to his face as she struggled to dislodge his grip. Damien could feel the terror radiating from her as she fought to free herself, and in desperation he uttered the words he felt certain would control her outburst.

"If you make too much noise, you will wake Catherine and Ian."

His words had the desired effect. Slowly Isabella ceased her struggles, but the wild fear did not leave her face. When he felt certain she would remain silent, he removed his hand.

"I'm sorry," he said finally, not sure how he could begin to explain his bizarre behavior.

Isabella blushed furiously, her hands clutching the ends of her nightgown closed. She barely acknowledged his apology, she was so flustered. She edged away from him toward the center of her bed, traces of fear still in her eyes. Her wary expression clearly indicated that she expected him to pounce on her at any moment.

Damien retreated from her, watching her struggle to conquer her fear with anguish in his eyes. He felt like an utter cad for allowing his raging desire to overcome his inbred sense of decency and honor. In retrospect, his humble apology seemed almost as insulting as his physical advances.

"What are you doing in here?" Isabella's voice was raspy with emotion.

"It's Maggie," Damien replied softly, thankful he was able to provide a legitimate excuse for invading her room. "Her labor has begun."

Isabella lifted herself off the bed in concern, her thoughts momentarily distracted. "Has the midwife arrived?"

"No. We can't ride into the village to fetch her. The creek has overflowed from the rains and flooded the bridge. It is impossible to get across."

"Merciful heavens! Is Mrs. Amberly with Maggie?"

The earl grimaced slightly. "Mrs. Amberly has been suffering badly with a toothache for two days. Unfortunately, she chose this evening to douse herself with brandy. I'm afraid she's passed out cold. Neither Jenkins nor I could revive her."

"My God." Isabella gave a nervous giggle. "I find that a difficult picture to imagine."

Damien briefly returned her smile, then leaned forward and spoke soberly. "Maggie is very frightened. Fran is with her now, but she is more terrified than Maggie. Can you help?"

"I have no experience with childbirth." Isabella's eyes went dark with fear. "When I was about nine years old, there was a dreadful carriage accident on the village road. There was lady in the coach, and apparently the accident triggered her labor. I remember the shouting and screaming and two men carrying her into our house. They brought her into my bedchamber. I hid behind the draperies and dared not reveal myself all through the long hours that followed. I shall never forget the raw pain and shear agony of that poor woman as she struggled to give birth."

Damien's eyes were sympathetic. "What happened?"

"The child was stillborn. The mother died the following day." Isabella bit her lip. "I don't think I can be of much help, Damien."

"There is no one else," Damien replied carefully. "Please, Isabella. Will you come?"

Isabella forced herself to breath slowly and deeply. It was imperative that she gain control of her emotions and her queasy stomach, she thought ruefully. Maggie needed her.

Isabella stared at the earl in the shimmering candlelight. Very slowly she nodded her head in agreement.

"Wait outside," she said softly. "It will only take a moment for me to dress." With obvious relief, the earl turned from her and walked to the door. As his hand touched the brass handle, Isabella whispered from the shadows of the bed.

"When this is all over, sir, and, the good Lord willing, Maggie is safely delivered of her babe, I expect you to explain precisely what you were doing in here before I awoke."

Chapter Thirteen

Fortunately, the scene that greeted Isabella and Damien when they entered Maggie's bedchamber was not as gruesome as Isabella's active imagination anticipated. Maggie, dressed in a loose flowing nightgown, was pacing the room slowly while her husband, Fred, impatiently watched. Fran was fussing over the bed, smoothing down the sheets, arranging and rearranging the pillows. Jenkins was hunched over the fireplace, methodically adding logs to an already blazing fire.

"It was very good of you to come, Miss Browning," Fred said the moment he spied Isabella.

Isabella smiled nervously at Maggie's husband. Although he was outwardly calm, she observed the sporadic twitching of Fred's hands. His eyes darted constantly to his wife, and Isabella saw him wince visibly as Maggie suddenly ceased her pacing and bowed her head in pain.

"Well, Maggie, I am told the moment is upon us at last," Isabella proclaimed brightly. She gave the maid a look that she hoped conveyed the confidence and reassurance she was far from experiencing. "If you gentlemen will excuse us, I believe Maggie and I can handle things from this point on."

The men shuffled silently out the door, and Fran hovered

expectantly by the bed, clearly torn between her desire to go and feelings of loyalty to remain. "It is best if you leave too, Fran. I promise I shall call if I need you."

Fran hesitated a moment, then bestowed a wavering smile on Maggie. "Do you want me to leave?"

"Would you please see to Fred for me?" Maggie requested. "I know he is trying to be brave for my sake, but I swear he turned paler each time a pain gripped me. I'd feel much better knowing you were watching out for him."

"Of course, Maggie," Fran replied, clearly thankful to be able to perform at least some useful task for her friend.

The room turned eerily quiet after Fran left. Maggie took a tentative step toward Isabella, but stopped short when a strong contraction overtook her body.

"Is it true the bridge is flooded, Miss Browning? The midwife won't be coming?"

"Yes, the bridge is impassable," Isabella confirmed quietly. She reached out and tenderly brushed the hair from Maggie's face. The maid looked so frail and frightened and alone. "But I'm here, Maggie. And I'm going to help you. Did I ever tell you my . . . father was a doctor?"

"I recall Mr. Jenkins mentioning it once." Maggie cautiously straightened her body and pressed a fist into her aching back. Isabella watched her every movement.

"You learn things growing up in a physician's household," Isabella lied baldly. "I have more experience than you might think." There was no point in scaring Maggie any further. What she needed was reassurance. As far as Isabella was concerned, a white lie at this point certainly seemed in order.

"What should I do?"

Isabella felt a tiny stirring of relief. Maggie accepted her. Isabella looked at the young girl hugging her cramping abdomen and prayed she was up to the task. "Does walking help ease the pain?"

"Some."

"Good. Then let's keep at it." Isabella moved next to Maggie and placed a comforting arm around her. "I'll help you."

The next few hours passed slowly for the two women. Maggie's pains were obviously increasing, though she made a gallant effort to hide it. When Isabella noticed Maggie tiring, she insisted they abandon the pacing in favor of the bed. She wiped the maid's face with a cool, damp rag and tightly held her hand when the contractions grasped Maggie's body. And Isabella talked. Endlessly.

She'd gotten it into her head that keeping up a constant stream of inane chatter would distract Maggie from her pain. So Isabella told amusing, and for the most part fictitious, stories from her childhood. She talked until her voice was nearly hoarse and her throat felt dry and raw.

It seemed to work for a while, but after a time Isabella noted a marked change. Maggie's contractions came closer together, and Isabella could tell by the way Maggie clenched her teeth that they were fierce and violent.

Isabella reached out a comforting hand and rested it on Maggie's abdomen. She could feel the intense tightening of the womb through the nightgown as the babe within lurched and quivered. As the pain washed over her, Maggie dug her heels into the mattress, arched her back and lifted her convulsing body off the bed.

"It hurts, oh, how it hurts." Maggie winced, twisting her head from side to side.

It was nearly unbearable to watch Maggie suffer so intensely, but Isabella forced down her own fright. Her torment was nothing compared to the agony Maggie now endured. Helplessly, Isabella pushed back Maggie's dark, sweat-dampened hair.

"Have courage, Maggie," Isabella whispered. "It will all be over soon."

For the thousandth time, Isabella again reviewed in her mind the few birthing instructions she knew. Over and over the stern voice echoed in her head, a memory of that long-ago day in her childhood when she had witnessed that awful birth. *You must push as hard as you can when the head appears, you must push as hard as you can when the head appears.*

Gently, Isabella lifted Maggie's nightgown and looked between her legs, praying for a glimpse of the baby's head.

Maggie moaned sharply, and her head sank back against the pillows in exhaustion. She closed her eyes and seemed to struggle for the strength to take a few shallow breaths. A sharp chill of fear ran down Isabella's spine. The maid was obviously tiring; Isabella was uncertain how much longer she could endure the pain. She desperately hoped Maggie would have the strength to push the child from her body.

"Everything is going very smoothly, Maggie," Isabella said in a soothing voice. "You must try to conserve your strength and rest between the contractions. Soon you will be able to begin pushing the babe out."

A slight movement startled Isabella, and she turned to find Damien by her side. The earl had slipped unnoticed into the room, and he stood now at the foot of the bed, his eyes riveted in horror and wonder on Maggie.

"She looks as white as the sheets beneath her," Damien whispered hoarsely. "Is everything all right?"

"How the devil am I supposed to know?" Isabella hissed in a loud whisper. Desperately needing to vent her fear and frustration, the earl provided a convenient target for Isabella. "In case you have forgotten, sir, my experience with childbirth is rather limited."

Embarrassed by her outburst, Isabella anxiously turned her head toward Maggie, fearing the young woman had overheard. She need not have been concerned. Maggie was oblivious to her surroundings. Her eyes were tightly shut, and she made low, whimpering sounds deep in her throat.

"I've sent Fred down to the stables to check on the horses," Damien told Isabella. "The poor man is frantic with worry and desperate not to show it."

"His fears are not unfounded," Isabella said solemnly. "Birthing can be a dangerous business."

"Mrs. Amberly is still out cold, but Fran and Molly have volunteered to help," Damien informed Isabella.

Regretfully, Isabella shook her head. "They are both expecting children of their own. As much as I would appreciate their assistance, I cannot subject them to this. After witnessing

Maggie's ordeal, I am sure they would dwell overlong on their own forthcoming births.''

"Then I shall stay," Damien declared softly.

Isabella's knees went weak with relief. "I suppose it would be too much to hope that you have done this before," she said with a curious mixture of sarcasm and elation in her voice.

"I've delivered some livestock," Damien replied in all seriousness.

"Perfect," Isabella snorted. "Your vast experience nearly exceeds my own." She turned with concerned eyes toward Maggie. "She is so tired. I only pray this will be a swift and normal delivery."

At Isabella's instruction, Damien took up a position at the head of the bed, behind Maggie. The poor woman was so consumed by her labor pains, she was barely aware of his presence.

Isabella climbed onto the mattress at the foot of the bed and gently raised Maggie's knees. "With the next pain you must bear down and push hard, Maggie."

Isabella placed her hand on Maggie's distended belly and waited for the tightening of the next contraction to begin. When she felt the muscles tense, Isabella calmly issued instructions. "Bear down, Maggie. Now."

Disoriented, Maggie struggled to obey, but she lacked the strength to lift her upper body off the bed while pushing with her lower extremities. Collapsing against the pillows in exhaustion, Maggie sobbed brokenly, "I cannot. Dear God, I cannot." Tears seeped from her eyes, wetting her temples and falling into her sweat-soaked hair.

Numb with fear, Isabella stared beseechingly across the bed at Damien. The earl was pale under his tan, but he did not hesitate once in his actions. He sat down on the bed, braced himself against the wooden headboard and carefully lifted Maggie so that her back rested flush against his chest.

Barely half-conscious, Maggie whimpered as the next racking pain gripped her body. Waiting for Isabella's silent cue, Damien whispered encouragingly to Maggie and, miraculously, the maid was able to follow his commands.

After an agonizing hour, Isabella began to panic. How long could this possibly continue? Maggie was almost beyond reality, awash in a constant sea of pain. The grim expression on the earl's face confirmed that Damien shared this view. But what could they do?

Isabella was so consumed with worry that she nearly missed the sudden appearance of the tiny dark crown of hair between Maggie's legs. "My God, it's the head! I can see the baby's head!"

"This is it, Maggie, the baby is finally coming," the earl elatedly announced.

Dazed, Maggie somehow managed to bear down once more. She let out a harsh, blood-chilling scream and pushed with every ounce of strength her overfatigued body could muster. A minute later, the infant slid into Isabella's waiting hands.

"It's a girl!" Isabella cried out in jubilation. The babe gave a tiny wail of indignation that soon grew in strength and volume. "She is tiny, but she appears healthy."

"Her vocal cords are certainly in working order," Damien commented as he craned his neck for a glimpse of the baby.

With a soft, clean sheet, Isabella tenderly began cleaning the infant's body. The baby was red and wrinkled, and to Isabella's eyes utterly beautiful. Tears ran unchecked down her cheeks as the baby squalled loudly with indignation. What a wonderful noise! Then she stopped suddenly in the middle of her ministrations and called to Damien in alarm.

"Good Lord, she is still attached to her mother!" Isabella exclaimed in fear. She lifted the baby so Damien could see the birth cord from the infant's stomach trailing down to the bed and ending somewhere under the thin sheet that covered Maggie's legs. "What should I do?"

"You need sever the cord, my little midwife," Damien teased with a grin of relief. Isabella held the squirming infant gingerly while Damien located the knife Fran had left for that very purpose. He brought it to the bed, deftly tied off the cord and returned the baby to an astonished Isabella.

Impressed, Isabella finished bathing the infant and wrapped her in a dry blanket. Eagerly she approached the bed and laid the precious bundle in the curve of Maggie's arm. The maid's eyes instantly filled with tears and she tried to speak, but her numbed throat would not cooperate.

"I'll go and summon Fred," Damien said. Clearly startled, Maggie turned her head at the sound of the earl's deep voice.

"Lord Saunders?" Maggie croaked in puzzlement.

"Is going to get your husband," Isabella stated in a soothing tone. Isabella walked Damien to the door. "I don't think she was even aware of your presence during the birth."

" 'Tis no wonder, with all that she suffered," Damien replied with sympathy. He shuddered slightly with the memory. "She has safely delivered her child and the afterbirth. If no fever develops, I believe she will be fine."

"Thank the Lord for that," Isabella replied, rapidly whispering a small prayer of thanks.

Fred appeared suddenly on the landing, his eyes alight with hope. "I thought I heard the babe cry," he began wistfully.

"So you did, Fred," Damien exclaimed cheerfully. "Congratulations. You have a daughter."

"A daughter," Fred repeated, clearly awestruck. "And Maggie. How is Maggie, Miss Browning?"

"Exhausted," Isabella replied with a smile. "But I know she wants to see you. Go inside."

Needing no further encouragement, Fred bolted inside the bedchamber, anxious to see his family. Isabella's throat tightened. How wonderful to be so loved and share such a special moment of joy with the man you adored.

"You're not going to fall to pieces on me now, are you, Isabella?" Damien chided gently. "Not after it is all over."

Embarrassed, Isabella averted her face from his contemplative gaze. She knew it was foolish to become embarrassed at this point, but she felt an odd closeness toward Damien. They had shared such an unusual, overwhelming experience. In a very real and strange sense, it was almost as if they had been the ones responsible for bringing this precious new life into the world, not Maggie and Fred.

"It was such an emotional ordeal," Isabella whispered in wonder. "So miraculous. So terrifying. I shudder to think how I would have managed without your help, Damien. I knew nothing of the birth cord or the afterbirth. If not for your assistance, the child might not have been safely delivered."

"It certainly was a humbling experience," Damien admitted.

They descended to the second landing in silence. Fran waited below, her face strained with worry.

"Maggie has a beautiful daughter," Isabella told her quietly. Breaking into a wide grin, the maid left quickly to alert the rest of the household.

"Now that Maggie is safely delivered of her child, Damien, it is time for us to have our discussion." Isabella turned to him, her expression frankly curious. "You have promised me an explanation of what you were doing in my room this evening."

The earl faced Isabella squarely. "Maggie was in labor and needed your help," he said with an innocent expression. "I knocked on your bedchamber door, and when you did not answer, I entered your room. I'm sorry if I startled you."

Isabella pursed her lips. "When I awoke you were . . . kissing me."

"Did you find it repulsive?"

"Of course not, but—"

"Father! Father! Have you heard the news? Fran just told us Maggie has a new baby."

Ian interrupted their conversation with a loud shout of excitement.

"It's a girl," Catherine added with breathless delight. The two children raced up the stairs to meet the earl and Isabella. "We haven't seen the baby yet, but we heard her crying. It sounded just like a kitten, didn't it, Ian?"

Ian nodded enthusiastically. "Fran said she would let us see Maggie and the new baby after they rested. Will you come with us, Father?"

"What in the world are you two doing up?" the earl asked in astonishment, ignoring his son's question.

"It's already past nine o'clock," Ian explained patiently. "We've been up for ages. Mrs. Amberly is still in her bed, snoring ever so loudly, so Jenkins gave us our breakfast. We had cake."

"Cake? For breakfast?" Isabella coughed slightly to mask her giggle. "It sounds as though you have had a most exciting morning."

"Indeed," the earl muttered. He glanced over at Isabella and smiled warmly. "I definitely need a strong cup of coffee. Children, I think you should accompany me down to the kitchen. I'm sure I can locate something more substantial than cake for us to eat."

"An excellent suggestion, sir," Isabella piped up, including herself in the invitation. "I find that I am suddenly famished."

The earl managed to disappear as soon as breakfast was finished. Mrs. Amberly arose from her bed in time to cook an uninspired lunch for the excited household. The housekeeper's surly temperament, along with her aching tooth, did not improve as the day progressed. Isabella was vastly relieved when Mrs. Amberly took Jenkins's advice and retired to her room directly after luncheon.

"I don't believe Mrs. Amberly is up to cooking dinner this evening," Jenkins confided to Isabella as they sat alone together in the kitchen, sharing a cup of tea. The earl was still out attending to estate matters, despite the constant rain, and the children were upstairs with Maggie and her baby. "I hope the maids and I will be able to provide something adequate for dinner."

"Of course, if all else fails, we can always have cake for dinner, Mr. Jenkins." The corners of Isabella's mouth curled up in a teasing smile.

"Don't be so quick to dismiss the notion of cake," Jenkins retorted with good humor. "Maggie is the only one of the four maids who possesses any culinary skills, and she is in no condition to do any cooking. Fran's idea of preparing a meal involves boiling everything until the last ounce of flavor and texture is gone, and Molly can only cook eggs and fry bread. If memory serves me correctly, Penny doesn't even know how to light the stove.''

''In that case, I should like to offer my services,'' Isabella volunteered.

''You can cook, Miss Browning?''

''I am far from a French chef, but I'll wager I can produce something more flavorful than a boiled dinner.'' Leaning towards the valet, she wryly added, ''I dare say, I might even be able to improve on the swill Mrs. Amberly usually serves us.''

''That hardly takes talent, Miss Browning.''

''True, Mr. Jenkins.'' Isabella laughed. ''I will rummage through the pantry and see what supplies are available. I suppose we can send someone to one of the nearby tenant farms if there isn't any fresh meat or vegetables.''

''Let me know what is needed,'' Jenkins said. ''I will see to it.''

Isabella began prowling around the kitchen to see what fresh food was on hand, feeling enthusiastic over the challenge of cooking a meal for the entire household. Pleased with the variety and quality of food she discovered, Isabella planned a dinner menu based on the recipes she could remember.

''After you have finished your tea, Mr. Jenkins, would you please go find Ian and Catherine? I suspect they will be on the third floor, pestering Maggie and the baby. There will be no time for lessons this afternoon, but I'll find something to keep the children busy. Maggie and the baby need their rest.''

Isabella mixed a stiff ginger cookie dough, and when the children joined her in the kitchen, she taught them how to roll and cut out cookies. They were intrigued with the entire process and spent several joyful hours at the task, although they ate more dough than they rolled.

Inspired by the variety of food she found, Isabella settled on a rather ambitious menu. Vegetable soup to start, followed by fillets of fish poached in white wine, roast beef with fried potatoes, and fresh greens. For dessert there was a luscious honey-wine pear tart that had been a specialty of Isabella's childhood cook, to be served along with Catherine and Ian's unusually shaped ginger cookies.

The kitchen soon filled with mouthwatering aromas. Fran and Molly drifted in to investigate, and Isabella immediately set them to work chopping vegetables while she delicately worked the pastry for the tart.

Though it entailed a great deal of hard work, Isabella enjoyed her day in the kitchen. Working in compatible ease with the children and the maids, she experienced the warm sense of family that had long since been missing from her life. And she gleefully anticipated Damien's pleasure at her culinary efforts. Deep in her heart, Isabella admitted that the need to prove herself worthy in Damien's eyes was strong, even in such a menial task as cooking.

The excitement mounted as the dinner hour approached. After ascertaining that all was under control, Isabella slipped away for a quick bath to remove the smells of the kitchen from her skin. Freshly bathed and dressed, she waited for the earl to return, hoping he wouldn't be too late to appreciate the sumptuous meal.

When the clock struck the hour, Isabella realized she could wait no longer for the earl to arrive. Reluctantly, she served the children their soup before going in search of Jenkins. She encountered the valet in the foyer, a open bottle of brandy in his hands.

"I have already begun the meal," Isabella reported with dismay. "Will the earl be returning home soon, Mr. Jenkins?"

"The earl is at home, Miss Browning," the valet replied with guarded eyes. "He is in his bedchamber."

"Go tell him that dinner is ready," Isabella insisted, not bothering to hide her delight. "I shall expect him in the dining room in five minuets."

"I don't belive the earl will be joining the family for dinner this evening," Jenkins replied with regret in his eyes.

Isabella was instantly suspicious. "Why not? Is something wrong?"

"I am not certain." The valet hesitated for a moment. "The earl was in a fine mood when he returned late this afternoon, but after reading today's post he became livid. He has ensconced himself in his bedchamber with a bottle of brandy and only emerged long enough to demand a second bottle.''

Jenkins's voice dropped to a mere whisper. ''I must confess, Miss Browning. I am worried.''

Chapter Fourteen

"I'll go to him," Isabella decided. She glanced ruefully down at the brandy bottle in Jenkins's hands, hesitated, then finally pulled the bottle into her arms.

She strode purposefully through the hallway and up the staircase, pausing a moment before the closed doors of the earl's bedchamber. She raised her hand to knock, but changed her mind and instead turned the latch. Shoulders squared, Isabella marched in the room, intentionally closing the door with a loud bang.

"Where is Jenkins?"

Isabella halted abruptly at the sound of Damien's deep voice. With slightly less confidence, she approached the earl. He was sprawled in a leather wing chair, his muddy boots carelessly propped on the low mahogany table before him. His discarded riding coat lay on the floor near the roaring fire, and his fine linen shirt was undone halfway down his chest.

Despite his languid pose, he looked powerful and dangerous, like a wild beast ready to attack its unsuspecting prey. Isabella's heart thudded erratically as she stared at him, mesmerized by the raw, masculine emotions she sensed within him.

Face expressionless, his steely gray eyes impenetrable, Damien repeated his question. "Where is Jenkins?"

With difficulty, Isabella dragged her eyes away from his bronzed, muscular chest.

"Mr. Jenkins is in the dining room with the rest of the household eating his dinner." She gave him an exasperated glare. "Which is where you belong. I spent the better part of the day preparing supper. I hope you will at least do me the courtesy of eating some of it."

Damien turned his head and gave Isabella an irritated stare. He mockingly lifted the half-finished glass of brandy toward her in a light salute before bringing it to his lips. Downing the contents in two swallows, he flung out his arm and presented Isabella the empty goblet.

"Would you be so kind as to replenish my glass before you leave?"

Isabella's eyes narrowed. "You drink too much," she ventured boldly.

"And you meddle too often, so I suppose that makes us a well-matched pair."

Isabella muttered indignantly under her breath. She moved toward him slowly, her eyes pinned to his handsome face. She reluctantly filled his glass, then set the bottle down, just a hairsbreadth beyond Damien's reach. Making a wide berth of the earl, Isabella paused before the fire, warming her hands over the flames.

The tension increased with the growing silence. Isabella was so acutely aware of Damien that she could feel her skin prickle. She cleared her throat.

"What is wrong, Damien?" she finally asked.

Pain flashed briefly in the earl's eyes, but her back was toward him and she did not see it. He felt a great need to confide this latest disaster that had befallen him to Isabella, but it was difficult for him to share the burden. Isolation and loneliness had been a part of Damien's life for so long that he'd become accustomed to the emptiness that governed his life. It was an almost impossible habit to break.

"Nothing is wrong, Isabella." A muscle knotted his jaw. "I only wish to be left in peace."

Isabella pivoted slowly, determined to face the underlying bitterness in his voice, and noticed for the first time the sheet of parchment Damien clutched tightly in his left hand.

"What is that?"

Damien gave her a crooked smile. "Are you referring to this document, per chance?" The earl held the offending piece of paper aloft, as though it possessed a noxious odor. "This, my dear Isabella, is a letter from my illustrious and disgustingly rich brother-in-law, Lord Poole."

Isabella did not miss the importance of the name. "What has Lord Poole done now?"

Damien took another fortifying sip of brandy before answering. "It appears that Poole has somehow managed to purchase all the remaining mortgages held against Whatley Grange. He has written this charming letter informing me of this fact and has given me fair warning that he intends to call in all debts in sixty days' time."

"Sixty days! Good heavens, Damien, what will you do?"

"I suppose I shall attempt to borrow the funds I need from a bank or even a moneylender, although I have nothing of sufficient value to place as collateral. Beyond that, I have not as yet formulated a practical solution. It seems I have as much a chance of holding on to Whatley Grange as I do of finding Lady Anne's treasure."

The earl's sarcastic tone betrayed none of his emotions, but Isabella knew his pain and frustration must run deep. Her heart constricted in alarm. Damien had devoted many years of his life to working hard to make The Grange solvent. It must be maddening to know he was so close to losing what he had worked so tirelessly to preserve.

Isabella sank slowly to her knees beside his chair. Her slender hand reached out and gently caressed his forearm, offering silent comfort, seeking in some small way to ease his torment.

"I am so sorry, Damien."

At the sound of her voice, the earl dropped his eyes to the delicate fingers softly stroking his arm. Her hand looked small and feminine against the stark whiteness of his shirt. Hers was a gentle touch, a comforting touch. A touch of understanding and kinship. Her tenderness wrenched at his chest, yet his male pride demanded a token resistance and he shifted in the chair, attempting to evade her.

Isabella felt his withdrawal and hooked her fingers firmly around his wrist, refusing to break the physical bond. Their wills clashed, but Damien soon relented and gradually relaxed, allowing her soft touch to sooth his bruised spirit.

The earl set his glass of brandy on the floor and closed his eyes. Leaning his dark head back against the chair, he let his mind wander aimlessly as Isabella's hand continued to lightly caress him. The unique way she touched him made him feel oddly cherished. It gave him a sense of strength that made him feel it was possible to triumph over any adversity. Even the despicable Lord Poole.

Isabella could feel the tension slowly leaving the earl's body. The building tension within her also eased. How she hated to see him suffer! Nearly overcome with emotion for him, Isabella moved her cheek softly against the back of his hand.

Damien eyes flew open. He twisted his head to glance down at her just as she turned his palm up and pressed a feather-light kiss on the inside of his wrist.

Tentatively, the earl reached across with his free arm. His hand hovered for several seconds before he succumbed to temptation and placed his hand upon her head. His fingers delved softly into Isabella's tight chignon, scattering her hair pins and releasing her hair from its strict confines.

"You are a wonder, Isabella," he whispered softly. When she turned her head up to reply, Damien swiftly leaned down and captured her lips.

His mouth was warm and spicy, and Isabella could taste the brandy on his tongue. His kiss was filled with restless urgency and hunger. Isabella shuddered heavily and wrapped her arms around Damien's broad shoulders. An almost unbearable sense of excitement washed through Damien as she slid her long fingers around his neck and kissed him back with sensual welcome.

He touched her hair, inhaling the scent of her as their tongues swirled together. His entire body was straining with need as he kissed her with all the passion building inside him. Isabella moved up from the floor, pressing herself closer to his hard, muscular body, instinctively seeking Damien's heat and strength.

Finally, the earl forced himself to break the kiss. He lifted his head and gazed into her violet eyes with a searing sense of longing. And a chilling sense of uncertainty. For he knew, deep in his soul, that his desire for Isabella was far more complex than mere physical need.

"If you are going to leave, you'd best go now, Isabella."

Damien's voice was harsh and raspy in his throat, and Isabella quivered at the sound. The intense passion in his smoky gray eyes nearly consumed her, but she saw beyond the desire to the vulnerability of spirit he could no longer hide.

Every moral fiber within her screamed for her to leave the room, but Isabella willfully shut out the sensible, practical side of her nature. She also consciously reined in her romantic imagination. She might love this man with a depth of feeling that was almost frightening, but she knew that did not mean he returned her love. Yet he dearly desired her. And needed her. For Isabella, a woman who had struggled through neglect and indifference as a child to intense loneliness as an adult, it was enough.

"I shall not leave, Damien."

To emphasize her response, she kissed him. Her tongue slipped past his startled lips, tasting him yearningly, curious to discover the power a woman held over a man's passions.

Damien laced his hands through her hair. He brushed a soft kiss along her temple, cheek, and jaw, then sought her trembling mouth again.

She was acutely aware of his masculine size and power as he knelt before her on the rug. The heat from his body was nearly as strong as the blaze from the roaring fire. Looking into Damien's smoldering eyes, Isabella felt her heart turn over.

"I want you, Isabella. Very much."

Swallowing with effort, she barely managed a response. "I am glad, Damien. I want you too."

Her boldness and honesty delighted him. The decision made and now verbally expressed lifted the burden of restraint from the earl. He paused a moment to remove his boots and then turned back to Isabella. His strong arm encircled her waist, and he pulled her roughly to him. He kissed her fiercely, crushing her supple form tightly against his straining body.

Isabella shuddered heavily as she felt the rigid proof of his desire leaping and throbbing against her thigh. His fingers slid through her hair, down the nape of her neck, then stopped, cupping one soft breast possessively. Even through the layers of clothing, Isabella could feel the heat of his fingers as he caressed her. She shivered and gave a soft, whimpering moan.

The small sigh broke him. Frenzied, Damien tore at her clothing, pulling at the fastenings of her gown, impatient to touch her silky flesh. In the flickering glow of the firelight, his eyes gleamed with possessive brilliance. Somehow he managed to remove the top half of her gown and pull her arms from the sleeves. Groaning in triumph, Damien swiftly lowered the lace-trimmed chemise to Isabella's waist.

He went very still as he looked at her breasts. She saw his eyes narrow and darken when his fingers reached out and traced the outline of her naked flesh.

"My God, you are beautiful," he muttered huskily. He kissed her again, hard on the lips, then drew back.

Isabella held her breath as she watched his dark head lean forward and capture one dusky rose nipple in his mouth. The tender tug of his caress sent a bolt of pleasure crashing through her body, and she moaned loudly, feeling a bewildering, urgent need deep within.

Encouraged by her response, Damien's teasing fingers glided down her neck, across her throat, and over to the other breast. She could feel the nipple quickly harden under his stroking hands. She felt the awakening stirring inside her, and she clung to the warmth that flowed so naturally between them.

She stared down in fascination at the dark head on her breast, and her heart swelled with emotion. She felt a rush of tears stinging her eyes. How completely she loved this man! Blindly following her emotions, she wound her arms around his shoulders, hugging him tightly, feeling a primal desire deep within her to never, ever, let him go.

"You are so sweet," he murmured softly, as he placed hot, wet kisses across her creamy breasts, traveling lustily from one to the other.

Isabella's breath spilled out in a rush when Damien's lips closed over her straining nipple. She arched her back instinctively, seeking more of the shivering sensations.

Damien gave a throaty laugh as he tenderly laved the exquisite bud. It had been a very long time since he held such a giving, passionate woman in his arms. It felt good. Damn good. He pursed his lips and suckled harder.

"Oh, my!"

Isabella unconsciously clenched her hand on the back of Damien's neck, under his dark hair, her grip tightening as her body quivered with excitement. Her now restless fingers moved down across his hard shoulders, feeling the sleek muscle and sinew. She tensed against him as the excitement within her grew to an almost unbearable level.

"Relax, sweetheart," Damien whispered throatily. "Allow your passionate nature its freedom. We will both profit from it."

Damien's words barely registered in her mind. He shifted abruptly and pulled her completely down onto the carpet, then rolled her onto her back. He settled his body intimately atop hers, staring into her eyes with an intensity that made Isabella tremble. The air felt suddenly closed and heated.

"I'm going to remove the rest of your clothing, Isabella." The deep, sensual timber of his voice made her shiver.

"Wait!"

A thunderous expression crossed the earl's face, but it quickly turned to sexy delight as Isabella's questing fingers splayed across his hard chest.

"I want to remove some of your clothing first," she insisted. When he offered no protest, she reached for the buttons. Curious and excited, Isabella began to open the last few fastenings on his shirt. Damien shifted his weight and gave her an odd smile as she struggled with the buttons.

"Just rip it," he whispered in a deep voice, and he inhaled deeply as Isabella followed his commands. Buttons spewed about the room, and Damien laughed with delight.

Nervous but determined, Isabella continued her explorations. Deftly she reached inside the linen and spread her hands across Damien's naked chest. The springy dark hair tickled her palms. The flesh beneath felt smooth and very hard. Experimentally she moved her hands lower, across the flat plane of his stomach to the top of his breeches. A long shudder ran through Damien.

"Enough," he said abruptly, yanking off the remains of his shirt and tossing it aside.

He briefly debated carrying Isabella over to the bed, but his blood was roaring in his ears. He kissed her deeply, his passion becoming more urgent with each kiss, his need more overwhelming with each caress.

Damien couldn't stop touching her. His skillful fingers reached under her skirts, tugging impatiently at the strong ribbons that fastened the drawers around her waist.

"Lift your hips," he commanded with a desperate plea of passion.

Dazed, Isabella obeyed, and the earl triumphantly pulled the flimsy garment from her heated skin. Her cotton stockings quickly followed, then her already unfastened gown. Damien's hand stroked boldly down her naked flesh, past her belly, finally coming to rest between her legs.

Isabella lost control of her breathing as she felt his fingers sliding into the moist triangle of curls. She made a raw choking sound as Damien tenderly spread the delicate folds of her flesh. His fingers slid lightly back and forth, spreading a throbbing excitement throughout her entire being. Clenching her eyes closed, Isabella fought back the rush of embarrassment and allowed herself to yield to the exquisite pleasure.

She felt the most incredible aching tension deep within her and arched convulsively in reaction, twisting to get closer to him as he intimately caressed her.

"Sweet, so sweet, my Isabella," Damien whispered sensually as his finger slid deeply inside her dampness. ''Let go. Just let go.''

For a moment Isabella lay motionless, gazing with mute astonishment into Damien's passion-darkened eyes, and then she cried out as the pleasure surged suddenly, wildly exploding within her.

He kissed her deeply, then held her tightly as the climax overtook her, his excitement mounting at each moan, each whimper, each shuddering breath she drew. Finally Isabella quieted.

Her release made her body feel limp and pliant. Damien knew he should wait until he brought her to the edge of passion again before coupling with her, but he was no longer capable of rational thought. Feeling the dewy feminine moisture of her body caused the earl's hard-fought control to dissolve. Savagely ripping his breeches away, he loomed over Isabella, his entire body straining with need. He kneed her legs wider apart and settled himself between them.

''I'm going to claim you now, Isabella,'' he whispered hoarsely.

Damien entered her as slow as he could manage, wanting to spare her unnecessary pain. Roused from her stupor, she caught at the hard arms braced around her and held tight. With a look of wonder in her eyes, she gazed deeply into his.

Her open trust and passionate acceptance overwhelmed Damien. He wanted to warm her with his flesh, to protect her with his strength, to cherish her with his heart. She deserved no less.

Moaning, he grasped her hips in his hands and pressed deeper. Isabella felt something tear inside her and give way, but she ignored the burning pain and lifted herself closer, wanting to feel him even deeper within her body.

Damien forced himself to take deep breaths and remain perfectly still even though his body was throbbing. He could feel her stretching, her muscles convulsing around him. It felt glorious.

''I'm sorry I hurt you,'' he whispered against her temple.

''It wasn't so bad.'' Isabella pulled her head aside and gazed

into his handsome face. "I can feel you throbbing inside me,"
she said with gentle awe. "Is it over?"

She shifted her legs restlessly, and Damien swore softly.
" 'Tis only begun, my sweet."

His lips descended on hers in a crushing kiss while his hips
drew back, then thrust forward, deep within her. He began to
raise and lower his body with slow, steady strokes, and Isabella
began to move with him.

The pain lessened, and Isabella gasped at the wonderful
sensation of him inside her. Yet she experienced more, much
more than the physical intimacy. She was merged with him in
her heart as well as her body. He was filling the emptiness in
her soul, coloring the drabness of her spirit. Isabella encircled
Damien with her arms, lightly stroking his back. She rose boldly
to meet his thrust and felt him grow even larger within her.

Damien knew it was too soon, knew she was not ready, but
his blood was afire and it was impossible to hold back. He
sank more deeply into her. Eyes closed, his body stiffened,
shook, and a long rattling cry emerged from his throat. Tears
rolled gently down Isabella's cheeks as she felt the warm wetness of his seed inside her body. Never in her life had she felt
closer to another living creature than she did at that instant.

For a long time, Damien lay sprawled atop her, seemingly
incapable of movement. His body was slick with perspiration,
his breathing uneven. He was heavy, but she paid it no heed.
She lay quiet and still beneath him, inordinately pleased that
even with her sexual ignorance, she had managed to give him
pleasure.

Damien raised his head and lifted his hand to touch her cheek
in a placating gesture, his steely gray eyes soft and apologetic.

"Next time it will be better," he promised mysteriously.

She dropped her eyes from his. Next time! Her face flushed
with embarrassment. Did that mean he expected her to share
his bed now as a matter of course? Isabella opened her mouth
and attempted to say something, anything, in response, but her
words were cut off as Damien gathered her in his arms and
took her with him as he rolled onto his back.

She lay atop him with her arms pressed against his chest

and her legs tangled with his. Her body still vibrating with awareness, it took a few moments to realize they were no longer joined together. But they were still very much connected.

Time passed. Gradually Isabella realized that his strong hands had begun to sweep enticingly over the small of her back and buttocks. The tingly, restless feeling started burning again low in her belly.

"We really should move to the bed," Damien announced in a deep, lazy voice. It took several long moments for him to follow through with his suggestion, his limbs too tired and content to obey his mind.

Eventually he lifted her in his arms and walked to the bed. Pulling back the counterpane, Damien laid her down gently, almost reverently. He kissed her long and ardently before gathering her close in his arms. She sighed contentedly and snuggled closer, wondering what was to happen next.

"Good night, Isabella," Damien said softly.

"Good night," she replied automatically, feeling her eyelids drooping. Before drifting off to sleep, she could have sworn she heard the carl mutter something else. It sounded suspiciously like "thank you."

A sharp, insistent knock jolted Damien awake. Disoriented, he sat up in his bed and glanced about the room in confusion. He couldn't read the time on the clock near his armoire, but the fire still blazed in the hearth. It couldn't be that late.

The bright flames of the fire kept the worst of the chill from the room and partially illuminated the bedchamber. Damien could clearly see the nearly full decanter of brandy alongside an empty glass and several piles of clothes scattered about the floor. His clothes. And Isabella's.

Damien turned, startled at the sight of her sleeping peacefully in his bed, even though he had carried her there himself.

The knock sounded again. Damien rose quietly from the bed, hastily donned his breeches, and answered it. Not surprisingly, Jenkins stood on the other side of the door, looking both curious and concerned.

"It has been hours since Miss Browning brought up your brandy," Jenkins said, stretching on his toes in an unsuccessful attempt to look above the earl's head and into the bedchamber. "We have all finished dinner. Mrs. Amberly was feeling well enough to get the children ready for bed. But they are expecting Miss Browning to tuck them in, as she does each night."

"Miss Browning has gone to bed early this evening." Damien stared hard at his servant. "Her *own* bed, Jenkins. Do you understand?"

"I hear you quite well," Jenkins replied shrewdly. The valet folded his arms across his chest. "And I *understand.*"

Damien dropped his chin to his chest. "No lectures, please. I'm confused enough without hearing your blistering opinion of my actions." The earl lifted his head, sighed deeply, and added, "I'll see to Catherine and Ian myself."

"I managed to save a bit of dinner for you," Jenkins said, his expression inscrutable. "Miss Browning made quite a feast that everyone thoroughly enjoyed. I suggest you stop by the kitchen after you have said good night to the children. It looks as though you could use some nourishment."

"I most likely shall. Good night, Jenkins."

"Good night, Damien."

Catherine and Ian were both pleased to see their father and detained him for as long as possible with repeated requests for stories and drinks of water. Damien finally insisted they go to sleep, and he left them both snuggled under the covers, with a long candle lit to chase away the gloomy darkness.

Once the children were settled, Damien proceeded to the kitchen and was amazed at the glorious selection of food he discovered neatly arranged in the larder. After helping himself to a large wedge of pear tart that literally melted in his mouth, Damien piled three plates high with food and set them on a tray. He added cutlery, napkins, and a bottle of wine. Then he carried his bounty up to his bedchamber.

Isabella was lying in precisely the same spot on his bed, but as he set their dinner upon the small table near the fire, she awoke.

"I've brought some food," the earl explained unnecessarily. "Come and eat dinner."

Isabella sat up warily in the bed, trying desperately to hide her embarrassment. She was lying naked in the earl's bed, her body still warm and sore from the passion they had recently shared, and he was acting as though this were a common, every day occurrence.

Her stomach rumbled from hunger. Scarcely believing she was thinking about food at a time like this, Isabella nevertheless decided that it couldn't hurt to eat something. Since there was no clothing within her grasp, she yanked the sheet off the top of the bed and wrapped it securely around her naked body.

Feeling utterly ridiculous, she joined the earl at the cozy table. Once seated, however, Isabella's embarrassment fled as her appetite took control. They ate dinner in silence, savoring each bite.

"This is truly delicious," Damien remarked as he finished the last of the pear tart. "Jenkins told me you prepared the entire meal. Where did you ever learn to cook?"

Isabella blushed and lowered her lashes to hide the glow of pleasure she thought was certainly reflected in her eyes.

"After my mother died, I felt terribly lost and lonely. I craved female companionship, but there was no one to give it to me, no aunts or female relations. Actually, we had no women in our household except for our housekeeper, who was also the cook. She wasn't overly fond of little girls, especially me, but I was determined to somehow place myself in her good graces.

"I decided that the fastest way to get her to like me was to pretended to be interested in learning how to cook. Luckily, my plan met with great success. So in addition to receiving some much-needed attention, I learned a rather useful skill."

"You realize, of course, that you have placed me in a sticky position, Isabella." Damien's mouth curved in a smile that brought a sparkle to his eyes. "Now that I have tasted your roast beef, I know the only sensible recourse is to sack you as the governess and hire you as my cook."

"You are nothing but a tease, my lord," Isabella answered with a laugh. Sobering, she continued. "I truly do not like speaking ill of anyone, but why do you employ Mrs. Amberly? She is a disaster cooking anything more complicated than toast and is surly to boot.''

The earl grew quiet. ''I know she is difficult, even impossible at times. The truth, as you may well have guessed already, is that Mrs. Amberly is not trained as a cook. She first came to The Grange as a lady's maid and served my mother for many years.

''She tried to perform the same duties for Emmeline, but since my wife was seldom in residence, there was little to occupy Mrs. Amberly's time. She developed a great fondness for Catherine when she was an infant, so eventually Mrs. Amberly became Catherine's and later Ian's nursemaid.

''When the rumors started and the other female servants left, Mrs. Amberly was the only one who stayed. She took on the role of housekeeper and cook because there was no one else to perform the tasks. Over the years, she has more than earned my support and, dare I admit it, even my regard.''

''I admire your loyalty,'' Isabella said softly.

Damien shrugged. ''Any man of honor would react the same.'' Though he acted nonchalant, Isabella could see that her words pleased him. He tilted his head and smiled faintly at her. ''I admire your inner beauty. And your passionate nature.''

Momentarily stunned by the abrupt change in the conversation, Isabella found it impossible to respond. Damien's eyes moved over her, and she sat very straight and very still. She could hardly breathe.

He leaned across the small table. Gently, he lifted a long curl from her shoulder and brushed the wisps of stray hair away from her face.

''What am I going to do with you, my darling Isabella?''

The emotion in his voice brought a rush of tears to her eyes. Suddenly she longed to place herself inside the circle of his arms, curl herself against his broad chest, and rest her head against his strong shoulder.

Love me, her heart cried.

He kissed her instead. A brief, tender kiss that teased and hinted at passion and romance. Her heart swelled with longing and she made no protest when Damien tugged insistently at the top of the sheet she wore until it loosened. He then slipped his hand beneath the fabric and stroked her naked breast.

"Your skin is so soft. Softer than the finest silk."

"Oh, Damien." She pressed herself boldly against him, a tantalizing combination of innocence, bravado, and desire.

His eyes fixed on hers, and this time she recognized the undisguised hunger that sprang into them. Her heart did a strange flip-flop when she realized she shared that hunger.

"Take me to bed," she whispered.

Their joining was slow and passionate and filled with heat. When it was over, Isabella's body felt fully sated, yet the yearning ache Damien had kindled in her heart grew stronger. He held her tight as he drifted off to sleep, and she felt strangely grateful to be lying in his arms, burrowed close to his warmth and listening to the steady rhythm of his breathing.

The hour grew late. Isabella felt herself falling toward sleep wondering with both excitement and fear what the coming dawn would bring.

Chapter Fifteen

The heavy velvet bed curtains were drawn tightly closed, and Isabella awoke to a world shrouded in darkness. Sleep left her momentarily disoriented, but when she realized she lay in the earl's bed and not her own, her body stiffened.

Not daring to utter a sound, she cautiously reached out an arm and gingerly felt along the mattress. Slowly, Isabella inched her fingers over to the far side of the bed, eventually discovering she was alone.

Tentatively, she rose to her knees, parted the bed hangings, and peered out. Half expecting the earl to be prowling around his bedchamber, Isabella felt oddly disappointed to find the room empty. Both her clothes and his lay scattered in wild disarray by the cold ashes of the fireplace, and memories of the previous night invaded her mind.

Her behavior had been wanton and bold, and she knew the complete, shatteringly beautiful acts of love they shared would mark her for eternity. She regretted none of it. Yet anxiety and doubt flashed strongly within her. What would happen next? Would they continue to be lovers?

Damien had implied that he intended to continue this new, intimate side of their relationship. But how long could she hide her feelings of love from him? Would she be able to sustain a physical relationship while struggling to conceal the depth of her emotional attachment? Did she even want to?

Realizing that just because she was in love with him did not mean he would ever return her love already brought a pang of remorse to Isabella's heart. Was she willing to settle for so little? Did she dare to dream there would ever be more?

Doubts continued to flood her mind, plaguing Isabella as she left the bed and went in search of her garments. She had no desire to linger naked in the earl's bedchamber.

Quickly she donned her gown, in her haste forgoing all the underthings. A final glance around the room confirmed that she had successfully removed all traces of her presence—until her eyes rested on the bed.

Although they had first made love in front of the fireplace, there were streaks of dried blood marring the pristine white sheets. The marks of her lost virginity were plain to read.

With a sharp intake of breath, Isabella whipped the sheets from the mattress and tucked them under her arm, along with her undergarments. Creeping soundlessly across the hallway into her bedchamber, Isabella decided to simply hide the evidence in her room. Let Damien explain to his valet why the bedding had mysteriously disappeared.

Despite the late morning hour, Isabella dressed unhurriedly. She longed for a hot tub to soak her strained and quivering muscles in, but she was loath to arouse the staff's suspicions. She might not regret her actions, but she was not eager to broadcast her indiscretion to the entire household staff either.

Isabella arrived at the dining room just before the clock struck the eleventh morning hour. She suspected the children were already running about the estate and fervently hoped the earl was off on business as usual. She was not prepared to face him. Hopefully, spending the night in bed with the governess was no cause to disrupt the earl's normal routine.

Catching the breath of nerves in her lungs, Isabella opened the dining room door and gracefully stepped inside. The earl sat waiting for her amid a collection of dirty breakfast dishes. He was reading a newspaper and did not notice her quiet entrance.

Isabella's heart somersaulted at the sight of him. He looked somber, rather distant, and utterly handsome.

Her heart continued to pound frantically and erratically. The urge to turn and flee ran deep and strong. She must have made a sound, for the earl suddenly looked up.

"Good morning, Isabella."

She moistened her dry lips and mumbled an appropriate greeting.

"How do you feel?"

Some of Isabella's hard-fought-for composure dropped away, and a surge of embarrassment struck her.

"I am fine," she mumbled, regretting that she did not have the courage to inquire how *he* felt this morning.

"Please, take a seat, my dear. We have much to discuss, but it certainly can wait until you have eaten something."

Effectively caught, Isabella had no recourse but to comply. Deliberately, she choose the chair farthest from him. She never imagined it would be so difficult to face him again. His look was unnerving her. As was the tone of his voice.

A strong flicker of guilt washed over Damien as he watched Isabella. He grimaced, but held his tongue. She was stiff and cold, like a statue. It was painfully obvious she did not wish to be in his company. The wrong word, the wrong gesture, might easily upset her. Clearly no cause would be served by enacting an emotional scene.

Damien was feeling alarming pangs of guilt over his seduction of Isabella. Although she had been a more than willing participant, he took full responsibility for what occurred between them last night. Not only had he taken advantage of the generosity of her spirit, he had enjoyed it with an intensity that bordered on criminal. Honor clearly demanded he make amends.

Damien did not consider himself an especially religious man, but it seemed a gross irony that a sin so enormous had yielded a passion and fulfillment stronger than any he had previously experienced.

He waited until Isabella had placed a cold piece of toast on her plate before speaking.

"We shall be married before the week is out," he announced, pleased that the idea, now spoken aloud, no longer held the repugnance it did in the early hours of the morning when he realized it was the only honorable course to pursue.

"It will not be difficult for my solicitors to draw up the documents and procure a special license," Damien said, choosing each word with deliberate care.

Isabella could not believe her ears. Marriage? He wanted to *marry* her? Of all the things she had anticipated hearing from the earl, this truly was not among them. Her heart soared, but her head urged caution. She fidgeted with the toast in her dish, breaking the bread into small pieces as she struggled to regain her equilibrium.

Finally she lifted her chin and gave him a steady, direct look. "It is hardly necessary to offer marriage," she replied in a quiet, firm voice.

Damien's face tightened at her refusal. "I beg to differ, Isabella. After the events of last night, honor demands I marry you."

Isabella closed her eyes in understanding. His honor. Of course. She should have foreseen this. Isabella suppressed an involuntary shiver. How could she have been so foolish as to overlook his sense of duty? It was one of the qualities she so often admired in him.

Isabella sat up tall in her chair, drawing her brows together in a questioning frown. "I was unaware, sir, that every couple who engages in . . . um . . . who acts . . . as we did last night then marries." She flushed and quickly popped a small piece of toast in her mouth.

"Isabella . . ."

She would not allow him to interrupt. Rapidly coughing down the dry crumb in her throat, she continued breathlessly. "Besides, how can you consider marrying me when it is common knowledge that you do not acknowledge Emmeline's death? I would not be sitting here today if you did not firmly believe your wife was still alive somewhere." Crumbling the last of the toast in her plate, she gave him a bold stare. "You cannot marry me if you already have a wife. It is my understanding that the law does not allow a man to have more than one at a time.''

Damien looked briefly startled. He scrutinized Isabella's face intently, probing for signs of distress, regret, even embarrassment, but Isabella kept her expression unreadable.

''My personal beliefs in this matter are not significant. Legally, Emmeline is dead. Therefore I can take another wife if I desire.''

Isabella turned away from the determination in his voice and struggled for a clear head, a voice of reason. There was nothing in the world she wanted more than to be married to Damien, but it was an unthinkable idea.

She reached across the table and gently covered his large hand with her own. ''You are missing my point, Damien. Truth be told, you don't want another wife, yet your honor demands you offer for me. I share equally the responsibility for last night. I place no blame on you, nor do I hold you to any obligation.''

Snatching his hand away, Damien pushed back his chair and paced the room in agitation. Instead of appeasing him, her nobility irked him.

''Damn it, woman, can you never react as I expect?'' he muttered in frustration.

A sad smile came to Isabella's lips. ''What sort of reaction did you desire, Damien? Shall I be flattered that your honor demands you sacrifice yourself and wed a woman you do not want and do not love because she had the poor taste to seduce you?''

''I take responsibility for my actions, Isabella.''

Isabella uttered a slight cry of distress. ''I know how it feels to be a man's unwanted responsibility. My stepfather and grandfather have taught me that lesson all too well. I—I simply could not bear spending the rest of my life as yet another one of your many responsibilities,'' she finished, her voice breaking with emotion.

She rose to leave the table, but Damien prevented it with a firm hand on her wrist. He pulled her down forcefully until they were seated side by side.

"You are not unwanted," he said softly. His gaze drifted from her tear-filled eyes and rested meaningfully on her flat belly. "You must be practical, Isabella. You might be carrying my child."

Her contained manner vanished as her mouth dropped open. "It cannot be possible to conceive a child so quickly." Isabella rubbed her fingers furiously across her brow. "It was the first time. Well, first and second time," she finished lamely.

"Once is all that is needed. Catherine was born nearly nine months to the day after I wed Emmeline."

Isabella refused to be intimidated. She cast him a stern look, hoping to convey her determination against being manipulated into amicably bowing to his authority. "That still means nothing. There certainly is time to wait and see if there is a child before we discuss what is to be done."

She astonished herself with her calm response. Inside, the terror had taken a deep hold on her emotions. Buried in the deep recesses of Isabella's fantasies existed the longing to bear a child for Damien. But facing the actual possibility of a baby brought only a sharp pang of fear. It was wrong to use a child to hold a husband.

"We should marry immediately," Damien insisted, somehow sensing a weakness.

Isabella was frightened, but not convinced. If there was to be a child, then there would be no choice but marriage. But until she knew with certainty that she carried Damien's babe within her body, she refused to consider it.

Isabella knew firsthand the pain of a loveless marriage. She had witnessed for too many years her mother's unhappiness and her stepfather's bitterness. She didn't want that kind of life for herself. And perversely she did not want that for Damien. They both deserved better.

Proudly she lifted her head and announced with brutal honesty, "I will only marry for love."

A long silence stretched between them while he stared at her. His jaw clenched, and his expression hardened.

"My marriage to Emmeline was considered a success by society's standards," Damien finally said. "We led separate and very different lives. Yet it was not a particularly satisfying arrangement for either of us. I believe a large part of our mutual unhappiness existed because Emmeline and I entered into the marriage with very different expectations. I would not want to make that same mistake with you.''

Damien reached out and brushed a wisp of hair back from Isabella's cheek. ''You're a romantic. I never suspected.'' A mere hint of a smile crossed his handsome face. ''I respect you, Isabella, and I confess I have a great fondness for you. But I cannot, in good faith, make the kind of promises of romantic love you require.''

''Then I cannot marry you,'' she whispered softly in an anguish of yearning.

All other feelings faded away, and for one endless moment Isabella was filled only with regret. The earl sighed loudly and turned his head. Silently Isabella studied his taut profile, desperately wishing she could read his thoughts, understand his emotions.

''Please try to understand,'' she said softly. ''I could never accept the fact that you would be marrying me without love.''

The raw emotion in her voice told him beyond a doubt that she was being honest. Still, he was shocked to discover the idea of losing her was simply intolerable.

''I still insist we marry,'' Damien stated firmly.

''And I insist there is no need,'' Isabella replied, wanting to cry. She knew she should be proud of herself for holding fast to her convictions. A loveless marriage was truly hell on earth. Yet, despite all her noble affirmations, all she really felt was utter loneliness.

''Damien! Where the bloody hell are you, man!'' Jenkins burst unexpectedly into the dining room, his face flushed with color. ''You're not going to believe what I have just seen,'' the valet proclaimed as he crossed the room.

For one hysterical minute, Isabella panicked, thinking the valet had discovered the missing bed linen from the earl's chamber. Thoughts of an embarrassing scene filtered through her mind, but she soon realized that absent sheets would hardly send the unflappable Mr. Jenkins into such a tizzy.

"What has happened, Jenkins? Is it the children?" Damien's face contorted with concern.

"Catherine and Ian are fine," Jenkins assured his employer. He paused a moment to catch his breath. "A carriage has pulled into the drive. I swear, you will be astonished when I tell you who is riding inside."

"How cruel of you to ruin my little surprise, Jenkins," a strong male voice drawled from the open doorway, making his presence known.

Three heads turned in unison to view the speaker. Jenkins looked both worried and shocked, while Damien's steel-gray eyes darkened noticeably with anger. Isabella looked closely at the stranger, beholding a fashionably dressed man, probably in his mid-thirties, of average height, with fair hair, a pleasant though not exactly handsome face, and an erect bearing. Since no one had yet spoken his name, she had no earthly idea who he might be.

Damien stared incredulously at the man lounging in the doorway for several seconds before his anger exploded.

"Poole, you mangy mongrel. What in God's name are you doing here!" The earl leapt from his chair and lunged toward the stranger.

Isabella let out an involuntary screech at Damien's violent movement, but Jenkins apparently anticipated the earl's reaction. Moving swiftly, Jenkins placed himself between the two men, planting his hands firmly on Damien's wide shoulders. "He would like nothing better than to provoke you," the valet whispered sharply. "For pity's sake, Damien, don't give him the satisfaction."

Ignoring the servant's advice, Damien attempted to move around Jenkins, but the valet successfully blocked his way.

"I give you fair warning," Damien snapped "Remove yourself from my house. Immediately!"

"I have traveled a good distance to see my sister's children. And I have no intention of leaving until I do."

Lord Poole! Isabella's eyes widened in amazement as she realized the stranger's identity. It was no wonder Damien and Jenkins were acting so oddly. Looking back and forth between

the earl and Lord Poole, she clearly read the smoldering animos-
ity. Isabella moved forward, hoping to somehow lend her assistance. Turning toward Lord Poole, she said beseechingly,
"Perhaps it would be best if you called on us another day,
sir."

At the sound of her gentle voice, Poole broke eye contact
with the earl and focused his attention on the woman who
spoke. He had absently noted her presence when he first entered
the room, but had paid her little heed. All his attention had
been centered on Damien.

Turning his head aside, Lord Poole looked curiously down
at Isabella. What little color he had in his face quickly drained
away.

"My God," he exclaimed in shocked disbelief. He took
a small step toward her and reached out to touch her arm.
"Emmeline? Can it truly be you?"

"If you so much as lay a finger on her, Poole, I shall take
great delight in breaking it," Damien declared, his voice low
and lethal.

"Emmeline?" Lord Poole repeated softly, ignoring the earl's
threats, his deep blue eyes, never wavering, fixed on Isabella.

For a split second, Isabella wished she possessed the fortitude
to enact the charade. How simple life would be for everyone, she
thought morosely, if she was in truth the damnable Emmeline.

" 'Tis said I bear a distinct resemblance to your sister, Lord
Poole," Isabella replied steadily. "You are hardly the first
person to remark upon it."

Isabella threw a challenging stare at Damien. He frowned at
her, the firm set of his jaw declaring his determination to neither
agree nor disagree with her remarks.

Isabella had no choice but to introduce herself. "I am Isabella
Browning, Lord Poole. Governess to your niece Catherine and
nephew Ian." She would have offered her hand in greeting,
but she was afraid Damien would not allow it.

Lord Poole looked puzzled, and for a minute or two was
quiet as he weighed the introduction heavily in his mind. Then,
giving Isabella a pensive, but not unfriendly look, he asked,
"Are you really the governess?"

"Yes, she is," Damien forced out through tight lips.

Lord Poole's hollow laugh rang out loudly. "God almighty, Saunders, only you would be perverse enough to hire a governess who is the very image of my late sister."

"Matters of my household are no concern of yours, Poole," Damien retorted hotly. He definitely did not like the marked interest Poole was displaying toward Isabella. In another moment he half expected Poole to bow ceremoniously and kiss her hand in greeting. He doubted he would be able to control his temper if Poole actually touched her.

Shoving Jenkins out of the way, Damien stood toe to toe with his uninvited adversary. The sound of laughter died quickly as the room vibrated with their barely leashed hostility. The intense dislike between the two men was a tangible thing.

A muscle leaped in Lord Poole's jaw, but he held his tongue. Damien's temper burned brightly in his gray eyes, and his fists were clenched at his sides.

Jenkins scowled at the two men, knowing the slightest hint of an insult, spoken or gestured, would erupt in pandemonium. Moving close to the earl he whispered, "Remember, Damien. Keep thy friends close, and thine enemies closer."

The valet's words caused Damien to hesitate, then capitulate. Jenkins was right. Lord Poole had already declared his intention to visit Catherine and Ian. Damien knew from experience that Poole would not be dissuaded once his mind was set. He could keep a far better watch on Poole's activities if the man was nearby. Yet the thought of sharing his roof with his former brother-in-law left a decidedly sour taste in the earl's mouth.

Slowly Damien's expression changed. He shrugged his shoulders. "If you truly have come all this way to see Catherine and Ian, I shall not prevent it," he announced magnanimously. "In fact, I insist you stay at The Grange with us." Damien's smile was lethal.

Poole cleared his throat and fixed Damien with a penetrating look. "What a surprisingly civilized thing to do," Lord Poole replied smoothly. "Naturally I shall accept."

And then, to everyone's mutual astonishment, Lord Poole smiled at Damien and offered his hand. Damien ignored it, but after a censoring glance from Jenkins, the earl grudgingly accepted.

"I feel certain this will be a most enlightening visit," Lord Poole announced, his blue eyes never leaving Isabella. "Most enlightening."

Chapter Sixteen

Isabella was fully prepared to despise Lord Poole. In a perverse way, she was almost looking forward to it. Here at last was something tangible toward which to project her feelings of anger and frustration. While it was true that the entire blame for Isabella's current predicament could hardly be placed at Lord Poole's feet, his accountability in her troubles was still significant and Isabella intended to make full use of it. Yet one obstacle to her plan quickly became apparent. Lord Poole proved to be both a charming and a likeable man.

"I've brought some trinkets for the children," Lord Poole ventured from the schoolroom doorway. "If you have no objections, I'd very much like to give these gifts to my niece and nephew."

He stood a respectful distance away, clearly awaiting permission to enter the schoolroom. Isabella could not think of a valid reason to refuse his simple request without appearing shrewish.

"We have finished with our lessons for this afternoon. Please, come in, Lord Poole," Isabella invited in a chilled tone. "Catherine, Ian, step forward so I may present you properly. This gentleman has traveled all the way from London to visit you.

He is your Uncle . . . ?" Isabella turned a questioning eye to Lord Poole.

"Thomas," he supplied readily. "I am your Uncle Thomas. It would please me greatly if you would address me as such."

Lord Poole entered the room casually, his arms laden with several parcels of various shapes and sizes. A few were tied with string, and one large box sported an impressive red bow with matching ribbons. Both Catherine and Ian moved toward the stranger curiously.

Isabella noted that Lord Poole had changed his travel-stained clothes and was now elegantly garbed in immaculate doeskin breeches, a starched white linen shirt, an impressive waistcoat patterned in silver and gold, and a handsomely fitted dark brown jacket. The intricate tie of his cravat suggested that Lord Poole's valet had also made the journey from London. No man could be so well turned out in such a short span of time without expert assistance, and Isabella highly doubted Jenkins had offered his services to their unexpected guest.

Isabella studied him openly as he presented his gifts with a flourish to Catherine and Ian, allowing that Lord Poole was an attractive man, in a polished and florid way.

"Oh, look, Miss Browning," Ian called out excitedly as he pulled out a lethal-looking sword from the box his uncle gave him.

"My goodness, is that blade made from steel?" Isabella questioned in alarm, attempting but failing to extract the toy from Ian's grip.

" 'Tis made of wood," Lord Poole responded, "and painted rather cleverly to resemble metal. I'll own I know nothing of small children, Miss Browning, but even I possess the good sense not to purchase something that would pose a danger to my nephew." He took the sword from Ian and swung it experimentally in the air. It made a swishing sound. "I saw the sword in the window of a shop on Bond street and couldn't resist buying it. It seemed like great fun. I do hope you will enjoy it, Ian."

"Oh, I shall," Ian assured his uncle reverently, his young eyes shining with pleasure.

Clearly impressed by her brother's toy, Catherine anxiously tore into the large box with the red bow. Her disappointment was audible as she drew out an exquisitely dressed doll, its long golden hair elaborately coifed.

"It is very pretty, Uncle Thomas," Catherine said quietly, replacing the doll back in the box. "Thank you."

Ignoring Catherine's lukewarm response, Lord Poole hunkered down on the floor beside Ian and Catherine, intent on making a positive impression. "There are several more boxes to open, children. I certainly hope you will find something more to your liking, Catherine," Lord Poole said gently.

Backing away, Isabella allowed them a bit of privacy as she set the schoolroom to rights, but her eyes and ears strained often to the group on the floor. It was obvious that Lord Poole had indeed spoken the truth. He had little experience with children, but clearly he wanted very much to increase his knowledge.

A gift box crammed full of intricately painted toy soldiers met with a cry of delight from both Ian and Catherine. Riflemen, horse soldiers, infantry, even artillery was brought forth and exclaimed over. Isabella could almost feel Lord Poole's pleasure at the genuine smile Catherine bestowed upon her uncle. The three began an immediate campaign, pressing the new recruits into active duty.

After a time, Lord Poole stood to stretch his cramped limbs. He noticed that Isabella had remained in the room, and with Ian and Catherine effectively occupied, he seized the opportunity for a private conversation with their intriguing governess.

"You must excuse my forward manner, Miss Browning," Lord Poole insisted, as he drew himself in front of Isabella. "Your resemblance to my late sister is nothing short of remarkable. Please tell me something of your family history. I feel certain we must in some way be related."

Isabella deliberately swept her head aside, shielding her eyes. Recalling the many hours she had spent staring at the alluring painting of Emmeline, she admitted it was an idea that often crossed her mind. There was a similarity between her and Emmeline, a resemblance around the mouth and nose. And of course they shared an identical rare shade of violet eyes. And Isabella did not know the identity of the man who had sired her.

Perhaps she was related to Lord Poole and his sister. The notion piqued Isabella's interest and stirred her fears, yet she felt uncomfortable discussing the matter with a total stranger.

"We have never met before, Lord Poole," Isabella said softly. "If we were in fact related, I feel certain we would be acquainted."

Lord Poole shook his head in doubt. "The resemblance," he repeated softly. His finger reached out and grasped Isabella's chin firmly. He slowly lifted her face toward the light. "You are her very image."

"Only a rather bizarre coincidence, I am sure," Isabella insisted, pulling away from him. Lord Poole was beginning to make her edgy. He had prominent, light blue eyes and a way of dropping his lids over them to effectively shield his expression when he desired. Yet, more often than not, his light blue eyes held a faint look of mockery and his lips an ironic twist as he skillfully probed a reluctant Isabella about her past.

"Where did you first meet Damien? In London?"

Before Isabella could reply, she heard a muffled curse behind her and turned to find Damien watching them with a cryptic expression on his handsome face.

"I so hope I am not interrupting anything of importance," Damien drawled.

"I was just leaving," Lord Poole interjected smoothly. "I look forward to continuing our discussion at dinner this evening, Miss Browning." With a lithe movement, he bowed at Isabella, then turned toward the children to bid them good-bye. Grinning slyly, Lord Poole sauntered out the door, all the while pointedly ignoring the earl.

Isabella stepped forward hesitantly to face Damien, half afraid of the anger she would see in his smoldering gray eyes. But the earl seemed unimpressed by his brother-in-law's snub. Instead, Damien's attention was centered entirely on her, casting her a look that gave her a melting feeling right down to her toes. Isabella's cheeks heated with the memory of the torrid, intimate passion they had shared, the message in Damien's eyes conveying his strong recollection of that same event.

"I thank you for not further provoking Lord Poole," Isabella said in a desperate tone, determined to ignore the strong sensual current between them. "I know what an effort it took."

"Yes, it is indeed difficult for me. Behaving in a civilized and tactful manner is quite wearing," Damien remarked with a wicked glint of amusement in his grey eyes.

"Especially when one is so unaccustomed to acting civilly, my lord," Isabella promptly retorted.

Damien merely smiled at her cheeky response, pleased that she felt comfortable enough to engage in verbal fencing. His pride was still smarting from her refusal of his marriage proposal, and having fixed the idea firmly in his mind, Damien was now determined to have Isabella as his wife. He knew he could never win her over if he allowed Isabella to withdraw completely from him.

"Good gracious, what is all this?" the earl exclaimed distractedly as he noted the new toys and boxes strewn about the room.

"Uncle Thomas brought them for us," Ian explained. He picked up his new sword and lunged toward the earl. "Isn't it grand, Father? I'll wager you have one just like it."

"My saber is safely packed away in the attic, where it belongs," Damien replied as he neatly dodged his son's enthusiastic sword thrust. "For pity's sake, be careful with that thing, Ian." The earl's scowl deepened as he stared at the offending toy. "On no account will you aim this sword at your sister, or Miss Browning, or the servants, or any other living creature. Is that clear?"

"I am sure Ian will exercise great restraint when playing with his new toy, won't you, Ian?" Isabella said. Efficiently scooping up the soldiers from the floor, she quickly straightened out the room.

"It is nearly time for afternoon tea, children," Damien remarked. "Run down to the kitchen and tell Mrs. Amberly she may serve tea for the four of us in the drawing room. I'm sure Lord Poole will be otherwise engaged and unable to join us. However, Miss Browning and I will be in the drawing room shortly.''

The room quieted when the children left. Damien peered curiously into the large open box on Isabella's desk, discovering Catherine's new doll.

"Poole always did have a keen eye for the expensive,'' Damien said soberly. He experimentally tugged on a long golden curl that sprang instantly back to the doll's head upon release. "I suppose Catherine was enchanted.''

"Not especially,'' Isabella replied. She carefully replaced the cover on the box, effectively hiding the toy. "I honestly think she would have preferred a sword like Ian's.''

"Don't tell Poole, or one will appear with the morning post,'' Damien said with a mocking laugh.

"Your place in their affections is hardly threatened by a few toys.'' Isabella reached out and softly stroked the earl's forearm, sensing his discomfort. "Lord Poole cannot buy your children's regard, no matter how elaborate or expensive the gift.''

"Perhaps,'' the earl responded, his eyes troubled. "Yet he most assuredly will try.''

"This seems like a good spot, children,'' Isabella announced. "Let's set up our picnic here.''

Last night's heavy rains had thoroughly soaked the ground, but the section of open meadow not far from the house Isabella had selected for picnicking was covered in thick grass. Brilliant late-afternoon sunshine and unseasonably warm spring weather had combined successfully to dry out the worst of the puddles, although there was a thin layer of mud clinging to Isabella's boots and hem.

As she arranged the blanket, Isabella conceded it was rather late in the day and a bit too soggy to be eating out of doors, but the children had been in such high spirits after meeting their uncle that it seemed like the perfect idea. An *al fresco* dinner. Away from the subtle tension and veiled hostility of the house. And the fresh air might even make Mrs. Amberly's overcooked fare a tad more appetizing.

"We shall double our blankets so the dampness of the grass will not seep through," Isabella informed the children. "It will make for a cozier seating arrangement."

As soon as the simple meal of cold beef, cheese, warm bread, and milk was unpacked the children began eating with gusto. Isabella poured herself a cool mug of cider and helped herself to a small wedge of cheese.

"I do wish you had allowed me to bring my new sword, Miss Browning," Ian said between bites of beef. "This is the perfect place to play pirate attack."

"Pirates is a stupid game," Catherine sulked. "Ooooh, that's horrid, Ian. Don't talk when you have food in your mouth. I can see inside."

"Hush now," Isabella commanded softly, suspecting Catherine was more upset over not having a sword like her brother's than having to watch him eat his meal.

The children had quarreled heatedly over the toy after tea, leaving Isabella no choice but to confiscate it. She had hidden the sword in her room hoping, yet not really believing, that Ian would eventually forget about the cursed thing.

Deciding to take advantage of the momentary peace between the children, Isabella opened the large book she had brought and began reading aloud. The quiet meadow soon echoed with the soothing tone of her voice and the enthusiastic munching of her charges.

"An early evening picnic? Lucky for me, I've brought something to share. May I join you?"

The earl's startling appearance caused Isabella to lose her place in the story. Flustered, she repeated a sentence twice, then finally gave up and ceased reading.

The children clamored to their feet and eagerly embraced their father.

Without waiting for an invitation, Damien sprawled down on the small blanket, insinuating himself next to Isabella.

Her nose caught the tantalizing sweet smell of fresh berries. Damien held out a basket of fragrant strawberries.

"Try one," he coaxed.

Isabella shifted uncomfortably. The deep, silky pitch of his voice brought to mind all manner of sensuous pleasures that had nothing at all to do with fruit. Blindly, she reached out and filled her hands with the luscious berries.

Lounging back against the blanket, Damien propped himself up on his elbows, crossed his ankles and inquired casually, "Is that one of the barn cats over there on the hill?"

"Where? Oh, where?" Catherine shrieked, whipping her head about and dropping a half-eaten strawberry on the ground.

Damien grinned. "Right there, on the hill."

The earl pointed toward the top of a small grassy knoll, where a substantial-looking cat was languidly resting in the grass, washing himself in a dignified manner.

Catherine and Ian both jumped instantly to their feet, exactly as Damien had planned.

"I can see it! I see the cat!" Ian shouted. "It's the big orange tabby, my favorite."

"I want to pet him first," Catherine insisted, nearly knocking her brother off his feet in her haste to reach the animal.

"But I saw him first," Ian retorted.

Yelling and shrieking with excitement, the pair raced riotously across the meadow.

"Be careful or you'll frighten the poor cat away," Isabella called, pushing herself upright. She attempted to rise, but discovered she could not. Damien held her hand tightly against his chest.

The children quickly vanished in hot pursuit of their quarry. Damien wasted no time. He pulled Isabella down until she was nearly reclining next to him. Just being so close to her brought him a shivering thrill of anticipation. He fitted his length close to hers, pressing his leg deliberately against hers, wondering if she could feel the power of his desire for her.

"The children are perfectly safe. Besides, I find I like having you all to myself," he said thickly.

He saw her take a determined breath, but she did not move away. In fact, she appeared to press herself closer to his side. Damien's palms started to sweat.

He released her hand, reached over, and brushed his fingers against her cheek.

"Isabella." He spoke her name softly, tenderly.

She lowered her eyes, refusing to meet his gaze.

"Isabella," he repeated, stroking her neck with his open palm, feeling her tremble beneath his sensuous caress.

"This is madness," Isabella whispered, tilting her chin toward him in silent invitation. "Sheer madness."

He kissed her. With wild abandon. Even though they were outside in the light of day, even though his children were only a few hundred yards away, Damien's mouth descended commandingly upon Isabella's lips with hunger and need.

He kissed her passionately, totally without restraint. The emotions of last night, the frustrations of the day, careened inside him, nearly out of control. He sought comfort in her arms, he sought understanding, he sought acceptance. He wanted, nay he needed Isabella to feel every bit of his desire for her. He only dared to hope she would return at least a small measure of it.

She didn't disappoint him. She was warm and willing, and her tongue boldly met his as she melted against him. Cupping her face between his hands, Damien deepened the kiss. He pressed closer, crushing her soft breasts against his hard chest, seeking relief from the heat suddenly building inside him.

"Father! Miss Browning! Look what I've found!"

At the sound of Ian's voice, Damien and Isabella sprang apart. Damien bent his knee to hide the painful swelling in his breeches while Isabella turned away to shield the flush in her cheeks.

Apparently oblivious to the tension, the little boy breathlessly stumbled over the edge of the blanket. He opened his closed hands and proudly displayed his prize.

"A frog. I found a frog."

The creature made a belligerent croak; then, with a flying leap, dove across the blanket and landed directly in Isabella's mug of cider.

"Ian!" Damien shouted, as he rolled out of the way. "What the devil are you doing?"

"I'm so sorry, Father." The little boy squatted down and

plunged his hand into Isabella's cup. "I was holding his leg tight, but he got away. My frog is rather slippery."

After several attempts, Ian managed to rescue his new friend. He pulled it gingerly from the liquid and held it up for examination. The frog hung limply in his hand, dejected and dripping cider on the blanket. Ian shook it sharply, then turned to his father with bright, questioning eyes.

Isabella coughed discretely behind her hand, trying to disguise her laughter. Damien refused to meet her gaze, certain he would be unable to contain his own mirth if their eyes met.

"I believe the frog will feel better if you put him back where you found him, son," the earl said solemnly. "He is most likely missing his fellow frogs."

"Come along, Ian," Isabella stood on her feet, shaking off the stray drops of cider that had landed on her skirt. "We shall return him together."

"I'm sorry he jumped in your mug, Miss Browning."

" 'Tis all right. I suspect your young frog was thirsty. Do you suppose he had enough to drink before you pulled him out? Shall we give him one last dunk in the cider?"

Ian giggled. He allowed Isabella to dry, then wrap the frog loosely in a linen napkin. He held the cloth tightly, in one fist, then with only slight hesitation clasped her outstretched fingers with his free hand.

Damien watched them leave, feeling unexpectedly light-hearted. She was good for the children. Kind, patient, understanding. He remembered the harsh dictates of his own governess and was glad he was able to provide a far more pleasant experience for his children.

She would be, without question, an excellent stepmother.

Dinner for the adults that evening began as a strained affair. Isabella had overseen the arranging of the table herself, ensuring that no unpolished silver or cracked china was pressed into service. At first glance, the array of food on the sideboard gave a favorable impression. Closer inspection, however, revealed overdone beef, undercooked pheasant, soggy vegetables, and sauces with a decidedly burnt aroma.

Lord Poole made no comment on the unappetizing food, instead making a valiant effort to consume as much of his dinner as possible. Damien was uncharacteristically silent during most of the meal, but could not resist a comment when a dry piece of beef flew off Lord Poole's plate as he was attempting to cut it.

''I do hope you are enjoying our simple English fare, Poole,'' the earl commented with a mocking grin.

''As much as you are, I feel certain, Saunders,'' Lord Poole retorted. ''Hearty English fare can have great appeal. I often find the French chefs vastly overrated, don't you, Miss Browning?''

''On occasion,'' Isabella commented, privately thinking how wonderful it would be to be feasting on some overrated French chef's efforts right now.

''I recall one evening dining with Lord and Lady Lofting,'' Lord Poole continued. ''They so often boasted of having the finest *chef de cuisine* in London, but the man was a fright. On the night I was in attendance, he deliberately threw an entire tureen of hot lobster bisque onto the kitchen floor.''

''How childish,'' Isabella commented. ''Why did the chef do such a thing?''

''Apparently he was piqued by tardy arrivals in the dining hall.'' Lord Poole lowered his head apologetically. ''Regretfully, I must confess to being among them.''

''Regretfully?'' Damien's brows rose slightly. ''I strongly suspect you had prior knowledge of the Frenchman's obsession with promptness, Poole.''

Lord Poole smiled broadly. ''Perhaps I did hear a rumor or two about it at my club.'' He took a long swallow of his wine. ''Still, I can't image a man would be so foolish to allow a servant to take such advantage.''

''Indeed. How utterly ridiculous,'' Damien responded in a mocking tone.

Isabella cleared her throat noisily at the remark, her mind filling with the endless occasions when she had clearly overstepped her role as the earl's employee.

Mustering her courage, she risked a glance at Damien. He stared boldly at her, his gray eyes challenging. A quickening sensation jolted unexpectedly through her. Isabella's breath caught in her throat and her mind went blank for a crucial instant. Their eyes met and held, and Isabella's heart swelled with emotion.

The earl's lips curved slightly in an intimate, secret smile that left her feeling as if she had done something that pleased him enormously. She shyly returned his smile, and Damien winked broadly at her. Isabella's fork clattered noisily to her plate.

Her hands trembled as she reached down to retrieve her cutlery, while the strange, heady feeling persisted. Pulse hammering, Isabella deliberately took a large bite of dry beef, waiting for her scattered senses to return.

Fortunately, Lord Poole appeared unaware of her predicament. Polite conversation resumed. Then Jenkins brought in a silver bowl filled with strawberries.

"Luscious, ripe fruit grown on my own land," Damien stated proudly, his eyes pinned on Isabella. "Sweet nectar from the gods."

Isabella felt his stare, but refused to raise her chin. She elected instead to gaze at the fruit on her plate and remembered, with almost sad longing, the tenderness, the passion, the gentleness of his kisses earlier in the evening.

"You sound just like a yeoman farmer, Saunders," Lord Poole said scornfully, but he filled his plate with the appetizing morsels.

"Farming is an honest, noble profession, Poole. One I am proud to be successfully engaged in. Over the years I've learned a great deal from the men who work my lands." Damien leaned back casually in his chair. "Did you know that the secret to such large, sweet berries is an abundance of aged cow manure mixed in the soil?"

Lord Poole quickly dropped the strawberry he had been about to put in his mouth. It remained untouched upon his plate alongside the other luscious berries.

"Shall we adjourn to the salon, gentlemen?" Isabella hastily suggested. It seemed pointless to suggest the men indulge in port and cigars together while she withdrew. They would most likely come to blows if left alone.

In anticipation of this moment, she had asked Fran to ensure that the room was properly cleaned, aired, and fit for company.

Determined to favor neither man, Isabella ignored the two outstretched hands eager to assist her from her chair and majestically sailed from the dining room. Damien and Lord Poole followed complacently in her wake, but Isabella was not foolish enough to believe impending disaster had been completely thwarted. It was absurdly early to suggest retiring, and there were still several hours left in the evening for the uneasy peace to be shattered.

With each clicking step she took across the unpolished oak-floored hallway, Isabella racked her brain, searching for a stimulating yet safe subject upon which the three of them could engage in conversation. A true challenge indeed.

Lord Poole unexpectedly came to the rescue. Spying the recently polished pianoforte by the salon windows, he asked, "Are you musically inclined, Miss Browning?"

"In a rather limited fashion, Lord Poole."

He smiled encouragingly. "Perhaps you will be kind enough to favor us with a song."

"I shall gladly play a tune, Lord Poole," Isabella replied with a twinkling laugh, "but I must forgo the song. My grandfather once likened my voice to fingernails scratching a chalkboard. I regret to inform you that it was, in truth, a kind comparison."

Isabella positioned herself in front of the pianoforte, fussing for a few moments before sitting down. She gave only a cursory glance at the sheets of music neatly arranged on the music stand, recognizing the first piece as a classical composition far beyond her talent.

Instead she played from memory, slowly picking out the tunes, gradually playing with greater certainty as she remembered the correct notes. She played the simple melodic ballads she enjoyed from childhood, releasing long-suppressed memories of her mother. Although not possessing a great talent,

Isabella played from the heart, and her music had an exalted, vibrant quality that touched both men.

The final note died away, but the mood created by the music remained until a log in the fire crackled, showering sparks over the hearth.

"That was lovely, Isabella," Damien remarked sincerely. "I recognized a few of the tunes—Irish ballads, I believe. But I never heard the final song. It was charming."

"My mother always played it," Isabella said softly, her mind still filled with memories of her mother. "I don't recall the title."

"You of all people should know the name of that particular tune," Lord Poole spoke out. " 'Tis an old Spanish folk song entitled 'Fair Isabella.' "

Isabella looked with surprise at Lord Poole. "However would you know such a thing?"

"Quite simply. I too have memories of that ballad. When we were children, my father often played the piano for me and Emmeline. He had a talent for music that was certainly far greater than my mother's, and he took great delight in indulging himself."

"And the song?" Damien inquired sharply.

"In memory of his mother, my grandmother. Apparently you are unaware of my family history, Saunders. My paternal grandmother was half Spanish, a strikingly beautiful woman with thick dark hair and unusual violet eyes. She had an equally lovely name. Isabella."

Questioning looks of amazement passed between the earl and Isabella. Pitching his voice low, Lord Poole added softly, "An interesting coincidence, is it not?"

Chapter Seventeen

"Damn you, Poole!" Damien's anger broke through the silence that had enveloped the room. "What sort of bizarre game are you playing at now? I for one do not believe a word of that preposterous story."

"Your opinion is of no interest to me, Saunders." Lord Poole's tone was icily polite. "My only concern is for Miss Browning."

"Your only concern is for yourself, Poole. What is your plan? Do you think to come into my home and steal Isabella away from me with your preposterous lies? I will never allow that to happen."

"You don't own her, Saunders. This woman, who might very well be my half sister, merely has the misfortune of being employed in your household. I fear for her safety, and fully intend to do everything in my power to ensure that she does not end up like poor Emmeline."

"You bloody hypocrite!" Damien lunged toward Lord Poole.

"Stop it! Both of you." Isabella sprang to her feet, clapping her hands tightly over her ears to shut out their angry words.

She gulped helplessly as she felt the tears welling in her eyes, and she trembled with the effort it took to contain them.

Her outburst had the desired effect of stopping the earl in his tracks. His head turned, and Isabella could see the blazing fury in his smoky gray eyes. She shifted her glance to Lord Poole. His expression was unreadable, but his stance was rigid and his shoulders stiff with tension.

"How dare you discuss me as though I were a piece of property to be fought and bargained over. Your behavior is insulting, and I refuse to listen to another word from either of you."

Lowering her hands from her head, Isabella picked up her skirts, defiantly lifted her chin, and strode across the room, not sparing so much as a glance at the two men. Throwing open the door, she banged loudly out of the room. Her speed increased with each step she took, and by the time she reached the staircase she was sprinting.

Her thoughts tumbled wildly as she ran. Was it possible that Lord Poole spoke the truth? Could she in fact be his half sister? Ever since discovering her striking resemblance to Emmeline, the notion had festered in the back of Isabella's mind, yet she had deliberately refused to examine it closely. Hearing Lord Poole voice the possibility had shaken Isabella. Frightened her. Filled her with an equal sense of longing and dread.

Her mind spinning with shock, Isabella stumbled up the staircase, letting out a sob of relief when she entered the private sanctuary of her room. She felt a mild sense of satisfaction as she slammed the door loudly, and for good measure, turned the key to lock the door.

She took a few small steps and stood in the center of the room waiting vainly for the feelings of panic and fear to subside. Warm droplets of water fell on her wrists and it took a few moments before Isabella realized she was crying. Feeling a strange sense of detachment, she removed a fresh linen handkerchief from her pocket and wiped away the tears.

Isabella moved toward the center of the room and caught a glimpse of her pale face in the mirror by her dressing table. She immediately closed her eyes, forcing away the reflected image, wishing she could so easily dismiss the turmoil in her heart.

The knock she had expected and dreaded came the moment she sank down upon the bed.

"Open the door, Isabella. 'Tis Damien."

"Go away, my lord. I do not wish to speak with you."

Isabella heard Damien's exaggerated sigh and concluded that he was attempting to master his temper. The brass doorknob rattled noisily, but the lock held. "Open the door, Isabella."

He continued rattling the doorknob, and Isabella knew he would not be easily dissuaded. Rising on unsteady legs, she opened the door slightly. Fixing her gaze firmly on the earl's cravat, she repeated quietly, "Go away, my lord."

"I shall leave the moment we finish our discussion," Damien said as he nudged the door open with the palm of his hand and moved into the room.

Shoulders slumped in defeat, Isabella eased the door shut and slowly turned to face the earl. She kept her face lowered, attempting to master her emotions. She was certain the pain and vulnerability she felt was still mirrored in her eyes. And she felt compelled to shield Damien from her distress.

"First of all, I must beg your pardon for my behavior downstairs. Lord Poole usually acts like a braying ass, but that does not excuse my conduct." A self mocking expression touched the corners of Damien's mouth. "I am sorry."

"Do you think it is true?" Isabella asked, ignoring the earl's apology. She raised her head. "Could I be Poole's sister?"

"Half sister," Damien replied. He narrowed his eyes. "I'm not sure what I believe, Isabella. Yet I can't stop myself from hoping this is merely another of Poole's attempts to bring misery into my life."

Isabella stood watching him in silence for a long moment. Her hands began to tremble, and her stomach felt queasy. "Would you hate me? If it were true?" she finally whispered.

"I could never hate you, my dear." Damien moved forward and lightly touched Isabella's shoulder. "But in all honesty, I must confess I would be very pleased to prove Poole a liar."

"I see." A heavy weight settled in Isabella's breast. She

breathed deeply, but it would not ease. "Ever since I was told that Charles Browning was not my real father, I've longed to learn the truth about my birth. Yet I never let myself hope I could discover my real family, because I knew it was an impossible task. The answers died with my mother all those years ago. But tonight . . . tonight Lord Poole brought that hope back to life."

Isabella shut her eyes tightly, willing back the tears. "I am afraid, Damien. I am terrified to learn the truth, yet I am drawn almost against my will toward it. If I am indeed Poole's sister, then I have finally found the family I've hungered to know for so many years. And that discovery will, by your own admission, bring you misery. I don't want to hurt you, Damien."

"Isabella." Damien reached out and pulled her closely against him. A wave of guilt engulfed Isabella at his affection and concern, and her shoulders shook as she sobbed noisily.

Damien held her tightly, murmuring soothing words until her sobs became sniffles. Isabella shifted her position slightly and laid her head against his shoulder. She felt so secure in his arms. Taking the handkerchief from her pocket, she dabbed at her tears and gulped back the few remaining sobs.

"I am sorry," she said softly. "I never meant to lose such complete control over my emotions."

"It has been a shocking evening for both of us. A few tears are understandable." He touched her cheek. "I might shed a few myself before the night is over."

Isabella felt her lips curve into a smile. "I highly doubt that, sir." She stared into his handsome face, finding it impossible to picture him succumbing to tears when faced with adversity.

"I won't lie to you, Isabella," Damien said solemnly, his penetrating gaze never faltering. "I'm not thrilled with the notion of having Poole for a brother-in-law again."

Isabella's brows shot up in surprise. "That is hardly the issue, sir. I have no plans to marry you."

"We will marry," he said.

A look crossed his face that caused a stirring in Isabella's heart. She held her tongue, realizing with surprise that she had no inclination to argue the point with him. Although she had been adamant in her refusal of his marriage proposal earlier, her mind, prompted by her heart, now wavered. Perhaps they should marry. It was clear that Damien cared for her, maybe even more than he realized.

Isabella knew he was capable of love, for even though she had often insisted he devote more time to Catherine and Ian, she never once doubted the depth of love Damien carried for his children. Perhaps someday he would come to love her. The thought thrilled and humbled Isabella.

She gently pressed her palm to Damien's chest and felt his heartbeat. For one tiny fragment of time she swore their hearts thudded in unison. She raised her chin and slowly lifted her face toward his. Damien smiled and touched his lips to hers briefly, but Isabella could feel his desire. His eagerness. His hunger. It exactly mirrored her own needs. Pressing herself against him, she returned the kiss passionately, holding nothing back.

Her tongue met his boldly, imitating the strong thrusts she remembered from their previous joining. Damien's hands roamed her body with urgent gentleness, his lips trailing sweet, succulent kisses down her sensitive neck.

"Tell me to leave," he whispered huskily.

Her heart was beating like a drum in her ears, and it took Isabella a few moments to realize Damien had spoken. She tentatively raised her head. She could hear his uneven breathing in the silence and see her own blatant need reflected in his stormy gray eyes.

"What did you say?"

"Tell me to leave before I throw you down upon this bed and thrust myself inside your warmth." He slipped a hand beneath her skirt and possessively ran his palm up her leg to the apex of her thighs, emphasizing his meaning.

Isabella became still. She did her best to focus her vision on Damien's handsome features, but she felt lost in an erotic spell. Damien's hand remained between her thighs, pressing, rubbing, stroking. Isabella let out a small cry when she felt the hot wetness he brought forth. It was shocking. Scandalous. Leaning closer to him, Isabella nipped playfully at Damien's earlobe. Her hands moved beneath his jacket and waistcoat, and she kneaded his chest sensually.

"Please stay with me tonight."

Damien smiled broadly, jolting the aching heat in Isabella's body. "An excellent suggestion, my dear."

He swept her up in his arms and laid her down on the bed. He bent down and kissed her lips fully, his tongue caressing her warm mouth. She drew him against her body, running her hands through his thick, dark hair. Isabella could feel his fingers unbuttoning her gown and she smiled. It felt so right.

Damien's firm hands pushed the gown off her shoulders. He hastily untied the ribbons of her chemise and reverently lowered it to her waist.

"You are so very beautiful," he whispered. The sleepy, sensual expression on his face made Isabella shudder. He kissed her lips sweetly and then bowed to run his tongue over her bare nipple.

Isabella felt the warm tingling between her thighs immediately. She sucked in her breath and arched her shoulders, thrusting her nipple deep into his mouth. Her hands clawed at his back, tugging ineffectively at his shirt.

Damien rose to his knees, pulled his shirt over his head and flung it across the room. Isabella giggled.

Damien flashed her a wicked grin as he reached down and peeled off her remaining garments. His hot gaze remained riveted on her naked splendor as he impatiently tore off the rest of his own clothing.

His tongue caressed her navel and she felt acutely conscious of her femininity as he kissed the inner softness of her thighs. His breath was warm against the tight curls surrounding her womanhood as his kisses lingered on her upper thighs.

"Open for me," he urged.

The husky edge to his voice made her shiver. She spread her legs wide, then screamed with shock and embarrassment as Damien began to run his tongue up and down the most intimate part of her.

"You mustn't," she cried out weakly, feeling the blush spread through her entire body.

"So perfect," Damien muttered passionately, ignoring her protests. His fingers opened the delicate folds of her body and the tip of his tongue laved the sensitive bud.

Isabella went rigid as the emotions washed over her, overwhelming her. How deeply and completely she loved him! After a few moments of mind-bending tension, Isabella reached her peak. At her cry of release, Damien lifted himself and plunged deep inside her. A moan of pure pleasure passed her lips as she arched her body to fit his, her arms stealing around his neck to cling to him.

Damien's hips bucked back and forth in a frantic rhythm. Isabella looked up at him through narrowed eyes, and he reached down to cup her buttocks, bringing her even closer. His breathing labored as he quickened the rhythm, thrusting deeper. With each hard thrust, Isabella felt the liquid heat flowing over her as the fiery tension began to build once again.

"Let me hear you reach your pleasure, my sweet."

She moaned throatily, unable to stop herself. The swell of sensations coursed through her, and Isabella screamed as release came swiftly, almost violently. At the same time she felt a great shudder ripple through Damien and then the cool air against her skin when he suddenly jerked away. His rigid shaft pressed tightly against her upper thigh, throbbing insistently as it spewed forth sticky, wet semen.

Damien abruptly turned from her and lay flat on his back, his eyes closed, his breath coming harshly.

"What happened?" Isabella asked.

After a few moments Damien rolled to his side and propped himself up on one elbow. Brushing her cheek softly, he said, "You will be my wife, Isabella. But I'll not force you into this marriage by getting you with child."

Isabella's throat tightened with emotion. "Thank you," she whispered.

The earl left the bed, returning with a damp cloth. He efficiently wiped Isabella's thighs, then resumed his place beside her. Isabella immediately moved closer and Damien gathered her into his arms. Lying against his chest, listening to the steady beat of his heart, she gradually fell asleep.

* * *

Damien woke first and watched the sleeping Isabella with troubled eyes. A single candle burned low by the bedside, the flickering flame illuminating her delicate features. Her brows were knit together, and occasionally she murmured small, incoherent sounds. His chest tightened when he saw a small tear slip down the outer corner of her closed eye, wetting the hair at her temples. Damien raised his hand and wiped the glistening drop with his fingertip.

''All will be well, Isabella. You mustn't cry, my dear. All will be well.''

The words appeared to soothe her. She stirred, then quieted, her eyes never opening, her features visibly relaxing. If only he could so easily prevent their lives from unraveling, Damien thought grimly.

Poole's calmly uttered words had shaken Isabella, yet Damien admitted he was partly to blame for her distress. The contradictions she felt were directly related to the adversarial relationship he had with Poole. Damien sympathized with Isabella's awkward position, and seeing her in pain brought forth a need in him to comfort her, to somehow lessen the burden this mass of contradictions caused her.

There was only one possible course of action left to take. He would find the information she needed to ease her pain. He would discover who her true father was.

Without fully considering the ramifications of his intended actions, Damien carefully slipped from the bed. Isabella's torment would not ease until she learned the truth about her parentage. And Damien was determined to somehow uncover that truth. If Poole's suspicions were proved correct, and he was her half brother, Damien would be faced with the unpleasant task of forming a tolerant relationship with Poole. It was a bitter, unappealing notion, but for Isabella's sake Damien was willing to try. He owed her that much.

Damien made a final adjustment to the bedcovers before quitting the room. He strode silently across the hall into his bedchamber, noting that it was still dark outside. He lit several candles, then began removing clean clothes from his armoire and placing them on the bed.

The bedchamber door opened. Damien whirled around and beheld Jenkins in the doorway, a branch of lit candles in the valet's hand.

"Rearranging your wardrobe at this hour of the morning, my lord?" the valet asked, looking about the room in frank curiosity.

The earl turned his back on the servant and resumed his activities. "I am packing. I need to leave at first light."

"Packing?" Jenkins repeated. "You are planning a journey? Where?"

"To York. I am going to pay a call on Isabella's grandfather, the Earl of Barton."

Jenkins gave the earl a shrewd look. "I assume this will not be a social call."

"Hardly."

"Are you going to ask for her hand in marriage?"

Damien turned so quickly, he banged his shin against the bed frame. "Damn!" Bending at the waist, he vigorously rubbed the bruised leg, his gray eyes pinned on his valet. "I need no one's permission to marry Isabella, least of all that of a self-important earl who lacks the good sense to appreciate what a truly remarkable person she is."

"Then why are you going?"

Damien pierced his valet with an exasperated stare. "You know everything that goes on in this house, Jenkins. Usually before I do. I can scarcely believe you missed the drama that unfolded in the salon last evening after dinner."

Jenkins grinned sheepishly. "Lord Poole certainly turned Miss Browning's world upside down with his revelations," Jenkins said. "Do you believe she is related to Poole?"

"I am trying not to think about the matter too closely." The earl threw three linen handkerchiefs onto the bed. "What I truly desire is to smash my fist into Poole's smug face," Damien said as the anger flared within him. "Unfortunately, that will solve nothing."

Jenkins reached across the bed and began neatly folding the

earl's clothes. "You do realize, Damien, that you could end up losing her. Poole can offer her a far more comfortable life. A place in high society, elegant clothes and jewels, evenings spent at balls and parties and the theater. Given her meager existence working as a governess these past few years, Poole's rich, pampered lifestyle could easily turn Miss Browning's head."

"She is not like other women. It will take far more than a few baubles to impress Isabella." The earl gave Jenkins a long, searching look. "She brings out emotions and feelings in me I never knew existed. Her pain affects me, Jenkins, and I am compelled to do whatever I can to help ease it."

"Are you in love with this woman, Damien?"

The earl lowered his gaze, shocked to feel his ears warming with embarrassment. "I don't know."

Jenkins stared at Damien's bent head with knowing eyes and concerned features. "Poole will try to turn her against you while you are gone."

"I suspect he'll try," Damien said with a philosophical shrug of his shoulders. "However, I am not a complete fool. You will be here, and in my absence I expect you to keep things under control. And make certain you pay particularly close attention to our unexpected houseguest."

The valet's back stiffened with pride. "I shall do my best."

"Excellent." Damien nodded his approval. "I will write a note for Isabella, explaining only that I have left The Grange on urgent business. I prefer that she not know where I am going. The last thing I want is to raise false hopes."

Damien removed a sheet of paper from his small writing desk and quickly dashed off the letter while Jenkins packed the satchel of clothing. Handing the note to Jenkins, the earl added, "Be sure to deliver it to Isabella when she is alone."

"Of course."

The two men left the room, heading for the stables after Damien vetoed Jenkins's suggestion of a hearty breakfast before beginning his journey. His course set, Damien was anxious to begin his trip and would not waste time waiting for an uninspiring meal from Mrs. Amberly.

Jenkins insisted on saddling the earl's horse, and Damien paced the stables impatiently. Dawn was slowly breaking, and a faint mist covered the grass, permeating the air with a clean, sweet smell.

Jenkins led the earl's large stallion out to the stableyard. Damien swung up on his horse and gripped the reins tightly.

"Is there anything else you want done while you're away, Damien?"

The earl thought for a moment. "Poole has said nothing about the mortgages he holds against The Grange, but I feel certain he will begin pressing me for the funds very soon."

"Shall I make some discreet inquires about the value of the artwork hanging in the long gallery?" Jenkins asked.

Damien looked broodingly off into the distance. "As much as it angers me to think of selling off Ian's inheritance a piece at a time, it might be the only way to save the estate."

"Of course I could always find Lady Anne's treasure," Jenkins said with a faint trace of humor in his voice. "Even if the treasure is only half of its reputed worth there will be more than enough funds to pay off Lord Poole."

"Why not?" The earl gave his valet a grim smile. "Then after you have discovered the treasure, you may as well round up a few unicorns. I daresay Catherine and Ian will be enchanted with the notion of keeping a pair of them in our stables."

"I'll see what I can do," Jenkins replied with good grace.

The earl shook his head. How like Jenkins to try to ease these difficulties with a spot of humor. Yet the valet's unwavering loyalty gave Damien a feeling of strength. It made the impossibilities of the situation seem slightly less daunting knowing he wasn't facing them entirely alone.

A shaft of bright sunshine hit Damien's sleeve, warning him that the hour grew late. Giving Jenkins a salute of farewell, the earl dug his heels into the horse's flanks and tore off down the drive at a clipping pace, trying hard not to think overmuch on the problems he was leaving behind and what truths he might discover at the end of this impulsive journey.

Chapter Eighteen

"He is gone? The earl has left The Grange?" Isabella stared at Jenkins in disbelief.

"A most urgent matter called him away early this morning," Jenkins said, glancing nervously at the floor. "He left this note for you."

"I see." Isabella studied the sealed envelope the valet hastily thrust into her hands. A cold dread swept through her, and she struggled against voicing her fears. She thought last night they had shared a moment that went far beyond pure physical pleasure, yet something must have gone terribly wrong to cause Damien to flee without even speaking to her.

With shaking hands, Isabella broke the seal and quickly read the note.

> *Urgent business calls me away, my dear. I shall return as quickly as possible. Watch over Catherine and Ian for me. Have faith. Damien.*

"Bad news?"

"No," Isabella answered, tensing warily at the sound of Lord Poole's voice. Determined not to be caught wallowing in self-pity, she turned her head toward him as he entered the dining room and smiled brightly. Crushing the note in her hand, she slipped it unobtrusively into the pocket of her gown. "Will you join me for breakfast, Lord Poole?"

"I would be delighted." Lord Poole glanced about the empty room with obvious interest. "No doubt Saunders is already outside mucking about the estate. I shall enjoy having you to myself this morning."

Isabella's smile disappeared. "The earl has been called away on business."

"Wonderful. I hope he will be gone a long time." Lord Poole removed the bread rack from the sideboard and placed it on the dining room table. He retrieved the butter dish and jam pot, set them cozily on the table, and then held out a chair expectantly. "Sit down, Miss Browning. I will ring for coffee. Or would you prefer chocolate?"

"Coffee will be fine."

A stone-faced Mrs. Amberly answered Lord Poole's summons, and Isabella watched in amazement as he charmed the housekeeper with a few softly spoken words and a dimpled grin. Leaving the room with a broad smile, Mrs. Amberly returned quickly with a steaming pot of coffee and a large dish of coddled eggs that actually looked appetizing.

Isabella selected a piece of bread, declining the offer of eggs. She sipped her coffee quietly and studied Lord Poole openly as he ate his breakfast. He seemed a man accustomed to being in the company of women, and he possessed an effective manner for dealing with them. She assumed he was unmarried since Damien had never mentioned a Lady Poole. Isabella strongly suspected Lord Poole was a favorite with the unattached ladies of the *ton* due to his pleasant face and polished manner, not to mention his wealth and title.

"You are rather quiet this morning, Miss Browning. I trust you slept well?"

"Fine," Isabella said. Swirling the dregs of her coffee in her porcelain cup, Isabella suddenly felt nervous and uncertain. "Actually, that is a lie, Lord Poole. I did not sleep well last night. And we both know why."

Lord Poole's expression was unruffled. He forked in a final bite of egg, then carefully placed his cutlery on his dish. "I upset you last evening with my outburst. I deeply regret any discomfort I inadvertently caused you."

"You showed little interest in my feelings last night. I was given the impression your words were meant for Damien, not for me, my lord," Isabella said. She glanced at him suspiciously, but his placid expression revealed nothing. "I wonder even now if you spoke the truth about your family."

"Of course I told you the truth." Lord Poole pressed Isabella's forearm urgently. "I would never lie about something this important."

"Then I suppose I must consider the possibilities." A nervous fluttering began in Isabella's stomach. "My mother died when I was eight years old, and I discovered the day I left my home that the man who married my mother was not my natural father. Perhaps we *are* related."

"I feel certain you are my sister," Lord Poole responded quickly.

"I find this difficult to accept, without proof of paternity. My resemblance to Emmeline coupled with my name could be a unique coincidence, Lord Poole."

"Please, call me Thomas. And I shall feel honored if you will allow me to address you as Isabella." He smiled broadly at her slight nod of acceptance, and Isabella felt the tension ease from his grip. "I require no additional verification of your identity, but naturally I shall pursue the matter if you wish. My father passed on ten years ago; my mother preceded him by a year. There was no reference to a child in any of his papers. Had I known of your existence, I would have moved heaven and earth to find you."

"Thank you." Isabella took a deep breath and released it slowly, realizing that the anger she had felt toward him last night was fading. It was difficult to remain aloof from him when he demonstrated such concern.

Lord Poole's glance shifted to his empty coffee cup. "I would like to know more about you, Isabella. What was your mother like? Your childhood? And how did you ever end up here, working for the earl?''

It was a strange and unusual sensation for Isabella to be the focus of such intense interest. She had rarely spoken about herself or her life with anyone. No one had ever cared enough to ask. Except Damien.

To her annoyance, Isabella's first inclination was to invent a cozy, carefree childhood and a gay, frivolous adolescence. Shaking off the impulse, she slowly refilled Lord Poole's coffee cup and her own before speaking.

''I've led a rather quiet life, Thomas. I have no doubt you will find it dull and uninspired.''

Lord Poole made no reply. And because he didn't press her, or ply her with cloying sympathy and insincere soothing words, Isabella gradually revealed the circumstances of her youth.

She spoke of her mother's death and her childhood fears. She told him of her grandfather's indifference, her great aunt's cruelty, her longing for a warm and loving family. She related tales from her life as a governess and revealed the bizarre events that had brought her to Whatley Grange.

Isabella nearly spoke of her love for Damien, yet managed to hold back at the last moment. She knew Lord Poole would be displeased, and she did not want to jeopardize the fragile bond she was forging with him.

''Life has treated you unfairly, Isabella.''

''There are many poor souls in this world that have suffered far more than I have,'' Isabella said, disliking the edge of pity she heard in Lord Poole's voice.

''Yes. But those unfortunate creatures are not my sister,'' he replied very quietly. ''I know I cannot change the past, but I will do everything in my power to guarantee that your future holds the fulfillment of all your dreams.''

Isabella's violet eyes widened. ''That is a bold promise, sir,'' she said breathlessly.

Lord Poole laughed. ''You will soon learn I follow through on all my promises.'' He stood up. ''Come along,'' he said, extending an arm to her. ''I know just where we shall start.''

Isabella rose to her feet. "Where are we going?" she asked as they entered the foyer, her mind whirling.

"To the village. To buy you a new frock," Lord Poole said.

"Oh, no." Isabella pulled up short. "I have far too many things to do today. And I must look after Catherine and Ian."

"They may accompany us."

Isabella shook her head vehemently. "No." She offered no further explanation. As much as she would dearly love a fashionable new gown, Isabella felt decidedly uncomfortable at the suggestion. It was far too intimate a gesture. Besides, Damien would be furious.

Lord Poole accepted her refusal, but Isabella could tell by his hardened expression that he was not pleased. To his credit, he did not press the matter and escorted her up the main staircase, his voice and manner extremely polite.

They rounded the second story landing, but instead of proceeding up to the third floor, Lord Poole pulled Isabella down a dark hallway. She had never previously ventured into this part of the house, but Lord Poole appeared confident of his destination. Eventually he stopped in the middle of the hall and stood silently before a closed door. Isabella could feel the trembling of his arm through his thick cloth jacket.

"Is something wrong, Thomas?"

"This was Emmeline's room," he whispered reverently.

He reached up, and with the tip of his finger gently caressed the intricate wood carving in the center of the door. Isabella placed a hand on his shoulder, offering silent comfort, but Lord Poole ignored her and continued staring at the door, his expression morose.

"The children are waiting," Isabella finally said.

The sound of her quiet voice appeared to awaken him from his catatonic state and Lord Poole jerked forward suddenly, thrusting open the door.

With a startled cry of surprise, Isabella followed him inside. The room was huge and cold and held a faint, though not unpleasant odor. Lord Poole took slow, even steps as he walked to the center of the room, his demeanor pious and somber.

"Everything appears to be as it was," he whispered softly.

Strolling about the room with a glazed expression, he touched each piece of furniture, dipping his fingertips into the layers of dust as if it were holy water. Stopping in front of the large mahogany armoire, Lord Poole yanked hard on the delicate knob. Isabella gasped when the door opened, and she caught a glimpse of frothing colors. The wardrobe was literally stuffed with women's clothing. Lord Poole pulled out a silver ball gown, his hands trembling visibly. Several other dresses fell out of the wardrobe onto the dusty carpet.

Drawn toward the amazing sight, Isabella ventured closer. She had never seen so many beautiful dresses. There were low-necked gowns of silk and satin with puffed sleeves and decorated hems, muslin dresses embroidered with small flowers and frilly flounces, and walking dresses of stiff cotton in vibrant patterns trimmed with buttons, lace, and bows. The colors were as varied as the styles and materials, shades of blue, silver, gold, green, red, and yellow.

Lord Poole continued riffling through the garments and several more dresses fell to the rug. He disregarded them.

"I don't recognize these gowns," he said in dismay. His movements grew frenzied as he searched among the clothing. "I cannot recall seeing Emmeline dressed in any of these garments."

Isabella watched in confusion while Lord Poole picked up the silver ball gown, held it close to his nose, and inhaled deeply. His eyes were sorrowful when he solemnly proclaimed, "Emmeline never wore this dress. I do not smell the sweet floral perfume she favored."

He quickly retrieved another gown from the pile on the floor and repeated the process.

"I don't believe she ever wore any of these dresses," he said, after sniffing several more.

"They are all so beautiful," Isabella said, fingering the smooth satin of a jade green ball gown. "And very costly."

"Naturally. Emmeline always had the best, the most expensive of everything. It was no less than she deserved."

"The earl was very generous," Isabella said dryly.

"I paid for these dresses!" Lord Poole's voice was harsh.

"That pitiful excuse for a monthly allowance that Saunders gave Emmeline wouldn't have kept her in new gloves. I handled all of Emmeline's personal finances. All the tradesmen sent their bills directly to me for payment. It was I who cared enough to make certain that Emmeline was given everything she desired, not her husband."

Isabella nodded her head silently, unsure how to respond. Turning away from the grief and passion in Lord Poole's eyes, she began retrieving the dresses from the floor and carefully returned them to the wardrobe.

Eventually Lord Poole joined her. He lifted a white muslin dress embroidered with small blue-and-red flowers and held it toward Isabella.

"Try it on," he urged.

"I couldn't!"

"Please, Isabella. For my sake. Try on the dress."

Isabella glanced at the lovely frock with misgivings. She had never worn such a delicate, fashionable garment. The high-waisted gown had long sleeves with ornamental ruches at the wrists and a blue velvet band that crossed beneath the breasts. Isabella thought the simple, elegant style was romantic without being too fussy. Lord Poole pressed the gown into her reluctant arms.

Isabella felt her resolve falter as she clutched the dress. She was being silly. What harm would it do to merely try the dress on? It seemed such a little thing to make him happy.

"I'll be back in a few moments."

Once in her own room, Isabella changed quickly, the front fastenings in the bodice of the gown enabling her to dress unassisted. After closing the tiny pearl buttons at her wrists, Isabella anxiously turned to view herself in the cheval mirror. The high neckline enhanced the slender column of her neck and the soft white muslin brought out the natural pink tones of her high cheekbones. Eyes sparkling with delight, Isabella modestly admitted the dress looked good on her. Smiling, she left to show Lord Poole.

He brightened visibly when she reentered the room and

rushed forward to greet her. Isabella felt the coldness in his hand when he touched her fingertips.

Still clutching her hand, he stepped back and studied her closely, his eyes narrowed. "You look charming, Isabella, yet something is not quite right." Lord Poole dropped Isabella's hand and circled her slowly, stroking his chin. "It's your hair. Emmeline always wore her hair down."

Without asking permission, Lord Poole yanked a pin from Isabella's tightly bound chignon. She was startled by the action, but when he reached for a second pin, Isabella threw her arm up in defense and grasped his wrist firmly.

"I am not Emmeline," she whispered softly.

Lord Poole stared at her long and hard. His pleasant features tightened in annoyance and his blue eyes darkened, deep and fathomless. Isabella shivered.

"Forgive me," he said finally.

"Miss Browning! Miss Browning! Where are you?"

Catherine appeared unexpectedly in the open doorway. "Ah-ha, I have found you. Ian and I are having a contest, and now I have won."

Isabella released her grip on Lord Poole's arm and backed away from him. His expression was once again kind and pleasant, but Isabella could not easily dismiss his former anger.

"If you have found me, Catherine, then Ian is still searching. We must go and tell him that the game is over," Isabella said, trying to keep her voice from giving away her confused emotions.

"May Uncle Thomas come also?" Catherine asked.

"He will join us in the schoolroom this afternoon," Isabella said. Composing her face into an expressionless mask, she addressed Lord Poole, "We all look forward to seeing you later, Thomas."

Lord Poole's eyes clashed with Isabella's, but he said nothing as she and Catherine escaped into the hall.

Lord Poole remained standing in the center of the empty room. His head felt light and he rubbed the back of his neck, trying to massage away the tension. He tried to focus on the events of the last few minutes, but random images of Emmeline flittered in and out of his mind.

A deep, terrible yearning filled his body. His chest hurt and his lungs burned. Slowly he released the breath he'd been holding. A ghost of a smile lit his mouth.

He was making progress, of that he felt certain. Yet he must be more careful in the future. Isabella had clearly been frightened when he tried to arrange her hair. He was sorry for that, but the excitement of seeing her dressed in a gown made for Emmeline had overwhelmed him.

How very much alike the two women were! The softness of their skin, the sparkle of their eyes, even the lilt of their voices were the same. Thomas closed his eyes, savoring the memory.

The images in his head were jumbled and confused, and they meshed and merged before a clear picture of Emmeline floated into his mind. He clung to it. It was a miracle, truly a gift from God. The fates had smiled upon him and he was grateful. He had found his beloved Emmeline. And he vowed never again to lose her.

Chapter Nineteen

"His lordship has consented to a brief audience."

Damien glanced up at the stone-faced butler and scowled darkly. After riding hard for two days, he had been kept waiting for nearly three hours in the Earl of Barton's great hall, with its painted and gilded dome, wide, sweeping staircase and richly appointed, uncomfortable furniture. His temper was stretched taut, yet he had managed to hold it in check by sheer force of will and alternatively pacing in front of the huge fireplace and sitting straight-backed on the edge of a wooden chair.

Damien now drew himself up to his full height and glowered at the butler, releasing some of his inner tension. The servant never flinched, but pivoted on his heel and silently led the way from the hall. Good Lord, Damien thought, the man's face would surely shatter if he ever did anything so frivolous as smile.

Eyes pinned firmly on the thinning patch of hair on the crown of the butler's head, Damien followed the servant from the room, his booted feet echoing on the black-and-white marble tiles.

He was ushered into a formal salon, vast in size, and furnished with impressive and expensive antiques. The Earl of Barton was seated on a large sofa near an open window, but he rose expectantly to his feet when Damien entered the room.

"Damien St. Lawrence, the Earl of Saunders," the butler announced, closing the door soundlessly as he left.

"Now that I've set eyes on you," Barton greeted him, "I'm certain I don't know you. What do you want?"

"Good afternoon." Though he was far too acquainted with adversity, even Damien was surprised by the openly hostile greeting. Deciding to counter the attack with overt politeness, he executed an exaggerated bow and said, "Thank you for seeing me so promptly, sir."

The older man stiffened. "State your business. And be quick about it." He resumed his seat on the sofa and airily waved his hand in the direction of a chair.

Damien surmised that half-hearted gesture constituted an invitation to be seated. He remained standing.

"I've come about your granddaughter, Isabella Browning."

"Gotten herself into trouble again, has she? She always was a high-spirited miss. Well, out with it boy. What's she done this time?"

"She hasn't *done* anything, sir. Isabella is currently employed as governess to my children and doing an excellent job."

"An excellent job, you say?" The earl lifted his gray eyebrows. "You arrive at my home uninvited and unannounced and wait three hours to see me. Judging by the mud spattered on your boots, you've traveled a fair distance. Do you mean to say you went to all that bother just to tell me that Isabella is a competent employee? I think not. I may be old, but I've still got my wits about me. What's she done? Has she gone and ruined herself like her witless mother?"

Damien felt his face flush. He took a deep breath and moved slowly toward the edge of the room, determined not to be bested by his own temper or this disagreeable old man. Stalling for time, Damien set himself near the fireplace and casually perched an elbow upon the mantel.

"I want to know who Isabella's natural father was."

The earl made no reply. Damien caught a glimpse of the

older man's reflection in the gilt-edged mirror at the opposite side of the room. His stoic facade had not cracked, but his face had become a hollow shade of ash.

"I cannot see how this is any business of yours, Saunders. Unless you object to having my bastard granddaughter caring for your children."

"You are a reprehensible old fool," Damien said, unable to dispel the flash of pure fury that sprang up within him. He leaned forward and stared steadfastly into the earl's eyes, exuding an aura of determination and power that momentarily stunned his adversary. "Tell me what you know about Isabella's father."

"Nothing. I know nothing." Damien watched the earl's face turn dark. "Marianne was my youngest daughter. Most folks said she was the prettiest. She was a shy, quiet girl who kept mostly to herself. Then one day she came to me and tearfully confessed she was going to have a child. She told me some nonsense about being in love with the babe's father, but she couldn't marry him. Blast it, she wouldn't even tell me the bounder's name. I was so furious, I refused to listen to her pathetic explanations and locked her in her bedchamber.

"After a week of isolation, I thought she'd crumble and tell me everything, but the stubborn chit wouldn't say a word. I knew I had to do something, so I took Marianne down to Kent, hoping to get Charles Browning, a local doctor I knew, to fix everything. But somehow she convinced the buffoon not to abort her child. I told her she could come home with me if she would reveal her lover's name, but the obstinate girl refused. I left her with Browning and never set eyes on her again. Eventually Browning married her. She wrote me once, when her child was born, but I saw no need to reply."

Damien felt his stomach turn. How could a parent be so harsh with his own child as to reject her during the greatest crisis of her life? Damien's heart filled with empathy for the frightened young Marianne, finding herself in such a dire predicament, having no one to turn to but this hard, unfeeling monster of a parent.

"And the child's true father?" Damien asked.

"I never found out. Browning sent Isabella here when the

girl reached seventeen. My sister Agnes questioned her, but the girl didn't know anything. She had always thought Browning was her father. I guess her mother never spoke of it. Marianne protected her lover to the end.''

The bitterness in the old earl's voice echoed through the vast room. Damien heard it, but failed to be moved. Clearly Isabella's grandfather was an unnatural parent. He had willfully abandoned his daughter and deliberately shunned his granddaughter. As far as Damien was concerned, these bleak memories were precisely what the earl deserved.

A odd combination of anger and pity swept through Damien when he thought of Isabella living in this household with her cold, unforgiving grandfather. How isolated and lonely she must have been. Feeling the need to get away, Damien bowed curtly in the earl's direction.

"Good day, sir."

Damien left quickly, not bothering to wait for a servant to escort him out. He had taken no more than three steps outside the room, however, before being ambushed by a woman with light gray hair and a deeply lined face.

"Where are you off to in such a rush?" the woman demanded. She stood directly in front of Damien, boldly blocking his path while leaning heavily on her gold-tipped cane. "I heard your discussion with my brother. Not all of it, mind you, but enough to understand the gist of it."

"You must be Isabella's Great-aunt Agnes," Damien decided. He remembered the cruel treatment Isabella had received from this woman and favored her with a stare that usually sent warning chills down a recipient's spine. "Goodbye, madam."

Damien made a motion to go around the woman, but Aunt Agnes thrust up her cane, laying it sharply against Damien's arm in a forestalling manner. "It will take more than a brooding stare to chase me off, young man. Of course, if you aren't interesting in finding out the truth, you'd best be on your way."

"You know who Isabella's father was?"

"Ah, so now I've caught your attention." Agnes lowered

the cane slowly, her eyes darting about the empty hall. "Who are you?"

"Damien St. Lawrence, Earl of Saunders."

"No, no. I heard all that already. I want to know *who* you are."

"I am a friend of Isabella's."

"A friend, heh?" Agnes grunted her opinion of his answer. "No matter. Come along, I've got something to show you."

She marched away from the drawing room, leaning on her cane yet keeping her spine stiff. She never once glanced over her shoulder to see if he followed. Damien ignored the doubts that crept into the back of his mind and accompanied Agnes. She led him through several grandly furnished rooms toward the private apartments at the back of the mansion. Eventually they entered a bedchamber decorated in shades of blue. The delicate furniture boasted a high polish, but the room had a closed, unused smell to it.

Agnes stared about the chamber vacantly for a moment, then advanced with great purpose toward a small trunk tucked away in the corner of the room.

" 'Tis over here, young man. Come along now, you can't expect an old woman like me to manage such a heavy burden."

"What is this?" Damien asked as he dragged the trunk into the center of the room, surprised by its weight.

"These were Marianne's things—at least, what is left of them. My brother had her room stripped and ordered all her belongings burned after he left her in Kent. But I bribed a footman to let me take what I wanted before they lit the fire. I stuffed this trunk full of anything I thought might yield me a pertinent clue. I've spent many an afternoon looking through these things, trying to determine who planted that seed in Marianne's belly."

Damien's mouth twisted. "You didn't send the trunk to your niece? Did it never cross your mind, madam, that Marianne, frightened and living among strangers, might have found comfort in having a few of her belongings?"

"Seeing the remnants of her former life would have reminded

the foolish girl of everything she threw away with her impetuous and immoral behavior.''

''What was Isabella's reaction when she viewed the contents of this trunk?'' Damien asked.

''I never showed it to her.''

That cold answer, coupled with the sharp tone of Agnes's voice, was all the justification Damien needed. Bending at the knees, he squatted down and hoisted the trunk on his left shoulder. Grunting loudly, he stood up, rocking back on his heels slightly until he regained his balance. Using his right hand to steady the burden on his shoulder, he headed for the open door.

''What are you doing? Where are you going with my trunk? I want you to open it here and tell me if you see anything of significance.'' Agnes pounded her cane on the floor. ''Put down that trunk, young man! I will not allow you to take it from this room.''

''Try and stop me,'' Damien said, glancing down at Agnes's horrified face. He stomped out the door, kicking it shut with his booted foot. Turning around, he leaned against the wall, a look of triumph on his handsome face. Fingers fumbling, he located the brass key and gleefully turned the lock.

Deliberately ignoring the sharp noises and indelicate language emanating from the other side of the door, Damien carried his booty through the house. He reached the main landing and smiled broadly, experiencing a sense of profound pleasure when he remembered the astonished expression on Agnes's face.

He entered the great hall and encountered several footmen, but no one questioned him. Damien was grateful the earl ran such a rigid household; these properly trained servants would never think to interfere with the behavior of any member of the nobility, even if he was a stranger to them.

An expressionless flunky obligingly opened the front door, and as Damien exited he took great delight in dropping Agnes's door key into the large potted plant by the entrance.

Damien found his horse tethered in the stables, and upon his command a young groom willingly saddled the animal. Damien mounted his stead and with the lad's assistance positioned the heavy trunk in front of him, resting it awkwardly on the saddle.

He would need to hire a carriage for the journey back to Whatley Grange, but Damien felt it prudent to put himself a fair distance away first.

Fishing into his pocket, he retrieved a coin. He flipped the crown in a high arc, and the groom caught the glittering silver piece in midair.

"By the way, Lady Agnes is locked in a second-story bed-chamber. Please be sure to inform the household of her unfortunate predicament." After a slight hesitation, Damien added with a sly wink, "In about three hours."

Precariously balancing the heavy trunk in front of him, Damien rode down the sweeping drive, feeling an enormous sense of relief at leaving the mansion and its occupants behind him.

Damien leaned out the carriage window and smiled. After four days of traveling in a hired coach, Whatley Grange at last loomed in the foreground, a towering fortress of gray stone. It was a marvelous sight.

When the coach drew nearer, however, Damien was struck by the unmistakable air of dignified neglect. Conditions that had existed for years without drawing his attention were suddenly brought to the forefront. The formal flower beds were choked with weeds, the waters of the lily pond murky and gray, the arbors and shrubberies wild and overgrown.

Yet in Damien's mind nothing could detract from the splendor of The Grange. He remembered the strict, expensive elegance of Isabella's grandfather's estate and realized he much preferred the reckless disorder of his own lands.

At least they still were his lands. Damien's mouth curled grimly. He did not regret his trip to York, but concentrating on Isabella's dilemma had relegated his own considerable problems to the background. Damien had no doubt that Lord Poole would make good on his threats and take control of The Grange if Damien was unable to secure the necessary funds to reclaim the mortgages.

The coach hit a deep rut and listed to one side. Damien

braced his feet on the floorboards as the carriage righted itself and glanced at the trunk perched opposite him on the cushioned seat. It did not budge.

Damien was sure the driver he hired thought him addle-brained for keeping the thing inside the coach instead of lashing it to the back, but Damien felt a strange reluctance to let the trunk out of his sight. He had not opened it, first because he was in haste to be away, but later because he felt he had no right. The trunk belonged to Isabella, and he intended to present it to her intact.

The coach slowed and drew to a halt at the front door of The Grange. Damien jumped down from the vehicle, then reached in to haul out the trunk. Cradling it in his arms like a child, the earl turned to the driver.

"You are welcome to spend the night. The stables are around back. Joe will assist you with the horses, get you some dinner, and show you where to bed down."

The driver accepted the invitation with a gap-toothed grin. Flicking the reins sharply, he drove the tired team toward the stables.

"Good afternoon, Mrs. Amberly," Damien said when the housekeeper finally answered his persistent knocking. He set the trunk down and removed his gloves and greatcoat. "It is good to be home. Be sure that someone brings this trunk into my study immediately. I trust that all is well with the children? And Miss Browning? Are they in the schoolroom having lessons?"

"Everyone's in the drawing room," Mrs. Amberly answered. She gave the earl a sidelong glance. "Having tea."

Damien was in too much of a hurry to take interest in the housekeeper's sullen tone, so he left without further inquiry.

As he entered the drawing room, he immediately noticed the changes. The room was sparkling clean and smelled like roses and beeswax. Yet that was hardly the only difference. Isabella, Lord Poole, and the children were enjoying an elegant tea. The silver gleamed, the napkins were snowy white, and the china unchipped. There were platters of small sandwiches, delicate pastries, flakey scones, fresh fruit tarts, and other elaborate confections that could not possibly have come from Mrs. Amberly's kitchen.

Ian spotted the earl and jumped up, nearly knocking over his overflowing plate of treats.

"Father! Catherine, look, Father is back!"

The children rushed to embrace him, and Damien felt his heart swell. It was good to be home.

"Ah, the master has returned," Lord Poole drawled in a censorious voice. "How delightful."

His tone was like the prick of a needle, but Damien refused to be baited. However, one look at Isabella, fashionably garbed in a charming gown of light green muslin trimmed with ribbons, sent all his good intentions flying out the window.

"Hell's teeth, what's going on here? And where the devil did you get that dress, Isabella?" The words were out before Damien could stop himself, and he hated how harsh and jealous he sounded.

"I gave Isabella these garments, Saunders," Lord Poole said. "Not that it is any of your business."

"Anything that concerns Isabella is my business, Poole." Damien's gray eyes were smoldering as he captured Isabella's eyes across the room.

The color washed into her cheeks. She lowered her lashes, picked up a light green lace-edged fan that matched her gown, and began moving it vigorously. Damien saw Lord Poole reach for Isabella's free hand and squeeze it in a gesture of comfort and reassurance. Then Lord Poole turned his eyes to Damien, his expression resembling that of a small boy gloating over a favorite toy.

A hot wave of resentment clogged Damien's throat, and he gave Lord Poole a violent stare. "I thought you'd be long gone by now, Poole. When are you leaving?"

"Whenever it suits me."

"Would you care for some tea, Damien?" Isabella interjected. Her face was set in grim lines.

"I have important matters I need to discuss privately with you, Isabella," Damien said, pointedly ignoring her offer of refreshments.

She lifted her teacup and took a leisurely sip. Damien felt the gloom wrap itself around him. He had suspected that while he was gone from The Grange, Poole would try to burrow his way into Isabella's good graces, and it was evident he had succeeded. There was an obvious bond of affection and respect between Isabella and Poole that made Damien feel excluded. And strangely hurt.

"I will await you in my study, Isabella," Damien muttered. Opening the door with a jerk, he escaped into the hall.

Chapter Twenty

Isabella stood outside Damien's study door fighting against the nerves that threatened to overcome her. She had been avoiding this encounter for nearly two hours, uneasy with the notion of being alone with him again. Much had happened during his absence, and if Damien's reaction in the drawing room was any indication of his mood, Isabella knew it would be a volatile meeting.

Deciding she could no longer stall for additional time, Isabella knocked sharply on the door, opened it, then forced her reluctant legs to move forward. Damien was seated behind his massive oak desk, an assortment of papers strewn around him. He turned toward her when she crossed into his domain, and for the briefest moment something fierce glimmered in the depths of his stormy gray eyes.

"So you have finally decided to grace me with your presence. What took you so long?"

The harshness in his voice roused Isabella's fighting spirit. "I saw no reason for haste, since I strongly suspected your greeting would be less than cordial. And now you have proven me correct in my assumption."

Damien gave a loud snort and leaned back in his chair. "You

can hardly expect politeness from me after that cozy scene I witnessed in the drawing room. Damn it, Isabella, I am gone for six days, and when I return I'm made to feel like a stranger in my own home. I hardly recognize the place.''

A twinge of guilt invaded Isabella's mind, but she was not about to indulge it. She folded her arms tightly across her chest and stood stiffly in front of him.

''We thought you would be pleased, Damien. When the opportunity presented itself to make a few improvements, we seized upon it. I'm sorry you don't approve. It was never our intention to annoy you.''

''Our intention?'' Damien slapped his hand down loudly on the desk and rose to his feet. ''How disgustingly intimate you and Poole have become in my absence.''

''Lord Poole? He took no part in these decisions. Three women from the village have been hired on as day maids, and a male chef is now installed in the kitchen. *Jenkins* asked for my assistance in this matter, and we interviewed these new servants together. He and I are responsible for the changes at The Grange.''

Damien returned Isabella's piercing stare. ''Is Jenkins also responsible for your new wardrobe?''

Isabella felt herself coloring, and her defiant stance withered fractionally. Although she enjoyed her lovely new gowns, she did not feel entirely comfortable with the notion of wearing garments that had once belonged to Emmeline. Jenkins had repeatedly assured her the earl would not object, but Isabella secretly feared Damien would think she had done something horribly inappropriate when he discovered the truth.

''This was Emmeline's gown,'' Isabella said quietly, her fingers smoothing the soft folds of the green muslin skirt. ''Lord Poole gave me several of her dresses. Jenkins thought it permissible for me to accept them, but I shall return the garments to Lord Poole if it upsets you to see me wearing them.''

Damien's mouth dropped open. ''What the devil is Poole doing with Emmeline's clothes? Does he travel about the countryside with her garments packed away in his luggage?''

Isabella let out a nervous giggle. "What a ridiculous notion, Damien. Don't be absurd."

The earl gritted his teeth. "I suggest you tread carefully, my dear. My patience has been sorely tried this afternoon."

"So has mine, my lord."

She had the satisfaction of seeing him momentarily speechless. Capitalizing on her advantage, Isabella quickly added, "This dress came from the armoire in Emmeline's bedchamber. It is filled with gowns, most of which were never worn."

"I remember now," Damien said, his eyes involuntarily sweeping over Isabella. "After Emmeline disappeared, Jenkins and I searched her bedchamber. I recall thinking it strange that she kept such an extensive wardrobe here, since she came to The Grange so infrequently."

"I will not wear the gowns if you object," Isabella reiterated.

As Damien pondered her words, Isabella saw the anger diminish from his eyes. "It seems a ludicrous waste to let the clothes become food for the moths," he finally said. "Besides, you look very pretty."

Isabella fought back a smile. The compliment was sincerely if begrudgingly given. "Thank you, Damien."

The earl shifted from one foot to the other, then walked out from behind his desk and began prowling around the study. He appeared restless and uneasy, but to Isabella's relief, no longer angry. Eventually Damien paused by the fire and idly picked up the poker.

The tension gradually eased from the air. Isabella found herself watching his hands, mesmerized, as they prodded the smouldering logs, sending showers of glittering sparks leaping among the flames. The heavy gold signet ring on Damien's left hand gleamed in the firelight, and the memory of the feel of cool metal on her warm flesh sent a tremor of excitement through Isabella.

She cleared away the lump in her throat. Damien turned at the strangled sound, and Isabella berated herself for being caught staring at him with such blatant expectancy in her expression.

Seeming to read her thoughts, Damien flashed her a wickedly inviting smile and moved nearer. Isabella's stomach clenched.

Damien looked so strong and vital, the romantic light cast by the burning fire emphasizing his handsome, rugged features. His broad shoulders and muscular chest filled her vision, and Isabella felt a tremor run through her body.

Unable to stop herself, she reached out a trembling hand and rested it upon his shoulder. Damien cocked his head to one side and looked down at her in a way that made her knees feel weak and her heart beat at twice its normal rhythm. His smoldering, heavy-lidded gaze made her achingly aware of how lonely she had been without him.

"I missed you," she whispered softly.

"Thank God," Damien murmured with relief. He stroked her cheek gently with his forefinger. "I thought about you constantly."

The room was warm, but Isabella could feel goosebumps on her arms. His gaze dropped suggestively to her mouth and she nervously flicked out her tongue.

"Where did you go?" she asked.

"I'll tell you later."

Damien bent his head and softly kissed her lips. Isabella eagerly welcomed him, shutting her eyes at the delicious pleasure she felt when his tongue explored her mouth.

She raised her arms, clasping them tightly around his broad back. He felt solid and powerful, inspiring a sweet sense of security. Damien had haunted her thoughts nearly every hour he had been gone from The Grange. Being held so lovingly in his arms made Isabella realize how much he meant to her, how truly incomplete she felt without him.

Worries about her future, her past, even this very moment, faded as Isabella savored the feelings of love that burned in her heart. It was a true testament to the mysterious power of love that she and this proud, worldly man shared a closeness that endured no matter what their differences. Isabella offered a silent, selfish prayer that this oftentimes bumpy, yet blissfully exciting relationship would continue.

Damien's teeth raked the delicate skin of Isabella's throat, causing a restless urgency within her. Smiling, she pressed herself closer to him, smelling the fragrant smoke from the fire mingled with the musky male scent of his body. It was pure heaven.

"Shouldn't you lock the door?" she whispered breathlessly.

Damien's gray eyes flared. "As much as I would dearly love to ravish you on this rather scratchy-looking carpet, my dear, I find myself compelled to exercise a modicum of caution. Even with the door locked, we could be interrupted at any moment."

She leaned against his broad chest, closed her eyes, and fought to control her ragged breathing. "What a damned inconvenient time for you to develop a sense of decorum, Damien."

He laughed heartily, and Isabella could feel the rumbling deep in his chest. "You are a refreshingly honest woman, Isabella. It is probably the quality I admire most in you."

"Two compliments in one afternoon. You will turn my head with your flattery, my lord."

"I wish it were that easy," Damien grumbled. He hugged Isabella tightly for a few moments longer, then gently eased her out of his embrace. "I left The Grange to travel up to York, Isabella. The purpose of my journey was to speak with your grandfather."

Isabella went very still. "You have seen the earl?"

"Yes. And Great-aunt Agnes too."

"Oh." Isabella lowered her eyes. Damien, her grandfather, and Aunt Agnes all together in one room. Discussing her, Isabella felt certain. How perfectly mortifying. "They are an interesting pair, the earl and his sister," she said, carefully examining the tips of her light-green shoes.

"They are mean spirited, rude, and dictatorial," Damien said. "After spending only a brief afternoon in their company I can understand how unhappy you must have been living there."

"Can you?" Isabella's head snapped up, her face suffused with color. Damien had endured merely a taste of the atmosphere at her grandfather's estate. The self-confidence and self-worth she had managed to achieve through years of struggle faltered badly when she recalled the unpleasant memories. "Toward the end, it became unbearable living at the estate.

Aunt Agnes scrutinized everything about me—my appearance, my actions, my conversations—and always found me wanting, while the earl either ignored me or dismissed me out of hand as being beneath his notice.''

"They are both fools," Damien said. "You are far better off without them."

"I know that," Isabella answered quietly. "Yet they are my only family."

"Perhaps." Damien took Isabella's arm and led her to the other side of his desk. She saw a small trunk resting beside his chair. "I brought this back from York for you, Isabella. It is filled with your mother's belongings."

"My mother's?" Isabella's eyes lit up with excitement. "How is this possible? I was told by one of the servants that my grandfather burned all my mother's possessions. Where did you get this?"

"I stole it from Aunt Agnes," Damien said, tipping back on his heels proudly.

"You didn't?"

"I did." Damien's gray eyes danced with merriment. "I marched straight through the house with the trunk perched on my shoulder. I can't imagine what the servants thought, but naturally no one said a word. Of course Agnes was not overly pleased with my actions. Apparently she had become rather attached to the trunk over the years and objected strongly when I decided to remove it. It became necessary to lock her bedchamber to prevent any interference."

"She must have been very angry," Isabella said, finding it difficult to image Aunt Agnes being bested by anyone.

"She was absolutely furious," Damien chuckled. "When I left her, she was spouting profanities that would make a sailor blush."

Isabella shrieked with childish laughter. "I wish I had been there to witness her defeat. Aunt Agnes finally met her match when she tangled with you, Damien."

"I hope my prize proves to be of worth," Damien said, shifting his eyes down to the trunk. "Agnes thought there might be something of significance in here that would name your true father.''

"Pray, don't keep me in suspense, Damien," Isabella said, clasping her hands tightly together. "What have you found?"

"I haven't opened the trunk yet, Isabella. I felt it was your right.''

She knelt down and ran her hand hesitantly across the top of the trunk. A heavy weight of impending doom and dread crept into her chest. It suddenly seemed as if her entire future depended on the contents of this mysterious trunk and the secrets it held. Fearing she would lose her nerve, Isabella took a deep breath, thrust the latch, unbolted the lock, and quickly lifted the lid.

Shades of brown, tan, and white swirled before her unfocused eyes. Isabella blinked hard several times, forcing herself to adjust her vision. Gradually she distinguished the shapes and colors—stacks of books, piles of correspondence neatly tied with colored ribbons, a small jewelry box, a writing box, a few garments.

Hands shaking visibly, Isabella pulled forth two packets of letters. "Please help me read through them," she asked, offering a pile to Damien.

The room fell to silence as they both concentrated their attention on the letters, the occasional spark and crack of the fire the only noise. Damien reclined in a leather chair near the fire while Isabella sprawled on the floor, leaning back against the open trunk as she read.

The first letter Isabella scanned was signed by a female named Pamela and was dated four years prior to the year Isabella was born. Impatiently she folded the missive and reached for another. When all the correspondence had been thoroughly perused, Isabella turned toward Damien. He answered her unspoken question with a slight shake of his head.

"I know it's absurd to feel so disappointed," Isabella said, slumping dejectedly. "I'm sure Aunt Agnes has read these letters a hundred times over, yet for some reason I thought the answer would leap out at us."

"Let's look through the other items, Isabella," Damien said soothingly.

She grudgingly nodded her agreement and picked up two boxes. Keeping the smaller jewelry box in her lap, she gave Damien the larger writing box.

"Damnation!"

Damien's husky voice jarred Isabella. Glancing up, she saw his strained expression. Her stomach did a somersault. "What is it? What have you found?"

"The writing paper," Damien said quietly, holding up a single sheet of parchment toward the firelight.

"It's blank," Isabella replied, knitting her brows together.

"Yes," Damien said. "And because it is not written on, I can easily read the watermark. I recognize it."

Isabella rose to her knees and awkwardly shuffled toward him. "I don't understand," she said, peering closely at the parchment. "I thought these watermarks were woven into the paper by the manufacturer to denote quality." She fingered the heavy cream colored paper. " 'Tis obvious this is a superior vellum."

"Aside from crediting the paper maker, watermarks of heraldic themes and armorial shields showing the bearing of the aristocratic owner are often used," Damien explained. "The paper I use is marked with a replica of my family coat of arms."

Isabella frowned. "Lord Poole wears a gold ring bearing his family heraldry. I don't recall the design exactly, but I am certain it does not resemble this mark."

"Of course not. If Poole's father and your mother were lovers, he would not have been foolish enough to present her with something containing his coat of arms."

"Yet you said you recognized this paper," Isabella said. "How?"

"Emmeline refused to use my parchment for her correspondence, preferring her family's unique creation." Damien traced the outlines of the watermark to emphasize his point. "The bull's head is a common symbol, but rising between the horns is a supporting symbol, a star. This paper is made exclusively for the Poole family. It cannot be purchased by anyone else. Finding it among your mother's personal effects establishes a firm connection between her and them.''

"Good Lord." Isabella sank back unsteadily on her haunches. "I don't believe it.''

"I agree the evidence is hardly conclusive, but given all the other circumstances, in conjunction to your striking physical resemblance to Emmeline, I believe we have finally discovered the truth.''

"The truth!'' Isabella jerked herself up to her knees, swayed drunkenly, then sat down hard on the floor. She looked at Damien's solemn face, and a cold, empty fear invaded her heart.

He would grow to hate her now because of who she was. Gone forever was the chance, the hope, that he would one day return her love.

Her vision blurred. The tears were close to the surface, and Isabella knew she was about to disgrace herself. Yet she couldn't seem to gather the strength to leave.

"Sweetheart.'' Damien reached down and lifted her into his lap. "Shhhh, don't cry.''

Isabella hiccuped back a sob. Damien smiled affectionately and kissed her temple. He rocked her slowly back and forth. She took a shuddering breath and rubbed her cheek against the soft silk of his waistcoat. He felt wonderful. Yet the turmoil in her heart continued.

Isabella felt disjointed, somehow out of touch with her true self. She absently twisted one of the gold buttons on the earl's jacket until the thread snapped. With a mute, apologetic glance, she handed him the button and he slipped it inside his pocket. Then his fingers began to stroke her head and shoulders in a soothing motion that gradually calmed her panic. And raised her passion.

Suddenly she wanted to kiss him. Everywhere. She wanted to loosen his cravat and nibble at the base of his throat, where his pulse beat strong and sure. She wanted to remove his jacket and waistcoat and shirt and run her fingers across his naked flesh. She wanted to make love to him. Now. But after all that had happened, would he still want her?

Isabella let her hand slide over the rock-hard muscles of Damien's arm and gave a firm squeeze. Then she bent herself seductively back over his other arm in a calculated pose of utter abandonment.

The earl squirmed in the chair, and her heart sang when she felt a familiar hard pressure against her bottom. She turned her head and looked him straight in the eye.

"The carpet might be scratchy, my lord, but your desk top looks invitingly smooth."

A dark brow arched up. "Are you suggesting that we test that assumption, my dear?" The heat in his eyes and the sexy timber of his deep voice stole her breath away.

"Oh, yes," she whispered in his ear.

"Right now?"

"Please." Her voice was husky and thrillingly coaxing.

Damien hesitated a mere fraction of a second, then lowered his head and took her lips in a wet, open-mouthed kiss. Isabella immediately responded by thrusting her tongue inside the warmth of Damien's mouth. She kissed him deeply, drinking in all of his heat and hunger. They kept kissing until her lips felt swollen, until the desire rose between them thick and urgent, tightening every nerve in her body.

Tearing her mouth free from his, Isabella drew her lips along the square line of his jaw, then flicked her tongue behind the lobe of his ear. Damien quivered and held her tighter against his chest. Even through the many layers of clothing, his body felt wonderful—strong, hard, and solid, offering her the comfort and security she so desperately needed, so desperately craved.

But she needed more. She needed to feel his naked skin against her own. She pushed Damien's jacket off his shoulders, released his waistcoat and cravat, and practically ripped his shirt away. Together they worked the buttons of her gown. She felt mindlessly insatiable, almost feverish, as the last button fell open. Naked, she rubbed her swollen breasts with their rigid nipples against Damien's chest in an agitated rhythm.

Her frantic urgency drove him wild. He caressed her breasts

with his tongue until she was sobbing with pleasure. He pulled her skirt up to her waist and plunged his hand between her legs. Ripping away the fragile barrier of her undergarments, his fingers sought and found the slick wetness of her desire.

"More," she pleaded, pushing herself closer. "I need to *feel* you."

Her raging hunger threatened to consume them both. Damien grasped Isabella's wrist and placed her hand on the front of his breeches. She felt his swollen manhood straining against the fabric. With unsteady fingers, she unbuttoned his pants and he spilled into her palm, thick, hot, and full. He growled deep in his throat, growing larger and more rigid as she pulled and stroked him.

"I can't wait," Damien said breathlessly.

He swept Isabella up in his arms, stood shakily on his feet, and quickly carried her across the room. He laid her across the desk, reached for her hips, and slid her to the edge. Isabella laughed. The wood did indeed feel smooth on her naked derriere.

Damien pushed her thighs wide apart and stepped between them. She bent her knees and lifted herself to receive him. He thrust himself inside her and she closed her eyes, rolling her head from side to side as he filled her, pounding hard against her with each exquisite stroke. Faster. Harder. Deeper.

It didn't last long. Isabella felt him begin to shudder and she tightened her legs, holding Damien closer. He cried out as he reached his peak, and she too let herself go, feeling wave upon wave of blissful sensations wash over her entire being.

Still breathing hard, they sagged together, clinging to each other in the turbulent aftermath of their passion. They stayed joined together for several countless minutes. Isabella felt wonderfully languid and numb. She barely stirred as Damien gently adjusted her clothing, covering her naked and still heated flesh.

He pulled her upright and she perched on the edge of the desk, her feet dangling. Framing her face in his large hands, Damien fingers brushed aside the damp tendrils of her hair before softly kissing her temple. Isabella sat patiently as he calmly rebuttoned her gown, her eyes never once straying from his beloved face. He tried repinning her hair, but the errant locks refused to cooperate.

"Let me do it." Isabella held out her palm expectantly, and he obediently deposited the hairpins in it.

She could feel his eyes intently studying her every move, and her fingers grew clumsy. How foolish to feel embarrassed in front of him *now,* after what had just occurred between them. She lifted her head, her lovely violet eyes shining brightly.

Damien gave her a heart-melting smile. "Christ, Isabella," he whispered softly. "We didn't even lock the door."

Isabella raised the wine goblet to her lips, startled to realize it was empty. *How odd,* she thought, *I just filled the blasted thing.* Shrugging her shoulders, she reached for the bottle of claret on her dinner tray. She juggled the glass and the bottle awkwardly on her lap, then raised both knees to steady her hands.

She clutched the glass upright between her legs and took a deep breath. Squinting her eyes, Isabella carefully adjusted her aim and succeeded in replenishing her glass. She took a cautious sip, pleased that the taste no longer made her grimace.

Isabella lolled her head back against the chair and sighed. Her mind was totally confused. After Damien had made the startling connection between the writing paper and her mother, she had nearly lost control of her reason.

Yet Damien had remained concerned about her, kind, sympathetic, loving. In fact their wild, uncontrollable passion was exactly what she had needed at that moment. An intense, emotional escape from the truths of the past. But once she was fully dressed and her hair neatly pinned in place, Isabella had shocked them both by racing from Damien's study as if the hounds of hell were on her heels. A most cowardly and unladylike exit, to be sure.

Isabella was at a loss to understand her own feelings. She had fantasized for years about her natural father. She thought she was prepared to learn the truth—nay, she thought she would welcome it. But it had overwhelmed her and thrust her into such a dark state of confusion and despair that she felt compelled to hide herself.

Her bedchamber offered Isabella a small measure of sanctuary, and she had not ventured from the room for the remainder of the day. At her request a dinner tray had been prepared, but it lay untouched, except for the rich claret.

A sharp knock at her door sent her heart thumping. She attempted to rise, but the room began swaying with an irregular motion. Isabella stumbled back into her chair and called out breathlessly, "Come in."

The earl crossed the threshold, and Isabella straightened her spine. Damien's unexpected presence dispelled her gloom.

"Damien." Her smile was a joyful welcome. "How delightful to see you. Please, join me." She indicated a chair near her own, but the earl remained on his feet. "I would offer you some wine, my lord, but I'm afraid there is no more. It must have been a very small bottle of claret. Shall I ring for another?"

"I don't think that would be a prudent idea, Isabella." Damien knelt before her chair and regarded her intently. "I came to see how you are faring. Are you all right?"

"I am fine. Perfectly fine." Isabella waved her arm through the air in what she hoped was a carefree manner. The dramatic gesture caused her eyes to cross and her head to swim. She shut her eyes tightly to stop the spinning. It didn't work.

Isabella sighed deeply, rested her elbow on the cushioned arm of her chair, and rested her forehead against the palm of her hand. It helped quell the dizziness. Slightly.

Damien was speaking. She raised her head, then frowned at him in exasperation. "I would appreciate it, Damien, if you would please stand still instead of dancing about the room. It makes my stomach alarmingly queasy."

"You should be in bed." His voice was hard, but his expression soft.

Isabella was instantly contrite. "What a lovely notion." She stood up, and the room immediately began spinning. Isabella swayed as the floor seemed to drop out from beneath her feet. She threw her arm back and braced herself against the chair.

"I definitely owe you an apology, Damien. Apparently the room is moving, not you."

She heard his deep laugh and smiled. He had such a wonderful laugh—rich, smooth and merry. Damien's handsome face blurred before her eyes. Damn! If only the room would remain still, she could kiss him.

Isabella was having great difficulty setting one foot ahead of the other until she felt a strong supporting arm guiding her. She sighed with gratitude at the assistance, since she could not, for the life of her, remember where she was going or why.

Her bottom touched softness, and Isabella realized she sat on the edge of the bed. Damien gently eased her backwards until her head touched the pillow, then lifted her legs onto the mattress. He was so kind, so gentle, she thought dreamily. She waited eagerly for his moist kisses.

He removed her shoes and dropped them on the floor. Isabella winced at the loud noise they made. Damien pulled the pins from her hair and it spilled over the pillows. His knuckles brushed the nape of her neck. She moved her head so she could feel his strong hand against her cheek. How she loved this man!

"Damien?" she whispered.

"Yes, my dear."

"I am going to be violently ill," she said in a panic-stricken voice, sitting straight up.

Miraculously, Damien produced a porcelain basin in the nick of time. He thrust it under her chin and held her head firmly as she heaved up her liquid dinner. Her body spasmed as she retched a second, then a third time. When she had emptied the contents of her stomach, he wiped her face with a damp cloth. He pressed a glass of cool water into her hand and told her to drink it. Isabella took one small sip, then collapsed against the pillows.

"Feeling better?" Damien inquired in a sympathetic tone.

Isabella groaned. "I cannot decide which feels worse, my wretched stomach or my injured pride. I am simply mortified, Damien."

"You drank a bit too much wine on an empty stomach, my

dear, that's all. There is nothing to feel embarrassed about. Close your eyes and try to rest. I'll stay until you fall asleep.''

Damien stretched out on the bed next to Isabella. He put his arm around her and drew her against his side. He kissed the top of her head and said softly, ''Go to sleep, Isabella.''

She snuggled nearer to his warmth, closed her eyes, and promptly fell unconscious.

Chapter Twenty-one

Isabella woke with throbbing temples and a queasy stomach. Not daring to move her head from the pillow, she cautiously allowed her eyes to travel around the bedchamber. She discovered she was lying in her bed, beneath the covers, completely dressed except for her shoes. An almost agonizing sense of relief entered Isabella's body when she realized she was alone. Her muddled brain sought valiantly to reconstruct the events of last night. Though all the details were unclear, she distinctly remembered certain occurrences with far more clarity than she desired.

The truth about her father. The wine. Damien. Isabella groaned loudly and pulled the pillow over her head. She had made an utter and complete fool of herself last night. And became revoltingly sick in the process. It was nearly unthinkable to imagine Damien's opinion of her behavior. Isabella groaned again when she remembered the time she had chastised him for overindulging in spirits.

A noise in the hallway drew her attention, and Isabella sat up. What time was it? The heavy drapes were drawn shut, and the bedchamber was in near darkness. Swinging her legs off the bed, Isabella gingerly walked to the window. Slowly moving the curtain aside, she peered outside.

"Oh, God!" The sunlight nearly blinded her. Isabella instantly dropped the curtain as a shooting pain tore through her head. She staggered back to the bed with her eyes closed. Fearing she would never regain her feet if she lay down, Isabella remained standing, rubbing her pounding temples vigorously.

She wanted to die. Right here and right now.

The door to her bedchamber slowly opened. Isabella lifted one eyelid a fraction, summoning up the barest interest when Damien strolled nonchalantly into the chamber, carrying a silver tray.

"Good morning, my dear. I thought you might enjoy having breakfast in your room this morning," he said cheerfully. He placed the tray on the same table where her untouched dinner had languished last night, then lifted the cover off one of the many platters.

Isabella's knees grew weak when she smelled the eggs and broiled kidneys, and she sagged against the bedpost. She took several deep breaths, shuddering with the effort. This was even more embarrassing than last night. "Please take that away, Damien," she whispered in a woebegone tone. "I vow to never eat another morsel of food."

Damien laughed, but when she turned her head to glare at him, Isabella saw he was watching her with genuine concern.

"Have some water," Damien suggested, handing her a filled goblet. "Use the first swig to cleanse your mouth, then drink the rest down."

She obediently filled her mouth with the water, swirled it about her tongue, then spat it out into the basin he provided. The same basin, she noted with ironic humor, into which she had emptied the contents of her stomach last night.

"Better?"

"No. My tongue still feels three times its usual size."

"That will pass. Come, at least sit and drink some coffee." Damien graciously held out a chair.

"I will sit down on one condition," Isabella said. "You

must replace the cover on the food platter. Better still, you will remove all traces of food from the room."

Damien obligingly picked up several platters and deposited them outside the room. As Isabella moved toward the chair with unsteady legs, she saw that he had left a rack of toast on the tray, but since it had no odor, her stomach did not object. She did object, however, when Damien threw open the drapes and flooded the room with light.

"Please, Damien, show a little mercy," she begged, squinting hard to avoid the irritating sunlight.

"Sorry."

A mischievous gleam crept into his silvery eyes as he closed the drapes, parting them only a fraction to allow a small amount of light into the chamber. Isabella felt too miserable to care much. Using both hands to steady her cup, she managed to take a tiny sip of coffee. She felt the warm, bitter liquid slide down her throat and fall into her sore stomach, then waited anxiously, her eyes pinned to the basin, for the coffee to come back up. When it didn't, she bravely took a second swallow.

"Of course, the real cure for a hangover is what Jenkins refers to as the hair of the dog," Damien said. "A large dose of good brandy."

Isabella dropped the small piece of toast she had been trying to force into her mouth. "I bow to your superior knowledge of the subject, Damien. However, I can assure you I would prefer consuming actual dog hair to swallowing another drop of liquor."

Damien laughed sympathetically. "Try to eat some toast. It will settle your stomach and help ease the pounding in your head."

"I don't believe that is possible," Isabella muttered, but she followed his advice.

Damien settled himself comfortably in the chair opposite her and poured a cup of coffee. While he picked up a piece of toast, Isabella stole a quick peek at him. He was dressed very casually in a loose-fitting white cambric shirt, dark brown breeches, and freshly shined riding boots. His jaw was newly shaved and his hair slightly damp, probably from a morning bath. He looked and smelled divine.

Sitting across from him, Isabella felt like a total mess. Her slept-in gown was hopelessly rumpled and her unbounded hair disheveled and tangled. Worse than her appearance, however, were her fanciful imaginings about last night. She had a vague recollection of drinking a few glasses of wine, Damien appearing in her chamber, and a thoroughly disgraceful incident with a wash basin, but was that everything? Did anything else occur that she should be aware of?

Isabella lifted her eyes to the ceiling. Last night was hardly a subject she was eager to introduce into the conversation, but curiosity won out over common sense.

"I must apologize for my behavior last night," Isabella muttered. "I hope I didn't cause you too much trouble. To be honest, I'm not quite sure what happened."

"You got drunk," Damien said bluntly. "On my best claret. Then you retched it up in a basin. When you were done, I put you to bed."

Isabella winced at the image. It was a harsh comment, but the unexpected warmth she saw in the earl's eyes softened the blow. "That is all that occurred?"

"Isn't that enough?"

"Yes, I suppose it is," Isabella whispered. "I made an utter fool of myself."

"Nonsense," Damien replied philosophically. "I've been drunker. And sicker. Just ask Jenkins."

Isabella smiled. Damien's matter-of-fact attitude went far in restoring her serenity. "We are quite a pair, my lord."

"I am finally beginning to realize that, my dear."

Damien's voice was husky. He stared steadily at Isabella for several long moments with a look she thought was almost hostile in its intensity.

"The children seem well," Damien said, suddenly breaking the mood. "I spent the majority of last evening teaching Catherine to play backgammon. I fear that with only a bit more practice she will succeed in beating me."

Isabella was rattled by the abrupt change of subject and

struggled to follow along. "Catherine is a bright child. I'm glad you have found something that so captivates her attention. Backgammon makes a refreshing change from artillery battles."

"She is still fighting Napoleon?"

"On occasion." Isabella wrinkled her nose and swallowed more of her coffee. "Catherine's interests usually turn to other matters when she spends time with you."

"I am trying," Damien said solemnly.

"I know." Isabella set down her cup. "You love your children, Damien—that is the most important fact. And you are very good with them—kind, patient, loving. They even enjoy your teasing. All they really need from you is more of your time."

The earl's face grew serious; then he grinned. "I guess you are feeling more yourself, since you have the strength to lecture me," he said. "How is your headache?"

Isabella managed a slight laugh. "No longer excruciating, merely raging."

"A vast improvement." Damien idly picked up a silver spoon and ran it between his fingers. "Shall we discuss what happened yesterday?"

Isabella nervously clenched her hands together. Her thoughts and feelings were a complex bundle of contradictions. She felt apprehensive, embarrassed, and totally unprepared.

"I feel lost, Damien. I am still the same person I was yesterday morning, yet I feel different. Everything has changed. The faceless family of my imagination is now real. It has a name. A name you disdain."

He looked keenly at her. "Knowing the identity of your true father hasn't made you a different person, Isabella. At least, not in my eyes. You can allow this knowledge to alter your life as much or as little as you desire. Remember, you are in control of your own destiny, my dear."

She wrapped her arms around herself. "What did Thomas— uh, Lord Poole say when you told him?"

"I said nothing to Poole."

Isabella grimaced with understanding. "I suppose you expect me to do the same."

Damien shook his head. "The decision is entirely yours, Isabella. I shall not interfere."

Isabella's violet eyes widened involuntarily. Damien was not a man who allowed events to control him; *he* controlled events. "Lord Poole will want me to leave The Grange. He has been hinting rather broadly at the notion these past few days. Once he learns the truth, he will be most insistent."

"I expected as much. Will you go?"

An aching lump in Isabella's throat made it difficult to breathe. The thought of leaving Damien brought forth physical pain. He made no mention of marriage, and that hurt. When she had discovered early last night that she was not carrying a child, Isabella's immediate reaction had been relief, but that was quickly followed by a puzzling burst of disappointment.

She knew it would be better to allow the budding affection between Damien and herself to grow without the added complication of an unplanned child, but now they were discussing the possibility of her leaving The Grange entirely. Isabella shivered. She had grown fond of this disordered, eccentric household. She held Catherine and Ian in genuine affection and their father close to her heart.

"I would leave here with great reluctance," Isabella said quietly.

"Don't look so downcast, Isabella. If Poole has his way, he will be the new owner in a few short months. You could return then."

Isabella flushed. She had been obsessing so much about her own dilemma, she had quite forgotten Lord Poole's ownership of the Whatley Grange mortgages. "Perhaps I can persuade Thomas to work out a more equitable settlement. I am certain that given sufficient time, you will be able to reclaim the mortgage."

"No." Damien stiffened. "Under no circumstances are you to bring this matter up with Poole. Is that understood, Isabella?"

"I only want to help, Damien." Isabella lowered her head.

She knew her offer had pricked the earl's pride, but the situation was sufficiently grave to dispense with ego.

"I know your motivation is pure, my dear. 'Tis Poole's I distrust." Damien rose to his feet. "I promised Catherine and Ian I'd take them riding this morning. Then I will leave them in Jenkins's care while I wade through the mountain of papers on my desk. I think you deserve the day off."

Isabella smiled wanly. "I would welcome a quiet afternoon. Thank you."

Damien took her hand in his, brought it to his lips, and softly caressed her upstretched fingers. His expressive gray eyes held hers in a sensual spell as he deliberately moved her fingers across his chest and over his heart before dropping her hand. It was an intimate, tantalizing gesture that left Isabella still feeling its effects long after the earl had left her alone.

Isabella's fingers quivered slightly as she struggled to fasten the small buttons on the back of her gown. She had consumed a second pot of coffee and an entire slice of plain toast, and she had soaked in a hot bath until the water lost its warmth. She was already ten minutes late to a rendezvous she had requested with Lord Poole, and her taut nerves were beginning to fray. By the time she managed to finish dressing and pin up her hair, Isabella freely admitted she was suffering from a full-blown case of cold feet.

She was genuinely puzzled at her hesitation. Thomas had shown her endless kindness and consideration this past week, offering her a sympathetic ear, entertaining conversation, and continuous pleasant company. He had spent many hours with Catherine and Ian, playing their favorite games and amusing them with humorous stories. Yet it was his constant unflappable good humor that struck Isabella oddly. No one was that nice all the time.

Her unaccountable sense of unease was probably a subconscious result of Damien's intense dislike of Lord Poole, Isabella decided. She suspected Thomas would be overjoyed when she told him they had discovered a link between her mother and his father, but a small hint of doubt was enough cause for her to worry.

Isabella ran lightly down the steps, determined to banish these thoughts and make this encounter with Thomas a festive event. Clutching a piece of the heavy vellum paper discovered among her mother's belongings tightly in her sweating palm, Isabella crossed the hallway and entered the drawing room.

Lord Poole was sitting by the window, reading a book. He was dressed as immaculately as usual in blue knee breeches, an embroidered silver waistcoat, and a light blue coat. His snowy white neckcloth was elaborately tied, and his fair hair was meticulously brushed.

"Good day, Isabella. I missed seeing you at breakfast this morning, but you look so enchanting, I believe the wait was worth it."

He smiled so broadly, she could see small creases at the corners of his blue eyes.

"Good afternoon, Thomas," Isabella said. She moved toward the sofa and Lord Poole politely stood up. "I have some good news to share with you. That is, I think it is good news, and I very much hope you will feel the same."

"This sounds rather serious. And intriguing. Come and sit by the window. 'Tis more comfortable here in the sunlight."

Isabella meekly followed Lord Poole to the sofa and sat down. He took a place next to her, so close that his knee was almost touching her own.

"Do you recognize this paper?" Isabella's voice shook slightly, but she was pleased she managed to keep her hands steady as she passed the sheet of vellum to Lord Poole.

He merely stared at the blank page.

Isabella reached over and gently lifted the vellum towards the sunlight. "Now does it seem familiar?"

Lord Poole looked hastily from the paper to Isabella and then back again. "This parchment is from my private stationery stock. It has my bull-and-star watermark. Did you find it in Emmeline's room?"

There was silence for a moment while Isabella fought to calm her thumping heart. "The writing paper was found among my mother's belongings. Damien and I both believe it proves a strong connection between my mother and your family."

Thomas grasped Isabella's hand and pressed it hard against his lips. "Isabella," he said breathlessly. "Oh, my dear, wonderful, darling sister. I am delighted. Simply delighted."

Isabella smiled with relief. His ready acceptance of her as his sister helped banish a bit of the loneliness and feeling of inadequacy that had haunted her whenever she was in the presence of her family. It was such a welcome change to be wanted by one's relations instead of barely tolerated.

"Thank you, Thomas." Isabella blushed and pulled back slightly from his hand. "You are very kind."

"My sweet Bella, I am exuberant—nay, I am giddy with excitement." Lord Poole jumped up from the sofa and paced the room with restless energy. "We must make plans. Can we leave today? No, perhaps it will be best to start out early tomorrow morning. Shall we head straight to London, or travel to my country seat? It is still early enough in the Season to spend a week or two in the country before arriving in London. You will be an instant success, I am certain. Of course, we must have a complete wardrobe made for you first. Would you like to go to Paris for your gowns? I would dearly love to see you dressed in the very latest fashions."

Lord Poole paused a moment in his pacing, and Isabella looked up at him, her eyes wide. She had long suspected that Thomas would want her to leave The Grange, but she was unprepared for the extent of control he seemed determined to wield over her future.

Isabella mastered the shock she was feeling. "I am deeply flattered by your offer, Thomas, but I must insist you temper your enthusiasm. I cannot imagine traveling to London with you, let alone Paris. And a season in London? It is out of the question. I am twenty-five years old, far too advanced in years to be making my entrée into society. Besides, how would I be introduced? As your newly discovered bastard half sister? It would be scandalous."

Isabella watched the light of excitement dim in Lord Poole's eyes. "You are right to scold me, Bella. I have gone off half-cocked without considering your feelings. We must plan your introduction to society very carefully. I will not tolerate even a hint of scandal touching your name.''

''I am not interested in entering society,'' Isabella quietly insisted.

''Nonsense. The beau monde will adore you. I will open up a world beyond your dreams, Bella, a world that has been unfairly denied to you.'' Lord Poole suddenly went very still. ''Bath! I will take you to Bath! It is a far less rigid environment, and the season does not begin until late summer. It will give you time to acquire a new wardrobe and refine your manners. Not that they need much study, but a few hints and tricks from me will make you feel more confident. I am certain you will be the focus of attention and admiration wherever we go. Most who gather at Bath are gentry, but many of the nobility also attend the assemblies and twice weekly balls. It is the ideal solution!''

''No, Thomas,'' Isabella said, keeping her voice strong and steady. ''I cannot imagine myself sitting among the matrons of polite society, drinking the waters and exchanging the latest on-dits with the fashionable world.''

''Please don't make a rash decision, Bella,'' Lord Poole said, earnestly regarding her. ''Promise me you will consider this very carefully before deciding.''

Isabella rested her hands at her sides and looked tranquilly at her brother, relieved to see the unbridled zeal had left his eyes.

''I promise to think about everything you have suggested,'' Isabella said. ''But I will not leave The Grange without giving the earl proper notice. You must agree not to press this issue with me.''

Lord Poole smiled fleetingly in her direction. ''As you wish.''

Isabella lowered her eyes. It was clear Thomas possessed a great deal of self-discipline. He behaved with perfect correctness, showing her deference, yet Isabella could see he was displeased.

It seemed that her newly discovered brother wanted her to become a glittering jewel in the crown of high society, a sparkling gem among the privileged. He wanted to cosset and protect her and also, Isabella suspected, treat her more as a fragile doll than an intelligent woman. The idea was unappealing and unrealistic. Isabella took a deep breath and absently rubbed her temples. Her headache had returned.

Chapter Twenty-two

"No, Ian, we cannot go in there. Father and Jenkins told us we must leave Miss Browning alone today."

Isabella glanced up from the book she had been staring at for the past half hour and saw Catherine and Ian hovering in the library doorway. Catherine had been speaking to Ian in a loud, childish whisper, but Isabella clearly heard her remarks.

"Children," Isabella said, smiling warmly at them, "please come in."

Isabella placed her book on a nearby table and waited expectantly as Catherine and Ian cautiously entered the room, hand in hand. *This is exactly what I need,* Isabella decided. Shutting herself away all morning had caused her to dwell overlong on her problems, and no matter how hard she tried, her brain would not be stilled from the difficult decisions she faced.

"We aren't supposed to disturb you," Catherine said. "It will make Father cross."

Ian nodded his head in vigorous agreement.

"You are not disturbing me," Isabella insisted, welcoming the children as both company and distraction. Patting the love seat next to her, Isabella gestured for the children to be seated. "Tell me what you have been doing all morning."

"We went for a ride with Father, and then Jenkins took us up to see Maggie and the new baby. The baby was sleeping, but Maggie let me rub her back. Ian did too. She felt very soft."

Isabella focused her complete attention on Catherine as the child continued describing the morning activities, successfully pushing the tumultuous events of the past twenty-four hours from her mind.

"It certainly seems as if you have had a busy morning. Would you like me to read you a story?" Isabella volunteered. She stood up and began searching the library shelves for an appropriate book.

"We'd rather go on an adventure, Miss Browning," Ian exclaimed.

"An adventure?" Isabella smiled and placed the book firmly back upon the shelf. "What sort of an adventure did you have in mind, Ian?"

"We want to hunt for treasure," Ian said, swinging his legs restlessly.

Isabella frowned in puzzlement. "Lady Anne's treasure?" It seemed such a long time ago that Damien had related the fascinating tale of his ancestor Lady Anne and the cache of gold and jewels legend claimed she had hidden somewhere on the castle grounds. And even longer since Isabella and the children had fruitlessly searched for it.

"Oh, yes," Catherine replied, her young face alight with excitement. "It has been ages since we last looked. We promised Father we would not go looking on our own. We need you to come with us."

Jubilant shouts of glee echoed off the walls at Isabella's nod of agreement. Feeling proud of herself for being able to make a decision that clearly brought someone happiness, Isabella allowed the children to drag her from the room.

Isabella followed Catherine and Ian up to the third floor. The children were most insistent about searching this rarely used section of the house, and Isabella willingly indulged them. The first obstacle they encountered was a sagging oak door that shut off the east wing. It creaked piercingly as Isabella opened it.

"You must be careful where you walk," Isabella warned. "I'm sure this part of the castle has been closed off for many years."

Isabella stepped carefully onto the scared floorboards, making sure they would support her weight before allowing the children to follow. They entered a huge hallway, the cool air smelling of dust and mold. Catherine opened the first door on the right, and Isabella felt a cold blast of air. She peered into the chamber. Shards of sunlight slanted dimly through the dirty, latticed windows which had several broken and missing panes. Everywhere were signs of damp and decay.

"I don't want to go inside," Ian said. Backing away from the open door, he reached out and took Isabella's hand.

"It is rather gloomy," Isabella agreed. "Let's keep on looking." She held tightly to Ian's hand, enjoying the warmth and trust she felt radiating from him. He really was a darling little boy.

"This room is ugly," Catherine declared, opening another door.

Isabella glanced inside and silently agreed with Catherine's assessment. The room was a vast, cold, and forbidding chamber with a gigantic fireplace along one wall that stretched to the paneled ceiling. Cobwebs clung stubbornly to all corners of the dismal room.

"I'm afraid all the rooms here will look much the same, children," Isabella said. "Perhaps we should try another part of the house. We might find chambers that are not in such a state of disrepair."

Catherine ignored Isabella's suggestion and continued opening doors. "Oh, this room is beautiful," she said with a touch of awe in her voice as she pushed the door wide open.

Isabella and Ian murmured in surprised agreement and followed Catherine inside. The room was bathed in the glow of soft, rose-tinted light, an effect created by the sunlight streaming through the numerous panes of colored window glass. Although dirty and dusty, this room did not have the same aura as the others. It was neither cold nor damp, and the cobwebs were barley visible.

"Roses! Look, Miss Browning there are roses cut into the wood. Aren't they pretty?"

"They are lovely, Catherine."

Isabella ran her fingers appreciatively over the delicately carved paneling. Ian bravely let go of Isabella's hand and imitated her movements.

While the children explored the intricate paneling, Isabella wandered slowly about the room, taking in the gentle calm and serenity created by the unusual rose-colored hues.

"I'm sorry. I didn't mean to break it, Catherine." Ian's voice was filled with remorse. Isabella turned to where the children were standing on the opposite side of the room and saw Ian frown dejectedly at his sister.

"You didn't break it, silly. You've found a secret passage." Isabella saw Ian's eyes grow as wide as saucers when Catherine pushed on a section of panel that was no longer flush with the wall. Slowly it creaked inward. "Isn't it marvelous, Miss Browning? I bet the treasure is hidden in here. I'm going to find it."

"Catherine, wait!" Isabella shouted and rushed forward, but she was too late. In the wink of an eye, Catherine disappeared behind the small door.

Isabella somehow managed to catch an edge of the door before it closed. It was heavy, heavier than she expected, but she pushed hard against it with her shoulder and opened the passageway. A strong odor of musty dampness wafted into the room.

"Stay back, Ian," Isabella commanded. The little boy needed no urging. He obediently stepped away from the wall.

"Miss Browning?" Catherine whispered in a timid, weak voice.

Isabella moved forward and caught a glimpse of Catherine's features in the shaft of light that reached into the deep cavity. The child's face was ghost-white, her blue eyes glazed over with an emotion too intense to be fear. "My goodness, what is it Catherine? What is wrong?"

Catherine shook her head vigorously, refusing to speak, seemingly incapable of moving her legs. Reacting to the terror in the young girl's eyes, Isabella lunged forward, intending to pull Catherine out. But she misjudged the distance, and as her hand closed protectively around Catherine's arm, her hold on the door slipped, and it quickly slammed, shutting them inside.

Isabella stood in the total darkness, immobile for several seconds. The passageway was low, little more than four feet high, and she had to stoop to avoid hitting her head. Isabella could hear Catherine's rapid breathing and feel the trembling of fear in the small arm she thankfully still held.

"Catherine?" she whispered softly.

The child's ear-splitting screams echoed off the stone walls. Isabella's heart pounded with fright as she reached out blindly with her free hand, took hold of Catherine's shoulder, and pulled the girl into her arms. She held the screaming child close to her breast, trying to quell the girl's hysterical sobs.

In the inky darkness, Isabella raised her hand to cup the side of Catherine's face and tenderly stroked her cheek. Speaking in a firm, soothing voice, Isabella gradually penetrated Catherine's terror. The child's deep, painful sobs lessened, then mercifully ceased.

"Gracious. I think this is a bit too much of an adventure. Don't you agree, Catherine?" Isabella spoke with forced lightness, seeking to control the sudden panic that caused her heart to beat painfully fast.

"I want to get out!" Catherine wailed pitifully. She buried her head against Isabella's shoulder and sobbed loudly.

"So do I, sweetheart," Isabella whispered, forcing the sense of impending doom from her voice.

Still holding Catherine in her arms, Isabella inched them both back slowly through the cold darkness, waiting breathlessly to reach the solid bulk of the door. After an eternity, she encountered it and dropped awkwardly to a squatting position while precariously balancing Catherine in her arms. Isabella flattened her shoulder against what she thought was the outline of the door. Taking a deep breath, she dug in her heels and pushed with every ounce of strength she possessed. Nothing moved.

Isabella leaned her forehead against the door, refusing to acknowledge the choking fear and sense of terror that welled up inside her. Shifting Catherine to one side, Isabella freed her right arm and slowly, methodically, ran her hands over the inside wall, desperately searching for a lever or lock or latch that would open the door. She found nothing.

Fighting down her rising panic, Isabella put her ear to the door, straining to catch the faintest sounds. "Ian? Ian, are you there?"

"I want you and Catherine to come out now, Miss Browning," Ian replied, his voice sounding muffled and distant.

"We cannot open the door from this side. You must do it, Ian. Can you find the latch?"

"No, no, I can't!" Ian's voice rose in volume.

"It's all right, Ian. You found the latch before, remember? You thought you had broken the wall. I know you can do it, just take your time," Isabella encouraged. "Try again."

"I can't find it," Ian screeched.

Even through the heavy door, Isabella could hear his whimpering sobs. Apparently, so did Catherine, for she began crying again.

"Don't fret, Catherine, all will be well," Isabella said with a show of false bravado. She kissed the top of Catherine's head and gently stroked her back, trying to calm the child.

Isabella shivered, wishing she believed her own words of comfort. This was fast becoming a highly dangerous situation. Ian was clearly incapable of freeing them. He must go for help, yet the thought froze her. Would he be able to find his way back to this chamber? If he couldn't, she and Catherine might be entombed for hours.

Firmly pushing that terrifying thought from her mind, Isabella spoke to Ian.

"We are going to need some help, Ian. Your father is working in his study. You must find him and bring him here. Do you understand?"

"Yes."

Isabella's heart lurched at Ian's woebegone response. "I know you are frightened, Ian. But you must trust me. Everything will be fine. Your father will be able to easily open the panel, you'll see. Go find him, tell him what has happened, and hurry back.''

"I don't want to leave. I want you to come with me."

Isabella bit her bottom lip hard. "Please, Ian, go find your father."

A chilling silence descended, grating on Isabella's already frayed nerves. Finally she heard the faint sound of Ian's footsteps as he left the chamber. Sagging with relief, Isabella sank down onto the cold, hard floor, pulling Catherine into her lap. She hugged the child tightly against her chest, as much to bolster her own waning courage as to comfort the little girl.

"I don't like it in here," Catherine said. "What is this place?"

"It is probably a priest's hole," Isabella replied, grateful for any distraction. "These chambers were built in many houses during the reign of the Tudors to hide members of the Catholic faith so they could escape religious persecution."

"Did the priests live in here?"

"No. They would only hide to escape arrest, then leave when the danger had passed."

"I think a priest is hiding in here right now," Catherine said, her voice rising in agitation. "I saw one lying on the floor when I walked in here."

Isabella felt the bottom fall out of her stomach. Surly it was fear and a vivid imagination that caused Catherine to imagine such a horrible thing.

"Put it from your mind, Catherine. I'm sure we are alone in here. What you saw was probably just a trick of the light when you opened the panel door. There is no need to be afraid."

She rocked the little girl to and fro, humming softly. She knew Catherine could not have seen a priest, but something had badly frightened the girl. And whatever it was, it was still there, lurking in the darkness. Isabella shivered.

Time passed slowly, the silence and darkness becoming even more oppressive. Isabella placed the back of her hand over her eyes as a cold chill ran up her spine. She felt as if she was suffocating. She had never been overly fond of closed spaces, and with each passing moment it felt as though the walls and ceiling were closing in on her. It was difficult to remain calm and rational when all she really wanted was to break through the wall and breathe some clean, fresh air.

Isabella blinked hard several times, trying to shake the atmosphere of unreality. She felt cold to the very heart, yet she clung stubbornly to the belief that Damien would rescue them. Soon. Ian was a bright boy. Although he was distraught, he would somehow find his way back. She must have faith. Cradling the trembling Catherine in her lap, Isabella's lips began moving in silent prayer.

Ian burst into the earl's study, running as if the very hounds of hell were chasing him. Damien rose to his feet in confusion and watched his son race across the room.

"Father!" Ian launched himself at the earl. Damien caught the little boy in his arms. "Oh, Father, you must come at once! Something awful has happened to Catherine and Miss Browning!"

A rush of anxiety filled Damien. Crouching down on his knees, he grasped Ian's shoulders tightly. The little boy's face crumpled in misery and tears spilled down his cheeks.

"Don't fret, son," Damien whispered, his gut wrenching with worry. "Tell me what has happened."

But Ian was too upset to speak. He threw his arms around Damien's neck, lowered his forehead to the earl's shoulder, and sobbed pitifully. The anxiety in Damien's chest increased tenfold. He had never seen the child so distraught.

Ian had latched onto his father with an iron grip. With difficulty, Damien gently released the boy's hold from around his neck. He held Ian's trembling hands reassuringly in his own moist palms.

"Tell me what has happened," Damien repeated, wiping away a trickling tear with one finger.

Ian took a shuddering breath and began speaking. "They are in the wall. Catherine and Miss Browning. I tried to open it, I really tried, but I could not. Miss Browning told me I must find you. She said you would be able to help them. You will save them, wouldn't you, Father?''

"You are not making any sense, Ian," Damien said with frustration. "How can Catherine and Miss Browning be inside a wall?''

"We were having an adventure, looking for Lady Anne's treasure. We climbed up lots of steps, and Miss Browning opened a big door that made noise. It smelled funny, and then Catherine found a pretty room. I touched the wall and it moved. Catherine called it a secret passage, and Miss Browning said to stop, but Catherine did not. She walked inside the wall. Then Miss Browning walked inside the wall too, and it shut closed. And Catherine screamed and screamed. And Miss Browning told me I must open the wall. But I couldn't Father ... I couldn't.''

Damien drew Ian's shivering body close against his chest and wrapped his arms about him.

"Do not cry, Ian. We will find them," Damien said softly, trying to think straight. Ian's bizarre tale was far from logical, but it did make some sense. And clearly the boy knew where his sister and governess were trapped. "You must show me where Catherine and Miss Browning are, so we can properly rescue them.''

Ian pulled out of Damien's hold. The earl tenderly framed the child's small face with his hands. Tears still brightened the little boy's eyes, and he tried to bravely blink them away.

"I remember the way, Father," Ian whispered.

Damien's throat closed with emotion. "Good boy. Let's hurry." Hoping to ease the fear etched in the child's eyes, Damien added, "Every gentleman knows it is bad form to keep a lady waiting.''

Hand in hand, father and son rushed from the room.

Damien tried not to dwell on the gruesome possibilities as Ian led the way. Were Catherine or Isabella hurt? Was that the real reason they couldn't exit from this "secret passage," as Ian called it? As a young boy Damien had searched many of the rooms in the old fortress and had never stumbled upon any hidden passageways. It was, however, quite possible that a room such as Ian described did exist, constructed long ago, perhaps during Cromwell's time to hide Royalists. That theory certainly fit nicely with Lady Anne's inclination for supporting and spying for King Charles.

"This is the room, Father."

Damien blinked with surprise when he stepped inside and beheld the rose-tinted room. He was certain he had never seen it before since he knew he would not easily have forgotten such an striking effect.

"Here is where the wall moves," Ian said.

Damien knelt where his son indicated and carefully examined the wall. He saw nothing unusual in the intricately carved paneling. Cupping his hands on either side of his mouth, he shouted loudly at the wall, "Isabella, Catherine, can you hear me?"

"Damien, is that you?"

The words were faint, but distinguishable. Damien smiled weakly as relief shot through him. He had found them.

"Ian brought me here, Isabella. Are you injured? Is Catherine with you?"

"I am here, Father," Catherine wailed.

"We are fine," Isabella said. "A bit anxious to get out, however. Ian originally found the latch that releases the panel. It must be fairly low to the ground."

With renewed determination, Damien continued poking and probing the panel, following Isabella's advice to search the lower half of the wall. Suddenly, his fingers found a small latch hidden within the carving of a thorny rose stem. Excited, Damien pulled on it and the panel miraculously popped open.

"You did it!" Ian cried with delight.

"Help me, son." The little boy moved forward and they pushed together on one side of the panel. It swung inward and Catherine and Isabella literally tumbled out with a shriek of alarm.

"Thank God," Damien murmured as he assisted them to their feet.

"Oh, Father, I was so scared." Catherine wrapped her arms

about Damien's waist and squeezed tightly enough to crack a rib.

Damien hugged his daughter fiercely. Over her head, he fixed his gray eyes directly on Isabella's pale face, dirt-smudged cheek, and untidy hair. Damien smiled broadly. She had never looked more beautiful. He offered her his hand and she grasped it without hesitation. An aching tenderness filled his soul, and he was stunned by the feelings that swelled in his chest. He loved her. With all his heart. *God help him.*

Chapter Twenty-three

"Catherine has fallen into an exhausted sleep and Ian will soon follow," Damien said. "I asked Maggie to sit with them. I don't want the children awakening from their naps and finding themselves alone. They might become frightened."

Damien spoke from the doorway of Isabella's bedchamber. He had stayed with his children until a peaceful sleep had claimed his daughter, her small hand clutched tightly in his own. The earl had slipped away when she was fully slumbering, after holding his son for several minutes in a warm, comforting hug.

"I pray Catherine and Ian will not have any lingering nightmares from the incident," Isabella replied in a small voice. Damien watched the swift play of emotions that crossed her face. Tears sparkled in her eyes, and she wiped them with the dusty sleeve of her gown. "It was all my fault, Damien. I should have been more careful. I'm so very sorry."

"You must not blame yourself, Isabella. If anyone is to be held responsible, it is I," Damien insisted. "I should never have told the children those preposterous stories about Lady Anne's treasure. Naturally they were curious."

Damien moved forward, feeling awkward as he approached

Isabella. The unexpected discovery a few hours ago that he was in love with her was nearly paralyzing him. He did not feel at ease with these new emotions. Damien was stunned and slightly overwhelmed at the enormity of the love and protectiveness he felt for Isabella. These strange, unexpected feelings made him uncertain. He felt vulnerable and slightly out of control.

Damien decided this must be the difficult, unpleasant side of love. Yet this same emotion had the power to make his heart, nay his very soul, leap with gladness just to be near Isabella. She brought forth the tenderness and joy buried deep within him. She brought lightness and laughter into his life.

Damien longed to reveal his heart to Isabella, but he was unsure. He stared at her in silence, this woman he loved, and wondered if this was the right moment to speak. She was clearly still shaken by the occurrences of the morning. In fact, the past twenty-four hours of Isabella's life had been nothing but turmoil. She had discovered the identity of her father, gotten drunk on a bottle of his best claret for the first and probably last time in her life, and been locked away in a damp, musty passage with a nearly hysterical child.

How would she react to his declaration? Would she welcome it or, God forbid, be embarrassed by it? Damien knew how important love was to Isabella. He remembered vividly her passionate speech the morning after their first intimate encounter. She had refused his marriage proposal because he did not love her. Would she now accept him? Would he finally have a chance at the life he had never before known he wanted?

Deciding he could not stand the uncertainty, Damien took action. He swung his foot and slammed Isabella's bedchamber door shut. He wanted complete privacy for this intimate moment.

Isabella jumped, clearly startled by his action. "Please don't," she whispered hoarsely. Crossing the room quickly, she reopened the door. "I find myself suddenly averse to closed spaces of any kind."

"Ah, sweet," he murmured. He reached out and drew her to him. "It pains me deeply to know you suffered."

Isabella gave a small cry of anguish, crushed her face to Damien's chest, and sobbed quietly.

"I was so frightened. It was cramped and dark, and Catherine, poor mite, was terrified. I knew you would come, Damien—I never doubted that for a moment. But it was so hard waiting."

Isabella's pain touched him, sending a wave of tenderness surging through him. Her blind trust that he would come to her rescue was a humbling thought. She was an independent, self-reliant woman, yet she turned to him for solace and strength. It was a good sign.

"I am going to send Jenkins with a crew of men to the east wing this afternoon and instruct them to seal off that panel," Damien said. "I do not want anyone else ever subjected to the torment you and Catherine endured today."

"You mustn't do that." Isabella's violet eyes were troubled. She took a deep, bracing breath. "I'm sure you will think me mad, Damien, but I believe there is something in that passageway."

"What!" Damien felt his stomach clench in shock. "What is it? What did you see?"

Isabella chewed briefly on her lower lip. "I didn't really see anything; it was far too dark. But something in there rendered Catherine motionless with fright. At first I thought it was just her imagination, but the longer we were trapped inside, the more I began to feel it too. Toward the end it became unbearably intense."

Damien sighed with relief. "I'm sure it was merely a reaction to being confined in such a small, dark place."

"Perhaps," she conceded. Isabella turned from him and twisted her fingers nervously. "As much as it pains me to suggest it, I think we need to go back inside the passageway and investigate."

Damien's brow rose. He found Isabella's request oddly disturbing. He was hoping to put the unfortunate incident behind them. He had never dreamed Isabella would want to return to the place that had brought her such distress.

"If you feel it is so important, Jenkins and I will do as you suggest,'' Damien said, not relishing the notion of entering the tomblike passage.

"Good.'' Isabella turned back to him and smiled sheepishly. "I'll only need a few moments to change into a fresh gown. I know it's rather foolish, since I will probably get all dusty and dirty again, but I would feel better if I cleaned up a bit. Of course, the best thing for me to wear would be breeches.''

"Absolutely not.''

Isabella's smile broadened. "I was only teasing, Damien. Naturally I will not be donning breeches. Where would I ever find a pair to fit me?''

"Isabella, there is no reason for you to come with us,'' Damien said, deliberately ignoring her quip. "You cannot tolerate a closed bedchamber door, how will you fare inside that passageway? Jenkins and I are perfectly capable of exploring it on our own.''

"You don't understand. I don't really *want* to go, I *have* to go. I swear I will never have a decent night's sleep if I don't see with my own eyes what is or is not hidden inside that chamber.''

Damien heard the edge of fear in Isabella's voice, but he also saw the glint of determination in her eye. And he knew from past experience that she would not be denied.

Damien heaved an ungracious sigh of defeat and forced himself to consider the one positive aspect of the situation. At least he would be with Isabella. He could protect her from any harm, real or imagined, and if he judged the situation too upsetting for her, he would abruptly end it. If she could not see to her own best interests, then he most certainly would.

Damien narrowed his gaze. "I'm going to gather the supplies we'll need and locate Jenkins. I will await you in my study. I'll expect you there in twenty minutes.''

Damien turned on his heel and stalked out of the room, deciding that being in love with an impetuous, willful woman like Isabella was going to age him quickly.

Fifteen minutes later, Isabella breathlessly arrived at the earl's study. She had changed into her oldest gown in record time, not wanting to give Damien any opportunity to change his mind about taking her along. Holding her arm against the stitch that cramped her side from running, she watched in quiet fascination as Damien packed a cloth sack.

Neatly spread out before him were three lanterns, four candles, a light box, a considerable length of heavy rope, a long-bladed knife, and several large stones. Isabella was surprised when she realized the earl meant to take all these items with him.

''My goodness, Damien, we are only going to explore one rather small chamber. We are not about to embark on a trip to India.'' Isabella fingered a foot-long gray stone in puzzlement. ''Rocks?''

''For propping the panel door open,'' Damien explained. He continued filling his sack as if Isabella had not spoken. ''There must be a release mechanism on the inside of the wall, but I have no intention of placing myself in the disadvantaged position of being forced to locate it in order to exit the passageway.''

''A sound idea.'' Isabella nodded her approval. ''But are all these other items necessary? Would not a few candles suffice?''

''I am preparing for any eventuality,'' Damien replied. ''Ah, here is Jenkins. I hope he has packed our lunch.''

''Lunch!'' Isabella exclaimed. Her eyes widened in disbelief, and Damien burst out laughing.

After a moment's hesitation, Isabella joined in. She supposed she deserved that. Lord knew she certainly didn't need her female instincts to tell her that Damien would prefer she not accompany him this afternoon. Given the earl's autocratic nature, Isabella was sure he did not appreciate her questioning his choice of supplies.

Damien finished packing the satchel and tossed the cumbersome bag easily over his shoulder. Isabella could not help but admire the way the strong muscles of his forearms rippled beneath his snug-fitting coat. She had always found his taut, muscular physique appealing, but the sight of his powerful body filled her with a sense of confidence. Damien was physically strong and mentally alert. Her fear of their forthcoming expedition lessened. At all costs, Isabella knew, the earl would keep her safe.

"Are we ready?" Damien asked. "Jenkins, Isabella, come along."

Isabella obligingly fell in step with Jenkins as Damien led the way. While crossing the great hall, the trio unexpectedly bumped into Lord Poole. Isabella could tell from the contemptuous glare Damien cast at Lord Poole that he was annoyed by the interruption.

"Where are you off to in such a hurry?" Lord Poole asked.

"This doesn't concern you, Poole," Damien said without breaking stride.

"If it involves Isabella, then it most definitely concerns me," Lord Poole retorted, stepping forward to block Isabella's progress.

Everyone stopped. Isabella lowered her eyes, avoiding the probing look Lord Poole sent her way. She said nothing. Risking a glance beneath her lashes, she saw Damien's expression darkening. She sighed loudly. Clearly both men were going to continue to make her the focus of their ongoing feud. Isabella felt as though she were a prized toy being fought over by two young lads.

This constant battle between Damien and Thomas for her undivided loyalty must cease. Isabella forced herself to stop twisting the folds of her gown between her fingers. It was high time she put her foot down. Lifting her chin, she spoke to her half brother.

"We are going to explore a hidden passageway the children and I discovered this morning. Would you care to join us, Thomas?"

Lord Poole appeared confounded by Isabella's invitation, but he readily accepted. Damien was silent for a long moment, and Isabella feared he would cancel the proposed expedition. Instead he gave her a level look, then began climbing the staircase.

Relieved at avoiding a scene, Isabella accepted Lord Poole's arm and they trailed behind Damien and Jenkins. Seeking a distraction from the palpable tension, Isabella began relating the morning's startling events to Lord Poole. When she discovered he had no prior knowledge of Lady Anne's treasure, Isabella launched into a spirited rendition of the fascinating tale.

"Egad, Saunders," Lord Poole taunted, " 'tis hard to imagine you've had the solution to your endless financial problems buried in this old relic for over a century."

Damien neglected to rise to the bait. He flashed Lord Poole the lethal smile that usually sent the faint of heart running for cover. Isabella felt a twinge of sisterly pride when Thomas returned the look measure for measure.

"This is it," Damien announced when they reached the proper room.

Everyone followed the earl solemnly into the chamber.

He strode directly to the correct wall panel and pressed the latch hidden in the molding. The panel clicked open.

"Fascinating," Jenkins said.

"Simply amazing," Lord Poole agreed. He moved forward, reached into his breast coat pocket, and drew out a quizzing glass attached to a black silk ribbon. Holding the magnifying glass up to his eye, Lord Poole peered intently at the panel door. "It is so simple, yet so ingenious."

"Easy enough for a child to find," Damien said with a rueful grin. "Help me with these things, Jenkins."

The two men spread the contents of the sack upon the floor.

"I want a lantern too," Isabella declared as she observed the valet lighting the wicks and carefully positioning the glass.

"You cannot mean to say you are going traipsing around in that tunnel, Isabella?" Thomas straightened up and gazed at her with acute alarm. "I expressly forbid it."

"For once we are in agreement," Damien said. "Isabella, you will wait here with Poole while Jenkins and I go inside."

"No. It is my decision to make." Straightening her shoulders, she announced calmly, "I'm going too."

"Then I must accompany you," Lord Poole declared. "Pass me a candle."

Damien snorted, but did not protest. Jenkins handed Lord Poole a lit taper while Damien propped open the panel with two of the large stones he had brought expressly for that purpose. Extending his arm forward, the earl held his lantern aloft and illuminated the dark cavity. Isabella moved behind him and peered around his arm. Dozens of spider webs overhung the passage, and the oddly shaped stone walls caused the lamp to throw strange shadows.

Ignoring the twist of dread that clenched her stomach, Isabella forced herself to take a small step forward. Her lit lantern dangled at her side. A steady stream of cool air emanated from the passageway, and Isabella wrapped her free arm tightly around her waist to ward off the cold. The utter quiet was eerie and foreboding, and she was certain all three men could hear her heart pounding.

"Watch your heads," Damien commanded, crouching low.

The passage opening was only a few feet high. Crawling on his hands and knees with his lantern thrust before him, Damien entered the tunnel. As he disappeared, Isabella's heart rose to her throat. She thrust her arm out blindly, groping for his hand, but he was already too far ahead. Mercifully, she managed to catch the edge of his coat.

Holding on tightly with nerveless fingers, Isabella took a lung-filling breath, bent low, and followed the earl. Lord Poole immediately took up the position behind Isabella, and Jenkins brought up the rear.

Something briefly scurried into the glare of Isabella's lantern light, then darted into the shadows. She shuddered violently. As terrifying as the dark had been, it was almost preferable. The lamplight seemed to be awakening mysterious creatures that in Isabella's opinion were better left undisturbed.

"Drat! My candle has gone out," Lord Poole exclaimed.

Everyone stopped moving. Nervously, Isabella looked to her own lantern, watching the flame intently. Protected on four sides by sturdy glass, the flame barely wavered.

"There's a strong draft," Damien said, lifting his head. "The ceiling appears to be a few feet higher up ahead. We should be able stand there. I brought a flint so we can light your candle, though I'm uncertain it will remain lit in this chilling breeze."

They all moved soundlessly to the point Damien had indicated. They were able to stand erect in this section of the passageway, though Isabella noted that the earl was forced to stoop his broad shoulders to avoid hitting his head. It was very narrow, so they remained in a single line.

Since she was standing behind the earl, Isabella held Lord Poole's candle while Damien struck the flint and lit the wick. The candle flame danced merrily for several seconds, then flickered and died out. Cursing softly, Damien tried again. After three attempts, he admitted defeat.

Isabella could tell from Lord Poole's dour expression that he was annoyed. She knew Damien would not relinquish his lantern; besides, he was in the lead and must illuminate the way. Jenkins had not volunteered to give up his lamp, and Isabella was not about to force the issue. She reluctantly spoke, "You may have my lantern, Thomas."

Lord Poole instantly accepted her generous offer, and with only a slight hesitation Isabella passed him the lamp. She pocketed the useless candle.

"Stay close to me," Damien instructed.

"I shall," Isabella replied, hoping he did not detect the nervous edge in her voice.

Damien continued leading the way. Isabella adjusted her grip on the earl's coat, and for good measure placed her other hand loosely on his waist. His solid strength and warm body stilled her nerves.

They moved forward together only three steps before the earl abruptly stopped. Isabella could feel the tension and shock suddenly rippling through Damien's body. Her hand, so tightly gripping his coat, went numb. Something was terribly wrong.

"Damien?"

Isabella shifted to one side, trying to look beyond him at what lay ahead, but his broad shoulders blocked her view. Flattening her back against the cold stone wall, she slowly moved beside him.

The odor was stronger here, choking and musty. Isabella's nose wrinkled in protest. Craning her neck, she squinted, determined to see what was causing Damien's strange reaction. As she swept the area with a slow, considering eye, she noticed a dark outline of fabric on the stone floor. Or was it something else?

"This morning when we were trapped in here, Catherine insisted someone was lying on the floor. Do you think this is what she saw?"

"It's impossible," Damien muttered.

Confused by the remark, Isabella lifted her gaze from the floor and stared at the earl. Through the eerie glow of the lantern, she could see the puzzlement in Damien's eyes that gradually changed to understanding, then rapidly to horror.

"It's Emmeline."

Damien's voice was a raspy whisper, but Isabella was standing close enough to distinguish the words. Her eyes shot down to the stone floor. It couldn't be! With a growing sense of dreadful premonition, Isabella studied the dark outline.

She could see now that the fabric had a distinct shape. It was a woman's gown, wider on the bottom, narrower near the center, then wide again on the top. There was a fan of five white sticks spreading out from the top of one narrow band of fabric that Isabella belated realized was the skeletal remains of a human hand. A thick gold ring encircled one of the finger bones.

Isabella's blood ran cold. She gasped in shock, her mouth forming a circle. Only through the conscious exercise of tremendous will was she able to remain on her feet.

One of the two great mysteries of Whately Grange was finally solved. Emmeline's body had been found.

Chapter Twenty-four

Damien had known fear. He had led men across the field of battle with sword drawn and fear pumping through his veins. He had faced down charging regiments of French cavalry, their eyes glazed with hate and vengeance. He had heard the thunder of cannon, seen the grass suddenly explode beneath the feet of unsuspecting soldiers, helplessly listened to their agonizing screams of death. He had smelled the thick smoke and blood of war.

Yet as Damien stood staring down at the skeletal remains of his wife, a wrenching cold invaded the deep recesses of his chest beyond any prior feeling. His mind and body were rendered motionless.

"Why have we stopped, Saunders? Have you found your bloody treasure?"

Poole. The tightness in Damien's chest leaped to his throat. He swallowed hard, struggling to dislodge it. A whispering touch on his forearm startled him. He jerked away reflexively, then turned and found himself looking into Isabella's wide violet eyes.

He saw her concern and her unspoken support. The tightness

in his chest eased a fraction. Her comforting presences was a flickering light inside his tormented darkness.

"Get Poole out of here," Damien muttered through clenched teeth, exhaling in relief when Isabella nodded in understanding.

"I want to turn back," Isabella said in a voice that sounded high and strained to Damien's ears. "Thomas, will you please escort me?"

For a split second, Damien thought Poole was leaving without protest, but fate refused to be so merciful.

"What is it? What have you found?" Lord Poole's voice was riddled with suspicion as he charged forward, seeking to wheedle his way into the confined space.

Damien moved to block Poole's advance, but Poole ignored the earl and pulled Isabella ruthlessly aside and successfully wedged himself into the small space she had previously occupied. Damien watched with sickening dread as Lord Poole lifted his lantern shoulder high, further illuminating the gruesome scene.

"Damn. It's a body," Poole said with surprise. He squatted down for a closer look. "I think it's a woman. These clothes look as though they might have once been a riding habit. Could it be Lady Anne?"

Damien forced himself to gaze down dispassionately while Poole continued his exploration. He knew that eventually Poole would recognize, as Damien had, the heavy gold signet ring still starkly in place on the bony hand. After all, Poole had given Emmeline the ring on her wedding day.

"The flesh has long since rotted from the bones, but 'tis strange to see her riding bonnet so perfectly placed on her head," Lord Poole remarked casually. Damien winced when Poole impersonally fingered the hem of the velvet skirt. "I suspect that if we remove the hat, we will find her hair still neatly coiffed."

"Don't touch it!" Isabella screeched. "Please, Thomas, come away from there."

"There is nothing to be afraid of, Isabella," Lord Poole said soothingly, flashing her a superior smile. "This poor creature cannot possible harm you."

"Please come away," Isabella pleaded. She tugged insistently on his shoulder.

Lord Poole furrowed his brow and looked again at the corpse. When Damien saw the mild curiosity flee from Poole's eyes and a wild hysteria burst forth, he knew the other man had realized it was not Lady Anne's, but Emmeline's, pitiful remains that were so grotesquely displayed.

"Mother of God, what have you done, Saunders? What have you done to my angel? I'll kill you for this, you bastard!"

Poole threw his lantern to the floor, leaped to his feet, and lunged for Damien with both hands extended.

"Thomas, no!" Isabella stepped between the two men and Poole crashed into her. Damien felt the woosh of Isabella's breath as she was crushed against his chest.

Crazed with fury and grief, Poole struck out with clenched fists. He swung fiercely, aiming for Damien's head, but Damien, braced for the attack, ducked, pulling Isabella down with him so she wouldn't be hurt.

"I am as shocked as you are, Poole. I never believed Emmeline drowned in the lake. These past years I have firmly believed she was alive," Damien insisted, having difficulty dodging Poole's blows in the confined space.

"Lies, all lies!" Poole shouted with a raging snarl.

Jenkins moved forward to lend assistance. When Poole tried landing another punch, the valet intercepted it, knocking Poole off balance.

Poole staggered back, but remained on his feet. He glanced down again at what remained of Emmeline's body, and in a flash the potent violence inside him seemed to vanish. Visibly trembling, Poole helplessly crumpled to his knees, buried his face in his hands, and began howling like a wounded animal.

The shrill keening echoed off the thick stone walls, permeating Damien's soul. He had never heard such cries of deep anguish and pain. Poole was delirious with grief.

"My little angel." With a shaking hand, Poole reached out and stroked the billowing skirt slowly, lovingly. "My darling Emmeline."

Isabella went down on one knee beside her brother. "I'm

so sorry, Thomas,'' she said tearfully, wrapping her arms around his shoulders. Poole appeared unaware of her gesture.

Damien watched them in silence. Poole's whole body shook with deep, racking sobs. Damien's vision blurred. He threw his head back and shut his eyes tightly.

The bitterness and resentment Damien had carried for so long in his heart toward his estranged wife was washed away, replaced by guilt and regret. No matter how ill suited they were, no matter how unhappy and miserable they made each other, Damien never would have wanted Emmeline's life to end in this horrible manner.

What had happened? Had she become accidently trapped in this passageway as Catherine and Isabella were this morning? Damien felt nauseated at the idea. It was an unthinkably gruesome way to die. He shuddered, barely able to imagine how greatly Emmeline must have suffered, locked away in this cold tomb waiting for death.

What in God's name had she been doing in here? The questions crowded Damien's mind, and he knew regretfully they might never be answered. Yet he owed it to Emmeline to try.

''Ride over to Glendale Manor at once and fetch our illustrious magistrate, Lord Rathwick,'' Damien said to Jenkins, noticing how pale and shaken the valet appeared. ''I want Lord Rathwick to see Emmeline's remains before we remove them. Perhaps he can assist us in discovering what happened to her.''

Jenkins frowned. ''Are you sure you want him here? We both know Rathwick is a braying ass.''

''There is no one else,'' Damien said simply.

''Do you want me to help you get Lord Poole out of the passageway before I leave?'' Jenkins asked. ''I doubt he will be able to walk out under his own power.''

''His reason might completely snap if I try to force him away,'' Damien replied. ''We will wait for the magistrate. Perhaps his presence will ease Poole's mind.''

Jenkins left the chamber quickly, leaving his lantern behind. Deciding he wanted no further illumination of the haunting scene, Damien carefully pushed it along the edge of the wall and stood in front of it. Poole's lantern had gone out when he

threw it away in such rage, so only a single lantern kept the
darkness at bay. Hunching his shoulders against the gray,
gloomy atmosphere, Damien forced his mind to empty while
he waited.

Isabella's knee was numb, her back stiff, her fingers cold.
Yet she did not move from Lord Poole's side. His pain and
misery had choked her tender heart with pity. She felt driven
to offer him whatever compassion she could, though she
doubted he was aware of it. He seemed utterly lost in his grief,
beyond even the simplest comfort.

Damien stood silently in the background, his distance seemingly a calculated attempt to keep an emotional barrier between
them.

"Please, Thomas, come away," Isabella said, repeating her
plea yet again, but to no avail. Lord Poole remained as he was,
his eyes swimming with tears, his hands stroking the fabric of
Emmeline's gown. He seemed oblivious to Isabella's concern.

Isabella turned to Damien helplessly and was surprised to
read the frustration in his eyes. Apparently the earl was not as
immune to the situation as his actions indicated.

"Jenkins has gone for the magistrate," Damien said, with
a grim stare. "They should arrive at any time."

"Thank God," Isabella muttered. She blew the wisps of hair
that had fallen on her face from her eyes. "I doubt any of us
can survive much more of this."

"Poor devil," Damien whispered, and Isabella's heart constricted at the genuine sympathy she heard in his voice.

After an eternity, Jenkins arrived with Lord Rathwick in tow.
Their presence relieved one problem but created another. The
space was too narrow, too confined, to make a thorough investigation with so many people inside. Someone had to leave.

Bracing herself for the difficult task, Isabella tried to make
Lord Poole understand. "Thomas, the magistrate has come.
We must go outside."

Several long, silent moments passed before Lord Poole
slowly lifted his head. His eyes were vacant and unfocused.
"We can't leave Emmeline alone," he whispered in horror.

"Of course not," Isabella said soothingly, speaking in much

the same manner she used when comforting Ian or Catherine. "Lord Rathwick will stay with her."

Capitalizing on Lord Poole's confused state, Isabella pressed her advantage, and with Jenkin's help assisted her brother to his feet. Thomas swayed momentarily, then caught his balance and stiffened his spine. He looked neither left nor right as Isabella led him from the chamber.

Isabella's legs felt heavy as she exited the hidden passageway, but she was so relieved to be free of the cloying chamber that she easily dismissed the pain. She took a deep breath and concentrated on retaining her composure. The rose-colored hues of the bedchamber had deepened in the afternoon sunlight, offering a comforting balm to Isabella's fragile emotions.

She seated Thomas on the floor with his back pressed firmly against the wall at the opposite end of the room. He remained quiet and docile, and Isabella noted thankfully that the tortured look had eased from his eyes. She joined him on the floor, extending her legs out in front to stretch the stiff, aching joints.

After a short time, the three grim-faced men emerged from the passageway. Isabella rose to her feet.

"What did you find?"

"Who are you, young woman?" Lord Rathwick demanded. He was a short, portly man whose generous jowls quivered when he spoke. He smelled of horses and tobacco.

"This is Isabella Browning, governess to my children," Damien interjected. "Miss Browning, may I present Lord Rathwick."

Isabella automatically sank into a curtsey. The magistrate returned her greeting with a short nod of his head, running a distrustful eye from Isabella's dusty shoes to her unkempt hair. His heavy, dark brows crinkled in confusion.

"I still don't understand why she is here, Saunders," he said in a gruff voice. Puffing out his chest, Lord Rathwick added, "It's highly improper having a woman around an official investigation."

"I have a right to be here," Isabella said, drawing herself up to her full height and bringing her eyes level with Rathwick's. "Emmeline was my sister."

The magistrate's jowls shook. He opened and closed his mouth several times, looking so much like a fish that Isabella was hard pressed not to laugh out loud. Instead she ignored Lord Rathwick and asked Jenkins, "What did you discover?"

The valet never hesitated. "Lady Emmeline's neck and ankle were broken and the side of her face pressing against the stone floor was smashed. There is a deep rut in the flooring. She must have tripped and fallen. We found a small candle stub and a thin line of spilled wax near her left hand. It was impossible to tell if the flame went out in a draft, as Lord Poole's candle did, and caused the fall, or if Lady Emmeline simply missed her footing and stumbled on the uneven ground."

"It was a horrible accident," Damien added solemnly.

"An accident, you say?" Lord Rathwick raised a skeptical eyebrow. "Now that's for me to decide. 'Course, ruling all this an accidental death would be a convenient conclusion for you, wouldn't it, Saunders?"

Isabella saw Damien's jaw tighten, but he refrained from answering.

"Just what are you insinuating, Lord Rathwick?" Isabella demanded.

"I am trying to discover the truth, young woman," the magistrate said pompously. "Since Lady Emmeline was your *sister,* maybe you can give me a reasonable explanation as to why she was alone in that dark, hidden passageway."

Isabella gestured helplessly, looking first to Damien and then to Jenkins for support.

"I think this will provide the answer. It was found in the pocket of Emmeline's riding habit," Damien said. He pulled from his coat a fragile, leather-bound book.

Lord Rathwick rubbed his chin thoughtfully. He took the volume out of the earl's hand and flipped through several pages. Squinting, Lord Rathwick moved into a rose-colored shaft of sunlight. Grasping the book tightly, he extended his arms as far as they would reach. "Can't read all that well without my spectacles, but this appears to a journal of sorts. Who the deuce is Lady Anne?"

"Emmeline had Lady Anne's journal?" Isabella felt a flush

of excitement. "Good heavens, Emmeline must have been searching for the treasure. That's why she was in the hidden passageway."

"Lady Anne's treasure? I remember hearing those wild tales when I was a boy, but I didn't think anyone believed that silly old legend," Lord Rathwick said with a frown. "And yet, there doesn't appear to be any evidence indicating a crime. Although I find it a bit of far-fetched thinking to say Lady Saunders was searching for treasure, I suppose it is a reasonable explanation."

"That is a completely far-fetched and totally ludicrous notion." Lord Poole's voice, strong and steady, fell over the room.

Isabella watched him rise on his feet, push himself away from the wall, then move to join them. She was glad his deep melancholy had faded, but she was alarmed to see the fire of revenge that now gleamed in his eye. "Emmeline would never have gone on such a harebrained escapade. She had far too much dignity."

"What do you think happened, Lord Poole?" Lord Rathwick inquired politely.

"I think it is obvious. Saunders killed her and hid her body in the wall."

"Oh, Thomas, you can't believe that," Isabella cried, appalled by the accusation.

"Why not? It is as good an explanation as the accident theory. 'Twas was common knowledge their marriage was not a happy one." Lord Poole gave Damien a shrewd look. "Divorce is a long, costly, and unpredictable process. Surely there are easier ways to rid oneself of an unwanted wife."

"How dare you," Damien said through his teeth. Isabella could see the earl's temper flaring, but he stood perfectly still, his hands in clenched fists at his sides.

"Oh, I dare, Saunders," Lord Poole sneered. "I vow you will pay for Emmeline's death, and pay dearly."

"You are still upset, Thomas," Isabella said gravely. She set her arm gently on his shoulder. "You don't know what you are saying."

"He is deranged," Jenkins said scornfully.

"Murder is a very serious accusation, sir," Lord Rathwick said. "It will be necessary for me to conduct a formal investigation. Question witnesses, search for clues, that sort of thing. Are you sure that's what you want?"

If the situation weren't so grave, Isabella would have laughed out loud at Lord Rathwick's abrupt change of attitude. He no longer seemed enamored of his position as magistrate now that it appeared the job would entail actual work.

But this was no time for levity. She needed to act and act quickly if there was any hope of avoiding disaster.

"Excuse us, gentlemen," Isabella said. "I must confer with my brother in private."

She grasped Lord Poole's arm firmly and led him to the far corner of the room. Isabella saw his eyes become wary, but she pressed on. She firmly believed that somewhere beyond the hurt and anger in Thomas's mind lay a measure of reason. Somehow she must convince him to abandon his pursuit of vengeance and save them all from unnecessary pain and grief.

She must chose her words carefully. The wrong turn of phrase might further inflame him, and the chance for a peaceful conclusion to this horrible incident would be lost.

"You must stop this, Thomas," Isabella began without preamble. "I understand that you are hurt and angry, but the course you are pursuing will accomplish nothing. It will only lead to more heartache for all of us, yourself included. If you force yourself to look deeply, honestly, within your heart, I know you will conclude that Damien would never commit such a heinous crime."

Lord Poole narrowed his eyes. "Pray don't tell me that monster has stolen your regard, Isabella. I could not tolerate losing both my sisters to him."

"You are misreading the situation. My relationship with the earl is not at issue. Lord Rathwick is willing to drop the matter; he will only pursue it if you insist." She reached for his hands and held them tightly in her own. "Don't make this into a spectacle. Think of the children. Catherine and Ian will suffer greatly. And so will I. Please, I beg you, do not allow that to happen, Thomas."

The silence stretched for an eternity. "How can I refuse you, Isabella? It would be pure torture for me to see you so unhappy."

The relief that washed through Isabella was so strong, it left her weak-kneed. She took a deep and audible breath before murmuring a simple, heartfelt, "Thank you."

Releasing his hands she turned, but Lord Poole pulled her back. "Ah—Isabella, there is one small favor I must ask of you in return."

"Of course, anything."

"I refuse to spend any more time than is absolutely necessary in Saunders's company. I shall make appropriate arrangements for our departure to occur as soon as possible. I hope you will be ready."

"Ready?"

"To leave," Lord Poole said. "I am firmly committed to your future happiness, and I am more than willing to indulge you, as I have amply demonstrated this afternoon. But there are limits to my endurance. I cannot possibly allow you to live here any longer." He gave her a sly smile. "Shall we inform Lord Rathwick of our decision?"

Isabella blinked. The room suddenly felt overbearingly stuffy and hot. Lord Poole's magnanimous gesture, which had seemed so noble and unselfish moments before, took on an ominous taint. Isabella understood the underlying meaning of his words. He was willing to do what she asked and drop the matter entirely. For a price. Her freedom.

"It will be as you wish, Thomas," Isabella heard herself saying, closing her eyes to conceal her distress.

Lord Poole spoke contritely when he told the others of his concurrence that Emmeline's death was an accident. Isabella stood by his side, too stunned to say anything.

Lord Rathwick looked at them strangely and pursed his lips. "Is that truly your final word, Lord Poole? Think hard before you answer, man, for once I rule the death an accident, I'll not be reopening the case for any reason."

There was a short pause. "I understand, Lord Rathwick,"

Lord Poole replied. "I thank you for your indulgence. Obviously this has been a difficult day for my family."

The magistrate left. Damien made a move toward Isabella, but Lord Poole pulled her away.

"Isabella and I shall be leaving as soon as the proper arrangements can be made. I must speak to my servants without delay to ensure that all will be ready," Lord Poole stated coldly. He then whisked Isabella out of the room before the earl or his valet had an opportunity to react.

Isabella went without protest, convincing herself she was doing the right thing. Thomas had left her little choice in the matter. Yet in her mind all she could recall was the confused expression of hurt and betrayal on Damien's face when he realized she was leaving. It mirrored the pain of her own heart.

The clouds threatened, but no rain fell as the small, solemn procession made its way across the great lawn to the family mausoleum. The earl had hastily arranged for the vicar to perform a brief, late-afternoon funeral service for his wife now that her remains had been properly entombed in the family crypt.

Lord Poole had vehemently protested his sister's final resting place, insisting that Emmeline should be buried beside her parents, but Isabella had successfully prevailed upon him to reconsider his objections. Catherine and Ian would want to be close to their mother, Isabella explained, and in the end Poole had reluctantly relented.

With the earl leading the way, they all filed quietly into the small vestibule of the mausoleum. Damien took up his position at the front of the room, flanked on either side by his children. Jenkins and Isabella stood directly behind them as the remaining Grange servants crowded and shifted together, maintaining a respectful distance.

Missing from the somber sea of faces was Lord Poole. He had refused to walk with the rest of the mourners and now forced them all to await his presence. The tension grew as the minutes passed, and Isabella felt the marble walls closing in around her. Just when the nerves she had fought to control since the early afternoon threatened to overcome her, Lord Poole arrived.

All eyes turned his way as he entered the small space, clearly taking advantage of the opportunity to make a grand entrance. He swept in like an avenging angel, dressed entirely in black, his arms laden with white roses. His valet and two footmen followed him. Each servant wore a black armband.

Lord Poole's belligerent feelings about the funeral service were clearly conveyed by his arrogant stance. He acknowledged no one and remained unnaturally rigid, head held high, spine stiff, shoulders back. From the corner of her eye, Isabella stole a quick glance at her half brother. She saw only the deep grief in his eyes and the bitter coldness on his face.

At the earl's request, it was a mercifully simple service. Isabella was proud the children were able to stand so still and quiet throughout the ceremony. Naturally, they did not completely understand the significance of the event, but they sensitively took their cue from the adults and remained subdued.

Lord Poole's composure broke at the end of the final prayer. He tossed the white roses dramatically on the ground, sagged forward, and began weeping. His two footman hurried to his side and caught him under the arms before his knees hit the cold stone floor. They held him between them, muscles straining in an effort to keep Lord Poole upright.

Isabella shivered. His sobs were too loud for the closeness of the stone vault, his pain too raw. Tears fell unchecked down his cheeks until he appeared to be too exhausted to produce any more.

"Why is Uncle Thomas crying?" Ian asked in a frightened voice.

"He is very sad," Isabella explained, wishing she could summon some deeply hidden sisterly emotion and do something, anything, to bring Thomas some measure of comfort in his grief. But his sorrow appeared so great, it was clear there were no words of sympathy that would adequately soothe his pain.

Isabella went limp with relief when Damien wordlessly

turned away and led his children from the scene, knowing if she had to listen to any more of Thomas's anguish, she would surely go mad. Gratefully, Isabella followed them, as did the rest of the mourners. Not surprisingly, Lord Poole stayed behind, seeking privacy for his final good-bye.

Ian skipped ahead of the crowd and Catherine also left her father's side, but instead of running along with her brother, the little girl waited for Isabella. They walked silently together, Catherine matching her stride to Isabella's. After a few moments, Catherine reached for her hand.

Isabella's hand trembled slightly as it closed over Catherine's. They had come a long way together. It pained her to be leaving when there was so much more she could have accomplished, but she knew she had to content herself with the knowledge that she had done her very best by Catherine and Ian. Still, she would miss them more than she even dared to consider.

Although the earl walked behind Isabella, he kept pace with her slower step, their feet crunching in unison on the flagstone and gravel paths. She could feel Damien studying her intently, and she glanced back at him, trying to gauge his mood. His eyes were dark with emotion, but his expression was unreadable. She knew he was hurt by her decision to leave The Grange with Thomas, but she firmly believed her sacrifice was saving the earl from real danger.

In his current state of anger and grief, Thomas was capable of doing almost anything. And his main target for revenge would most certainly be Damien.

Once back at the house, everyone went their separate ways. There had been no need to prepare a traditional repast of food and drink following the ceremony of internment, since it was, by design, such a sparsely attended service.

"Tonight we will dine upstairs in the schoolroom, children," Isabella announced in what she hoped would pass as a cheerful tone. "We shall go down to the kitchen and select whatever strikes our fancy. I'm sure the chef has prepared many lovely dishes to tempt us."

Intrigued, as always, by the promise of a new adventure,

Catherine and Ian enthusiastically invaded the kitchen. Isabella raised no objections to their outrageous selections, for once not really caring that the majority of their food choices would probably end up on the trash heap.

Isabella and the children met Jenkins on the staircase. They paused only momentarily, since Isabella carried a heavy tray laden with their dinner.

"Please ask the earl to join us in the schoolroom," Isabella requested in a slightly breathless voice.

"The earl has left The Grange," Jenkins said stiffly. "I'm not certain when, or if, he will return."

Isabella nearly dropped the tray. Gone! Her brain reeled while her heart twisted, but there was nothing she could do. She could only feel robbed, cheated somehow. Knowing she was to leave in the morning made each moment she stayed at The Grange more crucial, more precious. She had never once considered that Damien would prefer to maintain a distant silence between them.

"Please tell Damien that I must speak with him." Isabella chewed on her lower lip and looked away. "Ask him to find me, Jenkins. No matter what the hour," she added softly, throwing all pretense of pride out the window.

The valet gave her a sharp glance, but Isabella was too distraught to notice. Her footsteps made a hollow echo as she slowly climbed the staircase.

It was going to be far more unbearable than she imagined, Isabella realized. She felt wounded inside. Her eyes burned with unshed tears, but she refused to let them fall. It was useless, foolish really, to lament what could never be. Yet all she could think about was being separated from Damien and knowing that over time, her heart would most likely wither and die.

Chapter Twenty-five

"It's not fair," Catherine protested. "Why must we go to bed when we aren't a bit sleepy?"

"Can't we stay up until Father comes home?" Ian pleaded. "We want to say good night to him."

Isabella averted her eyes, fearing that her distress over the earl's absence would be too obvious and further upset the children.

"I am not certain when your father will return home, so I think it is best if you prepare for bed," Isabella explained. "He will come and see you as soon as he is able."

After a few expected grumbles of protest, Catherine and Ian obeyed Isabella's orders. Once the children were settled in their beds, they shared a conspiratorial look, then turned towards her.

"A story will probably make us very, very sleepy," Ian declared innocently.

"Oh, yes, a story," Catherine repeated, shifting her legs restlessly beneath the bedcovers. "One about a princess, please."

Ian made a face. "No princess. I want to hear about the huntsman and his wishing cloak."

"Huntsman are nasty." Catherine shook her head vehemently. "It must be a princess."

"No!"

"Yes!"

"No, no, no! No princess!"

"No huntsman!"

"Children, please stop it!" Isabella interjected.

"I don't want to hear a story about a princess," Ian complained.

"Then don't listen," Catherine countered.

"There will be no stories at all if you don't cease shouting at each other. Immediately."

The bickering stopped. But the quiet didn't last.

"Maybe we should have two stories tonight?" Catherine ventured, rustling her bedcovers again.

"Yes, two stories," Ian shouted, bouncing excitedly on his knees. "Tell the princess story first."

Isabella smiled in spite of the calamity. Catherine and Ian's two story compromise reeked of conspiracy, but she didn't mind, especially considering this was the last time she would share this favorite bedtime ritual with them.

"All right. If you promise to be very quiet and go straight to sleep after we are finished, we shall have two stories tonight." Isabella dragged a comfortable chair to a spot an equal distance between the two beds and sat down.

The children obediently lay back in their beds, heads resting against their pillows, eyes open and alert.

"I want to hear the story about the young maid with the pretty hair as fine as spun gold, who was locked in the tower by the evil witch," Catherine declared.

"Rapunzel?" Isabella asked.

"Yes, Rapunzel." Catherine hugged herself with delight. "She lowered her long, braided hair out the tower window so the prince could climb up to see her, and then he married her and she became a princess!"

Isabella sighed. How ironic that Catherine should choose a story about a young woman shut away in a lonely tower, separated from the world. It bore too uncomfortable a resemblance to the bleakness of Isabella's own future.

Shaking off those strange thoughts, Isabella threw herself into the telling of Rapunzel's tale, changing the pitch of her voice for each character and the volume of her delivery to add mystery and suspense. The children lay wide-eyed at the edge of their beds, eagerly listening to every word. But when she reached the part in the story where the evil witch casts Rapunzel from the tower prison and then waits to catch and harm the prince, Isabella had difficulty keeping her voice steady.

She felt an odd kinship and understanding of the suffering endured by the mythical Rapunzel, a woman banished from the man she loved and forced to live in the greatest grief and misery. With a true feeling of joy, Isabella related the triumphant ending of the tale, when the lovers are once again united and Rapunzel's tears of happiness cure her prince's blindness.

Isabella sighed. Of course, in the world of legend and fairy tales, there was always a happy ending. If only she possessed the power to write a happier conclusion to her own story, Isabella thought, but alas, in life one was rarely given the chance to live long and happily with a loved one.

Following Rapunzel, she launched immediately into the account of the huntsman whose kindness to an ugly old crone brought him a gold coin under his pillow each night and a magical cloak that would grant all his wishes.

At the end of Ian's huntsman tale, Isabella noticed the children's eyes beginning to droop, but they struggled valiantly to fight off sleep. Quietly she rose from the chair and extinguished all but one candle before walking over to Ian's bedside. Still and silent, Isabella stared down at him for several long minutes.

The little boy's eyes were shut, and his steady breathing indicated he was drifting off to sleep. Reaching out with a trembling hand, she tenderly smoothed the soft curls off his brow, then secured the covers tightly around his chest. Finally she bent low and kissed his cheek. She did the same for Catherine, all the while fighting hard against the tears shining in her eyes.

Returning to the chair, she swallowed determinedly past the lump of regret and sorrow lodged in her throat.

"Since you have behaved exceptionally well, I shall treat you to one last story, a tale that I have never before shared with you," Isabella whispered. She filled her lungs with air, then slowly exhaled. "There was once a man who had to take a long journey, and when he was saying good-bye to his daughters . . ."

It was nearly dawn when Isabella awoke. The heaviness in her heart made movement impossible at first, so she lay in her bed staring out the window. She made an effort to disregard, at least for the moment, the burdens on her mind and concentrate instead on nature's beauty. The first faint rays of pink and yellow light burst upon the horizon, bringing the magnificent fields of green to life. It was a glorious sight. Truly, there was no place in the world like Whatley Grange.

Isabella realized she was biting her lower lip when she tasted the blood on her tongue. Defeated, she succumbed to her emotions and turned her head away from the outdoor splendor. Burying her face in the pillow, she wept loudly, but her many tears brought her heart little relief.

After a while, Isabella forced herself to sit up on the side of the bed and dangled her bare feet over the edge. A headache was beginning to form behind her eyes, but she willed away the discomfort. The earl had not returned to The Grange last night, and thoughts of him flooded her mind.

She had waited for Damien in Catherine and Ian's room until the wee hours of the morning, lightly dozing in a chair. Dimly hearing the clock strike three, in the early morning hours she had brazenly gone to the earl's bedchamber, but he was not there. His bedding was undisturbed, and she could not help but be curious about where he had spent the night.

Isabella's thoughts remained on Damien as she removed her nightgown and put on her clothes. Her traveling clothes. Since she had refused to pack her belongings last night, Isabella next faced that unpleasant duty.

She arranged her clothing methodically upon the bed, then pulled her worn satchel from the wardrobe. She began packing her bag and belatedly realized that Lord Poole had given her so many gowns, she would not have enough room in her case to take everything.

Leaving a generous space for her undergarments and personal effects, Isabella haphazardly stuffed whatever old and new gowns would fit inside the case. She stacked the remaining dresses in four neat piles, knowing that Fran, Maggie, Penny, and Molly would be speechless at the thought of owning such expensive, fashionable clothes. It seemed fitting somehow that the four young maids should wear these lovely garments. She would receive great satisfaction presenting the gowns herself to each girl before she left.

Before she left! Isabella's heart turned to stone as the words echoed in her mind. Whatley Grange was the home she had always longed for, and she loathed having to leave. Here she had found peace and contentment. Here she had loved—the children who were so fiercely independent, and their father who defied ordinary convention.

Yet it was because of that very love that she was leaving. At all costs, she must prevent her brother from creating a horrible scandal or, far worse, have Damien prosecuted for a crime Isabella knew he could never have committed. She feared for more than Damien's reputation if Lord Poole succeeded in exacting his revenge. She felt certain he would contrive to have a charge of murder brought against the earl. In a community that already believed an outrageous assortment of lies about Damien's behavior, Isabella doubted he would be treated to impartial justice.

Lord Poole's mercurial moods yesterday afternoon also troubled Isabella. He had gone from rage to grief to manipulation all in the space of a few short hours. It would be necessary to tread delicately over the next few days so as not to set him off again.

Isabella chafed at the notion of being under Lord Poole's control, especially now that she had seen his darker side. Yet his grief for Emmeline had been so genuine, his love and loyalty for his sister so extreme, Isabella held out some hope for the future. He was acting in what he believed was her best interest. Perhaps in time his possessive attitude would lessen.

It was an impossible dream to hope that she could one day return to Damien and The Grange, but perhaps Thomas might eventually be persuaded to give her a small allowance that would enable her to live independently.

As she faced her uncertain future, Isabella knew that by far the most difficult adjustment would be losing Damien. The earl had not renewed his offer of marriage since his return from visiting her grandfather in the north. Perhaps it was a blessing that Damien had not spoken again of his intentions.

In light of the current circumstances, an alliance between them was a total impossibility. Lord Poole would never allow it. And surely her heart would break if she were forced to decline his offer yet again. For this time, given the freedom of choice, she would follow where love lead her. She would marry Damien. Gladly.

Jenkins arrived to take her baggage.

"The rest of the household has finished breakfast. Mrs. Amberly wants to know if she should continue holding the morning meal for you."

"I couldn't possible swallow a morsel." Isabella's already queasy stomach revolted at the thought of food. She grinned timidly at Jenkins. "Especially one of Mrs. Amberly's dishes. I remembered that the new cook is taking this morning off, which means she is once again preparing the household meals."

"Very well." Jenkins didn't even crack at smile. "Lord Poole's coachman is awaiting your luggage, Miss Browning. Is it ready?"

The censure and disappointment in the valet's tone caught Isabella by surprise. From the beginning, he had been Isabella's friend and supporter, her staunchest ally. It hurt deeply to hear his blatant disapproval.

"I would stay at Whatley Grange if it were possible, Mr. Jenkins."

"Your actions speak otherwise," Jenkins replied coldly, his mouth curled in disgust.

"You judge me unfairly," Isabella said quietly. She looked at him with wide, remorseful eyes. "I leave only because Lord Poole demands it. He is a wealthy, influential man, and his current thirst for vengeance makes him very dangerous indeed."

"Have you so little faith in Damien?"

"I have every faith in the earl. 'Tis the neighboring nobility who lack judgment and honor. I could not stand idly by and allow my brother to place Damien in such an untenable position. In my heart I have wavered constantly over this decision, yet I sincerely believe that this course of action, while painful, is the only way to ensure Damien's safety."

"I still think you are making a grave mistake," Jenkins said, but his voice was less harsh.

"I have no choice," Isabella insisted with true remorse. Yet she was relieved the valet's hostility had lessened. Her departure was going to be difficult enough without adding a heavy dose of guilt.

Isabella swallowed back her emotions, knowing she would never be able to make any coherent farewells if she did not gain some measure of control over her regrets.

"My luggage is ready. You may bring it downstairs at your convenience," Isabella said. She gathered the large assortment of gowns she had left on the bed in her arms. "I'm going to take these gowns upstairs. Maggie should be there with the baby. I . . . I need to say good-bye."

"The others—Fran, Molly, and Penny—are waiting outside to speak with you. Will you see them first?"

"Of course."

Isabella placed the gowns for Maggie in a chair and brought out the dresses she had saved for the other maids. The girls were clearly grateful for the extravagant gift but markedly upset over Isabella's departure. Teary-eyed, they left her bedchamber just as Jenkins reappeared to carry the luggage down to the traveling coach.

"Has the earl returned to The Grange, Jenkins?" Isabella inquired, asking the question she feared most.

The valet's expression softened slightly. "Damien and the children await you in the front salon."

Isabella nodded her head in acknowledgment, not trusting her voice. When Jenkins had departed, she struggled up the narrow staircase with the bundle of clothes for Maggie.

Maggie's delight and excitement over the beautiful gowns quickly changed to sadness when Isabella said her final good-bye. Maggie hugged her tightly and sniffled loudly.

"Fred and I are so very grateful for everything you've done for us and the baby. I don't know how we'll get on without you. Catherine and Ian will miss you so much. And so will I. And Fran and Penny and Molly. Goodness, everyone will miss you."

"Even Mrs. Amberly?" Isabella joked, blinking back the moisture from her eyes.

"Oh, miss!" Maggie smiled. "That's just what I mean. Who will make us laugh when you are gone?"

Isabella smiled weakly. After a several minutes of fussing over the baby and more hugs from Maggie, she finally quit the room. Nerves frayed and resolve waning, Isabella proceeded to the front salon. Marshaling the courage she knew she would need, Isabella paused before entering the room.

Her expression remained contained, but she flinched inwardly when she saw Damien, Ian, and Catherine. God help her, this was going to be difficult.

"Father told us you are going away," Catherine said without preamble in the typical forthright manner of children. "Why are you leaving us?"

"I have important business I must attend to that forces me away from The Grange," Isabella replied, giving as much explanation as she dared. She was relieved that Damien had spared her from informing the children of her departure, but was unsure what the earl might have told his children. "I shall miss you, Catherine. And you too, Ian."

"But we don't want you to go away," Catherine cried.

"I know," Isabella whispered, impulsively dropping to her knee and opening her arms wide. Both children rushed forward without hesitation. Isabella hugged their small bodies tightly, committing to memory the joyful feel of their clinging arms and sweet, wet kisses.

"You must promise to behave yourselves and mind your father," Isabella said. She sat back on her heels but still held the children loosely in the circle of her arms. "I want you to practice your numbers, Ian. Catherine, you must continue with your alphabet and letters. I'm sure your father will be glad to help you."

Isabella risked a glance at the earl, but Damien's expression gave no hint of his inner thoughts.

"You may go down to the kitchen, children," Damien said. "Cook prepared a special treat for you last night and has left it in the larder."

The children didn't budge, clearly reluctant to leave, but after a commanding nod from their father they sprang into action.

"Good-bye, Miss Browning," Catherine said.

"Good-bye, Miss Browning," Ian repeated.

With one final hug, the children dashed from the room. The door slammed loudly at their exit, the room silent except for the lingering sound. Isabella slowly rose to her feet. She straightened her traveling cloak, looking down at the buttons that adorned the front.

"I waited for you last night," she said softly.

"My mood was not very congenial." Damien flexed the fingers on his left hand. "I would have been rather unpleasant company."

"I wouldn't have minded," Isabella said honestly. Screwing up her courage, she asked. "Where were you?"

"I rode for several hours around the grounds of the estate before eventually heading toward the village. By nightfall I found myself at the town square. I went inside the church." Damien swallowed so hard she could see his Adam's apple move. "And spent the night there."

"In church?"

A ghost of a smile flashed across his face. "Unbelievable, is it not?"

"Not really." Isabella leaned close and laid her hand on the earl's arm. "I hope it brought you some measure of peace, Damien."

"At this moment, I don't think that is either humanly or divinely possible."

Isabella gripped his arm. She wanted to lean her head forward until it rested against his broad chest. She wanted to tell him that she shared his pain, his grief, his distress. She wanted to offer comfort and be comforted by this strong, noble man whom she loved beyond all reason. But she did not move.

Damien cleared his throat. "We spoke once of the possible consequences of our physical relationship. If, after you leave, you discover—"

"There will be no child," Isabella whispered, dropping her arm.

"I see." The earl's voice was smooth and emotionless. "Are you all packed?"

"Yes." Isabella bowed her head.

"Has Jenkins or one of the other servants brought your luggage down?"

"Yes."

"Then I suppose you had best be gone. It is already several hours past the early morning start that Poole demanded."

"Yes," Isabella whispered, her voice a thread of misery. She could feel him looking at her. She wanted desperately to lift her face and stare into his one final time, but her eyes were swimming in tears and she vowed he would not see her cry.

"Good-bye, Damien." A great weight was pressing down on Isabella's chest, and she had difficulty catching her breath. She turned to leave.

"I will miss you, Isabella," he said quietly. "I have no doubts that I shall think of you far too often for my own peace of mind."

"*Oh, Damien!*" Her legs nearly gave out. She turned back to the earl, hesitated, then rushed into his arms. Burying her head in his shoulder, she finally allowed herself the luxury of tears. The unexpressed emotions and unspoken words of love remained hidden deep in her heart as she cried for all they had shared and for all they had lost.

Damien's fingers twined in her hair. He held her close, and she welcomed his protective, possessive touch. His warmth eased away some of the bitter coldness in her soul. Isabella felt her heart thumping in slow, painful beats, wondering why it did not simply split in two.

"I know it is selfish, yet I'm glad you will also miss me," Damien said hoarsely.

Isabella gulped back her sobs and raised her tear-swollen face. Damien smiled down at her, but she saw the bleakness he could not hide clearly in his eyes. He leaned down and kissed her lips softly, gently. It was a kiss of affection, not passion. A kiss of tenderness and comfort. A kiss of love.

She closed her eyes against the pain. All too soon the kiss ended. Isabella felt Damien take her hands in his own. They were warm and solid. She clung to them tightly. Slowly he led her out of the room, across the great hall, and into the sunlight.

A fine traveling carriage stood waiting in the drive, the steps lowered and door opened. It was a warm morning despite the breeze, but Isabella barely noticed.

Damien handed her into the carriage. She was glad of his support, for her feet faltered on the small steps. She settled on the near side and blindly thrust her arms out the open window. She felt Damien take her hands. He lifted one, then the other, to his lips.

"Farewell, my lord," she said.

"Godspeed, Isabella."

He dropped her hands abruptly, and the carriage lurched forward. Panic clawed at Isabella's throat as the wheels crunched down the gravel drive. Within minutes they had cleared the gates and turned onto the road.

Lord Poole gazed broodingly across the coach at her, but held his tongue. Isabella supposed he was chafed at the delay her long farewell had caused. She sighed deeply, allowing numbness to overtake her bruised emotions. She had left The Grange at her brother's command, because she had no other choice. But her heart would forever remain behind.

* * *

The sound of shattering glass brought Jenkins to the library at a run. He opened the door, fearing what he might discover, but the drapes were shut tight, bathing the room in darkness. Jenkins could barely discern the earl's tall silhouette.

"Are you all right? I thought I heard glass breaking."

"I didn't throw anything this time, Jenkins." Damien gave a hollow laugh. "I was merely holding my goblet when it suddenly broke."

"That goblet was made of leaded crystal," Jenkins grumbled. "You must have been pressing on it awfully hard for it to split like it was a ripe melon."

The valet lit a brace of candles, then crossed the room to assess the damage. "You've cut your hand," he exclaimed. "And in more than one place."

"So I have," the earl replied absently. "Strange, I didn't even feel it." Damien looked down with detached interest as the blood dripped steadily onto the rug. "Poor Mrs. Amberly will be distressed. I've gotten blood all over the Aubusson carpet. It leaves such a nasty stain. I hope she will not have too much difficulty removing it."

"Have you gone completely daft?" Jenkins pulled the earl's hand toward him and examined the wounds. There were several cuts on Damien's palm and a few slashes across the finger pads. After dousing the wounds liberally with whiskey, Jenkins wrapped the hand with a clean handkerchief. The earl remained silent through the entire procedure.

"After all that has happened today, the one thing that troubles you is the damn rug," Jenkins said with exasperation.

"You are missing the point, my friend," Damien said. He poured himself a fresh glass of whiskey. "If I concentrate long and hard on the inconsequential occurrences of today, I can ignore all the important ones. It is a technique I have subconsciously employed for years, yet I only realized that today. However, this afternoon I deliberately turn my attention toward the minute details."

"You are talking nonsense."

"I am not." Damien sighed heavily, and twirled his whiskey glass restlessly in his uninjured hand. "I have lived most of my life chasing after the unimportant details. My marriage to Emmeline was unhappy, so I ignored her and invested all my energy and time in making The Grange a profitable estate. If I had put half as much effort into my marriage, Emmeline might still be alive."

"You are not to blame for her death," Jenkins insisted, watching the earl's expression change from indifference to regret.

"Oh, but I am." Damien made a small, guttural noise and bit down on his lip. "She was my wife, my responsibility. And I failed her. God only knows what she was doing in that passageway, and so it shall remain. We will never learn the truth. But if I had cared more, if I had concerned myself more with her happiness, if I had protected Emmeline properly, she would have been safe. I failed her, Jenkins. And she paid the ultimate price for my neglect."

"Emmeline never sought or wanted your involvement in her life," Jenkins said. "Her friends, her social activities, pursuing her own interests—that is what occupied Emmeline's days. She wanted little to do with you or The Grange or even her own children. She spent far more time living in her brother's house than she did in yours, even after you were married."

"She was my wife, Jenkins. She was my responsibility," the earl repeated stubbornly.

Jenkins shook his head. "Are you going to wallow in guilt and self-pity for the rest of your life to atone for this great sin? Is that why you let Poole drag Miss Browning away? Are you punishing yourself?"

"God, I hope not," Damien replied honestly. He crossed the room and pulled one drape panel open. He stood looking out the window for several minutes. "I have nothing to offer her, Jenkins. I know Isabella left because she thought it would forestall Poole's revenge on me. She is a noble and unselfish woman."

"She is," Jenkins agreed.

"I doubt Lord Rathwick would have been able to bring me to trial without a shred of evidence, but Poole certainly would have pressed him hard to prove that I murdered Emmeline. Now Poole will have to content himself with my financial ruin. I feel certain he will demand payment of the mortgages by the end of the week."

Jenkins looked at the earl consideringly. "Can you pay them?"

"No." Damien shrugged expressively. "I have some funds put aside, but it is not enough. I've tried, but have been unable to secure any additional loans." The earl squared his shoulders. "We will have to start over."

"Miss Browning would rise to the challenge," Jenkins said, knowing it was true.

"It hurts a man's pride to offer so little to the woman he loves," Damien said quietly.

"I'd say that depends on the woman." Jenkins's lips tightened. He watched the earl closely, but Damien's expression never faltered. Gritting his teeth, the valet turned to leave. "Think hard, Damien. Don't allow Poole to take Miss Browning from you. Then he really will succeed in having his revenge."

Jenkins shut the door quietly as he left, hoping his words would propel the earl into action. It was so unlike Damien to remain passive when challenged. He had always lived by the creed that no obstacle was insurmountable.

Apparently, the shocking events of yesterday afternoon had hit the earl hard, and he wasn't thinking clearly. Jenkins prayed he would come to his senses quickly before he lost the chance to claim the happiness he so richly deserved.

Damien drummed his fingers on the windowsill. He pushed the heavy drapes aside, and as he watched the brilliant streaks of red and gold sunlight begin to disappear from the sky, a terrible loneliness invaded his soul. Isabella was gone. And somehow he was going to have to learn to live without her. Without her radiant smile and sparkling wit. Without her unflagging loyalty and unselfish regard. Without her willful attitude and outspoken tongue.

Damien turned sharply from the window and began pacing restlessly about the room. How he wished he could ignore the pain gnawing in his chest—and deny the fear creeping into his heart. Had he made a dreadful mistake? Was Jenkins right? The question nagged at his brain, refusing to quit. Should he have asked Isabella to stay?

The future stretched before him, empty and unappealing. Damien did not doubt that Isabella held a deep affection for him. He had seen and felt her pain when she bade him farewell. Did he have the right to accept her regard? Was he worthy of her love?

He clasped his hands behind his back to keep them still. He searched his heart and his conscience and considered all he had lost. He had lost the chance to share his life with an honorable, beautiful woman. A woman he admired. A woman who made him laugh, who challenged his intellect, who fired his blood.

A woman who was affectionate and nurturing to his children. A woman who was as at ease with the maids as she was with the nobility. A woman who stood up to his temper and forgave his occasionally incorrigible behavior. A woman he loved.

Lord, he was a fool! Pride be damned. And Poole be damned too! Damien's fighting spirit emerged. He was not going to allow his one chance at true happiness to escape unchallenged. He was going to do whatever was necessary to claim the woman of his heart.

"Jenkins! Jenkins!" Damien raced from library shouting loudly for his servant. His heart pumped with excitement as the rightness of his decision resonated through his being.

"Send someone to the stables and have them instruct Fred to saddle my horse immediately. I need to change my clothes and I require your assistance."

"Planning a trip?"

"A rescue." The earl grinned at his valet, then took the stairs to his dressing room two at a time. "Hurry, Jenkins," he called over his shoulder. "The coming darkness will hamper my pursuit, and they have already been on the road for most of the day."

A rueful smile tugged at Damien's lips as he envisioned his quest. He was going to ride hell for leather to find Isabella and Poole. He was going to bare his heart, nay his very soul, to the woman he loved.

His smiled dimmed slightly. All he could do now was pray that she would have him.

Chapter Twenty-six

The promise of sunshine quickly faded, and the weather turned gray and dreary. By late morning a light drizzle was falling, growing steadily heavier as the day wore on.

The weather mirrored Isabella's mood, for she soon discovered she had neither the strength nor the heart for conversation. She could feel Lord Poole's eyes upon her, but she chose to ignore him. Yet he continued looking at her with a faintly glowering expression on his face.

Hoping to avoid him entirely, Isabella leaned her head back against the velvet squabs and closed her eyes, listlessly waiting for the residual pain in her chest to ease. It did not.

"We should be arriving at a comfortable posting inn shortly," Lord Poole said in a brusque tone. "I shall send one of my servants ahead to ensure we have a proper selection of food prepared for our midafternoon meal."

"Please don't go to any special trouble on my account, Thomas," Isabella replied. The swaying of the carriage was making Isabella queasy, and the mention of food merely increased her distress. "The last thing I wish to do is eat."

Lord Poole edged to the end of his seat and leaned closer.

"You are very pale, Isabella. I must insist that you eat a substantial lunch."

"I cannot."

"But I insist."

"Thomas, please."

"Forgive me for my concern over your lack of appetite, Isabella," he said with a haughty air of aristocratic arrogance she instantly disliked. "But you must understand my feelings in this matter. You are my responsibility now; therefore I must see to your welfare."

"I have managed very well for the past twenty-odd years without having someone looking after me," Isabella snapped. "Let me assure you, the very last thing I require is a nursemaid."

Lord Poole gave her a hard look. Isabella's angry words seemed to shimmer in the air between them. She locked her hands together in her lap and stared down at them.

"My only thought is your happiness and well-being," he insisted in a stilted tone.

Her head shot up at that statement, but the fight soon left her. What was the point? Quarreling with Thomas would only make this difficult journey even harder.

"I am sorry," Isabella said, struggling to remove all traces of anger from her voice. "I'm an independent woman and unused to this sort of . . . of consideration. Above all, I do not wish to become a burden to you, Thomas."

"You are my joy, dear sister," he replied softly. Lord Poole sighed and shifted his legs. "However, since you prefer not to have lunch today, we shall continue on our journey and stop when darkness falls."

Relieved as she was that he had dropped the matter so quickly, Isabella still felt a lingering unease. It seemed impossible that Thomas felt as casual as he was acting. His mouth curved up in a smile and the creases around his eyes softened, but the eyes themselves seemed to sharpen. Isabella shuddered. It reminded her of a cat when he's spotted a mole in the lawn.

She rubbed her fingertips against her temples. Nothing had seemed real since the moment she left The Grange, and now

Thomas's possessive attitude was almost more than she could bear. The silence and tension within the carriage grew.

"Goodness, look at the rain," Isabella commented, trying to sound genuinely interested in the weather. Any sort of banal conversation was preferable to the uncomfortable silence. "If it continues to come down this heavily, we will most certainly get bogged down in the mud."

"The condition of some of these roads is deplorable," Lord Poole agreed. "But you mustn't worry about a thing, my dear. I will make certain that you come to no harm."

Isabella smiled stiffly and turned her face to the rain-soaked carriage window. She was simply too tired and too emotional to cope with these unexplained, uneasy feelings Thomas inspired.

It was still all so new, so strange, accepting the fact that she had a brother who felt it was his duty to take care of her. It was going to take time to make the necessary adjustments. Eventually it would get easier. Wouldn't it?

Isabella glanced out the carriage window with fleeting interest as the coach pulled into the courtyard of a modest inn.

"I apologize for the humble accommodations," Lord Poole said when the carriage stopped. "The inn is small and unfashionable, hardly up to my usual standards, but I will not risk your safety by traveling these roads in complete darkness. I was forced to frequent this establishment on a prior occasion, and I can assure you that although the food and service are rustic, the rooms are clean and the linen free of vermin."

"It is fine," Isabella replied wearily. Bedbugs were the last thing she was concerned about. The heart-wrenching grief she had first felt upon leaving The Grange had settled into a quiet lethargy. What she craved most was solitude.

Lord Poole climbed down from the carriage first and waited while the coachman assisted Isabella. They stood together in silence on the uneven cobbles for several minutes, stretching their cramped legs. Lord Poole extended his arm, and after a slight hesitation Isabella took hold of it. She bit her lip when his other hand clamped possessively over her fingers, but said nothing.

Shoulders held firmly back, chin high, Isabella entered the taproom. One lone customer was slouched in his chair with a brimming glass of ale set before him. A tired-looking barmaid was scrubbing off a table. The innkeeper rushed forward to offer assistance. Isabella could almost feel the man's nervous anticipation as Lord Poole cast a critical eye about the room.

"We need two rooms for the night," Lord Poole said. "And a private dining parlor. I trust you can accommodate us?"

"Yes, your lordship," the innkeeper replied with a low bow. "We always keep our best chambers ready for our finest guests."

Lord Poole waved a dismissive hand at the innkeeper and turned his full attention to Isabella.

"You must go to your room and refresh yourself before dinner, Isabella," Lord Poole commanded. "I regret that our haste to leave this morning has caused you the lack of a personal maid. I would have tried to secure the temporary services of one of the wenches from The Grange if I had believed them capable of performing the job adequately."

"As I have told you before, I am used to fending for myself," Isabella replied. It seemed a waste of breath to point out that all of The Grange's maids were married women and therefore unable to make such a journey even if asked.

The burly innkeeper insisted on escorting Isabella to her chamber personally, and she wearily followed him up the narrow, winding staircase. He led her to a corner room on the third floor. The room was of modest proportions, with a large window that overlooked the front of the inn. There was an ancient-looking chair to one side of the fireplace, and the coverlet on the bed was shabby, though it appeared clean.

Isabella sat on the edge of the lumpy mattress the moment the landlord left, struggling to hold the desperate sense of loss she felt at bay. It would serve no useful purpose to indulge in these lonely and morose feelings. Life at The Grange was now a part of her past. She must resign herself to that and turn her attention to the future.

Oh, Damien. A wave of longing rushed over Isabella. She flopped back on the bed and brushed back the tears that sprang to her eyes. How foolish to succumb to tears. One lesson Isabella had dutifully learned was that when there was no hope of achieving your heart's desire, it was madness to long for it.

But her stubborn heart refused to cooperate this time. The desperate longing did not ease—nay, it had increased. The love she felt for Damien, the need she possessed to be near him, physically and emotionally, were not easily denied. Being separated from Damien made everything else in the world look bleak and bare.

Isabella lifted her eyes to the ceiling. The tears slipped freely down her temples and wet her hair. Crying would accomplish nothing, she knew, but it made her feel less helpless to acknowledge the depth of her grief and loss.

When her tears had subsided, Isabella rose from the bed. She picked up the lit candle from the table near the bed and brought it to the washstand. She poured fresh water into the pitcher, then bathed her swollen eyes with the wet cloth.

Returning to the bed, Isabella lay back down and fell into a light sleep. Soft knocking on her chamber door woke her an hour later. A chambermaid had been sent to fetch her for dinner. Politely declining the maid's shy offer of help, Isabella left to join her brother, her emotions still in a tangle.

Lord Poole smiled brightly when Isabella entered the parlor and inclined his head in a brief greeting. "I took the liberty of ordering dinner for us, Bella. I knew, since you ate no lunch, you would be hungry. I hope I have selected items that will tempt you."

Isabella glanced at the generous platters of food but could summon up little enthusiasm for the fresh pigeon pie, stewed carrots, roasted mutton, meat pasties, buttered potatoes, wedges of cheese, and basket of fresh bread.

"It looks lovely, Thomas," Isabella remarked. She sat quietly while Lord Poole filled her dinner plate.

"The wine is tolerable," Lord Poole decided, taking a generous swallow. "Shall I pour you a glass?"

Isabella's stomach revolted at the innocent offer. "No, thank you. I prefer water."

Lord Poole attacked his food with enthusiasm while Isabella nibbled on her carrots. After appeasing his initial hunger, Lord Poole relaxed and poured himself another glass of wine. He leaned back in his chair and eyed Isabella critically.

"You have eaten very little," he said. "Is the meal not to your liking? Shall I instruct the innkeeper to bring you something else?"

"I am not very hungry," Isabella replied. She forced herself to take a bite of pigeon pie.

"Your appetite will return once we are at home," Lord Poole said. "I am eager to show you our family estate."

Isabella smiled faintly. Lord Poole talked for several moments about the grandeur of his properties, then switched to the social activities they would soon be enjoying. He spoke of the balls and parties, the theater, the delightful weekends spent in the country with friends.

As he spoke, Isabella's depression increased. It would be an empty life, she thought with remorse. A bleak, colorless existence.

Isabella dashed a single tear from her cheek impatiently. Feeling Thomas's keen gaze upon her, Isabella quickly moved her hand to the side of her head and smoothed an errant strand of hair behind her ear.

"Emmeline was also reluctant to enter society," Lord Poole said quietly. "Yet with my guidance, she was a smashing success. It will be the same for you, Bella."

Isabella lifted her eyes. She was startled to hear him speak so calmly about Emmeline. "What was she like?"

Lord Poole's eyes grew misty. "She was sheer perfection. A paragon of feminine gentility and refinement. She had a sparkling wit and a natural charm that enthralled everyone. She was greatly admired and envied by many in society."

"I'm sorry I never knew her," Isabella said truthfully.

"You would have adored her," Lord Poole replied. "Everyone did." His expression darkened. "Except Saunders. He never appreciated what a jewel Emmeline was. I blame myself for that. Emmeline had countless offers of marriage, but I insisted she make the match with Saunders."

Isabella's eyes widened in surprise. "You chose Damien for your sister?"

"Yes. He had recently returned from the war and was badly in need of funds, but he was different from the swarm of fortune hunters that prey on young women of society. I thought he was a decent man, and I believed he would give Emmeline the freedom she needed to be happy. Alas, my lack of judgment in character proved a fatal error for my darling Emmeline."

"We agreed Damien did not have anything to do with Emmeline's death, Thomas."

Lord Poole gave Isabella a disbelieving look. "I think it should be obvious to an intelligent woman such as yourself. Emmeline was desperately unhappy in her marriage. She was running away from her husband."

Isabella frowned in confusion. "You believe she was using the hidden passageway as an escape route?"

"No, no. I believe she was searching for Lady Anne's treasure. Emmeline needed the treasure to be free of him. You can't get far in this world without money."

"But you told me that you always saw to Emmeline's financial needs," Isabella protested. "Why didn't she come to you if she needed funds?"

Lord Poole's hand trembled slightly as he lifted his wine goblet. "That is the very question I have been asking myself ever since we discovered her body. If only she had come to me, all would have been well. I would have protected her. I would have given her anything, done anything to please her. I loved her."

Isabella shook her head, unable to let it go. Something in Lord Poole's version of events did not ring true.

"Damien told me he saw Emmeline infrequently in the year preceding her death. Why would she feel the need to run from the earl? She rarely saw him. Their marriage was considered successful by society's standards." Isabella sat back in her chair, her arms on the rests. Her eyes grew luminous. "Perhaps Emmeline had a lover."

"Never!" Lord Poole slammed his hand down on the table with such force that the dishes rattled. "Emmeline swore to me she had only been intimate with her husband. A great part of her reluctance to accept my affections was due to her lack of sexual experience."

His words puzzled Isabella. She studied him carefully. His anger had gone, and the wistfulness in his expression sent a tingle of alarm down Isabella's spine. Her voice dropped to a whisper. "What are you saying, Thomas?"

"I loved her!" he shouted. "I would never have hurt her, never have forced her. I kissed her one night. A full, deep kiss of passion. It was glorious. But she said it frightened her. She began avoiding me. She refused to be alone with me. She told me I was being hopelessly fanciful to believe there would ever be any sort of romantic involvement between us. She said it was sordid and ugly." He lifted his head and stared at Isabella. "But it was not. How can love be ugly?"

Isabella closed her eyes and clenched the arms of the chair. It was impossible. Certainly she was misunderstanding Lord Poole's remarks. What he implied was indecent, unnatural. It went against all the laws by which any civilized society lived. Physical love between a brother and sister? Isabella shuddered.

"I agonized when Emmeline disappeared," Lord Poole admitted, hanging his head. "I knew she had run from me, but she couldn't go far. Not without money. I was filled with pain and regret. I thought she had drowned in the lake, although Saunders refused to believe it. I never dreamed she had become trapped inside that horrible passageway. My poor little angel."

He looked up at Isabella and his expression brightened considerably. "We will speak no more of these distressing occurrences. It is all part of the past. Now I have you, fair Bella. Nearly the image of my lovely Emmeline. I vow I shall do everything within my power to make you happy. We will share a wonderful life together."

Isabella's stomach lurched, and the room spun wildly for a moment. She gazed at him, tense and terrified, her mind whirling in a desperate attempt to formulate a plan of escape. She must get away!

"I'm feeling rather tired, Thomas," Isabella said anxiously. "I'd like to retire for the evening."

"It's barely nine o'clock," Lord Poole protested. He rose to his feet and came to stand in front of Isabella's chair. " 'Tis far too early to go to bed."

With an effort, Isabella held her tongue. His presence surrounded her, suffocated her. She could feel the heat of his body, though they touched nowhere.

"I'm going to bed," she announced, standing up abruptly.

He took a step forward, deliberately blocking her exit. Lord Poole's face blurred before her eyes, and Isabella suddenly felt as if there were no air left in the room. There was a buzzing in her head, and she feared she would faint if she did not get away.

Thomas touched her arm and Isabella screamed. She could not help it. Her mind filled with vulgar images, and her flesh crawled at his touch. She wrenched her arm free and backed away from him. She was cold with horror.

"Do not touch me," Isabella said with jaws so tense, she could barely speak the words.

Lord Poole frowned with incomprehension. "What is wrong, sweet Bella? Are you unwell?"

Isabella was barely able to contain a second scream. She clenched her hands into fists and tried to form a response. Thomas stood in front of her, blocking the exit. Her eyes remained riveted on the heavy wooden door. Somehow she must escape.

Then, miraculously, the door swung open. Isabella nearly collapsed with relief, waiting anxiously to see the innkeeper or barmaid in the doorway. She was saved. She moved forward gratefully, then abruptly halted. Her mouth dropped open in astonishment. "Damien!"

The earl had ridden hard for hours, and his appearance reflected that fact. Sweat lined his brow and his coattails were splattered with mud from the wet roads. Isabella doubted there had been a time in her life when she had been more gratified to see anyone.

Their eyes met, and Damien looked at her measuringly for

a long moment. Lord Poole's back was toward the door, but it was obvious from the grim set of his mouth that he had heard Isabella's identification of the intruder. Isabella made a move to walk around her brother toward Damien.

Lord Poole pushed Isabella aside with such force that she lost her footing and landed in a heap upon the floor.

"How dare you lay a hand on her!" Damien bellowed with rage.

"I will not allow you to take her from me," Lord Poole hissed, pivoting on his booted heel to face Damien. "Isabella is mine."

Thomas hurtled himself at the earl, his teeth bared in a savage snarl. Cold hatred was etched on his face as he swung his closed fist viciously at Damien's head. Damien successfully dodged the blow and managed to catch hold of Lord Poole's arm.

Spinning his adversary around, Damien threw a punch at him. Isabella, sprawled on the ground behind the men, watched with fascination as the earl's fist landed squarely on her brother's lip. Thomas's head snapped back, and he staggered sideways but remained on his feet. Blood dripped steadily onto his silver waistcoat. He seemed unaware of it.

Lunging forward, Thomas swung again at the earl, and this time his fist caught Damien on the jaw. Isabella winced at the sickening crunch of bone and flesh. Damien weaved a bit, shook his head vigorously, then neatly sidestepped a second punch in the nick of time.

"Stop it! Both of you!" Isabella's cries were ignored by both men.

Damien's fist connected with Thomas's jaw. He fell back under the impact. Struggling to steady himself, Lord Poole reached out and grabbed the edge of Damien's coat. The earl lost his footing, and both men toppled to the floor. They landed heavily, and Isabella could hear their grunts and groans as they rolled on the floor.

They separated, both men scrambling to their feet. The fight resumed, with each man landing several more strategic blows.

Then, in a flurry of movement, Damien hit Thomas with five quick jabs, two to the head and three to the stomach.

Isabella saw Thomas's legs buckle under him, and he fell to the floor in a heap. Damien stood over Lord Poole, breathing hard, his fists poised and ready to continue the fight. Lord Poole groaned and rolled onto his back. He made no move to get up.

Crawling over on her hands and knees, Isabella crouched beside Lord Poole's inert form. The bleeding had slowed on his upper lip, but it was puffed and swollen. The flesh around his left eye was bruised and discolored, and his nose was bent at an odd angle. Isabella decided it was probably broken.

" 'Tis over, Thomas," she whispered.

"Bella." Lord Poole struggled to lift his head.

"No, don't speak, Thomas. Just listen." Isabella swallowed convulsively. This was her chance to set things to rights, and she seized upon it. "I am in love with Damien, and I am going to marry him." She held up a staying hand when Lord Poole opened his mouth. "No, don't say anything. I will marry the earl, and there is nothing you can do to prevent it."

Isabella's eyes narrowed as Lord Poole placed his hands over his ears to stop the sound of her voice. She pried his fingers away and squeezed his hands.

"Hear me well, Thomas," Isabella commanded. "I will never acknowledge the kinship between us. I demand that you keep yourself out of my sight and out of my life. You will leave England as soon as possible. Forever."

Isabella watched the agitation change to defiance in Lord Poole's face.

"You will leave," Isabella repeated, her voice turning hard, "for if you do not, I will tell the whole world the truth about Emmeline's death and the part you played in her suffering. The scandal and malicious gossip will be beyond endurance, Thomas. You will be ostracized, shunned completely by the society you so admire."

"Why, Bella? Why are you so hateful?" Lord Poole's voice was agonized.

"I do this for my sister," Isabella replied, her expression stiff. "To bring her a small measure of justice." She cleared her throat and continued. "Before you leave England, you will cancel the mortgage debts you hold against Whatley Grange. That is the price of my silence, Thomas. Do you agree to my terms?"

There was a long silence. Isabella fixed her eyes on Lord Poole's ashen face and waited expectantly for his reply.

"It will be as you say, Isabella." Looking utterly dejected, Lord Poole turned his head away from her.

Isabella hardened her heart against his suffering. "I expect you to be gone from this inn by daybreak. Farewell, Thomas."

Emotionally drained, Isabella staggered to her feet. She blindly reached out a hand for Damien. He caught her by the arms and pulled her roughly against him. Isabella closed her eyes and rested her forehead against his broad, muscular chest.

"Please, Damien," she whispered softly, "take me away from here."

Chapter Twenty-seven

Damien carried Isabella up the inn staircase and into her bedchamber. She did not protest. He kicked the door shut with his booted heel, then gently placed her on her feet.

"Thank you, Damien."

Isabella's tone was quiet and contained. Damien tilted his head to one side and looked closely at her face. The paleness had eased, but her eyes were still wide and pain-filled. His heart ached, knowing she had suffered, even though he did not yet fully understand what had occurred. He watched Isabella with concerned eyes as she crossed the small chamber and stood at the window, staring out into the darkness, her body turned toward it.

Desperately needing to touch her, to somehow assuage her pain, Damien stepped forward and circled Isabella's small waist with both arms. She leaned back against him, and he heard her drawing a deep breath.

"I don't want any secrets between us, Damien. Yet I know not how I can repeat the unspeakable things I have learned tonight."

Damien forced himself to rein in his impatience. When he entered the private dining parlor, he had felt the tension gripping the room, had seen the fear etched on Isabella's face. But he had been ignorant of the cause.

Finally, in a halting voice, Isabella revealed the truth of Emmeline's death. At first Damien was certain he had misheard, but when Isabella haltingly repeated the tale, the shock within him turned to pure horror.

Poor Emmeline. How lonely and bewildered she must have felt, having no one in whom to confide this horrible secret. Damien's stomach revolted at the image of Poole and Emmeline together.

"I should have killed him," Damien snarled. "I should have beaten him senseless."

Isabella lightly touched the forearm that was wrapped about her waist. "No, Damien. I don't want this ugliness to have any more power over our lives. Thomas has agreed to leave England. I pray that in time we will be able to forgive him."

"I hope I shall be able to forgive myself," Damien said, "for failing to protect Emmeline when she needed me most."

"Don't blame yourself. Emmeline made the choice not to tell you what was happening. You cannot be held accountable for what you did not know." Isabella turned around to face Damien. "Goodness, your jaw is turning purple. Does it hurt a great deal?"

"I barely feel a thing," he answered honestly.

She gave him a watery smile and placed her arms around his neck. He rested his hands comfortably on her hips. He found himself grinning back at her.

Leaning into him, Isabella said softly, "I want to marry you, Damien. Will you still have me?"

"Oh, I'll have you, Isabella," Damien replied with a wide smile. The warm contentment burgeoning in Damien's chest spread through his entire body like wildfire. "And I vow I shall keep you."

Isabella's smile broadened, and her face brightened with unmistakable joy. Damien's heart somersaulted and a deep, healing peace seeped into his soul.

He grazed the skin of her brow with his thumb, then ran the palm of his hand over the curve of her cheek. Her skin felt soft and silky beneath his touch. Cupping her beloved face in his hands, Damien bent down. He kissed her eyelids, her temple, her chin and throat, then finally claimed her sweet mouth.

Her lips were trembling, but they parted willingly. He pushed the tip of his tongue inside and caressed her moist flesh. Isabella made a deep sound in her throat and leaned closer. She returned the kiss, her mouth ravishing his tenderly, igniting his senses. He tasted her urgent sweetness and understood her need, for it matched his own.

Damien's hands stroked her back and shoulder, then moved forward to capture her breast. With thumb and forefinger, he gently pinched the nipple of her left breast. It peaked and hardened instantly, and Isabella moaned softly.

With a fervent effort at control, Damien guided Isabella to the edge of the bed. Three lit candles illuminated the small chamber, and Damien was glad of the light. He wanted to see her face when he made love to her. He wanted to watch her eyes darken with pleasure, her face strain with delight as he brought her to release. He wanted to gaze deeply into her violet eyes when he proclaimed his undying love for her.

He quickly removed his jacket, waistcoat, cravat, and boots before coming to the bed. He applied a slight pressure to her shoulder, and Isabella obediently lay back against the pillows. He slid his arm beneath her back and pulled her against his chest. Against his heart.

She curled close to him and kissed his shoulder. He smiled. He could not remember ever feeling such happiness. He clasped his arms tightly around her back and rolled over on top of her. He kissed her again, then came up on his elbows so he could look down at her. His eyes roamed her beautiful face, and he delighted in the sweet yearning he saw in her eyes.

"I love you, Isabella," he whispered softly. "I love you beyond reason."

"Oh, Damien." Her eyes welled with tears. "I love you too."

The euphoria building inside him grew to near bursting. He knew she cared for him, yet he dared not hope he would so readily achieve that which he most desired—Isabella's love.

He reveled in the certainty that they now belonged solely to each other. It brought his emotional and physical desire up to a level he had always believed existed only in the abstract. Romantic love, tender-hearted concern, deep and binding commitment—these phrases were no longer merely words for Damien, but truths.

Tenderly he removed her clothing, pausing to kiss her each time he removed a garment. Soon she was naked, the sight of her passion-flushed skin incredibly erotic and alluring. Isabella's eyes were shining with merriment and love, but he felt her hands tremble slightly when she reached up to unbutton the top of Damien's shirt.

"Nervous, my sweet?" he asked.

"Impatient," she replied.

Damien smiled wickedly and ripped the remaining clothes from his body. He stretched out beside her and lowered his head to her breast. He pressed feather kisses along the generous curves, then slowly licked the rosy nipple to a taut peak.

The tips of his fingers glided lightly up Isabella's inner thigh. He smiled with satisfaction when she sighed with pleasure and parted her legs. She lifted her hips against his hand and whimpered quietly as he stroked her softness, quickly bringing forth her slick, feminine essence.

The coiling tension inside Damien could wait no longer for release. He came down on top of her with the full force of his heated body, spread her legs wider with his knees, and thrust himself inside her softness.

Isabella gave a loud cry of passion and clung to him. Damien felt her legs twine around his calves and pull him even deeper into her body. She moved beneath him in naturally perfect harmony.

Damien's hips pumped rhythmically, his passion incited by the love burning in his heart. He looked down into her eyes, wild and filled with passion, and he knew he would love her until he no longer walked this earth.

Damien struggled to maintain his control, seeking to prolong this perfect moment. But Isabella peaked suddenly and her climax sparked his release. His hands came beneath her and he lifted her even closer, grinding himself against her softness as he spilled his seed deep within her.

With a sigh of fulfillment, Damien collapsed on top of Isabella. After a few moments he slowly opened his eyes. The spicy scent of passion invaded his nostrils, and he grinned like an idiot. Isabella's fingers were trailing soothingly across his shoulders, and her legs were still curled around his. He felt magnificent, totally sated in mind, body, and soul.

Reluctantly, Damien carefully eased himself out of Isabella's warm body. She protested at his leaving but appeared to lack the energy to do much about it. She garbled something, then turned to press the full length of her body against his. Her deep, even breaths told him she had fallen asleep.

Damien grinned with masculine pride. He had exhausted her with his passion. It was a truly satisfactory notion, knowing he could so completely love her. He moved closer to Isabella and curved his arm protectively around her waist. He kicked the covers up with his foot and rearranged the blankets around Isabella's shoulders. Then he turned his body until he could feel her cheek resting against his chest and fell asleep in the circle of peace and joy they had created.

Isabella awoke with a start, momentarily disoriented. She gazed with slight confusion at the sunbeams that streamed through the window and onto the unfamiliar bed. Her confusion turned to a smile of contentment when her memory also awoke.

Damien loved her. They were going to be married. A surge of elation swept through Isabella. She could not believe her good fortune.

Her eyes traveled the length of the bed and filled with admiration as she beheld Damien's uncovered, naked form. Indelicate thoughts of a decidedly carnal nature invaded her mind, but they fled the instant she heard footsteps outside her door.

Isabella clutched the blanket to her naked breast, poised to shake Damien awake the moment she heard someone fumbling at the locked door. The sound never came. Instead Isabella saw the gleam of white paper as a thick letter was passed under the door and into the chamber.

Isabella left the bed, but feeling uncomfortable in her nudity, she searched among the clothes scattered on the floor for her chemise. Pulling the garment over her head, she padded barefoot to the door to retrieve the letter. It was addressed to her.

"What is that?"

Damien sat up in bed and sprawled nonchalantly against the headboard. The sight of his muscular, naked chest made Isabella's blood sing. She cleared her throat and answered the earl's question. "It appears to be a letter for me."

There was a short silence as Isabella broke the seal.

She shuffled through the many pages to read the signature even though she was fairly certain who had sent the missive. "It is from Lord Poole."

"What does he write?" Damien inquired.

"He apologizes for any hurt he may have caused me and humbly begs my forgiveness. Thomas left the inn at daybreak this morning and plans to sail for the Americas by the end of the month. He has enclosed the mortgage vouchers to Whatley Grange."

Isabella gave Damien an anxious look, but his expression remained stoic.

"Oh, goodness—Thomas has signed the mortgage vouchers over to Ian, not you, Damien." Isabella scanned the rest of the letter quickly. "Is that legal?"

Damien shook his head. "How like Poole to be so difficult. I suppose he just couldn't bear handing them directly over to me. As Ian's father, I have control of his fortune until he reaches his maturity. And yes, in answer to your question, sweetheart, it is perfectly legal."

"You are not angry?"

"No." Damien stretched his arm above his head. "I didn't expect Poole to capitulate with so little resistance. I confess, Isabella, I feel he has escaped his reprehensible behavior with small punishment."

"I disagree, Damien." She crossed the room and sat on the edge of the bed. Her brows came together in a serious line across her forehead. "Thomas has suffered greatly by Emmeline's death, and in time I believe he will feel guilty for the part he played in it. He will now be separated completely from the life he has known and enjoyed. It will not be easy for him to start fresh, in a strange country."

Damien quirked a brow. "That hardly seems fitting revenge."

"You and I will be married soon, won't we, Damien?" Just speaking the words aloud gave Isabella a deep, warm feeling.

"I plan on obtaining a special license today, sweetheart. We shall marry tomorrow."

"And we will have a long, happy life together, won't we, Damien?"

"God willing." Damien's hands closed around Isabella's waist. He lifted her up and settled her in his lap, then kissed the sensitive place behind her ear. "We shall be joyously happy, my love."

"Then the best revenge is to be happy, dearest," Isabella said, smiling at Damien. "And we are!"

Epilogue

"I have been reading Lady Anne's diary again, Mama."

Isabella glanced up from her embroidery, slightly startled at hearing herself called *Mama*. Although Ian had been addressing her by that name for nearly a year, Catherine had only recently begun using it. Isabella was touched and honored to have finally earned such an important place in Catherine's life. It made her feel even more joy at the coming birth of her own child, knowing this newborn babe would be a welcome addition to an already loving family.

"Have you made a new discovery while reading the diary, Catherine? I hope you will share your latest theory about the treasure with me."

Catherine sat up tall in her chair, the pink ribbons on her new gown shaking with enthusiasm. She had changed in the two years since Isabella and Damien's marriage. She was no longer an intensely self-contained child existing in a narrow world. There were visits to neighboring estates and interaction with other children. Catherine had formed a special friendship with Lord Simmons's daughter, Elizabeth, and the two girls spent a great deal of time in each other's company.

Isabella was delighted that Catherine had become more frivolous and inclined toward mischief, although the family's governess, Miss Ballinger, found Catherine's high spirits trying at times.

"After much thought, I agree with Father's theory that the poem, which is the final journal entry, contains the secret of the treasure," Catherine informed Isabella. *"Oh Gloriana of titan hair, thy savior I shall be; for through the rose of the noon day sun, thy enemies shall flee.* The poem tells us we must search for the treasure at noon. But I believe the time of year we search is also important. Miss Ballinger has recently taught us about the sun, and she says it is higher or lower in the sky according to the season of the year."

"That is correct." Isabella pursed her lips and considered Catherine's theory. The treasure story had once again become a focal point of interest for the children, and both Damien and Isabella agreed it was a harmless diversion. "The time of year could be the essential factor that has been missing in prior searches. Have you figured out what time of year we need to search?"

"Oh, yes." Catherine jumped up from her chair with girlish enthusiasm. "According to the journal, Lady Anne fell ill on the second of July and the family bible says she died on July fifteenth. She must have hidden the treasure soon after she became ill."

"That is very sound reasoning," Isabella said, impressed with Catherine's logic.

"I found another passage in the journal where Lady Anne writes that her favorite room in the house 'glowed with rosy warmth.' Elizabeth and I have talked about this, and we agreed that if we were going to hide something very important, we would put it in our favorite room. I think that is what Lady Anne did."

Isabella experienced a moment of concern. The room Catherine was referring to was well known, for in that very chamber they had become trapped inside the hidden passageway. And later discovered Emmeline's remains.

"It has been a long time since we entered the bedchamber

with the 'rosy glow,' '' Isabella said gently. ''Would it not trouble you to explore it again?''

''No. I will not feel troubled. I want very much to find the treasure,'' Catherine insisted.

''Then we shall search for it.'' Isabella stood up and placed her sewing on the chair. ''Today is the sixth of July. That falls within the appropriate week. What time is it?''

''Half past eleven,'' Catherine whispered, her eyes round with excitement.

''Come along, Lady Catherine, we have some treasure hunting to do.'' Isabella held out her hand, and Catherine took it eagerly.

The renovation of the east wing had begun in early spring, and the workers had achieved marvelous results in a short span of time. All the rooms had been thoroughly cleaned, broken panes of glass repaired, chimneys swept, and fireplaces restoned.

As Isabella walked the hallway with Catherine by her side, none of the memories of her previous trips to this part of the castle gripped her thoughts. It was as though she had never walked these floors, so complete were the changes and improvements.

There were other happy changes at The Grange, too. Maggie was expecting her second child soon, and the three other maids had successfully given birth, Fran to a boy and Penny and Molly each to a daughter. Mrs. Amberly had retired to a cozy cottage on the estate, and Catherine and Ian visited her faithfully every week.

Damien had mentioned to Isabella only last week that Mrs. Amberly had been hinting rather broadly about returning temporarily to The Grange when their child was born. Isabella amazed herself by seriously considering the idea, for despite her past rocky relationship with Mrs. Amberly, she knew in her heart that she would never find a more loyal, devoted nursemaid for her baby.

Isabella and Catherine entered the rose room just as the clock in the great hall struck noon. The bedchamber was bathed in a rosy glow, but when the final gong struck, the glow faded, and a single shaft of rose sunlight fell across the floor.

"Mama, look!" Catherine shouted in awe.

"It's amazing," Isabella agreed. The tip of the sunbeam fell nearly in the center of the empty room, directly on a square of parquet flooring. It looked like a giant, rose-colored arrow.

"*Through the rose of the noon day sun*," Isabella whispered. " 'Tis just as Lady Anne's poem says, Catherine."

The little girl clapped her hands together with delight. "The treasure must be hidden under the floor."

Shaking her head in agreement, Isabella knelt down to examine the floor. The inlaid wood was in good condition and had not been replaced during the renovation, but it had been cleaned, scraped, waxed, and buffed to a high shine.

Isabella ran her hand cautiously over the smooth, polished surface and through the sunbeam. The section of wood was flush to the floor, no different from any other panel.

Balling her hand into a fist, Isabella rapped her knuckles sharply on the floor. A deep, solid sound echoed through the room.

Catherine sat beside Isabella. Imitating Isabella's actions Catherine tapped the surrounding floorboards, then hit the floor again directly in the beam of light. There was a hollow, thumping noise, distinctly different from the others.

Catherine's head shot up in triumph. "We found it!"

"We have found something," Isabella corrected, trying to keep the excitement from her voice. "If we lift the flooring, we might find only an empty space."

"But we must look," Catherine insisted.

"Of course we shall look," Isabella agreed with a grin. "If we do not pry this floor open, we will never be able to sleep tonight. Quick, run and find your father and Ian. They should be out in the stables. The new horses from Tattersall's were expected this morning."

Catherine left with an undignified flurry of skirts. Isabella sat back on her heels and glanced about the room. The sun had shifted again as the minutes passed. The rosy glow created by the many panes of colored glass set in the windows now replaced the solitary beam.

In the space of a few short minutes, the single shaft of light was no longer pointing the way. Isabella sat directly in front of the floor panel, vowing not to move an inch lest she forget which panel the sunbeam had marked.

As she waited, Isabella's eyes wandered involuntarily to the wall on the far side of the room that once hid the secret passageway. It no longer existed. Damien had ordered the entrance bricked closed and the latch removed from the wall.

The children had asked questions about their mother's death and were told she had died accidentally, as was the truth. By coming here today, Catherine had amply demonstrated that she suffered no lingering effects from her previous ordeal of being trapped inside the cold, dark passageway.

Isabella had received a brief letter from Thomas, who had resigned himself to a quiet life in America. She thought occasionally of her half sister and half brother, but did not dwell on the past. There were too many important things happening in the future. Isabella's hand rested comfortably on the slight swell of her stomach. If all went well, there would be a new baby to love by Christmas.

"What have my two favorite girls discovered?" Damien asked a few minutes later as he breezed into the room with Catherine and Ian hard on his heels.

"It is the most miraculous thing, Father," Catherine said enthusiastically. "There is a beam of light that points to the floor. That is where Lady Anne hid the treasure!"

Isabella saw the confusion and disappointment mar Catherine's face. "What happened to the beam, Mama? It has disappeared!"

"It is past noon, Catherine," Isabella said. "The beam only appeared briefly, but I have sat directly on the spot so we would know where it was."

"How clever," Catherine said with approval. "Hurry, Father. We must break through the floor."

Isabella noticed that Damien carried an ax, hammer, and chisel in his hands. His gray eyes sparkled with good humor. He was dressed in the comfortable attire of a country gentleman in buff breeches, a rust riding coat, and a white cravat neatly yet unostentatiously arranged.

He was still the most tantalizingly attractive man Isabella had ever known. Her heart skipped a beat when he cast her a loving gaze that sent a riot of warm feeling coursing through her veins.

"Are you sure about this, Catherine?" Damien asked. "I should hate to ruin this beautiful floor for no good reason."

"Father!" Catherine screeched. "You must break the floor to find the treasure!"

"Stop teasing her, Damien," Isabella said. She shifted her position and pointed to the wooden floor. "Start here."

"Stand back, all of you," Damien commanded, helping Isabella rise to her feet. They all obligingly stepped away. The earl took careful aim and swung the ax in a high arc over his head. It hit the panel dead center. The wood split and cracked.

"It's hollow underneath," Damien said with some surprise. He knelt on the floor. Using the hammer and chisel, he removed the square completely.

Everyone crowded around the small opening and peered inside.

"I don't see anything," Ian said.

"Neither do I," Isabella chimed in. "Put your hand inside and feel around, Damien."

The earl grimaced at his wife, but did as she requested.

"Can you feel the treasure, Father?" Catherine hopped from one foot to the other, looking as if she would burst from the suspense.

"I can feel lots of dust and spider webs on my hands," Damien reported.

"Spider webs! May I try?" Ian asked, inching closer to the earl hopefully.

"Your arms aren't long enough, son," Damien replied. He

spread himself flat against the floor and stretched his arm inside the hole.

"Anything?" Isabella asked.

"More dust, I think. No, wait—there is something solid. It is probably a cross beam." Sweat lined the earl's brow as he pushed and strained his body to reach farther inside the hole. "It moved."

Catherine's small scream of excitement ricocheted through the room.

"Don't tease us, Damien," Isabella said, striving to contain her emotions. "Have you truly found something?"

"Yes, I have," Damien said. "It appears to be a wooden box, and it is too heavy to lift with one arm." The earl picked himself off the floor and brushed the dust from his jacket. "Run and fetch a rope, Ian. I will try to tie the cord around the box and pull it up."

Ian returned with the rope in record time. It took the earl a while, but eventually he fashioned a noose and successfully looped it around the mysterious wooden box.

Isabella could barely breathe as she watched Damien slowly drag the box from beneath the floor. It was not overly large, but Damien's grunts and groans indicated that it was very heavy.

The earl placed his find in the middle of the room. Everyone stood in silent awe for several moments and stared at it.

"There is a big lock on the front," Ian said. "We don't have a key. How will we open it?"

Damien stepped forward and whacked at the lock with his hammer. It came apart on the fourth hit.

"Since you made the discovery, Catherine, 'tis only fitting that you do the honors," Damien decided.

Wide-eyed Catherine lifted the lid, and when Isabella saw the child's lower jaw drop, she knew they had discovered Lady Anne's treasure.

"It is so shiny," Catherine whispered, putting her hand inside and coming up with a fistful of gold coins.

Ian immediately plunged his hand inside. "It feels cold," he giggled, waving an emerald necklace. "Does this mean we are very rich?"

Damien smiled at his son and daughter and placed a loving arm around his wife.

"I hope you will learn, as I have, that true wealth is measured in many ways. I believe we already possess riches beyond price," Damien said with emotion. "This treasure is a mere trifle in comparison."

Please turn the page for
an exciting sneak peek of
Adrienne Basso's
newest Zebra historical romance
HIS NOBLE PROMISE
coming in February 2000!

Chapter One

Devon, England—June, 1816

The Earl of Rosslyn's ballroom sparkled with glittering candlelight and lavish colors as the dizzying number of festively costumed guests mingled amongst themselves. The assembled crowd danced to the strains of lighthearted music, indulged in the sumptuous buffet of rich food, and flirted with carefree abandon from behind the anonymity of their masks.

Laughter and muted conversation drifted out through the French windows along the length of the ballroom, which had been opened to allow in the evening breeze. There was an atmosphere of gaiety punctuated with an air of excitement among the guests that was almost contagious.

Clearly everyone was having a marvelous time. Except Lord Mulgrave. He was the single point of incongruity in the entire ballroom as he stood alone and brooded, observing all the elegance and fanfare with growing annoyance. *Where the devil was she?*

"Must you stand so near the entrance to my ballroom, Richard?" the Earl of Rosslyn asked with a sarcastic twist in his voice. "Your expression is set with such furious determination that it is frightening many of my guests."

"Shut up, Ian," Lord Mulgrave replied darkly. "I have been waiting over two hours for Nigel's darling Miss Paget to arrive. Apparently she lacks the wit to tell time correctly, for she is far beyond fashionably late. I am in no mood for joviality."

Richard tried scowling at his host and lifelong friend, but was unable to keep from grinning. The former Captain Simons was now the current Earl of Rosslyn, and Richard was pleased that Ian had taken his unexpected role as an earl so seriously. With only the occasional lapse in good judgment. Such as this evening.

Ian should have looked ridiculous in the white Roman toga trimmed in gold, sandals on his feet and a laurel wreath encircling his blond head, but amazingly he didn't. He looked strikingly commanding and regal.

Of course, only Ian could have invented such a bizarre reason for a costume ball—the anniversary of Wellington's victory at Waterloo—and gotten the entire neighborhood of nobles, along with a smattering of the beau monde, to attend. Most of them dressed in outrageous outfits ranging from a swashbuckling pirate to Henry VIII.

"Ah, yes—Miss Paget." Ian signaled a passing footman and snagged two flutes of champagne off the silver tray the servant carried. He handed one to Richard. "I remember. You want to speak with Miss Paget the moment she arrives. What exactly are you planning to do to the poor thing?"

"Scare her away from Nigel, I hope. If she is as shallow as I suspect, it should not be that difficult a task."

Ian lifted his goblet in a mock salute, and the two men clinked glasses. But Richard sipped his champagne distractedly, his eyes never leaving the rounded archway entrance to the ballroom. The steady stream of newly arriving guests had dwindled to a mere trickle, yet Richard knew Nigel's little darling had to descend these steps to enter the ballroom. And Lord Mulgrave would be waiting.

Surprise was the key element in Richard's plan of attack this evening. It was imperative that he reach Miss Paget before

Nigel had an opportunity to introduce them. He wanted time alone with the little schemer without her knowing with whom she was speaking.

"Do you want me to distract Miss Paget?" Ian volunteered. "I met her last week at the Tollies' dinner party. She is rather attractive in a pretty, girlish way. It would not be a great hardship to lavish attention on her. I can be most charming when pressed, especially with the ladies."

"I know." Richard laughed under his breath. "From barmaid to noblewoman and across all continents."

"It might work," Ian persisted, taking a large swallow of champagne. "After all, I inherited the title of earl from my brother, God rest his soul, last year. I am already an earl, while Nigel is merely a baron and will have to wait many years before he inherits. If Miss Paget throws in her lot with me, she will not have to wait eons to become a countess."

"She would have to wait an eternity." Lord Mulgrave tipped the remaining drops of champagne into his mouth. "If Miss Paget is only half as clever as I think, she will already be well aware of the fact that you are an outrageous flirt, and an occasionally charming and experienced rake. The type of man known for browsing among unmarried females, but never seriously considering making a permanent selection. The prospect of marriage has always made you jittery."

"Your cruel words wound me, Richard," Ian replied lightly.

"I know from years of experience that it is impossible to penetrate your foolish hide," Lord Mulgrave commented with a smile. "By the way, you look ridiculous in that getup." Julius Caesar, my arse."

"I like how my costume shows off the strength of my legs," Ian remarked mildly. He straightened his broad shoulders and adjusted the laurel wreath in his hair. "I recently discovered that women have an affinity for men's muscular bare legs. Capitalizing on that weakness left me with a choice of Roman emperor or highland warrior, but I had trouble fastening the damn kilt. That left Rome the victor."

"You are impossible," Lord Mulgrave said fondly. Ian was probably the only person in the entire room who could bring a genuine smile to his face tonight. "And I refuse to ask how you acquired this insane knowledge about females' interest in men's bare legs. Frankly, I don't want to know."

Shifting his attention away from his host, Richard once again scanned the crowded ballroom. There were actually several people he recognized, despite their costumes and masks. Of course, not all the gentlemen were dressed up. Many, like himself, were garbed in black formal evening clothes.

"I have not seen Miles all evening. Is he here?" Lord Mulgrave asked.

The humor immediately receded from Ian's eyes. "Yes, Miles arrived last night," Ian replied tersely. "We need to discuss our mutual friend. I am worried. I have heard rumors about Miles since he returned to England, but paid them no heed. I should have. He has developed quite a reputation as a reckless gamester with a violent temper. Most recently he has been banned from White's for one full year for brawling in the card room."

"Miles? Our own level-headed Captain Nightingall brawling? And gambling? It seems impossible."

Ian shook his head. "He is not the man we knew. Miles has changed, and not for the better."

Richard grabbed Ian's arm. "Why haven't you told me?"

"You have other, more immediate problems to manage at present. We will both confront Miles when the time is right."

Ian stiffened suddenly. Richard turned his head, following his friend's gaze. A gaily attired group of guests were converging on the steps leading to the ballroom.

"Is it her?"

Ian smiled softly. "Brace yourself, Richard. Miss Paget has finally arrived."

"Oh, here comes our host, the Earl of Rosslyn. Is he not handsome in that costume? He has the most enchanting smile." Nicole squealed. "Good heavens, you can see his unclothed legs!"

Anne ceased fussing with the folds of her gown and raised

her head. The earl's costume did indeed afford a splendid view of his muscular calves, but after a brief admiring glance, Anne's attention was drawn to the man by his side.

They were quite a contrasting sight. Although both tall, attractive men, the stranger possessed an arrogantly commanding air that bespoke obedience. His power went beyond his obvious physical strength. Anne knew without a doubt that here was a man whose wishes were seldom thwarted.

"Who is that tall, serious man beside the earl?"

"I do not know," Nicole whispered. "He is rather formidable looking."

Conversation between the sisters ceased as the earl and his companion drew near.

"Welcome, welcome," the earl called out merrily. "I am indeed honored to count you among my guests this evening. Lady Althen, you make a positively smashing Marie Antoinette. I fear it will be us poor gentlemen who lose our heads around you tonight."

Anne's mother snapped opened her fan in response, clearly pleased with the earl's teasing flirtation. "Good evening, my lord," she said pleasantly, dropping a low, elegant curtsey. "I believe you are already acquainted with my husband, Baron Althen, and my daughters, Nicole and Anne. Although I shall not spoil the surprise and tell you who is behind each mask. I leave that discovery to you, my lord."

"Mystery has always been a female's most powerful ally." The earl shook hands with the baron and bowed to the ladies. "I am delighted you can attend my humble gathering. May I present a close friend who has specifically requested an introduction to the Miss Pagets."

The earl turned to his companion, and Anne saw the warning look in the stranger's eye. Apparently so did the earl, and he must have reacted as silently commanded because when he began to speak, the warning look in stranger's eyes was replaced by appraising interest.

"Although my friend has chosen to forgo the ritual of a costume," the earl said calmly, "at my request he has agreed to join in the spirit of the evening by keeping his true identity a secret until the midnight unmasking. Therefore I shall simply introduce him as my dear friend, Lord Richard.''

Lord Richard gave a proper, albeit swift bow while the earl finished the introductions. Anne took the opportunity to study him. Up close, the stranger was even more attractive, she quickly decided. He had deep green eyes that contrasted strikingly with his dark brown hair. His strong, lean features were classically handsome, and his smile, though briefly seen, was nothing short of dazzling.

He carried himself with arrogant purpose, and there was an air of military command emanating from him even when he was standing still. Who was this mysterious stranger? Anne wondered.

Lord Richard turned his perceptive gaze toward her and Anne's heart began a steady, maddening thumping. His look was almost accusatory, but Anne convinced herself that was impossible. She had just met the man. Determined to prove she was merely being fanciful, Anne lifted her chin and boldly returned his stare.

He gave her a dark, seductive smile that revealed a depth of raw masculine virility far more appropriate for the bedchamber than the ballroom.

Anne's jaw nearly dropped. Unnerved, she flashed a brief, restrained smile and pulled her eyes away from the stranger. Nicole was chatting animatedly with the earl and her parents, and Anne pretended great interest in their conversation. In truth, she was desperately attempting to regulate her breathing.

"May I escort you into the ballroom, Miss Paget?"

His voice—deep, strong and masculine—seemed to come from far away. Yet when Anne shifted her attention toward Lord Richard, he stood no more than a few feet directly in front of her, his vivid eyes holding her captive once again.

An obvious silence greeted his request.

Even Nicole ceased speaking, in midsentence. Anne's entire family stared at Lord Richard as if he had taken leave of his senses. Anne? He had requested Anne's company? This simply did not happen, especially when she was in the presence of one of her sisters.

Anne was always the last one chosen, if at all. More often than not, she sat among the elderly matrons and chaperones, keeping a sharp eye on the activities of her sister as they danced and flirted until the wee hours of the morning.

The earl cleared his throat. "Um, Lord Richard, would you kindly escort Miss Paget, the charming Grecian goddess, to the buffet so I may dance with the lovely Queen Elizabeth?"

Anne pressed her lips together nervously, realizing her host was probably trying to smooth over an awkward misunderstanding. Naturally Lord Richard really meant to ask Nicole to accompany him. Didn't he?

"I would be delighted to bring Miss Paget to the buffet after I claim the first dance with our good Queen Bess," Lord Richard countered.

Anne's father coughed. Her mother began fanning herself with a short, fluttering motion, launching puffy clouds of powder from her wig into the air. Nicole stood completely still, her mouth visible beneath her mask, shaped into a perfect oval.

Anne felt a trickle of sweat run down her back and hoped the stain would not show. She hated being so conspicuous, the object of everyone's undivided attention. Yet was it so completely extraordinary to imagine that this handsome stranger had chosen her over her sister? Especially since they were both wearing masks, and he could not possibly appreciate the full impact of Nicole's fair beauty.

Drawing herself up, Anne stared hard at Lord Richard. His expression was one of open innocence, but she suspected there was a very deliberate reason for his request. She was genuinely puzzled, but also intrigued.

"I would be honored, my lord," Anne replied in a soft voice.

He bowed politely before offering his arm, yet his deep green eyes did not leave her face. Anne was immediately glad the matching mask she had crafted for her costume was the one component of the outfit that fit her perfectly. It covered most of her face except her eyes, mouth, and jaw. Combined with the elaborate red wig she was wearing, it somehow seem to protect her from Lord Richard's penetrating gaze.

With her fingers resting lightly on his sleeve, Anne slowly

descended the staircase. It was difficult to walk smoothly. The skirt of her costume was widely flared and jutted out stiffly from her hips, which were padded by great folds of cloth creating a drum shape. The stiff ruff that fanned out behind her head made quick turns of her neck impossible.

The dress might have been considered simple in Queen Elizabeth's time, but it was a far more elaborate and cumbersome outfit than Anne had ever worn. She only hoped that she would be able to move about the room with at least a hint of grace.

Lord Richard brought her to the edge of the ballroom, and they watched the glittering, brightly dressed crowd swirl pass them. The lack of conversation should have been unnerving, but instead Anne felt oddly calm. When he wasn't scrutinizing her, Lord Richard's powerful presence gave her an almost protected feeling.

Then he touched her arm. The warmth of his fingers easily penetrated the thin material of her sleeve, and pleasure flushed through her. How strange. The tingling sensations seem to run from the top of her head down to her toes. Anne took a deliberate breath and told herself to calm down.

She was acting like a green girl, an innocent child at her first grownup party. Lord Richard was merely leading her onto the dance floor. There was no need to be so flustered. Yet how odd that the warmth of his fingers had sent her heart racing.

Striving to gain her equilibrium, Anne muttered the first thing that popped into her head.

"Do you have an affinity for queens?" she inquired as they joined the set forming on the dance floor. "Is that why you partnered me for this dance instead of my sister?

"Redheads," Lord Richard answered with a sly grin.

Anne felt herself blushing behind her mask. "Then I must in good conscience tell you the truth, my lord. I am wearing a wig."

"I know."

The rhythm of the music came together, and their dance began. Lord Richard slid his arm possessively around Anne's waist, and she stifled the cry of surprise in her throat, realizing for the first time that their dance was to be a waltz.

Anne chided herself for being so foolish. What was wrong with her? She had never been the belle of any ball, but she had danced the waltz countless times with many different men. She swallowed the apprehension in her throat and fixed her eyes on an imaginary point over Lord Richard's left shoulder. When the dance began, she was ready. Or so she thought.

It was like being awake during a glorious, exciting dream. He danced beautifully. Anne followed his lead naturally, gliding and twirling gracefully about the floor. As they whirled around the crowded room, Anne tried not to dwell on how Lord Richard made her feel. Every nerve ending was more taut, every touch more intense, every smell more pungent. He was somehow able to heighten all of her senses just by his close proximity.

He was so tall and broad and muscular. Even with her considerable height and even wider padded skirts, he easily dwarfed her. There was something intimate, almost forbidden, about the way he held her in his arms. She felt like his possession and was completely puzzled why that feeling brought her an unexpected rush of excitement instead of a logical sense of dismay.

A young buck sporting an eye patch and a lace-ruffled shirt barely missed colliding with them, but on the second circuit around the ballroom he knocked squarely into Anne.

The hand at the small of her back drew her closer.

"I've got you," Lord Richard whispered softly.

Flustered, Anne raised her eyes. The tips of her breasts were touching his black evening jacket. A wave of acute tension fluttered through her chest and stomach. The voice of strict, proper training inside her head told her to pull away immediately, but Anne ignored it. Softly she pressed herself forward, helpless to control these crazy, newly awakened feelings.

The muscles across Lord Richard's shoulders went rigid beneath her fingers and his eyes grew dark. The look he gave her made Anne's skin feel hot, then cold.

He is going to kiss me, she thought wildly. Rattled by the preposterous notion, all Anne's fogged brain could register was the simple truth that she very much wanted him to do so. *And I shall delight in kissing him back!*

"Pardon me," the young pirate sang merrily, "I do hope I

missed smashing your feet.'' He grinned sheepishly as he danced away.

The cheerful apology effectively shattered the mood. Anne pulled herself back to a respectable distance, struggling to adopt an air of nonchalance that was total affectation. She nervously flexed her fingers and felt Lord Richard's strong muscles shift beneath her hands.

How very different his body was from hers. She remembered the time she had seen a group of farm workers laboring in the fields striped of their shirts, bronzed backs and chests, muscles straining with effort as they lifted and hauled.

Yet Anne strongly suspected that Lord Richard's unclothed form would put them all to shame. He was the very essence of male beauty. The artist in her longed to see and feel and explore this strange, intoxicating man at her leisure, yet the woman she was did not dare.

''That clod has stepped on your gown and torn a section of the hem,'' Lord Richard growled.

Anne shrugged her shoulders. ''He is merely enjoying himself. The pirate and pretty young shepherdess make a rather fetching couple, do they not?''

''With feet like that, he should be dancing with the sheep, not a shepherdess,'' Lord Richard muttered, ''in a barnyard.''

Anne smiled. ''When the dance is finished, I shall order him to be imprisoned in the tower. Will that be sufficient punishment for his accidental crime of gown tearing?''

''You should hack off all his toes and feed them to the hounds,'' Lord Richard insisted. ''In retribution for his clumsiness and to ensure the safety of all the other dancing couples.''

Anne gasped. Lord Richard turned his head sharply, as if realizing for the first time that he had just expressed such a graphically violent sentiment to a lady.

He cleared his throat. ''Forgive my lack of sensibility, Miss Paget. When one has witnessed the type of cruelty towards humanity that war brings, you occasionally forget that gentility still exists in the world.''

Anne's initial shock at his blunt words disappeared.

''Ah, but you forget, my lord, I am a warrior queen, accustomed to such violence,'' Anne replied in a quiet, sensitive voice. She stroked his sleeve in a calm, comforting manner. ''Did you fight at the battle of Waterloo?''

''No. I returned to England shortly after the battle of Talavera.''

''Talavera? It was a great victory for our cause, yet I suspect the newspaper accounts glossed over the horrors.''

''It was truly a respectable representation of hell itself. Nothing but fire, suffering, blood, and human sacrifices.'' A distant, blank coldness entered Lord Richard's beautiful green eyes. ''In the aftermath of other battles I had fought before that awful day, the usual salutation given upon meeting an acquaintance of another regiment was, 'Who has been hit?' After Talavera I simply asked, 'Who is still alive?' ''

''Were you wounded?'' Anne asked in an emotional voice, feeling every ounce of Lord Richard's despair in her own gentle heart. ''Is that why you returned to England?''

''I was unharmed.'' Lord Richard's stoicism quickly returned. ''My family needed me. So I came home.''

Anne's stroking hand of comfort stopped. An unexpected knot began to curl in her stomach. What sort of family had he returned to? A wife? The notion that he was married left a sour taste on her tongue, yet she could not in all honesty understand why she should care if he had a wife.

Perhaps it was because she felt such an intense attraction for him, and while it was madness to dream that Lord Richard might also find her attractive, it was a harmless fantasy. If he was married, however, the situation would become utterly distasteful, certainly immoral in Anne's unfashionable opinion.

''Is your wife here with you this evening, my lord?''

''I am a widower.''

Anne released the breath she had been holding. She was so intent upon hearing his answer that she barely noticed he spoke of his widowed state without any trace of emotion in his voice.

They twirled gracefully around the ballroom one final time. Anne felt a pang of regret pierce her heart when the last strains of the music died away. She had so enjoyed being held in his arms. She curtsied low and waited to be escorted to a quiet corner where she strongly suspected she would spend the remainder of the evening craning her neck searching for Lord Richard while pretending disinterest in his whereabouts.

But instead of returning her to the sidelines, Lord Richard steered her away from the crowd and out the open French doors. Heart thumping madly, Anne allowed herself to be led into the garden to a more secluded spot among the flowers and trees.

Now what? Would he pull her once again into his arms and steal a kiss? With uncharacteristic recklessness, Anne secretly hoped that was his intent. Still, she cautioned herself to be sensible.

She had never been overly disappointed by her lack of male admirers, but tonight she felt a perplexing need for Lord Richard to find her desirable. She wondered how it would feel to be wanted, just once, especially by this extraordinarily powerful man.

If she indulged this strange temptation, however, it must only be on this one magical night. Her future plans of freedom and independence would not be jeopardized by the complication of a male relationship.

" 'Tis a lovely evening," Anne volunteered, "though perhaps a bit warm. Is it usually this warm in Devon at this time of year?"

"It's July."

"Well, of course I know what month it is," Anne replied with a slight laugh. "I can assure you, my lord, the summers in Cornwall are never this warm."

"Is that where you are from? Cornwall?"

Anne's step faltered slightly. "No. I grew up in Hampshire. We keep a house in London, but with the season nearly over Papa gladly accepted Sir Reginald Wilford's kind invitation to visit. He is a distant cousin of my mother's."

Anne turned her head up toward the sky, deliberately avoiding Lord Richard's sharp green eyes. She had never before questioned the unusual way her family lived. Especially since the plan was of her own devising and necessary in order for them to remain members of polite society. Yet she felt uncomfortable telling Lord Richard the half-truths she had grown so accustomed to uttering.

"I am rather surprised," Lord Richard replied. An undercurrent of accusation crept into his voice. "I have known Sir Reginald since I was a young boy. I always found him to be a somber and reclusive man, something of a hermit. I find it difficult to imagine him inviting a parcel of energetic relatives for a prolonged visit."

"Goodness, you make us sound like a tribe of primitives," Anne said. Her hand fluttered to her neck and she adjusted the stiff collar of her costume. "Sir Reginald has been most welcoming. My father has a keen eye for horseflesh and has been advising him on the acquisition of several prime mares. Mother has generously lent her assistance in the running of the household and shared some of her best recipes with Sir Reginald's cook. He remarked just last evening that he has never sat down to a finer table."

Anne deliberately paused for a breath. Gracious, she was babbling. He must think she was the biggest fool, but Lord Richard's inquires into her personal affairs made her very nervous.

"I stand corrected, Miss Paget. Sir Reginald is indeed fortunate in his choice of houseguests. Pray tell me, what exactly do *you* do to enhance Sir Reginald's dull life?"

Anne decided she did not appreciate the mocking edge in Lord Richard's voice. She stiffened her spine and held his gaze steadily as she spoke.

"I keep my two sisters and my two young brothers out of doors as much as possible, and when they are inside the manor house I move them to an unoccupied section so Sir Reginald can enjoy the quiet he so treasures."

Anne knew she had struck home with her answer by the slight frown that appeared on Lord Richard's handsome face. "You are a most resourceful woman," he said at last.

"You need not sound so astonished, my lord," Anne countered. "It takes only good manners and common sense to remain a pleasant houseguest."

They came to a secluded section of garden surrounded by

hedges. Without speaking, Lord Richard grasped her elbow and sat her down on the stone bench strategically placed inside the small maze. He immediately joined her, sitting closer than was strictly proper.

Anne breathed deeply of the night air. It was filled with the distinctive scent of rose mingling with an edge of expectancy. Senses heightened with almost unbearable anticipation, she waited.

"Will you remove your mask?" Lord Richard asked, reaching boldly for it.

Suddenly Anne felt frightened. She knew she wasn't beautiful or enticing or provocative. Fearing that once Lord Richard saw her pleasant but plain features, he would no longer find her worthy of his attentions, she held up her hand to forestall the removal of her mask.

"Please?" he coaxed.

Honesty won out over curiosity. It had been an exhilarating flirtation, and if it was to end now, then so be it. She grasped the mask between her fingers and slowly pulled it away from her face.

"You are so very lovely, my dear," he whispered in a deep, strong voice.

Anne suddenly felt weak at the knees.

Richard held her gaze and fought to keep his eyes as blank as his expression. She was not at all as he imagined. Listening to Nigel describe his darling Nicole, he had pictured a tiny woman with a provocative stare and an annoying giggle. Rather like her older sister, the busty Grecian nymph.

But she was none of those things. Intelligent, amusing, even kind. A woman who lived by her wits. He saw immediately how Nigel would be smitten with her, but what could she possibly see in his nephew? He was far too young and spoiled to stimulate the bold Miss Paget.

Lord Mulgrave reached out his hand and gently traced the curves of her face. She wasn't conventionally or strikingly beautiful, but he had been completely honest when he told her she was lovely. She had smooth, flawless skin, expressive light brown eyes, a straight nose, and generous lips on a pretty mouth.

A very pretty mouth. A very pretty enticing mouth. Knowing he shouldn't, yet unable to resist, Richard held her face softly between his fingers, bent his head, and captured her lips in a searing kiss.

He wasn't sure how she would react. He half expected her to push him away and slap his face. After all she was supposed to be in love with Nigel.

He could feel her initial surprise. She stiffened and pulled back for a fraction of a second. He splayed his hand against her back and held her in place, effectively cutting off her retreat. But he did not force himself on her. Instead he waited with mounting desire for her to make the next move.

"I really should not," she choked out in a harsh whisper.

Frustration surged through him at her words. Tamping down his rioting passion, Richard shifted uncomfortably on the stone bench, resigning himself to accept her appropriate response.

Then, to his utter delight and astonishment she sighed deeply, lifted herself forward, and kissed him back. Without restraint.

She parted her lips slightly, and Richard ran his tongue slowly, sensually, across the seam of her mouth, tasting her sweetness. His heart beat in a wild pulse of need as she softened and molded herself against his chest, clearly aroused by their embrace.

His disappointment over her apparent lack of morals was quickly overshadowed by the incredible sensations streaking through him. Their kiss was an intoxicating blend of pleasure and fascination. The thrust and stroke of his tongue was met with equal fire, and Richard felt the heat and coiling tension rise inside him.

She was incredible! Soft and warm, hot and sweet. Knowing it was wrong, but not caring one wit, Richard tightened his embrace.

"You are truly beautiful." He whispered the words against her neck before pressing his lips against the white column of her throat.

He set his arms tightly around her, one on her waist, the

other on her shoulder. He pushed aside the cumbersome ruff collar around her neck. It crumbled like a deck of cards, revealing the luscious creamy white skin beneath. She was not a voluptuous woman, but her feminine curves easily inflamed his senses.

He trailed a line of soft, wet kisses down to her breasts, expertly drawing down the top of her gown with his thumbs. Her skin felt hot against the moisture of his tongue and he could hear her harsh breathing even though her face was turned down against the top of his head.

By the time the rustling sound of clothing and footsteps approaching registered in Richard's passion-hazed brain, it was too late. His immediate reaction was protective, and almost without thinking he stood abruptly on his feet, thrusting himself in front of the disheveled Miss Paget.

Ian stood before him and alongside the earl was Lady Althen. Their expressions of stunned disbelief informed him that he had in no way concealed the fact that he had been kissing Miss Paget. Rather thoroughly.

"Good evening." It was difficult to smile with clenched teeth, but somehow Richard managed.

"What in heaven's name is going on here?" Lady Althen exclaimed in a high-pitched squeal. "Anne, are you all right?"

Anne? Richard spun around and glared at the woman on the bench. This delectable creature he had nearly seduced was not Nigel's darling Nicole?

"Gracious, Mother, I am fine," she replied breathlessly. She struggled momentarily with the neckline of her gown before succeeding in covering her lovely breasts. "Please refrain from becoming hysterical. I don't have any smelling salts with me."

Lady Althen humphed with annoyance, but her daughter ignored her. Remarkable. She had just been caught in a compromising position with a man she barely knew, yet she was lecturing her parent.

Ian spoke, but Richard was not listening. Anne? He felt his mind spiral into a dark, dizzying vortex. Who the devil was Anne, and where in the hell was Nigel's darling Nicole?

ABOUT THE AUTHOR

Adrienne Basso lives with her family in New Jersey and is currently working on her newest Zebra historical romance set in the Regency period, *His Noble Promise* (to be published in March 2000). She is also working on a short contemporary, *Sweet Sensations,* which will be published in Zebra's Bouquet line in November, 1999. Adrienne loves to hear from readers and you may write to her c/o Zebra Books. Please include a self-addressed envelope if you wish a response.

Put a Little Romance in Your Life With
Fern Michaels

__Dear Emily	0-8217-5676-1	$6.99US/$8.50CAN
__Sara's Song	0-8217-5856-X	$6.99US/$8.50CAN
__Wish List	0-8217-5228-6	$6.99US/$7.99CAN
__Vegas Rich	0-8217-5594-3	$6.99US/$8.50CAN
__Vegas Heat	0-8217-5758-X	$6.99US/$8.50CAN
__Vegas Sunrise	1-55817-5983-3	$6.99US/$8.50CAN
__Whitefire	0-8217-5638-9	$6.99US/$8.50CAN

Call toll free **1-888-345-BOOK** to order by phone or use this coupon to order by mail.

Name_____

Address_____

City _____ State _____Zip_____

Please send me the books I have checked above.

I am enclosing	$_____
Plus postage and handling*	$_____
Sales tax (in New York and Tennessee)	$_____
Total amount enclosed	$_____

*Add $2.50 for the first book and $.50 for each additional book.

Send check or money order (no cash or CODs) to:

Kensington Publishing Corp., 850 Third Avenue, New York, NY 10022

Prices and Numbers subject to change without notice.

All orders subject to availability.

Check out our website at **www.kensingtonbooks.com**